THE WATCHER IN THE PINE

Also by the author

Death of a Nationalist
Law of Return

THE WATCHER IN THE PINE

Rebecca Pawel

Published by
Soho Press, Inc.
853 Broadway
New York, NY 10003

Library of Congress Cataloging-in-Publication Data

Pawel, Rebecca, 1977-
The watcher in the pine/Rebecca Pawel.
p. cm.
ISBN–10: 1-56947-409-5
EAN–13: 978-156947-409-9
1. Spain—History—Civil War, 1936–1939—Fiction.
2. Police—Spain—Fiction. I. Title.

PS3616.A957W38 2005
813'.6—dc22   2004048192

10   9   8   7   6   5   4   3   2   1

Acknowledgments

My grateful thanks to all the members of the *foro de Juanín*, especially Alfredo Cloux and Pepe Sala. And to Pepe and Carmen and Emma García, *la de Valmeo,* for sharing both their homes and their memories with me when I was writing this book. Discovering friends while doing research is a rare blessing. *Gracias. Un abrazote.*

"Yo me subí pino verde
por ver si la divisaba
y solo vi el polvo
del coche que la llevaba."
"I climbed a green pine tree
to see if I could glimpse her,
and saw only the dust
of the carriage that carried her."

—"Anda, jaleo," Spanish folk song

"Yo me subí un pino verde
por ver si Franco llegaba
y solo vi un tren blindado
lo bien que tiroteaba."
I climbed a green pine tree
to see if Franco was coming,
and saw only an armored train
that strafed the countryside."

—"Anda, jaleo," Spanish folk song,
Civil War version

Chapter 1

The baby didn't like the blizzard. At least, that was how Elena thought of it. She sat up a little clumsily, to pay closer attention. Her husband, whose shoulder she had been resting against, straightened also, and adjusted his arm, so that his cloak covered her as well. "What's the matter?"

Elena huddled against him, seeking protection from the cold. "Nothing. The kid's awake."

Lieutenant Tejada laid a thoughtful hand on his wife's stomach. "How can you tell he's awake?" he asked after a moment. "Maybe he's just kicking in his sleep."

"Because it's an awake sort of kicking." Elena sighed. "Although it is past his bedtime."

"I'm sorry." The reproach in Tejada's voice was mostly directed at himself. "You should have stayed in Salamanca."

"I thought it would be easier to travel with a guardia and without an infant," Elena replied dryly.

"Obviously a misapprehension." The lieutenant's voice was just as dry. The wind whistled through the broken windowpane opposite them, whirling a few more flakes into the gradually widening puddle of snowmelt. Tejada felt his wife shiver again, and struggled with a futile anger. It was just after ten, but darkness came early in the winter, and the snowstorm had cut off all light long before the train had dropped them off in this cheerless waiting room over four hours ago.

The train connections had been almost suspiciously good, and Tejada had not been overly worried when they had reached the tiny junction of Unquera and found that their ride was not waiting for them. After all, driving was difficult, and doubtless their chauffeur had assumed that the train would be late in this weather. But a four-hour wait was too long. A southerner by birth and temperament, the lieutenant disliked the storm on principle, but had he been alone he would have been less impatient. Elena had been a remarkably good sport, but she needed food and sleep and warmth, and none of those would be forthcoming at Unquera. He kissed her forehead, wishing that he had insisted that she stay behind with her parents until the child arrived. But she had wanted to come with him, and he had not really wanted to be separated from her less than a year after their wedding.

"How did I get talked into this?" he said aloud.

"Rodríguez." His wife was succinct.

The lieutenant snorted. A month ago, the transfer had seemed like an answer to all of his difficulties; a move away from his overbearing and incompetent captain and a promotion to his own command, so that he would have no direct contact with another irksome superior. Moreover, much as he had denied it to himself, Elena was unpopular with his colleagues in Salamanca. She was too much of a leftist. In Potes, she would not be the daughter of a known political dissident, but merely the wife of the commander.

"Of course it's only a little post," Captain Rodríguez had said, with a slight sneer. "But if you'd condescend to take a command outside of Madrid, Lieutenant, I think you'd be ideal." And Tejada had ignored the hostile sarcasm, and had said that he would be delighted to command the Guardia Civil post in the Cantabrian village of Potes.

His ears caught something besides the bitter whistling of the wind, and he hurried to the door of the deserted waiting room, hoping that their ride to Potes had finally arrived. For a moment he could make out nothing in the swirling whiteness, and then the tramp of hooves and the creak of harness leather attached themselves to a pinpoint of light that became a wagon, carrying a single lamp, which trundled out of the darkness and toward the station. *Oh, God,* thought Tejada, who had studied the map and knew that a good fifty kilometers, mostly uphill, lay between the train station and their final destination. *Don't they even have a truck?*

As the cart rumbled nearer, Tejada saw that the driver was huddled in an ancient wool overcoat that by no stretch of the imagination could be considered a guardia's uniform. Frustrated, he glanced back toward the shelter of the station. Elena had not risen from the bench. Her weary indifference decided him. He stepped out into the road and held up one hand.

The driver of the wagon saw the lieutenant at the last minute and pulled on the reins so hard that the horse neighed in protest. "Good evening, Señor Guardia." The words were whipped away by the wind.

"How far are you going?" Tejada demanded curtly.

"To Argüébanes, sir." The driver fumbled inside his coat and produced a faded wallet. "I live there. See, here are my papers."

"Is that in the Liébana Valley?" Tejada absently took the wallet, flipped it open, and glanced down at the man's safe conduct. The gesture was a formality. It was next to impossible to read anything by the dim light of the wagon's lamp, and he did not intend to waste energy trying.

"Yes, sir." The man shivered in his overcoat. "I'd hoped to be back sooner, but with this weather . . ."

Tejada nodded. "We're going to Potes," he explained. "And our ride seems to have been lost in the storm as well. Can you take us?"

The words were not really a question. So the lieutenant was caught off guard when the driver said nervously, "Of course, Señor Guardia, I'd be honored to take you and your partner but I'm afraid you won't find it very comfortable. Or very dignified."

"I'm not spending any more time in that damned waiting room," Tejada said, making it clear that his statement had been a command rather than a request. "Just a moment." He turned. "Elena! Come on."

The lieutenant had not particularly noted the driver's reluctance to take on a passenger, but it was impossible to overlook the man's surprise at the sight of Elena. "But who's she?" he ventured.

"My wife." Tejada's voice was at its most forbidding.

"Of course. Of course. I only thought—that is, I assumed when you said *we* that you meant another guardia. That is, I thought you were on duty, sir."

"If I were on duty," the lieutenant said, as he heaved his luggage into the back of the wagon, "I would walk. Let's get going."

It was a long, gloomy journey, the silence broken only by the plod of the horse's hooves in fresh snow, and the creak and rattle of the cart. The snow eased as they turned inland, into the dark gorge that provided the only access to the Liébana Valley, where Potes was located, but the wind intensified, whistling violently through the narrow slit cut by the river. Although impatient at the cart's speed, Tejada soon was grateful for its stability as they crawled along the hairpin turns of a nearly invisible road, with the bitter gale threatening to sweep them over the narrow ledge into the roiling white water below. As they passed through the gorge, the snow that had accumulated on Elena's coat began to melt through it, and she was shivering uncontrollably long before they reached the first village hidden under the folds of rock. Tejada squeezed her shoulders. "Almost there," he said gently, privately resolving to make whoever had left them waiting at the station clean latrines for the next six months.

"I'm all right."

He shifted position, trying to shield her from the worst of the wind, and reflecting that one of the things he loved about her was her unfaltering courage. "Someday I'll take you on a proper honeymoon."

"Biarritz, maybe?" she suggested, through chattering teeth.

Tejada, who had spent an unforgettable and not entirely pleasant night with her in Biarritz the preceding summer, snorted slightly. "I don't think so," he said, aware that he also loved her sense of humor.

"Are you newlyweds, then?" The driver joined their conversation unexpectedly.

"Last summer," Elena explained.

"And you're new to Potes, sir?"

"Yes." Tejada knew that there was no reason to vent his irritation on the driver. "My name is Lieutenant Tejada. I'll be commanding the Potes post."

"Oh!"

The only emotion Tejada could definitely identify in the monosyllable was surprise. The driver lapsed back into silence, and his passengers, who were tired, did not speak further either. The jolting of the cart was too uneven to allow either of them to doze off, although Tejada feared that his wife would succumb to the cold if she fell asleep, and Elena dearly would have liked to have been unconscious for part of the ride.

The driver broke the monotonous silence a few hours before dawn. "This is Potes, Lieutenant."

At an indeterminate hour of the morning, in the midst of a blizzard, the town was not prepossessing. A cluster of largely roofless buildings huddled together on either side of the bumpy road signaled the center of the town. Tejada thought longingly of the Plaza Mayor in Salamanca. "Where's the post?" he demanded, glad that the journey at least was finishing.

"Just across the river, sir." The driver raised an arm and pointed. "The building with the flagpole."

Tejada mentally measured the distance, considering the

possibility of walking it with baggage in the dark. "Take us over there," he ordered.

"I'm sorry, Lieutenant." The driver sounded frightened. "I can't. The wagon's too heavy for the bridge. "

"Then how the hell do the Guardia vehicles manage?" Tejada snapped, exhaustion wearing his patience thin.

"There was another bridge before the war. But it was destroyed when the town was burned. There's another bridge about a kilometer down that way, sir, that can carry trucks. The road loops back. But in this weather . . ." The man stopped, his voice pleading.

"He has to get home, Carlos," Elena interjected. "We can't take him that far out of his way."

"You're in no condition to walk that far!" her husband retorted, annoyed that she was undermining his attempts to protect her. Courage was one thing. Pigheadedness was quite another.

Elena's breath appeared in a cloud, as it hissed between her teeth, but she said nothing. Tejada frowned, wet, cold, furious, but fighting with her was the last thing he wanted to do. To his surprise, the driver of the wagon coughed. "There's a *fonda* a little ways further, on this side," he offered. "It's mostly a bar, but there are a couple of apartments upstairs that Anselmo used to rent in the summers to hikers. Maybe you could put up there for the night, and your men could pick you up tomorrow, sir."

"I'm expected tonight," Tejada said harshly. It occurred to him that if he had waited for appropriate transportation the issue would not have arisen.

"Yes, sir." The driver was meek. "I only thought your lady might want to get out of the cold faster."

On the other hand, Tejada thought, *if I'd waited for official transport we might still be at Unquera. And if they'd been so anxious for their new lieutenant to arrive they would have sent someone to meet the train.* He nodded capitulation. "Set us down there," he ordered.

Elena heaved a sigh of relief as the cart halted. The driver jumped down with startling spryness. It occurred to her that she had been thinking of him as an old man, and she wondered, with the light-headedness of the sleep-deprived, what had given her that impression. His hair (or his baldness) was hidden under a cap, and his throat and hands were muffled against the cold. Perhaps his voice had sounded old to her? Or the way he had hunched over the reins? Regardless of his age, he was heaving their suitcases out of the back of the wagon without apparent difficulty. *Just as if he were a taxi driver, depositing us at the Ritz,* she thought, amused. She saw her husband climb down and go to help him, and heard the man say easily, "Don't worry, sir. I'll get these. You'd better start hammering on the door. Anselmo sleeps like a stone."

Obediently, Tejada moved toward the door and rapped on it, first with his knuckles and then with the heel of his hand. There was still no answer by the time the wagon's owner had deposited their suitcases on the ledge and helped Elena down. The lieutenant shrugged and hit the door with his rifle butt. "Hello!" His voice carried in the storm, and echoed around the valley. "Wake up!"

"Anselmo!" The wagoner added his voice to the lieutenant's. "Anselmo! Oy! The new lieutenant's here and needs a room! Anselmo!"

A light finally went on inside, and the door creaked back to reveal a thin woman wrapped in a robe, with her hair in gray twists around her face. "What are you—?" she began, and then blanched. "Luis? The Guardia?"

"This is the new lieutenant," their driver, Luis, explained. "I can't take him over the footbridge, and he doesn't want to spend more time in the snow. Can you put him up until dawn?"

"The rooms aren't made up." The woman was shivering in the wind, which was blowing into the doorway. She turned to Tejada. "I'm sorry, Señor Guardia. We weren't expecting—that is, you'd have to wait."

"Look," Tejada interrupted her. "My wife has been traveling for almost twenty hours. She's expecting a child, and it's snowing. All we need is a room."

"Or a manger," Elena murmured, unable to repress a grin.

"Don't blaspheme!" Tejada growled. "You're exhausted, and you need rest! There's nothing funny about it."

"Sorry."

The innkeeper's wife had listened to this exchange without changing expression, but now she smiled slightly. "Come in, Señora. I'm afraid it won't be much warmer than a manger, but at least it's out of the wind."

Elena stepped inside with relief. The room was dark except for a lamp in one corner, but she received the vague impression of a long rectangular space, with a bar counter at the far end, and a few rickety tables, with chairs piled on top of them for the night. As she made out the shapes of the upturned chairs, she remembered how much her feet hurt, and realized how sorry she was that she could not sink into one of them. The truth of her husband's comment about twenty hours of travel suddenly struck her, and she wondered a little vaguely how much longer she would be able to remain upright. Carlos was setting the bags inside the doorway, and the innkeeper's wife was ushering her toward a stairway, talking all the while. "The fire's banked for the night, so hot-water bottles will be difficult, but I can offer you extra quilts." She heard her husband thank the man who had driven them from Unquera, and heard the innkeeper's wife say, "Good night, Luis," as the door to the street closed.

She turned to the gray-haired woman, swaying with weariness. "I'm sorry. The bathrooms are . . . ?"

"This way." The woman smiled comprehension, and took her elbow. "I'll show you. It's the second floor, Lieutenant," she added over her shoulder, as Tejada picked up the first of the suitcases.

Elena made her way to the bathroom. She was too tired to

feel more than a bit disappointed to discover that it was a latrine. Somehow she found the strength to drag herself up two flights of stairs, following her hostess's directions. A door off the upstairs hallway opened into a large room with a table shoved under a shuttered window. She passed through the room down a passage too short to be called a hallway, but just wide enough to accommodate a closet, and saw lamplight flickering off a bed. The gray-haired woman was tucking in a sheet, and there was a pile of folded blankets stacked beside it. Elena went toward the bed and sank onto the mattress, begrudging the effort it took to kick her shoes off her throbbing feet. The room was freezing, and she hastily decided against undressing further as soon as she took off her coat. She wormed her way under the sheets, pulled the blankets the woman had given her over the bed as best she could, and closed her eyes, relieved simply to be dry and lying down.

She was already asleep when the lieutenant brought up the last of their bags a few minutes later. He spread the blanket a little more completely over the bed and inspected Elena before turning out the lamp on the night table. Her face, always thin, seemed more sharply drawn in the dim light. Only the curve of her stomach was generous. He sat beside her and touched her belly lightly. Neither she nor the baby stirred. Very gently, he pulled the pins out of her hair, and uncoiled the long braid onto her pillow. She shifted, murmured his name, and then sank back into deeper sleep. The lamplight glittered off the single diamond set in a tiny gold cross that nestled in the hollow of her throat.

Tejada looked at the forgotten ornament, and smiled in spite of his own exhaustion. He had given her the necklace when she had first confirmed her pregnancy, and she was seldom without it, although she wore no other jewelry. He stroked her hair for a moment, and then forced himself to his feet one more time. His pistol became unbearably heavy as soon as he unbuckled the holster, and it was once more a weight separate from his clothing. He stooped, ignoring his aching back, and slid first his rifle and then the pistol under the bed. He undressed, shivering, and then slid into bed, profoundly grateful that Elena was already warming the icy sheets. *At least we're here*, he thought, as his head touched the pillow and he snaked an arm around his wife. *And after a trip like this, what else can go wrong?* Then he was asleep.

lena woke up reluctantly. She needed to pee but was unhappy about the idea of leaving the warmth of the quilts. The steady breathing beside her told her that her husband was still asleep, but light was leaking in between the slats of the wooden shutters in one corner. *It must be only a few minutes before reveille anyway,* she thought, and then she recalled that the barracks in Salamanca did not have shutters like these, and she remembered where she was.

The knowledge that she would have to go downstairs to reach the bathroom did not make her more eager to get out of bed, but her body was insistent. She sat up carefully, doing her best to avoid waking Tejada. She was only partially successful. He flinched at the rush of cold air when she pushed back the covers. "'s cold," he mumbled.

"Shh-shh." Elena hastily stood up and drew the blankets back up to his chin, hissing slightly as the cold of the floor tiles leaked through her socks. She would have appreciated slippers and a bathrobe, but since these useful items were buried in her trunk she reluctantly squeezed her feet back into her shoes and tiptoed toward the chair where she had flung her coat, hoping that it would provide some protection against the chill in the air. Her coat was still slightly damp. She slipped out of the room as quietly as possible, hoping that she would find a stove in her explorations. The room outside the bedroom narrowed at the far end into another passage, this one leading to a small room with a woodstove, a sink, and several cooking implements. Elena sighed and headed for the hallway. The door closed softly, without squeaking hinges, and she smiled, glad that Carlos at least would be able to enjoy an uninterrupted sleep.

She was in a darkened corridor, with another door identical to the one she had just left opening off it and a staircase that she vaguely remembered from the night before at the far end. The door was set directly across the hallway and probably led to another apartment, similar to theirs. She crept toward the stairs, hoping fervently that the guardia's quarters had running water. The steps were stone slabs, worn smooth with age and hemmed on either side by walls without a banister, and she felt her way down them carefully. A square of light on the wall at the landing just above the bar and the subdued murmur of voices below encouraged her. She had almost reached the landing when one of the voices was raised in sudden annoyance. "*Idiotic* thing to do!"

". . .didn't have much choice." This voice was a deeper grumble. "We can't afford trouble with the Guardia."

Elena froze where she stood, flushing slightly, and wondering if the speaker knew that a Guardia officer was asleep upstairs. "But to have them spend the night *here*? Of all places?" The first man spoke again, as if in answer to Elena's question.

"It's only one, and for one night." The deeper voice was soothing.

"I don't know what Anselmo will say." The tone was dubious now, waiting to be convinced.

"Which brings us back to the main point: Where *is* he?" The deeper voice subsided into an unintelligible mumble.

Mentally cursing the frailties of pregnancy that made it impossible to go back upstairs and lie down again, Elena coughed loudly and marched down the steps, hoping that her silhouette on the stairway wall would announce her presence if her footsteps did not.

She was unable to judge the success of her strategy, but no one seemed too startled by her appearance. It was full daylight in the room below. The chairs were still reversed on top of the tables, but a trio of men were hunched over the bar, and the gray-haired woman from the preceding evening was behind it. It was the woman who noticed Elena. "Good morning, Señora. I hope you slept well?"

"Yes, thank you." Elena hesitated, somewhat embarrassed. "I'm . . . er . . . sorry to disturb you." She marched in the direction she remembered from the previous night, running the gauntlet of the men's silent stares. Semihostile scrutiny had become a constant since her marriage, and by now it was more an annoyance than a threat. And the men at the bar wore neither arms nor uniforms. She did not bother to try to listen to their conversation again. She was sure that they would be absolutely silent until they knew she was gone.

Tejada was up and nearly fully dressed when she returned. "There you are." He smiled. "I was worried."

"Toilet," Elena explained succinctly.

He looked up and stopped buttoning his coat. "Are you all right? Were you nauseous?"

"I haven't been nauseous in weeks."

He nodded, still looking anxious. "You're sure? Did you sleep well?"

"Like a stone. And you?"

"Fine. And the baby?" Tejada stooped, and fished under the bed for his rifle.

"Fine, as far as I can tell."

"Good. No, no, sit back. I'll get that." The lieutenant twisted, still kneeling, and began to retie his wife's shoe.

Elena swallowed a smile. "I'm not sick, you know. Or made of porcelain."

"You shouldn't strain yourself. Do you want breakfast?"

He was still occupied with Elena's shoelaces and thus did not see her mischievous face as she said soberly, "Wild strawberries would be nice."

He stood and headed for the door with a sinking heart. "I'll see what I can do."

Elena's laughter stopped him. "Carlos! It's March! And it's snowing! I was joking!"

"Ingrate," the lieutenant said, looking slightly sheepish.

Elena relented. "Sorry. Coffee?"

"God, I hope so." Tejada held the door for her. "They should have it at the post, at worst. But let's see if we can find our host."

The barroom was empty except for the gray-haired woman when they reached the bottom of the stairs. Elena wondered briefly where the men had disappeared to. Perhaps it was later in the day than she had thought. Perhaps they had decided to avoid the impending presence of a guardia. Elena suppressed a sigh. Not so long ago, she would have avoided the Guardia also. But it was going to be difficult, being so isolated in a town where she had no friends or family.

Tejada, as usual, did not notice the effect of his presence. He nodded at the woman. "Good morning."

"Good morning, Lieutenant." She was courteous, if not friendly. "Can I help you?"

Tejada glanced at his watch. It was a few minutes before eleven. "Where's the telephone? I'd like to call the post."

"I'm sorry, sir. We don't have one."

The lieutenant blinked. "Oh. Well, then, we'd like some coffee. And if my wife could stay here while I walk over to the post, I'd be grateful."

"Of course, Lieutenant." She brought them coffee silently and stood by the entrance to the hallway, watching them as they drank. Elena was sorry for the scrutiny. She would have liked to communicate to Carlos the conversation she had overheard. But she had a shrewd suspicion the woman had taken part in the conversation, and to admit to eavesdropping would not be a good way to begin an acquaintance.

Tejada finished drinking quickly and stood up. "I'm going over to the post. I don't know what the mix-up was last night, but I want it sorted out as soon as possible. You'll be all right here?"

"Of course."

The lieutenant looked at his wife sharply. There was the faintest hint of constraint in her tone. He saw her eyes flicker to the woman who had brought them coffee. He leaned over, kissed her lightly on the cheek, and breathed. "We should talk later in private?"

"Yes." Her voice was soft, pitched for only his ears. "I'm all right for now though."

He gave her a smile that he hoped did not look anxious, and then put on his cloak and hat. Their hostess saw him to the door. "The footbridge is just up that way, Lieutenant. And you can't miss the post."

"Thank you." Tejada set off in the direction she had indicated. The snow was lighter now, barely more than a few flakes, but the wind was still bitterly cold. The street—or rather track—was completely empty, although a few cart tracks in the snow suggested that traffic had passed in the last few hours.

When he reached the bridge, Tejada understood the carter's reluctance to cross it with a vehicle. It was a rickety-looking structure that hardly looked wide enough for a man on horseback. The buildings surrounding it were thatched and Tejada guessed that the fire their driver had mentioned the night before had not reached this corner of the town. The bridge creaked under Tejada's weight as he hurried across. It was impossible to tell what was paved and what was not beneath the unplowed snow, but a few buildings were planted at a respectful distance from a businesslike medieval tower in the center of a vaguely rectangular space that Tejada guessed to be a plaza on the other side of the river. A bare flagpole stuck up in front of one of them. Tejada headed toward it, remembering the carter's directions the previous evening, and was rewarded by the sight of the familiar crest of the Guardia over the door. He rapped on the front door, wondering with half his mind if the lack of guards in front of the post was due to understaffing or to laziness, and noting absently with the other half that the man who had taken them to Potes appeared to have given accurate information. The man had mentioned that the *fonda* was run by an Anselmo, though he had thus far not appeared. Tejada wondered briefly if Anselmo would present himself when they settled their bill. *Maybe he lets his wife handle the business,* Tejada thought. And then, as a particularly malicious blast of wind nearly blew his hat off, *Maybe he hibernates in the winter, lucky bastard.*

The door to the post opened a crack, and Tejada was confronted by a man in his midtwenties, holding a leveled rifle. "What do you want?"

Tejada saluted, mentally noting that it would be desirable to make the Guardia's challenges a little more formal. "Lieutenant Tejada. I'm here to relieve your current commander."

"Sir!" The door swung back, and the guardia saluted, looking uncomfortable. "I'm sorry, sir. We weren't expecting . . . that is, Ortíz and Carvallo went to the station this morning, sir, to pick you up. But if you're here . . ." The young man turned away to shut the door as he spoke, perhaps relieved to have an excuse not to finish the sentence.

Tejada was inspecting his surroundings with interest. He was in a small cold hallway, lit by a single lantern. The lack of windows was more than compensated for by the poor insulation. Most of the hall was taken up by a square staircase on his right. On his left was a small table, a patently ineffectual stove, and a chair that he guessed the guardia at the door had been occupying. Beyond the stairs, a closed door signaled an entrance to the rest of the building. The guardia bolted the outer door behind the lieutenant, and then hurried to the door at the back of the hallway, opened it, and called, "The new lieutenant's here! Go tell Sergeant Márquez!" He turned back to Tejada. "My partner, sir," he explained. "Corporal Battista."

Tejada nodded. "And you are . . . ?"

"José Torres, sir."

The lieutenant took off his cloak, in spite of the chill in the hall. "And how many men are there at the post, Torres?" he demanded.

"Five in all, sir. Well, six, now that you've come."

Tejada frowned for a moment. "And they are the guardias you mentioned earlier, Ortíz and Carvallo, was it? And yourself and your partner, and the sergeant?"

"Yes, sir."

"And Sergeant Márquez has been the ranking officer?" Tejada asked, wondering why he had vaguely assumed that the post, however small, was commanded by someone of his own rank. It was common for rural outposts to be under the command of a sergeant, after all.

Guardia Torres looked embarrassed. The opening door saved him the necessity of answering. A burly man in his mid-forties emerged. He wore a sergeant's uniform and was followed by another, slightly younger man, whom Tejada guessed to be Corporal Battista. "Sir." The sergeant saluted. "Márquez. At your orders." Tejada nodded without speaking, and the sergeant added in a slightly aggrieved voice, "We thought you were at Unquera."

"I was, last night." Tejada forced himself to keep his voice mild. "The cable must have mistaken the time I arrived."

"I'm sorry, sir." Márquez did not sound overly apologetic. "We had an emergency last night."

Tejada breathed through his nostrils as he understood that someone had casually decided to leave him to wait in a train station all night in a snowstorm without word. "What sort of emergency?" he asked, sounding somewhat grim.

"A manhunt." Sergeant Márquez sounded disgusted. "Which came to nothing, of course. And then I had to send Ortíz and Carvallo to pick you up, which also seems to have been unnecessary."

The lieutenant kept his face blank. Sergeant Márquez was more than ten years his senior and had doubtless fallen into the habit of command. And nothing Márquez had said was actually insubordinate. It was unlikely that he intended to be disrespectful. Tejada had always relied on good relationships with his subordinates. He did not want to start off on the wrong foot with Márquez. Still, there was a slight edge to the lieutenant's voice as he said, "I'm sorry for the inconvenience. When no one arrived last night I thought we'd better hitch a ride."

There was a short silence. "You hitched a ride, sir?" Corporal Battista said, sounding slightly disbelieving.

Tejada turned. "Yes. With a local farmer on his way home. Why not?"

Battista shifted uncomfortably. "No reason, sir." He cleared his throat and added more strongly, "After all, it's not as if a pair of uniformed officers can't travel the country safely."

Battista's last words suddenly recalled Torres's greeting. *He's frightened*, Tejada thought. Now that it occurred to him, the sergeant's sullenness had the quality of fear as well. The lieutenant could think of nothing the guardia should find scary, but the signs were unmistakable. Instinctively, he searched for possible perils. "Our driver didn't want to cross the bridge just across the square with a cart," he said experimentally. "He said it was only fit for pedestrians. Is that true?"

"More or less, sir," Sergeant Márquez agreed. "A mounted man can cross it. And maybe a light motorcycle, although that would be chancy. We usually use the proper bridge, about a kilometer west of here. Devastated Regions is working on another one, but when they'll get it done . . ."

Tejada nodded, resigned. The Department of Devastated

Regions had more than enough work to do, and although Potes was clearly in need of its help, the reconstruction of the town could easily take years. "I'll need to take a truck back to Anselmo's *fonda*," he said. "I understand Torres and Battista are normally partners, Sergeant, but I don't want to take them both from the post. Which one do you think should come with me?"

"We don't have a truck, sir." Sergeant Márquez looked slightly embarrassed. "Ortíz and Carvallo took it."

Tejada blinked. "How do you do patrols?"

"Horseback, sir. Or on foot."

Tejada breathed through his nostrils again. "Fine. When they return, I'll go and collect our luggage."

"Surely you and your partner can carry your kits, sir? It isn't far, after all." Márquez's voice was faintly mocking.

Tejada's nostrils flared again. His voice was tight as he replied. "I can carry my kit. But we have several suitcases. And my wife is not fit to carry them."

For an instant, Tejada had the satisfaction of seeing Márquez look startled instead of smug. "Your wife?" the sergeant repeated. "You brought your wife with you, Lieutenant?" His voice held the same disbelief as Battista's, and also a faint suggestion of reluctant respect.

Tejada, always sensitive about his marriage, missed the respect. "Yes," he snapped, out of patience. "Is there a problem?"

"No. No, sir. Of course not. We could requisition a cart if you like." Márquez was looking at the new commander as if he had suddenly grown two heads but he sounded less self-satisfied. He turned to the corporal. "Doesn't old Aponte have a cart and horse?"

"Yes, sir," Battista nodded. "Should I go over now and get it?"

"There's no need." Tejada spoke before the sergeant could reply. "I assume that Ortíz and Carvallo will be back by this afternoon. And while I'm already here I'd rather take a tour of the post, Márquez."

Faced with a direct order, the sergeant nodded. "At your orders, Lieutenant."

"But, sir!" To Tejada's surprise, Battista objected. "If your lady's alone at Anselmo's—"

"I'm sure Señora de Tejada will be fine," the sergeant interrupted, glaring at his subordinate. Turning to the lieutenant, he added, "No doubt she'll find very congenial company there, sir."

Tejada would have sworn that there was malice behind the friendly words. He was just conscious enough of his own discomfort whenever any of his colleagues referred to Elena to discount it. Márquez was not an instantly likable man, Tejada reflected, as the sergeant led him through the far door and down a corridor, explaining the layout of the post as they walked. Yet there was no reason to suppose that the sergeant had any active reason for being hostile, much less that he had any ulterior motive in speaking of Elena. "And this is our office," Márquez finished, throwing open the door to a cluttered room, where a wood stove emanated welcome warmth.

Tejada ran his eyes over the pair of desks, shoved up against each other to form a large table. There was a covered typewriter in the corner by the stove. "Who generally works here?" he asked, noting that both of the desks had locks on the drawers.

"We do, sir," Márquez explained patiently. "This desk is mine, and the far one is yours."

"Mine?" Tejada echoed, noting the welter of papers and the cup of inky pens and chewed pencils on the desk that the sergeant had indicated. "It looks like someone's been using it. Whom did it belong to?"

"Your predecessor, of course." Márquez looked puzzled. "It's the lieutenant's desk."

Tejada frowned. "I understood from Guardia Torres that you were the ranking officer in Potes."

"Only in the interim, sir." Márquez's tone was too deferential to be believed.

"And why didn't Lieutenant—?" Tejada paused expectantly. When the sergeant said nothing, he sighed and added, "What was my predecessor's name?"

"Calero, sir."

"Why didn't Lieutenant Calero remain here until I arrived, Sergeant?"

Tejada knew, watching Márquez's face, that he had finally asked the question the sergeant had been waiting for. Márquez's sympathetic tone was grotesquely at odds with his malicious smile as he said, "You mean they didn't tell you, sir? Lieutenant Calero was murdered by Red guerrillas, nearly six months ago."

Chapter 3

"A bad winter we're having, no?" Elena spoke the words out of sheer desperation. She had been sitting in the barroom of Anselmo's *fonda* for the last hour, accompanied only by the gray-haired innkeeper's wife. It was, Elena supposed, only natural that the locals did not frequent the restaurant in the middle of the morning, when, presumably, they had work to do. But, Elena, accustomed to the constant noises of the city, was unnerved by the total silence, and her hostess had not been communicative.

"Yes, Señora. But we've had worse."

There was a pause. Then Elena said awkwardly, "How do the children get to school in this weather?"

"The school was burned during the war. It hasn't been rebuilt yet." Seeing Elena's expression, the woman relented and added, "Father Bernardo teaches the kids their catechism, and to read and write a bit at the church. But mostly folks that can afford it send their kids away to boarding school in the city, anyway."

"The city?" Elena echoed, imagining sending a defenseless child away, alone, for the sake of schooling and unconsciously putting a protective hand over her stomach.

"Santander." The woman noticed the gesture, and smiled. "You won't have to worry about that for a few years yet though, Señora."

Elena smiled back, then put her foot in her mouth. "Do you have children?"

"Grown." The hostess's face became shuttered.

Although it was obvious she did not want to say anything more, Elena was unwilling to let silence descend again. "It's nice there's someone to take over the business," she suggested, for lack of anything better to say.

"My sons were taken four years ago." The woman's voice was strained.

"I'm sorry." Elena reflected on the multiple meanings of "taken" and felt slightly sick.

The silence stretched and became uncomfortable. Elena stared at the frosted windows, wishing that she had the courage to rub a pane with her palm, so that she could see out of it. A shadow passed behind the glass and came to rest, with a creaking noise that was distinct from the wind. A moment later the door banged open, and Tejada entered. "You're all right?" He crossed the room toward her, holding out his hands.

"Yes." Elena smiled, pleased to see him, and then blinked as he gripped her hands, almost hard enough to hurt.

"Good." He sounded relieved. "Just wait here for another minute, and I'll get the bags."

His shoulders were tense. Elena watched him disappear up the stairs, moving with the deceptive speed that made distances seem shorter than they really were. He returned, carrying suitcases, and addressed himself to the woman behind the bar. "Our bill, Señora?"

She blinked, obviously disconcerted, but recovered herself enough to scribble something on a pad and hold it out to the lieutenant. He nodded and reached for his wallet. "Here. And . . . you're Bárbara Nuñez de Montalbán?"

"Yes, sir." She sounded frightened. Elena frowned, wondering how he had acquired the information she had been too shy to ask for in the intervening hours.

"Tell your husband to stop by the post this afternoon," the lieutenant ordered. "We have a couple of questions. Just a formality, really."

Bárbara de Montalbán had been a little nervous before. Now she was terrified. "Yes, sir," she managed. "I-I'll tell him as soon as I see him."

"Thank you." Tejada turned to his wife. "Come on." Then, seeing that she was glaring at him, "Come *on*, Elena. It isn't far. Slow and steady, remember."

Elena bit her lip, suppressing a series of questions. "Slow and steady" was a code phrase. She thanked the woman and received only a vague wave in reply.

Then she made her way outside, buttoning her coat and blinking in the brighter natural light. A few snowflakes brushed her hair. She turned her head, looking for a truck or even a cart like the one that had brought them to Potes, and saw only a sturdy bay horse, wearing a dark red blanket and stamping in the cold. Tejada was already pulling the blanket off the horse and looping rope through their suitcases to fasten them to the saddle in a makeshift pack. Elena watched him, startled by his competence. He straightened, caught a glimpse of her face, and gave her a lopsided smile. "I grew up on a farm," he reminded her, taking the reins, and leading the pack animal out of the half-ruined arcade that sheltered the sidewalk from the worst of the wind and toward the footbridge.

She nodded, and followed him. "This is a funny time to get in touch with nature, though."

"We don't have a truck available." His voice was sober. "And I wanted to get you out of there as quickly as possible. You don't mind a short walk?"

"Of course not," Elena said automatically. Then, unable to contain herself any longer, she added, "Why did you want to get me out of there? And why did you frighten that woman . . . Señora Nuñez? And, now that I think of it, why isn't there transport available?"

"Because the truck was sent to pick us up at Unquera this morning and is probably fighting its way back through snowdrifts."

Tejada answered the last question first. "Because Sergeant Márquez didn't send it last night because he was using the entire post for a manhunt. And because Anselmo Montalbán may well be involved in . . . the crime Sergeant Márquez was interested in."

"What crime would this be?"

"Devastated Regions is doing a lot of work here," Tejada explained, eyes fixed on the tracks in the snow. "To fix"—he waved an expressive hand at the roofless and flame-blackened buildings around them—"all this. There's a plan to rebuild the plaza and restore the bell tower. And they're building a hospital and post office, and laying pipes for a municipal water system, and we're hoping to have a new post soon, which we could really use."

"I heard the town doesn't even have a school," Elena commented, momentarily sidetracked.

"I didn't hear anything about a school, but it's something to think about," Tejada answered, glad that she was distracted. "I'm afraid the guardias' temporary quarters are a little rustic, but look at it this way: We'll be able to design our dream home."

"What does this have to do with a crime?" Elena demanded, suspicious.

Tejada sighed. "A couple of the workers escaped yesterday," he explained grudgingly.

"Escaped?" They had reached the bridge, and Elena's voice sounded unnaturally loud over the running water.

The lieutenant gestured toward a rectangular wooden structure, obviously new, that squatted on the far side of the river above a snow-covered cemetery. "You see that big building with the barbed-wire fence?" he asked, keeping his eyes fixed on it to avoid his wife's gaze.

"The one that looks temporary?"

"Yes. It *is* temporary. It's the barracks for Devastated Regions' workers. Most of the construction in Potes is being done by men doing penance."

Elena did not answer immediately, and the lieutenant found

himself regretting the use of the standard euphemism "penance." He wondered if he should have simply said "by Red prisoners" or "by the losers." He liked the phrase "doing penance." Liked the idea that some kind of redemption was involved. He usually tried to avoid the knowledge that his wife's brother would probably have been one of those serving the mandatory seven years and a day for fighting in the Red army, had he not fled to Mexico at the end of the war. "The two men who escaped were both from Valencia." Tejada spoke again, to drown out his wife's silence. "They're probably headed home."

"And you think that Anselmo Montalbán may have helped them?" Elena asked, remembering the conversation she had overheard in the bar that morning.

"It's possible." Tejada shrugged, evasive. He absently patted the horse's shoulder and added, "Easy, boy. Soon have you back in your stable, all cozy."

Elena had been a city dweller all her life, and did not particularly care for horses. But, as far as she could tell, this one was plodding along absolutely quietly, and required no reassurance. And her husband's tone of voice was odd. "You *don't* think Anselmo helped them?" she asked, secretly hoping that he had simply decided to let the escaped prisoners make for home.

Tejada sighed. "There's really no point in your getting mixed up in Guardia business."

Elena snorted, in an unusually good imitation of a horse. "Carlos."

"You shouldn't worry. Not in your condition."

"*Carlos!*"

"Montalbán may be part of a network that's responsible for a good deal more than this escape," Tejada explained. "We'd like to catch the two who got away yesterday because they may be able to tell us something about the people who helped them. Up here in the mountains there are. . . ," he hesitated, in deference to his wife's political convictions. "Well, they call themselves maquis."

"Guerrillas," Elena breathed.

"Terrorists," her husband corrected firmly.

"You're not going to—" Elena stopped, wondering whether she should tell him what she had overheard.

"I'm going to make sure they can't harm anyone else." Tejada's voice was even, but his grip on the leading reins tightened suddenly, making the horse toss his head and snort in annoyance.

Elena took a deep breath, remembering her mother's words just before her wedding: "You can't stay on both sides, Elenita. And if you marry him, you'll become one of Them." She shivered a little, and walked more quickly. "What do you mean harm anyone *else*?"

"They murdered a man named Calero this past October." Her husband spoke gently.

He knows how much I hate this, Elena thought, grateful for the gentleness. They had reached the square across the river by now, and the cheerless post was directly in front of it. "Are you sure it wasn't personal?" she asked pleadingly. "Had this Calero made enemies?"

He shook his head. "I'm afraid not. Come on, the stables are this way, and I want to put Bruno away before he catches a chill."

"How do you *know*?" Elena persisted, following him. "Why do you think maquis killed him?"

Tejada sighed. She was sure to find out the truth from one of the guardias if he did not tell her. "He was the lieutenant of the post here," he said quietly. "He was ambushed on a mountain patrol, and shot to death."

Elena's gasp was a ghostly puff in the air. *Good*, said a vicious internal voice. *He probably had it coming*. And then her husband's arm was around her shoulders and he was saying, "Come on, love, you shouldn't be out in the cold," and she pictured the arm that enfolded her flung out, lifeless, in a snowbank, and the damp woolen cloak around her shoulders falling open, bloodstained, around Carlos's motionless body.

Tejada could feel his wife shivering, and strongly suspected that more than just the cold was affecting her. "Our quarters are on the second floor," he said as he ushered her into the stables, deliberately searching for something to take her mind off Lieutenant Calero's murder. "Sergeant Márquez says they aren't prepared really, because no one thought that you would be coming with me. But they're quite large, and it looks like they have lovely views of the mountains."

"As long as they're heated," Elena said, allowing herself to be distracted.

The lieutenant coughed apologetically. "Well, there's a fire-place in the living room." He unhooked their luggage, and led the ever-patient Bruno into his stall.

Elena gulped. "Oh. How . . . quaint."

He indicated the door that led from the stables into the main portion of the post, and from there up the stairs to their apart-ment, doing his best to be cheerful. Elena was eager to match his good humor, and agreed a little overenthusiastically that the entrance from the stables would be really convenient in bad weather or at night. She opened the door to the apartment and found herself in a room so long and narrow that it almost felt like a corridor. Three doors stood open along the opposite wall, and at the far end a fireplace sat beside another door. Elena moved toward one of the open doors. Beyond it was a large rec-tangular room, bare except for two cots, and distinctly chilly. As Tejada had promised, the mountains rose dramatically outside the window. But the prison for Devastated Regions workers sat squarely in the foreground of the view. Elena turned away from the barbed-wire-trimmed panorama. "What do we do about fur-niture?" she asked, trying to block out the sight of the prison.

The lieutenant took a deep breath. "I understand there is a good carpenter in Tama. Or we could order it from Santander."

"Tell me you're joking."

It was Tejada's turn to gulp. "Most men don't bring their

wives," he explained, flushing. "It's considered an . . . unpleasant posting. No one expected you to come. These are the only beds available, but I was planning to drag in a few chairs this afternoon. It's only temporary." He sought for something encouraging to say. "The fire's only been going for a few minutes. I'm sure that the whole apartment will be very cozy in a couple of hours."

Elena was far less sanguine, but focused on other possible sources of warmth. "Where's the kitchen?"

Her husband coughed. "There isn't actually a proper kitchen. Sergeant Márquez explained that the guardias usually all eat together, but we could maybe set one up in one of the other rooms. They're all the same as this one."

Elena nodded slowly. "And the bathroom is?"

Tejada had dreaded this question. "Actually, there are just latrines attached to the men's quarters. The sergeant thinks maybe we could partition one off for you. . . ." He trailed off, worried by her expression.

Elena sank onto one of the bare cots. It was lumpy, and smelled unpleasantly musty. "You did say Devastated Regions was working on another post?"

"Yes."

"When will it be done?"

Tejada was afraid to meet his wife's eyes. "It's scheduled for the spring of 1945," he said.

Elena began to laugh, a little hysterically. "And we get to design our dream home!" she gasped, when she could speak again. "Why not build a school onto it! It should be done around the time the baby starts kindergarten!"

Tejada, who had feared that she would be angry, sat on the other cot and began to laugh also. "And I thought things couldn't get worse last night!"

"Come on. I'll help you bring in some chairs." Elena pulled herself together.

"You most certainly will not." Tejada gave her a quick hug. "You're in no condition to be dragging furniture around. Why don't you try to unpack a little?"

"Into what?"

The lieutenant sighed. "I think there are a few hangers in the closets. I'll be right back."

Elena did not argue with her husband. But as the door closed behind him she sighed and looked around the cold bare room again. *Oh, dear*, she thought. *I hope this wasn't a mistake.*

Chapter 4

Two days after the Tejadas' arrival in Potes the temperature shot up nearly twenty degrees, causing a massive thaw that transformed everything from snow to mud. Then, after two days of sunny blue skies and perfect spring weather, the thermometer plunged below freezing again, coating the streets with slick and treacherous ice patches. Tejada felt that the unexpected slippery spots were an apt metaphor for his experience of his new command.

The first unpleasant surprise was the sole vehicle at the disposal of the Guardia. When Guardias Ortíz and Carvallo returned from Unquera, Tejada was disconcerted to notice that the ancient truck had several suspiciously round dents in the doors and hood, and a small hole in the front headlight. "Those look like bullet holes," he said.

"Yes, sir," Guardia Ortíz agreed. "Corporal Battista and Torres had a little problem with the maquis a few months ago."

Tejada frowned. "Define 'little problem.'"

"Well, Don Virgilio—that's the mayor of Trillayo—called them over there to make a complaint about poachers, and they came back after dark." Ortíz's tone made it clear that any guardia fool enough to do such a thing deserved what happened to him.

"They were ambushed?"

"I wouldn't say it was really a formal ambush." Ortíz spoke judiciously. "More that some of the maquis happened to be in the neighborhood, so they took a few shots at the truck. The corporal had the sense to just step on the gas, and of course Torres returned fire as best he could in the dark. There's a report on file somewhere, if you'd like to look at it."

"Does this happen often?" Tejada asked, starting to understand why his subordinates had been startled by his decision to trust his safety and his wife's to a stranger on the road.

"Oh, no, sir." Guardia Ortíz spoke quickly. "If we have to take the truck mostly I drive. I grew up over in Cillorigo, you see, so people know me around here, and the maquis know there'd be a lot of ill feeling if they hit me."

Tejada let the subject drop, although he was less than pleased with Ortíz's logic. His annoyance increased into outright discomfort when Carvallo and Ortíz returned several hours late from a routine patrol the next day, with the news that they had been fired at from the woods. "We took cover, of course, and did our best to shoot back," Ortíz said. "But I don't think they were really aiming to hit us. Just trying to scare us a little." Tejada was irritated by Guardia Ortíz's calm assumption that being fired at while on patrol was normal, but it was preferable to the ill-concealed fear of Guardias Torres and Carvallo. The lieutenant had never seen such a miserably demoralized post.

Under the circumstances, it was not unexpected that Anselmo Montalbán did not report to the Guardia Civil when ordered. His wife, questioned the next day by Guardias Ortíz and Carvallo, insisted that she did not know where he was to be found. The morning of the thaw, Tejada gave orders for her arrest and hit another slippery spot.

"How, sir?" Sergeant Márquez asked.

Tejada stared. "What do you mean, how? Go over to the *fonda* and tell her she's under arrest."

"And then what?"

"Bring her back to the post and lock her up until we get some news of Montalbán!"

"Where would we put her, sir?"

For a moment Tejada was dumbfounded. Then he said slowly, "You're telling me that we have *no* cells available?"

The sergeant coughed. "They're only temporary quarters," he reminded Tejada. "They weren't built with a full prison attached."

"But you must have had prisoners in the past!" Tejada protested.

"Yes, sir. But we've never had married officers, sir. We were using you and your wife's quarters for cells."

The reason for his apartment's inadequate heating and somewhat bizarre floor plan suddenly became clear to the lieutenant. He struggled with a desire to laugh, wondering at the same time if he could safely tell Elena. He was unsure whether she would share his amusement or be disgusted. "Are you telling me we have *no facilities at all* for holding anyone?" he demanded, returning to the problem at hand.

"I'm afraid not, sir."

Tejada considered for a moment. "What do you suggest we do then, Sergeant?"

"It's not my place to say, sir." Márquez was wooden.

The lieutenant struggled with unreasonable annoyance. His sergeant in Salamanca had combined intelligence and goodwill. When Tejada had asked for his opinion in similar cases, he had given honest and well-considered answers. Although Tejada had known that he was exceptionally lucky to have Sergeant Hernández, he could not help feeling that Márquez was an exceptionally unfortunate substitute. He would have sworn that the sergeant's unhelpfulness was deliberate.

The lieutenant considered forcing his subordinate to express an opinion, and then gave up the idea as futile. "Bring her in for questioning," he ordered, "and don't tell her that we have no place to put her. If we don't get anything out of her, let her go with a warning, and then tell Ortíz to go and keep an eye on the *fonda*."

"By himself, sir?" Sergeant Márquez had apparently forgotten that it was not his place to have opinions.

"Yes, by himself," Tejada snapped. "And 'keep an eye on it' does *not* mean go and stand in front of it prominently. It means look discreetly from a distance, and don't make it obvious that you're looking. Send Carvallo in a few hours to take over from Ortíz. They can spell each other until tomorrow. If they don't pick anything up, pull in Bárbara Nuñez again."

"The pair system of the Guardia—" Márquez began.

"Is famous and venerable," Tejada interrupted. "Which is exactly why I do *not* want it used now. Do I make myself clear?"

"Yes, Lieutenant." Márquez saluted and went to give the guardias their orders. Tejada was left with the feeling that they would not be well executed.

He spent the next hour composing two letters, one to the local director of Devastated Regions and one to the mayor, respectfully asking about the possibility of providing a prison for the town as soon as possible. When he was ready to make copies, he discovered that there was no carbon paper in the office. Disgusted, he sent for Guardia Torres. "Is Anselmo Montalbán's wife here?" he demanded.

"Yes, Lieutenant."

"Good. I want to talk to her." Tejada stood up and held out the pad he had been writing on. "Type these," he ordered. "Two copies of each. When you're finished, leave one copy of each on my desk and bring the others to me to sign. Then deliver them."

Guardia Torres looked uncomfortable. "Type them, sir?"

"Yes. I'm sorry about the two copies, but I can't find carbon paper." Tejada saw that the young man looked nervous and added reassuringly, "You can drag my chair over to the typewriter, if you like."

This kindness gave Torres the courage to stammer, "I-I can't type, sir."

Tejada was annoyed, but not amazed. "You'll have to hunt

and peck then. Get as far as you can and if you haven't finished when I come back I'll finish them."

He was gone before the guardia had a chance to explain that he had never actually used a typewriter, was uncertain how to insert such niceties as capital letters, and was frankly terrified by carriage returns. Torres was a bold and enterprising young man, and managed to figure out the complexities of the battered Corona before the lieutenant's return, but he was barely past the salutation of the first letter when Tejada relieved him of his task.

The attempt to question Anselmo Montalbán's wife had been unsuccessful and had consumed the lieutenant's lunch hour, as well as running into the afternoon. Tejada took a certain satisfaction in banging the typewriter keys to ease his frustration. It was nearly six when he finished. He sent for Guardia Torres once more and told him to deliver the letters and inform the recipients that he would call on them the following day to discuss their contents. Made cautious by previous experience, he checked that Guardia Torres did in fact know where the mayor and the director of Devastated Regions were to be found.

Then he considered what to do next. Ortíz was watching the Montalbáns' *fonda*, probably uselessly. Carvallo was officially off duty until he relieved Ortíz of the Montalbán surveillance. Márquez and Battista were on patrol and would not be back until nightfall. The lieutenant had spent the last six hours in windowless rooms, and he felt that he deserved a break. He shut the office door a shade more firmly than necessary and marched out into the spring thaw. The Quiviesa, swollen with melting snow, burbled loudly. The peaks of Peña Vieja and Peña Sagra guarding Potes to the east and west loomed, snow-covered, in the still-warm afternoon light. If one overlooked the general charred rooflessness of the town, it was a pleasant evening. *Elena should get some fresh air*, the lieutenant thought. *And I've worked enough for one day.*

He hurried up the stairs to their apartment, smiling a little ruefully at the knowledge that his day would have been more productive had he escorted Bárbara Nuñez up them earlier instead of releasing her, and wondering again how to tell Elena that they were lodged in the Guardia's prison.

She was seated at the tiny square table he had dragged into the space they called the "living room," writing a letter, when he entered. "Care to go for a stroll?" he asked cheerfully.

She started and then looked up at him gravely. "Do I have a choice?"

He dropped into the chair beside her, concerned by her tone. "We don't have to if you're tired. But I think it's warmer outside than in at the moment. And I was just thinking of walking along by the river a bit. Why? Are you feeling all right?"

"That wasn't what I meant." She shook her head, impatient.

Temperamental, Tejada reminded himself. It's natural for her to be temperamental in her condition. He decided an apology for any outstanding sins might be in order. "I'm sorry I couldn't get away for lunch. Something came up."

"Bárbara Nuñez."

The lieutenant winced. "It was just a routine interrogation, Elena."

"I know. I overheard."

"You overheard?" Tejada repeated, disconcerted and less than pleased.

"The living room's right above where you questioned her." Elena spoke dully. "I wasn't trying to listen."

Nicely designed for a prison, Tejada thought. *Oh, damn.* "We didn't hurt her," he said aloud. "Márquez turned over a table, but he was just being theatrical."

"You frightened her, though." Elena wrapped her arms around her stomach and hunched one shoulder, turning her head away from him.

"Well, I hope so!"

"She's lost her sons, and now her husband's disappeared and she has nothing and you're persecuting her."

Tejada, who had gathered that one of the Montalbán sons had been executed for Communist sympathies four years previously, while the other was currently in a Devastated Regions work crew in Málaga, focused on the second half of his wife's statement. "It's likely she knows where her husband is," he said. "And it's likely her husband's a murderer. Or at the very least involved with people who are."

"She doesn't know where her husband is!"

"That's possible," Tejada agreed, watching carefully for signs of hysteria. "But we don't *know* that."

"*I* know it," Elena retorted. "The morning that we spent at the *fonda* there were three men there talking when I came downstairs and one of them said something like 'Anselmo won't like it' and the other said, 'Which brings us back to the main point: Where *is* he?' and she was there, and I think they were worried about him disappearing. So she *doesn't* know where he is."

Tejada blinked. "Are you sure?"

"Yes."

"Why didn't you tell me earlier?"

"I was going to," Elena sighed. "But then you were talking about maquis and I thought . . . I was afraid . . ."

"Elena." Her husband put an arm around her. "Have I ever. . . *ever* hurt anyone because of anything you've told me?"

"No, but . . . but there's always a first time." The words sounded childish in Elena's ears as she spoke and she smiled involuntarily.

Tejada smiled back. "Suppose we take that walk," he suggested. "And you can tell me what you remember. And I promise that no matter what you say I won't rush to beat the hills for bandits."

"You'd better not." Elena's smile was a little tremulous. "I don't want you to end up like Lieutenant Calero."

"I don't either," Tejada agreed. "Come on, the exercise will keep you from moping." He helped her into her coat and followed her down the stairs, one hand hovering above her shoulder in case she slipped.

Elena took a deep breath as they stepped out into the evening. The air smelled of water and new leaves and cow manure. It was as warm outside as indoors, and considerably less musty. "The road to Espinama runs along the Deva for a little ways," the lieutenant said, taking her arm. "Why don't we head that way?"

She nodded, and they turned their backs on the ruined town and walked out into the countryside. They walked silently arm in arm for a little while, Elena marveling at the stillness, and Tejada relaxing as they left man-made construction—and destruction—behind.

Then Tejada said gently, "Now, suppose you tell me what happened that morning at the *fonda*? You were upset, I remember, and wanted to talk in private. But then I heard about Calero, and was worried about the quarters not being ready, and I forgot about it. And then you didn't want to tell me."

Elena hesitated, and looked up at him. The sun lit his face from the side, illuminating one cheek with a warm yellow glow and casting the other into the black shadow of his tricorn. "You promise it won't hurt anyone?"

"You know I can't promise that. But I . . . promise I won't be in a hurry to do anything."

Elena smiled. "You are abominably honest."

"Are you sorry for that?"

"No." Elena sighed, and leaned against his arm. "But there really isn't much to tell." She quickly related as much as she remembered of the conversation she had overheard in Anselmo's *fonda*.

"Did Señora Nuñez say anything?" Tejada asked when she had finished.

"Not that I heard. But she must have been in the room with them. And surely she would have said if she had known where her husband was."

"And they shut up when they saw you." Tejada frowned. "You're sure you didn't hear anything more specific about *why* they didn't want trouble with the Guardia?

"No, but the whole thing took only a few seconds."

The lieutenant sighed. "So Anselmo has been missing since Tuesday morning. And maybe before that. At least as far as his underground contacts know."

"You don't *know* that they're underground," Elena protested. "Lots of perfectly honest people avoid the Guardia."

"His *possible* contacts," the lieutenant amended, unwilling to argue with her. He remembered something and added, "Elena, do you remember that old man we hitched a ride with? Luis?"

She nodded. "What about him?"

"We had to hammer on the door because he said that Anselmo 'sleeps like a stone.' So *he* thought that Anselmo was there. So if we could find Luis, and find out the last time he saw Anselmo, we'd know how long Anselmo has been missing."

Elena shook her head. "He could have just assumed that Anselmo was in. He's not even from Potes, remember."

Tejada sighed. "You're right. But I'd like to know if he's been missing for several months. Since Calero's murder, for instance."

"Surely it couldn't be that long. Wouldn't Sergeant Márquez have told you if there had been such an obvious suspect?" Elena was dubious.

"I'm beginning to suspect that Sergeant Márquez likes watching me blunder my way to answers he's known all along," Tejada said dryly. "Speaking of which, how would you feel about finding an apartment in town, separate from the post?"

"Fine with me. But why?" Elena hoped that she sounded only moderately pleased, instead of desperately eager. Her husband's colleagues had studiously ignored her since her arrival, and her conversation with Bárbara Nuñez three days previously had been her only contact with the people of Potes. Her long letters home were no substitute for human contact, especially since she knew that they would be heavily censored.

Tejada coughed. "Well, it's not as if our quarters are terribly convenient. And the post is a bit cramped." He hesitated, and then took the plunge. "And actually, it might be convenient to have a place to . . . keep people overnight at the post."

The sunset was turning the glacier on the slopes of the Peña Sagra to gold. Elena looked up at the silent mountain thoughtfully, working out her husband's meaning. "You mean you want to use our apartment as a prison?" she said finally.

"According to Márquez, it *was* the prison," Tejada admitted, shamefaced. "It could be awkward to not have any place to hold criminals. In the best interests of the town—"

"Do the townspeople feel that way?" Elena asked, sarcastic.

Tejada shrugged, annoyed. "Don't be dense, Elena. This isn't some sort of utopia. There's petty crime here, the same as everywhere else. It's not as if everything's political."

"Vandalism?" Elena raised her eyebrows. "Theft?"

Tejada smiled reluctantly. "All right, I admit that there isn't much left to vandalize. And maybe not a lot left to steal. But still—"

Elena noticed the smile and relented. "An apartment in town would be lovely. I just hope the neighbors don't treat me like a total pariah." She sighed. "It's hard having no one to talk to."

"We'll find lodgings in a place with a mistress," the lieutenant said encouragingly. "It will be good for you to have some women friends. And perhaps if there are little ones you'll be able to help each other with looking after the children later on."

"I'd like to find a midwife, too," Elena said.

Tejada nodded, although he had privately decided that the Guardia's only vehicle would be used to transport Elena to the hospital in Unquera as soon as necessary. He had been rather upset to learn that the hospital in Potes had been one of the casualties of the fire of 1937, and that the town still had no doctor. "I'm ready to head back whenever you are," he said aloud, mindful of his wife's delicate condition, and unwilling to tire her with a longer walk.

Elena's face clouded as they turned back toward the ruined buildings. "So little left," she murmured.

Tejada remembered reading that the fire that had devastated Potes had been set by the Reds. He felt that not pointing this out to his wife was an act of truly noble self-control. "We'll rebuild it," he said, emphasizing the "*we*" a little more than necessary.

"And while *we* are rebuilding *we* will quarter ourselves in citizens' homes, won't we?" Elena asked, turning toward him with a faint smile.

"You talk as if we were some kind of ravening horde out of *The Mayor of Zalamea* or something like that," Tejada said, torn between amusement and annoyance. "We've stayed one night in town already, remember?"

"Mostly I remember being dragged out of there because you were so afraid of how the townspeople feel about the Guardia!"

The lieutenant sighed. "It was an overreaction. I didn't mean to worry you. It's just that Márquez had just told me about the bandits and I was tired, so I made a snap judgment. I'm sure we weren't in any actual *danger*."

"I wasn't worried," Elena said dryly. "I was just reminding you why I thought the townspeople might not be thrilled to have us as guests."

Tejada saw her point, although he was unwilling to admit it. "We don't have to commandeer space," he said. "I'm sure that someone in town will be happy to have paying boarders."

"And given how prosperous everyone is, I'm sure every family has a spare furnished apartment," said Elena sardonically.

"The Montalbáns do!" Tejada retorted. He stopped abruptly, remembering that their one night outside the post had produced an interesting piece of information. "I wonder . . ."

Elena's eyes narrowed. "You wonder?" she prompted, half-guessing what he was about to say and disliking it already.

"The Montalbáns have plenty of extra space," her husband said neutrally. "And Señora Nuñez was very hospitable."

"Carlos, you just arrested the woman!"

"We brought her in for questioning," Tejada corrected primly. "And we let her go."

"Because you didn't have any place to hold her!"

"You make too many inferences," he said.

"What will you do if we move back into the *fonda?*" Elena demanded, smiling but earnest-voiced. "Arrest the owners and move them into our quarters?"

"It does seem a bit like musical chairs," Tejada admitted. "But look, Elena. At the moment, I've got Ortíz and Carvallo watching the *fonda* in shifts. Ten-to-one nothing will happen, because twenty-to-one Ortíz and Carvallo will make a mess of the surveillance. And . . . well, you know how unpleasant it is to have a shadow."

Elena nodded. Her father had been tailed by the Guardia for a number of years, sometimes more obtrusively and sometimes less so. "So you're proposing to live with them and take away whatever shreds of privacy they have left?"

"No." Tejada shook his head, serious. "I'm proposing to live with them because we need a place to live. I can take Ortíz and Carvallo off surveillance duty then, and still feel that someone is there just in case. I won't pry into their personal lives. *I* won't even be around most of the time."

Elena turned red with indignation. "*I'm* not going to spy for you!"

"I wouldn't ask you to," replied Tejada. "But you did say you'd like someone to talk to. And Señora Nuñez must know other women in town. It would be a chance for you to socialize a little."

"Socialize! As the lieutenant's wife? I'll be a leper."

"Everyone in town will know you're the lieutenant's wife anyway," Tejada pointed out gently. "But I don't see why that means you should be a leper."

Elena rolled her eyes. "What were you doing this afternoon?"

"My job." Tejada's mouth was tight.

"And that's guaranteed to make friends!"

"For goodness' sake, Elena, I'm trying to be civilized about this." They had almost reached the post, and Tejada lowered his voice. "We can find lodgings elsewhere if you like. But you seemed to like Señora Nuñez, and I thought this might be a way of giving her a little breathing space. Of making everything . . . a bit less official. And after all, times are hard. It will be money in her pocket."

Elena sighed. She knew that Carlos was doing his best. "I imagine her husband will be dropping by for dinner and to play checkers, too?" she said lightly, as they reached the Guardia building, and he held the outer door for her.

Tejada laughed. "Darling, I'm an optimist. Not an idiot."

"I'm not sure there's that much difference these days." Elena laughed also.

"Thank you very much!"

They had reached the door to their apartment. Tejada unsnapped the padlock and drew back the bolts that prevented intruders from entering in their absence, reflecting as he did so that it might be pleasant to live in a place with a more conventional lock. Elena still smiled, but her voice was serious as she said, "I don't want to spy on anyone. But I'd like to live somewhere else. I'll think about it."

Chapter 5

"With all due respect, Señor Alcalde, it would be to the advantage of the town if the Guardia had adequate facilities *now*." Tejada, watching the blandly benevolent face of the Honorable Don Eduardo Caro y Peña, knew that his words were useless.

"I understand completely, Lieutenant." The mayor of Potes was courteous. "But any construction work in the town falls under the purview of Devastated Regions."

"I spoke to the director of Devastated Regions yesterday," Tejada said. "He informs me that while any long-term construction is, of course, the responsibility of his directorate, the civil administration is responsible for the allocation and maintenance of space in existing public buildings."

"And that is correct, Lieutenant," Caro agreed. "However, as you must have seen by now, Potes's facilities are stretched to the breaking point as it is. It's simply impossible to allocate more space to the Guardia. Even if all the decisions regarding the use of municipal lands and buildings hadn't been already made for this calendar year," he added as an afterthought.

Tejada gritted his teeth. A week in Potes had convinced him that the village had a more ornate and immovable bureaucracy than the Ministry of the Interior in Madrid, but it had also taught him that the only way to deal with this bureaucracy was with the kind of dogged persistence he had previously associated with prisoner interrogation. And during interrogations he was allowed to smack people if they tried his patience too far. As he stood in Don Eduardo's well-heated and comfortably furnished office, he wondered—not for the first time—if the determination to be unhelpful was a general feature of Potes's civil administration or if it might be directed at him personally.

Once again he tried to appeal to the mayor's self-interest. "It's not that I'm ungrateful for the facilities we have," he explained. "They're more than adequate for administrative purposes, and the barracks are ample enough for my men. But there aren't enough cells for prisoners."

The mayor spread his hands in a gesture of defeat. "I'm not arguing with you, Lieutenant. We all see the need for a jail. There were plans for an independent one last year, and then Devastated Regions had the idea of attaching it to the new town hall and courthouse, off the plaza. It should be more than sufficient."

Tejada's hopes sank. It was, he had learned, worse than useless to denigrate Potes's mythical "plaza"—currently two elongated trapezoids of bare land that sloped steeply down to the banks of the Quiviesa River and still bore traces of the debris of previously demolished structures. The director of Devastated Regions had proudly shown him blueprints of the fine public buildings—including courthouse and prison—that would surround the plaza, and had then waxed lyrical over several artists' renderings of Potes's hypothetical city center in what appeared to be high summer. When pressed, he had admitted that groundbreaking for the town hall was slated to begin at the end of April, once the weather was reliable. "Although with this late snow, perhaps we'll have to put it off until May, and by then they'll probably have pulled most of our workers for rebuilding Santander, because of the fire," he had finished, so mournfully that Tejada had not bothered to ask when the plaza was supposed to be finished.

"Yes, Señor Alcalde," Tejada agreed patiently. "I've seen the plans. But, unfortunately, as you know, criminals do not wait on architects' plans. I'm sure you don't want miscreants loose on the streets until the new jail is finished."

"This isn't a town with much criminal activity, Lieutenant," the mayor said comfortably. "Of course, the convicts that Devastated Regions has brought in aren't our type of people, but they're penned in. Well, most of the time anyway." He paused significantly, giving Tejada a chance to suppress his rage at the unfair aspersion. "And, of course, the more of them there are, the sooner the work gets finished. In fact"—Señor Caro stood up, ending the interview—"I think you should talk to the director of Devastated Regions. He has that barracks set up for workers, and I'm sure that he'd be willing to let you use the space if you do see the need for any arrests."

The need for arrests also would be obviated if the Guardia simply shot suspects on sight, Tejada reflected, but that was probably not the best way of obtaining information. He thanked the mayor for granting him an interview and left.

Sergeant Márquez was waiting for him outside the mayor's office. "Did you make any progress, sir?" he asked, as the two men left Señor Caro's home, which was also currently serving as the town hall.

The question was perfectly reasonable, and the tone of voice could not have been called disrespectful, but the sergeant's calm moderation irked Tejada. Márquez had dutifully accompanied his superior on three such visits in the last two days (two to the mayor and one to the director of Devastated Regions) and had been the silent witness to Tejada's lack of success. Tejada felt that a normal human being would have shown sympathetic frustration, or at least some amusement. The lieutenant would even have been grateful had Márquez stooped to saying, "I told you so." But Tejada was beginning to take the sergeant's bovine indifference as a personal insult. "He suggested that we use space in the Devastated Regions barracks," the lieutenant said, as they headed back across the river to the office of the director of Devastated Regions. "And he implied that we weren't doing enough to capture the Valencias."

"I'm sure you've done everything possible, sir."

Tejada thought that the sergeant's tone implied that someone else would have done more and better. He told himself that he was imagining things. "So am I," he said dryly, as they stepped out into the street. "Goodness knows, I'd have more time for trying to find them if I didn't have to keep worrying about space," he added, hoping to force Márquez to express some sympathy.

"You're moved in all right?" Sergeant Márquez succeeded in misinterpreting the comment in such a way as to imply that Tejada was neglecting his duties to take care of personal business.

"Yes," the lieutenant said shortly. To justify himself he added, "It's only common sense to have some place to hold prisoners. And we're comfortable at the Montalbáns'."

Márquez nodded. "Yes, sir. You explained that when you moved."

"Besides, I thought it would be a good way to keep an eye on the *fonda*," Tejada said, wondering why Márquez always went out of his way to be hostile.

"Good thinking." From the sergeant, this was high praise. "At least you're there nights. And probably no one who's actually wanted would come into town in daylight."

Tejada's mouth twisted, recognizing what Márquez was not saying. The guerrillas in the hills obviously were receiving a good deal of support from the townsfolk. Passing messages along would still be possible. Sergeant Márquez had eloquently refrained from comment when his commander had dropped the surveillance of the Montalbán house. Márquez was not easy to work with, but the lieutenant felt that his subordinate deserved some explanation. "My wife is there during the day," he said, hoping that he would not have to amplify the statement. Elena had strenuously resisted all pleas to help with what she referred to as spying and Tejada preferred to think of as simply keeping her eyes open.

"I hope she's comfortable." The sergeant was unusually solicitous.

"She seems to be settling in all right," Tejada said.

"A little town like Potes must be quite an adjustment, after the capital."

Tejada turned toward his colleague, startled. "We'd been living in Salamanca, not Madrid."

"Of course." Márquez was wearing a faintly malicious smile. "But I meant before her marriage." His smile widened a little at Tejada's raised eyebrows. "I was the interim ranking officer, remember, Lieutenant? I read your files, in Lieutenant Calero's place."

"Naturally." Tejada forced himself to smile back, although he wondered a good deal what the Guardia's files said about Elena. *Not that there's anything incriminating,* he told himself firmly. *No one could think that a girl alone in Madrid at the outbreak of the war could have done anything except go along with the Reds, for her own safety. I hope.*

They had reached the incongruously impressive administrative headquarters of the directorate for Devastated Regions. The director's office was in the Torre del Infantado, the squat medieval tower that sat in the center of Potes's as yet unbuilt plaza. The tower's businesslike crenellations and narrow window slits bore witness to its history as a fortress. Its red-gold stones had been scorched by fire many times, and the devastation of 1937 was imperceptible here. The tower's facade was broken at ground level by only one massive wooden door. Tejada rapped on the rusty hinges as he spoke. He was too preoccupied to notice that they bruised his knuckles.

"Of course it could be awkward if—" Márquez began. He stopped as the door swung backward and a man in a ragged overcoat greeted them with a resigned expression.

Tejada, discomfited by the topic and by Márquez's unusual tendency to talk, cast a sharp glance at the sergeant, but it was too late for further conversation. The director's assistant was already holding out his hand and saying, "Can I help you, Lieutenant?"

Tejada made a mental note to find out what Márquez thought might be awkward, and then fell into a by-now familiar routine. "Is Señor Rosas in?" he asked. "We'd like to see him."

"He just arrived a few minutes ago, Lieutenant. It's—"

"Through that door," Tejada finished. "I know the way, thank you."

He pulled open a door that creaked on ancient hinges, before Señor Rosas's deputy could say more. The regional director of Devastated Regions was huddled in a greatcoat by a fireplace built on a magnificent scale fit for roasting deer, and currently home to a miserable, smoky excuse for a fire. His desk was littered with papers of all shapes and sizes, from torn scraps of notepaper to scrolls of blueprints. "I told you I'm not—," he began irritably, turning around. His voice did not noticeably alter when he saw who his guests were. "Oh, it's you. Good morning, Lieutenant. Sergeant. What is it now?"

"I'm sorry to intrude, Señor Rosas." Tejada was not in the least sorry, and his tone perhaps hinted this. "But I've just spoken to the mayor, and he suggested that I speak to you about housing prisoners."

"If Caro is listening to complaints from those bastards, he's soft in the head," snapped Rosas. "They're housed properly. My God, they're probably better off than I am! Would you believe those idiots made a woodpile in the mud? Look at this!" he gestured to the fire. "It'll never burn. And the rest will probably take until next winter to dry out."

"Black birch burns when it's green," Tejada said absently. "You might try that. And I didn't mean your prisoners. I meant mine."

Rosas turned fully away from the fire for the first time. "Martin!" he bawled.

His assistant stuck his head around the door. "Yes, sir?"

"Go find some birch." The director returned his attention to Tejada. "Sit down. You've found the Valencians?" he asked hopefully, in a slightly more conciliatory voice.

Tejada sat, cautiously encouraged by the invitation. "Not yet, I'm afraid," he admitted, hoping that he was not about to undo any goodwill he might have created. "We're doing our best. But at the moment we have exactly three cells at our disposal. If we were—for example—to want to hold someone for interrogation regarding the Valencians' escape, we could easily run out of space."

Rosas frowned. "Why aren't you talking to the mayor? He's responsible for allocation of space."

"I have spoken to him," Tejada said patiently. "He suggested that you place some of your facilities at our disposal. Only until other space is available," he added hastily, seeing Señor Rosas's mouth open to protest.

The director considered. "How much space would you need?" he asked finally.

Tejada, who had been expecting another denial, was caught off guard. He had to think a moment before replying. "Our current facilities can hold ten men, maybe a dozen in a pinch. I'd like to have room for at least twenty. Could you spare space for ten?"

"You mean keep cells open just in case?" Rosas's voice was dubious.

Tejada shook his head. "No. I don't want to be unreasonable. But could you house more on short notice if necessary? I'll try to avoid it, but I don't want a riot on my hands and no place to stash people."

"We have the space," the director admitted. "But I'm not sure we have the other facilities."

"They don't need beds," Tejada said reassuringly. "Just floor space. And naturally if we park them with you we'll provide guards."

Rosas was silent. Then he said slowly, "I'd like to help you, Lieutenant. But under the circumstances . . ." He trailed off, looking unhappy.

"What circumstances?" Tejada demanded. "I doubt we'd leave anyone with you for the long term, but if it's a question of rations?"

"No." The director shook his head. "No, it isn't that. It's just that I thought there might be some security issues. But I suppose you know your own business."

Tejada disliked having civilians tell him his job, but the director's modest coda made him think a moment about what kinds of security issues the director of Devastated Regions might consider worth worrying about. He wondered if Rosas was worried about prisoners' making contact with a specific man working for Devastated Regions. But the men in Señor Rosas's camp were all from other parts of Spain, unlikely to have any local contacts. Unless one of them was so well known that his name would mean something even in these mountains. "You don't have any big fish among your workers?" he asked.

"No, no, they're all just common soldiers." Rosas spoke hastily. "But"—he turned to Sergeant Márquez. "I assume you've told the lieutenant about the, er, the difficulties we've been having this winter?"

Tejada turned his head toward Márquez and raised his eyebrows.

The sergeant had the grace to look embarrassed. "No, sir," he said. "The Valencians were our first priority when Lieutenant Tejada arrived, and then there were routines to go over, and since there hasn't been any action recently . . ." Márquez wilted under his commander's stare, and added humbly, "I should have followed it up with you, sir. It's just that the business of the escape came up, and it slipped my mind."

"Not your fault," Rosas said reassuringly.

Tejada, who had come to the conclusion that Márquez suffered from convenient amnesia when a good memory would make work for him, was less inclined to be forgiving. "Did this issue with Devastated Regions suggest anything about the Valencians' escape that might have prevented it?" he asked sharply. As he spoke, Tejada thought that he was already accustomed to taking the blame for the escape, though it had occurred before his arrival in Potes. It was pleasant to have a chance to shift the responsibility a little. And he certainly did not mind an excuse to reprimand Sergeant Márquez.

"No, Lieutenant," Rosas answered for the discomfited guardia. "It's an unrelated problem." He sighed. "We've set up a brick factory, and we're doing our best to use traditional techniques, using materials native to the region, but we still do need metal pipes for the water system, and then there are tools that speed the work. With no railroad, everything has to be brought through the gorge, and with the highway being what it is, it's a real headache."

"This was what you called the Guardia about?" Tejada interrupted, before the director could begin a full recital of his grievances. Perhaps Márquez had been justified in not reporting the conference with Señor Rosas, if the director had only sought him out to complain. At the back of his mind Tejada wondered if Señor Rosas held the Guardia responsible for the state of the roads. *We should hold* him *responsible for that, really,* he thought. *After all, that's his department. And now I'm starting to sound like the mayor.* The thought amused him enough to prevent him from being irritated.

"No. I was just explaining the background," Rosas said. "So you can see how inconvenient it is that our supplies are being stolen."

"Stolen?" Tejada was instantly alert. "From here, or before they arrive?"

"That was the issue," Rosas spoke confidently now, a professional on his own ground. "I believe our deliveries were being waylaid by bandits as they went through the gorge. It's a perfect place for highwaymen. But it was cleverly done. We've had a hard winter. A lot of blizzards. And to make things worse, a lot of our materials come via Santander. Did you pass through Santander on your way here, Lieutenant?" Tejada shook his head, and Rosas clicked his tongue against his teeth and continued. "It's a disaster area, worse than some of the cities that were bombed during the war. The fire last month took out the whole city center. So when a few shipments here and there didn't arrive in bad weather, I thought they were simply delayed. I couldn't get through to Santander right away to confirm that they had been shipped, and we were out of contact with them for a few days anyway when the fire started, so I decided to wait until spring. Then, about a month ago, two crates of dynamite disappeared from one of our construction sites. When I investigated, I found that there were other things missing from our warehouses. Pipes. Tiles. Stuff that had arrived as scheduled, but had disappeared since. We don't have as good an inventory as I'd like, but I also strongly suspect that a pair of wire cutters and several cans of lubricant have been stolen. That was when I contacted Sergeant Márquez."

Tejada turned on his subordinate with fury. "You didn't tell me dynamite was stolen?"

"If the thefts occurred between here and Santander, they're not really our jurisdiction." Márquez shifted uncomfortably. "And, as I said, with the Valencians . . ."

Tejada's mind was racing. If dynamite had been in the hands of the bandits for a month already, then there wasn't a bridge or barracks in the province that could be considered secure. He turned to Márquez. "Go back to the post and call Santander," he ordered. "Tell them two crates of dynamite were stolen." He glanced at Rosas. "Do you have the date?" he demanded.

"I found out about it February sixteenth," Rosas said promptly. "Make it the fourteenth as an outer limit."

"February fourteenth," Tejada continued. "It's presumed to be in the hands of Red guerrillas. They should take appropriate security measures. And find out if anything's blown up since then. If not, we may still be able to stop them."

"Sir." Márquez saluted and turned to leave.

Wire cutters, Tejada thought, suddenly nervous. "Márquez!"

"Sir?"

"If you can't get through, tell Ortíz and Carvallo to take the truck and bring the information to Santander personally."

"Personally, sir?" Márquez stared.

"Yes," Tejada snapped. Then, since Márquez was still goggling at him, he explained rapidly. "The Reds may have cut the phone lines. Or they could be down because of the blizzards. Or because some damn peasant's sheep got caught in one. Who knows? But *I'm* not going to be responsible for the damage a missing crate of dynamite could do, so unless you have a homing pigeon to send to Santander with a message, we have to use the truck. Get moving."

Márquez left, and Tejada turned back to Señor Rosas, who was looking aghast.

"I'm terribly sorry, Lieutenant," Rosas stammered. "I'd communicated with the Policía Armada, of course, since they're responsible for guarding the materials, and I thought that they'd talk to you. It's just that when they finally put out the fires in Santander I got a call that I was going to have to design a whole new street grid for the city center, and lose half my workforce, and it drove everything else out of my head. I'm an architect, you see. I only thought of it as building materials."

Tejada nodded, waving away the faltering explanation with one hand. "I take it you are afraid that some of your prisoners have somehow made contact with the guerrillas, either through local people or directly?"

Rosas nodded. "Exactly. That was why I thought imprisoning local people might create a security problem."

"It seems to me you already have a problem," Tejada said frankly. He did not intend to waste breath in recriminations about the missing dynamite. Rosas should have reported his suspicions earlier, and Márquez was clearly a raving incompetent, but there was no point in crying over spilt milk. However, Tejada saw no need to mince words. *Be fair,* the lieutenant reminded himself, although his stomach was still clenched with tension. *After all, the man made a report over two weeks ago. It's not his fault the Valencians escaped when they did.* Aloud he said, "Give me the details of the dynamite theft. When did you first miss it?"

"I told you. February sixteenth." Rosas sat behind his desk and opened a drawer. He continued speaking as he rummaged through files. "We're pushing the highway through to Espinama, and ultimately we plan to have the major routes to all the towns in the valley paved. Mostly we follow the valley, but sometimes we do need to clear rock, and we're up to one of those points now." He drew out an accordion folder and pulled a sheaf of papers from it as he talked. "I verified that we had the materials on . . ." He riffled through the papers and then found the date. "February fourteenth. That was a Saturday. We scheduled blasting for Monday. Only the foreman came and told Martin that he couldn't proceed because the dynamite was missing."

"Where was it being stored?" Tejada asked.

Rosas winced. "We have a storage shed for all our materials next to the garage. It's convenient. And since it's inside the perimeter of the worker's barracks . . ."

Tejada sighed, anticipating what Rosas was about to say. "It's not guarded."

"Well, the perimeter is guarded by the Policía Armada," Rosas said apologetically. "Of course I spoke to them right away. But they're mostly concerned with men, not materials. So I talked to Sergeant Márquez."

It was on the tip of Tejada's tongue to retort that they were obviously none too meticulous about guarding men either. "Well, it wasn't elves who moved the dynamite," he said instead. "I'd like to look over the site when we're finished here."

"Of course, Lieutenant." Rosas half-rose, and Tejada gestured him back to his seat.

"First I want to know about the other thefts," he explained. "The dates the shipments were supposed to arrive, exactly what they were, and when you first learned they were missing."

Rosas was already scrambling through files. "Here you are, Lieutenant." He held one out. "This was the first, I think. Just before Christmas. A shipment of stonecutter's tools."

Tejada was already scanning the requisition form and jotting down particulars. An hour later he had digested the better part of four similar forms, and was beginning to feel puzzled. He had been alarmed by the theft of dynamite, and had initially looked for other materials that could be used for terrorist activity. But two of the shipments were for lead pipes. Short of melting the lead down and casting it into bullets, Tejada could not imagine what violent purpose it could serve. One was a shipment of wire. Mass garroting seemed similarly unlikely. He had initially been alarmed to see that the final missing consignment had been over one hundred liters of gasoline. Then he had reflected that there was no way the bandits could be using vehicles in the forest, and had been simply puzzled. The only thing the missing goods seemed to have in common was their portability.

Sergeant Márquez returned with the news that the phone call to Santander had gone through without incident, and that the colonel was preparing appropriate security measures. Tejada was momentarily relieved until Márquez added, "He was pretty upset about it, sir. He said that according to the best intelligence available, the guerrilla nucleus was right here in the Liébana *comarca*, so capturing the bandits was our responsibility. And that it should be our first priority."

"No argument," Tejada said. "Did you ask him what he was basing his intelligence on? I'd like any reports we have."

"Yes, sir." Márquez nodded. "He said he'd send someone with them tomorrow."

"Well done," Tejada said, glad that the sergeant had for once taken the initiative. Márquez might be useless as the commander of a post, but he was performing a sergeant's duties capably. Perhaps he was one of those efficient but limited men who are superb subordinates, but disasters when promoted beyond their competence. Tejada turned back to the director. "Suppose you take us over to the site now. I'd like the sergeant to see the scene of the thefts as well."

"Yes, Lieutenant." Rosas was already standing up and digging his gloves out of his coat pockets.

The barracks and storage space used by the Department of Devastated Regions in Potes stood only a few minutes' walk from the Torre del Infantado, but the buildings formed an obscene contrast. While the tower projected the firm security of centuries, the hangarlike structure for the workers was pathetically fragile and strikingly ugly. It was made of unpainted wood that had weathered to gray and looked like a dirty heap of snow. The longest side of the building sat along the highway to Espinama, broken only by high barred windows. The driveway and entrance to the structure faced the tower. An extension had been built onto this side of the building, turning it into an *L* shape. The majority of the extension, Tejada noted with envy, was devoted to a garage currently holding three vehicles, with space for a fourth. A member of the Policía Armada stood on guard outside a narrow doorway.

Señor Rosas waved to the guard and led his companions toward the garage. "We can go in this way," he explained. "It's quicker."

Tejada took a deep breath. "There's an unguarded entrance?" he said, hoping that his voice sounded neutral.

Given the amount of local cooperation the guerrillas were receiving, Devastated Regions might as well have put up a FREE HARDWARE sign as leave an unguarded entrance during working hours.

"Oh, no, not when the workers are here," Rosas reassured him. "The garages are all locked when the men come in. But for now it's quicker to head out back this way."

He led them quickly into the shelter of the garage, past the trucks, to a door fastened with a padlock.

"Who else has the key?" the lieutenant asked as Rosas fumbled in his pockets and drew out a fat ring of keys.

"The foremen. Well, three of them." Rosas was inspecting keys as he spoke. He selected one and fitted it into the lock without pausing. "There are two more who are skilled masons, but they're also prisoners, so we don't let them have keys. And my assistant Martin. And Ladislao. He's the chief engineer. So that's five, altogether."

"Six, counting yours," Tejada corrected. "Where do you keep yours normally?"

"In my desk drawer. It's locked, and so is my office when I'm not there." Señor Rosas pushed open the door and gestured them toward the storeroom.

Tejada nodded and stepped forward, recalling that Señor Rosas had not bothered to lock his office before escorting them to the storeroom. *He must go between the tower and the barracks several times a day,* the lieutenant thought. *And probably he doesn't lock up if it's just for five minutes. Although Martin is there. And whoever got into that office would be taking an awful risk. Unless they knew what they were looking for. I'll have to talk to the foremen as well. And if they're using prisoners as foremen, I bet they can borrow keys. My God, what a setup! It's a wonder there's anything left!*

There was really very little to see in the storeroom. It was piled with tiles, lumber, coils of wire mesh, and lengths of lead pipe. Tools were put away in cabinets along one wall. The abundance of materials gave a false impression of chaos, but Rosas's evident confidence as he detailed the inventory made it clear that the storeroom was reasonably well organized. Clumps of sawdust and debris littered the floor, but the room was obviously too heavily used to harbor distinguishable footprints. The missing dynamite, Tejada learned, had been stored in a little alcove. The crates had been clearly labeled. "A safety precaution, Lieutenant," Rosas explained to him. "We really had no choice. Especially in a wood building." Tejada could not deny the point.

The lieutenant asked a few more questions before leaving the storeroom. Señor Rosas answered them readily. Tejada left Sergeant Márquez to interview the three foremen who had keys to the storeroom, and returned to the tower with Rosas to interview Martin. The lieutenant would have liked to interview the unknown Ladislao as well, but Rosas explained that the engineer was in Santander and only expected to return that Friday. He had, to the best of Señor Rosas's knowledge, taken his keys with him. Tejada spared a moment to hope that Ladislao's keys had not been stolen on the road to Santander, then turned his attention to Martin.

Martin, Tejada learned, had been a military engineer during the war. He was an ardent Falangist, and had apparently decided that his subordinate position in a tiny outpost was a result of his devotion to the glorious National Movement. His tendency to answer simple questions with inspirational quotes from "our founder, the great José Antonio" made him rather difficult to interview. Tejada, who had read a fair amount of José Antonio Primo de Rivera's work, and knew the quotes already, could not help thinking that the great José Antonio would probably have had the sense to use less rhetoric and more facts with regard to missing weapons.

Nevertheless, the lieutenant was cheerful when he returned to his office that afternoon. He had succeeded in wringing a promise from Señor Rosas to hold hypothetical extra prisoners segregated from Devastated Regions workers, and he had managed to worm a few facts out of Martin. When he met Sergeant Márquez, they compared notes on their interviews. The sergeant had received a fair amount of information as well. More to the point, he shared it readily, and seemed less sulky than Tejada had ever seen him. He had even gone so far as to talk with the guard provided by the Policía Armada. "Much good I got out of him!" Márquez snorted.

Tejada nodded, sympathetic. The Policía Armada, in the considered opinion of the Guardia Civil, was a waste of uniforms and weapons. "You might try writing to them to ask for reinforcements, though. After all," he smiled, "*they're* responsible for guarding Devastated Regions' people."

"Huh! They'll probably give us some crap about being overextended and say the Guardia should clean up their mess." But Márquez obediently reached for a pad and began composing a letter.

"Probably. I'll send word to the colonel and ask for reinforcements," Tejada agreed. "And it wouldn't hurt if we had another truck."

The two guardias finished their letters and mailed them. Then Márquez began skimming the reports filed by Battista and Torres, and Tejada went to speak to the post's civilian cook, who had complained that rations were not arriving promptly. *All in all, it had been a surprisingly productive day,* Tejada thought, as he headed back across the river to the Montalbáns' *fonda.* The inn was deserted when he pushed open the door to the bar, but the fire was burning cheerfully in the fireplace. Since his wife was not in front of the fire, the lieutenant headed upstairs, wondering if the upper floors were that much warmer. "Elena?" he called, as he reached their room. "Did you have a good day? I thought we might—"

He stopped as he opened the door and saw that the room was empty. There was a note propped up against a book on the table. "WENT TO TAMA. BACK SOON.—ELENA."

Tejada shook his head, unsure whether to laugh or be annoyed. He was fairly sure that normal women did not set off on two-kilometer walks through the snow by themselves when they were heavily pregnant. And there was the question of dinner. His Elena was certainly unique. Or possibly incorrigible. *Fine behavior for a respectable married lady,* he thought, smiling. *It comes of those years on her own in Madrid.* And then, more seriously, *I wonder what Márquez was going to tell me when he said, "It could be awkward if—" I wonder if he knows about Elena's life in Madrid, before I met her. And if he does, is there something he's not mentioning?*

Uneasy for reasons he could hardly identify, Tejada turned and headed down the stairs. There was only one road to Tama, and Elena was in all likelihood already on her way back. He put on his hat again, and set out to meet her.

Chapter 6

Although their move back to Anselmo and Bárbara Montalbáns' *fonda* had solved their most pressing problems with regard to furniture, the Tejadas' room still lacked a decent table for writing, and anything in the way of shelves. Elena, whose luggage consisted of nearly as many books as clothes, felt the lack of shelf space acutely. She had spent the first few days after their move making herself as comfortable as possible with the existing furnishings, and futilely trying to talk to Bárbara de Montalbán. At noon, after her morning chores she had dutifully eaten lunch and done her best to follow her husband's injunction to take a nap. *We need a table and shelves*, she thought, staring at the ceiling. Then, with a strange mixture of fear and exhilaration, like someone who has just turned the key in the ignition of a car for the first time: *And I suppose we'll need a cradle soon.* The idea made sleep impossible. She got up, dutifully wrapped herself in sweaters and scarves against the cold, and set off for Tama to find a carpenter.

Elena had not traveled along the road to Tama since her arrival in Potes in the predawn blizzard nearly two weeks before. Now, although the wind was still sharp enough to take her breath away, she was in a far better position to appreciate it. The road sloped uphill gently for perhaps fifty meters from the *fonda*, lined on both sides with houses made of the same tiny, painstakingly assembled stones as the Torre del Infantado. At the top of the crest the houses stopped suddenly and the road leveled out, curling around the base of the mountain that bordered the valley to the east in a leisurely curve shaped like a swan's neck. The land beyond the town was bare. To her left, in the valley, lay fields that would surely be cultivated in a few weeks' time. To her right, barren scrub marked the hillside, broken occasionally by shepherds' huts made of windowless stone. The first houses of Tama sat in the curve of the swan's neck, just over a kilometer away.

Elena was content to meet no traffic as she trudged along. She had a destination, and a pleasant sense of purpose, and she did not mind being alone. She was far more lonely among the hostile stares of Potes's townsfolk who whispered about the lieutenant's wife, or the equally hostile stares of the guardias under her husband's command. The exercise warmed her, and the clean-smelling wind brought color to her cheeks even as it made her eyes water. By the time she reached the center of Tama, the village was once again coming alive after siesta. Hopeful that she would not be recognized as the lieutenant's wife, Elena stopped at a tiny dry-goods store that had just reopened its shutters and asked timidly if anyone knew where the carpenter's workshop was.

"Quico's, you mean?" The man behind the counter nodded. "Yes, Señora. You take the first left, three doors down. You can't miss it."

"Thank you." The man had spoken to her as if she was simply a normal stranger, and Elena was grateful. "Do you know if he's likely to be open for business now?"

He laughed. "This isn't Bilbao, Señora. Quico is open when he's home, providing it's a decent hour."

Elena smiled, thanked him again, and set out. She took the first left, and headed along a narrow street, cautiously sniffing the dry air for the scent of wood shavings. It was too cold to smell anything, but the third house on her left had a set of wooden shutters on the ground floor, and over the shutters hung the neatly lettered sign: FEDERICO ÁLVAREZ. CARPENTER. The door was shut. Elena hesitated, wondering if she should knock, when a howl of outrage shattered the quiet of the street, and the door opened inward rapidly. A girl of about five emerged at full speed, followed by another perhaps a year older. "I-hate-you-I-hate-you-I-hate-you!" The howls resolved themselves into words. Elena stepped to one side quickly to avoid being bowled over, and the smaller child fled past her, hardly noticing her presence. The girl's pursuer had the advantage of longer legs, however, and rage animated her. She tackled her opponent with a flying leap, and the two of them collapsed in the street, wrestling ferociously.

Elena had spent a fair amount of her life as a schoolteacher, and her instinct was to intervene at once. But she was painfully conscious of the damage a carelessly aimed kick could do to her baby. For a moment warring impulses held her still. Then she said sharply, "That's enough. Both of you."

Even as she spoke, the door opened again to reveal a middle-aged man, who leaned on a shepherd's hazel-wood crook. "Girls!" The man's voice was quiet but firm. "Stand up and apologize to the lady."

Confronted with overwhelming authority, the combatants separated and scrambled to their feet. There was, Elena saw as they bobbed rebellious curtsies and muttered apologies, a strong resemblance between them. Both had the round cheeks and fair hair typical of the region, strikingly combined with dark, almond-shaped eyes. Both wore much-faded cotton skirts, thick wool sweaters, and injured expressions. The man in the doorway had gray hair, but the same almond-shaped eyes. He nodded gravely to Elena. "I hope my girls didn't trouble you, Señora?"

Elena shook her head. "No. Not at all."

"Good." He looked at the girls. "Upstairs."

"But—" the older one began.

"Upstairs," he repeated.

The children filed past him, both making an effort to hold

back tears. He turned back to Elena, looking slightly embarrassed. "I'm sorry, Señora. My wife has been tied up with our
youngest. You mustn't think . . ."

"I like children," Elena said honestly, as he trailed off. "And I
know on a day like today when it's too cold to play outdoors,
and they don't have much to do, they get cranky."

"True enough," he agreed with a slight smile. "But I don't
know what the neighbors will say, with them making an exhibi-
tion like that in the street."

Since Elena was not prepared to vouch for what the neighbors would say, she murmured something noncommittal and
then asked hopefully, "Are you Señor Álvarez?"

"At your service. How can I help you?"

"I understand you make furniture," Elena explained. "My
husband and I have just moved, and—" She hesitated for an
instant. "And my husband is very busy at the moment. Do you
have time to do some work for us?"

"Of course," the carpenter agreed readily. "Come in." He
stepped backward and gestured toward the hall.

As Elena entered the hallway, she saw that a steep staircase
led up to a door that stood ajar. Light and the warm smell of
lamb stew spilled down the stairs. Señor Álvarez opened a door
beside the stairway that led to a much colder room, with a work-
bench in one corner, trails of sawdust on the tiles, and the faint
sweet scent of pine emanating from planed boards piled
along one wall. "What do you think?" the carpenter asked, gesturing to the center of the room, where an almost completed
rocking chair and an apparently finished end table sat.

"They're beautiful," Elena said truthfully. "Do you do bookcases as well?"

"Yes, ma'am. Do you have the dimensions you want?"

"Yes." Elena had left the sheet of paper with her penciled jot-
tings in an inside pocket and had to unwind herself from several
layers of clothing to get at it. She located it finally and held it

out. "Here they are. The top measurements are for a table, and the lower ones for shelves."

He inspected the paper, and then seemed to notice that Elena was shivering. "I could do these. But the shop's cold right now. If you'd like to come upstairs to the fire, we can talk business in comfort."

"Thank you." Elena followed him with relief. The walk had tired her more than she liked, and the idea of sitting down somewhere warm was attractive.

"Through here." Señor Álvarez pushed open the door at the top of the stairs. "Marta," he raised his voice. "Company."

A woman carrying a baby came forward to meet Elena. She had obviously just left a rocking chair by the woodstove in the far corner, a finished version of the piece Elena had seen in the workshop. A thin-faced boy bent over several sheets of paper at a table pushed against one wall looked up curiously as they entered and then got to his feet. The two little girls Elena had seen earlier stuck their heads out from behind a door to what she guessed was a bedroom. "My wife." Señor Álvarez gestured to the woman.

The woman nodded, and held out her free hand. "Marta Santos. Nice to meet you."

"Elena Fernández. Likewise."

"Señora Fernández is interested in furniture," the carpenter explained, ushering her toward the table. "Shelves and a table, isn't that right?"

"You're new to Tama?" his wife asked, as Elena nodded and sank gratefully into the chair Señor Álvarez offered.

"To Potes, actually. I understand there's no one who makes furniture there, though," she added.

"There isn't call for many of us," Quico Álvarez explained. "Most folks just buy lumber and do simple stuff on their own."

Elena flushed. Both Álvarez and his wife were too polite to ask, but she could feel their unspoken curiosity about her absent husband who had no time for carpentry. "You work on your own then?" she asked, to distract him.

Álvarez smiled, and indicated the boy beside him. "Simón helps me. He's a good little apprentice." The boy looked at the floor, obviously embarrassed by his father's praise.

Elena addressed her next remark to Simón, knowing that children hated being discussed in their presence as if they weren't there. "Do you want to be a carpenter when you grow up?"

Simón shrugged and muttered something inaudible. "Of course he does," said his father firmly. He turned back to business. "Did you have a preference for the type of wood, Señora? Pine would be cheaper, but oak is more durable. A nicer finish for the table, too."

"How much cheaper?" Elena demanded.

Señor Álvarez handed the sheet of paper with Elena's notes on it to his son. "Can you do the calculations?"

Simón took the paper with alacrity, picked up the pencil he had been using before, and began to scribble. His father smiled at him, and then said, half-apologetically and half-proudly, "The boy has a head for figures."

"It's a useful skill," Elena said, feeling the inanity of the comment.

"That it is." The carpenter looked at the boy with fondness. "In a way, it's a shame he can't go to school. Father Bernardo's been kind about showing him all kinds of tricks with numbers."

"Algebra," Simón put in helpfully, animated for the first time. "And a little geometry. He says carpentry is mostly geometry anyway but that he doesn't remember it much because it never made sense to him. Here." He slid the paper to his father, shaking his head at the priest's forgetfulness.

"Give it to Señora Fernández, not to me," Álvarez gently corrected the boy. "Can you read his handwriting, Señora?"

"Yes, of course." Elena, who had deciphered handwriting far worse than Simón's, read the estimates without difficulty.

They were unexpectedly and almost embarrassingly moderate. She was torn between a distaste for unnecessary haggling and the knowledge that airily ordering the most expensive furniture would mark her as relatively wealthy, and mean an end to the easy familiarity of her dealings with the Álvarez family.

Álvarez misread her hesitation. "These are just estimates, Señora. I'll accept payment in kind, whenever it's convenient, of course."

Elena blushed, doubly embarrassed by her wealth and the uselessness of her husband's profession, which created nothing that could be offered in exchange for furniture. "No, it's fine. I think we can afford the oak." She tried to soften the words.

"Maybe you'd like to consult with your husband?" the carpenter suggested.

Faced with the choice of explaining her husband's finances or his job, Elena opted for the former. "I'm sure it will be no problem." She hesitated and then said, "Also, I should have mentioned it before, we—" irrationally, she blushed, "we need a cradle."

"Of course." Álvarez nodded. "Say another—" He frowned in thought. "Seventy-five pesetas."

Elena nodded. "I-I suppose that will be fine." She hesitated, still feeling awkward. "Do you want a deposit?"

The carpenter smiled at her. "If you'd like to pay for the materials in advance, you can. But it's not necessary, Señora."

Elena, used to the more businesslike practices of the city, was once more embarrassed. "Well . . . then . . . thank you."

"It will take a few weeks." Álvarez spoke calmly. "I can make the pieces you need most urgently first and you can pick them up. Or would you rather come and collect them all together?"

Elena thought a moment. "It depends a little on how easily my husband can borrow a truck."

Marta Santos spoke up from her place by the stove. "It would have to be a cart. The only trucks in the valley are government vehicles."

Elena sighed. Sailing under false colors any longer would be unwise as well as difficult. "Actually, my husband is the lieutenant of the Guardia Civil post in Potes."

There was a little space of silence around her words. Then Quico Álvarez said in a slightly overly hearty tone, "That will likely be no problem then."

Elena nodded, looking at the ground. It had been so pleasant to talk to people without the invisible barrier that enclosed her in Potes. "No." She stood up reluctantly. It was time to go. "Thank you for—thank you."

"You're welcome." Álvarez stood also, to shake hands with her.

Elena dawdled putting on her coat, unwilling to step out into the cold loneliness of the afternoon again, even though her hosts' hospitality had given way to wariness. The baby kicked, and she was inspired to say suddenly, "Señora Santos, I wonder if you—if you know of a midwife? Since we've just arrived, I don't know anyone and . . . " Her voice trailed off. She looked more as if she was pleading than she realized.

"This is your first?" The carpenter's wife thawed slightly, speaking with the faintly approving condescension of the experienced mother.

"Yes."

"There aren't midwives here, the way you'd get in the city. Mostly the neighbors come and help. After all, once a woman's been through the whole thing a few times she knows how it works." Marta's voice was sympathetic as she added, "I don't suppose the guardias' wives . . . ?"

"They're unmarried." Elena paused, and then added, "We're staying at the Casa Montalbán. I know Señora Nuñez mentioned she'd had children. Maybe . . . "

Marta shook her head. "I don't think Bárbara's a good choice."

"She . . . she seems a little hard to get to know," Elena admitted, unwilling to ask for help outright, and hoping that it would be offered.

"You can't really blame her." Señora Santos took pity on her guest. "Bárbara's had troubles with the Guardia."

"Marta." Señor Álvarez's voice held the same note of quiet warning he had used with his daughters.

She glanced at him and shook her head. "It's no secret, Quico." To Elena, she added, "The younger Montalbán boy was killed on the orders of the old lieutenant."

Elena bowed her head. "I'd heard that after the town fell there were some reprisals."

Because her eyes were lowered, Elena missed the quick look that passed between the carpenter and his wife as she said, "after the town *fell,*" so she was both gratified and intrigued when Señora Santos added, with some bitterness, "This had nothing to do with the war. Jesulín Montalbán was going with a girl Lieutenant Calero had his eye on. Everyone knew they'd quarreled about her. But when the soldiers came and the lieutenant said Jesulín was a Red, who could argue with him?"

Elena met Marta Santos's eyes, horrified. "And the girl?"

"Poor Señorita Laura," Marta sighed. "She wouldn't give Calero the time of day until he threatened that the soldiers would come for her brother as well."

"He deserved what happened to him!" Elena's voice was trembling with rage.

Quico Álvarez nodded, almost unconsciously, but stopped himself from agreeing in words. A nod could always be denied later. "It broke Anselmo's heart," he said quietly. "Jesulín always was his favorite."

Elena leaned on the table, trying to control her sudden nausea. She remembered Bárbara Nuñez saying tightly, "My sons were taken four years ago." And then, with sickening clarity, she heard her husband's voice saying, "It's likely her husband's a murderer." "I'm sorry," she said, knowing the words were both true and meaningless, and wanting to make some reparation. "I . . . I won't ask Señora Nuñez."

Marta nodded, accepting the words and the intention for what they were worth. "Bárbara's had troubles," she repeated. "Don't be too hard on her."

Elena desperately looked for something to say that would prolong her visit to the warm room, among people who did not seem to hate her. Something to put off the return to the *fonda* where she would have to face Bárbara Nuñez with her new knowledge. She took a deep breath and met Marta Santos's eyes. "M-may I come see you again?" she stammered. "I don't have very much to do in Potes, and I-I might be able to help Simón with geometry or something."

"You've studied geometry?" Simón interjected hopefully.

"I used to be a teacher," Elena explained. "Only of younger children, of course. But I might remember a little math."

Simón considered the offer. "Could I show you how to draw a line from an equation?" he offered. "If Papa lets me?"

Elena smiled. "I'd like that. It's been a long time since I've calculated slope."

Simón's eyes were sparkling. "Can I, Papa? Please?"

The carpenter looked amused. "I don't think you know what you've let yourself in for, Señora."

"I don't mind," Elena reassured him. "That is . . . if it won't be taking Simón away from his chores?"

Quico Álvarez shook his head. "I can manage without him for a day."

"Thank you!" Simón was quivering with impatience. "When can we start?"

Elena hesitated. Simón's parents had not issued an invitation, and she was unwilling to push further. Simón's mother spoke first. "You're welcome to stay for a little while now," she said, accurately reading the desires of both her son and her unexpected guest. "The girls have been in a foul mood all day, and it will give me a chance to deal with them."

"I'll get my slate." Simón made a rapid exit.

"If you'll excuse me, I have work to do." Álvarez stood up. Laugh lines deepened around his eyes as he said, "I was going to ask in what order you'd like me to make the furniture, but seeing how well you get along with the boy, I'm guessing you'll want the bookshelves first."

"I guess so." Elena laughed.

The carpenter let himself out, and Simón returned with his slate. Elena spent a happy hour dredging her memory for half-forgotten facts and watching with amazement as Simón drank them in like a thirsty sponge. The boy flitted cheerfully from the Pythagorean theorem to what Father Bernardo had told him about classical architecture to how he had heard that if you dammed the Quiviesa all of Santander could have electric lights for practically nothing, and back to the aqueducts of the Romans, practically without pausing for breath.

Simón was, he admitted, going to be twelve in June, although his reproachful look at this eminently conventional and irrelevant question told Elena that she had sunk in his esteem for asking it. He submitted to her questions and to her idiotic comment that it was a shame that he could not go to school regularly in return for information on more interesting topics. Was it true that everyone had telephones in Salamanca? And indoor bathrooms? Where did the water come from? Was it like in the Roman aqueducts? How fast did trains travel generally? Where did the coal go in the locomotive?

Elena, faced with a host of questions that she was having some difficulty answering, was grateful for the interruption of Simón's younger sisters. He introduced them as "the brats" and their mother presented them somewhat more formally as Teresa and Ramonita. The girls had overcome their shyness and wanted a chance to look at the visitor they had ignored earlier. To Simón's annoyance, Elena politely asked their ages as well.

Teresa appointed herself spokesperson. "I'm almost eight. And she's only six."

"And do you study with Father Bernardo too?"

"I know how to read already." Teresa was complacent. "But Father Bernardo says I have to keep coming for catechism until I'm confirmed."

Elena smiled, trying to stifle her wave of sadness. It was criminal that this child thought that learning her letters and catechism was the beginning and end of schooling. And Simón was a bright boy. He would have been at the head of his class if a school had been available. "What about you, Ramonita? Are you learning to read too?"

The child nodded but said nothing. Simón made an impatient noise. "They know enough already," he said, tired of attention being diverted into social matters. "They're just girls."

"So what?" Elena retorted.

Simón struggled with this concept for a moment. "If Father Bernardo wasted all his time trying to teach girls, he wouldn't have time to show *me* anything," he offered finally.

Faced with this perfectly unhypocritical logic, Elena was forced to laugh. "Maybe Father Bernardo could use some help," she suggested. "That way everyone could learn more."

"That would be something to take up with him, Señora." To Simón's surprise, his mother entered the conversation. "I know he's spoken of a school before."

"Really?" Elena made a mental note to track down the priest.

Teresa took a deep breath. "Señora?"

"Yes?"

"How—?" The girl gathered her courage in both hands. "How old were you when you stopped playing with dolls?"

Elena had enough experience to guess the reason for the question. "I don't remember exactly," she said gravely. "I played with them less by the time I was Simón's age. But I know that I still had my favorite doll when I went to university."

"See!" Teresa muttered to her sister.

"I'm sure you're not too old to play with them," Elena said

encouragingly, suddenly enlightened as to the cause of the fight she had witnessed earlier. "Has someone been telling you that?"

"No." Teresa raised her head. "But Nita ruined my Victoria."

"She's not ruined the least littlest bit!" Ramonita protested.

"She *kidnapped* her," Teresa continued implacably. "And then she *broke* her arm."

The smaller girl began to sniffle. "It was an accident!"

"Well, people break their arms sometimes," Elena pointed out reasonably. "Maybe Victoria's arm could be set. You could play you were at a hospital."

Teresa looked suddenly hopeful. "Simón, do you think Papa has glue?"

"He won't let *you* use it," Simón said firmly. "But he might let me fix it for you."

"Would you? You're good at fixing things." Teresa looked appealingly at her older brother.

"I'll get it." Simón slid out of his chair and hurried down the stairs.

Teresa disappeared briefly and returned, carrying a beautifully carved wooden doll in one arm and a snapped-off forearm in her free hand. "This is Victoria." She made a face at her cowering little sister and added in a whisper, "Kidnapper!"

Elena had taught in wartime, and wounds and amputations had been grim realities for too many of her students. During recess periods her classroom had at times been filled with "wounded" dolls, some of them actually broken for verisimilitude by their frightened and enraged owners. She was an expert at supervising doll hospitals. By the time Simón returned with glue, Victoria had been laid out on a rag bed, and Teresa was vigorously persuading her to swallow imaginary morphine. Forgetting his disdain for girlish matters, Simón was persuaded to act as a surgeon. The operation was successful, and the hospital administrator was smothered in thanks, not only from the three children but from Marta Santos. "I don't know what I'd have done if Teresa and Nita had stayed at each other's throats," she added in an undertone. "I imagine their father would have fixed Victoria eventually, but they're happy this way. I hate it when it's too cold for them to play out-of-doors properly."

Elena modestly disclaimed thanks, and silently thought that she would have to actively pursue the unknown Father Bernardo about starting a school. She remained, playing with the children and chatting with their mother, until striking church bells made her start up. "I should go," she said regretfully. "I've taken up far too much of your afternoon. And my husband will be wondering where I am."

Marta politely said that she had not noticed the time at all, and the children unanimously agreed that her visit had been a pleasure. The carpenter's wife saw her to the door. "It was nice to meet you, Señora Fernández," she said, holding out her hand. "Come again."

"Thank you." Elena set out for home happier than she had been since her arrival in Potes. The sun was already low behind the mountains, and the path was more uphill than she remembered, but she felt like singing as she hurried along, her breath making little steam puffs in the evening air. Friends, she thought happily. People to talk to. And I'll find Father Bernardo and ask him about the school. And we'll have shelves soon.

She came around a curve in the road and saw the familiar silhouette of cloak and tricorn coming toward her. For a moment she was troubled, remembering what she had learned of the late Lieutenant Calero. Then her sense of contentment reappeared. She raised one arm and waved, saw her husband wave back, and hurried forward to meet him and tell him about her afternoon.

Chapter 7

Tejada relaxed as he came near enough to see Elena clearly. Her face was red with cold, and the wind at her back was whipping little tendrils of hair out from her scarf and plastering them against her cheeks. But her eyes were glowing and there was a laugh in her voice as she hailed him and gave him a quick hug. *She's settling in,* he thought with relief. *I suppose it is an adjustment to come here if you've only lived in cities.*

"You look good," he said, when they had exchanged greetings. "Although I'm not at all sure it's normal for women in your condition to wander off into the snow."

"You know I like to travel on my own." Her voice was teasing.

"A habit I've frequently deplored. But in this instance no harm done. What took you to Tama?"

"Furniture. I ordered bookshelves. And a table, and cradle." Elena hastily summarized the business of the afternoon.

"Sounds like you got a lot done," Tejada said, guessing that her good humor was as much a result of a productive day as his own. "But it's after seven. You must have started late."

Elena shrugged. "I ended up visiting with Señora Santos and her children a bit."

"Good," Tejada approved. "I told you it would be a good idea to have some female friends. Although I wish you had found some nearer to home!"

Elena made a noncommittal noise, unhappily reminded of

Bárbara Nuñez. "How was your meeting with the mayor?" she asked, to distract him.

Tejada, who had almost lost track of the morning's meeting in the wake of subsequent events, shook his head. "We didn't get anything out of him. But I talked to Rosas again."

"Was he helpful?" Elena asked, conscientiously trying to hope that her husband's plans for incarcerating their neighbors had been advanced.

"I suppose so. But in the meantime he's dropped a nice little crisis into our laps."

"Not another escape?" Elena exclaimed. She was unsure whether to be pleased or worried. She knew that the Guardia was still making an effort to capture the escaped Valencians, but she also guessed that the men were well out of Liébana and on their way home by now, and that Carlos was not wasting too much effort on their case. A more recent escape meant a chance at freedom for more men, but it also meant that Carlos would be instrumental in trying to track them down, and Elena found herself hoping that no strain would be placed on her loyalties.

"I wish!" Tejada shook his head. "Most of the prisoners just head home and the Guardia picks them up when they get there. But Rosas has misplaced a shipment of dynamite."

"Misplaced?" Elena raised her eyebrows.

"Left totally unguarded in countryside crawling with bandits," Tejada said with disgust.

Elena winced. "I suppose you're worried the guerrillas might use it for sabotage?"

"The war's *over*," Tejada said, a little annoyed. "So they're *not* guerrillas. They're just thugs."

"Who blow up military targets."

"They kill innocent people, Elena!"

"All right, all right," Elena sighed. "You have to get it back. When did it go missing?"

"Just over three weeks ago. That's the problem."

Because he was still nervous about the missing dynamite, Tejada ended up rehashing most of his day with his wife. He did his best to talk about other subjects during dinner, because he felt that it was inconsiderate to inflict too much of his work on Elena. He tried to listen attentively to his wife's description of her afternoon, but he was preoccupied, and it was a relief when the plates were cleared away and Elena settled into an armchair, dug out the baby sweater she had been knitting, and let silence fall. Tejada stretched, and lit a cigarette. He inhaled deeply, and some of the frustrations of the day began to seep out of him with the smoke. It was good to be warm and fed and home. He glanced over at Elena, and saw that she looked happy and maternal and domestic. He leaned back comfortably in his chair, and closed his eyes. "The thing is," he said meditatively. "We're so shorthanded. I *have* to keep sending Ortíz and Carvallo out on routine patrols or we'd have no one covering the entire district. And really Battista and Torres should be out also. And Márquez and I should do patrol duty once every two weeks at a minimum. But if I do that, then we have no one who can investigate the thefts from Devastated Regions, or do surveillance. And if I divert men into surveillance or investigation, then we lose the information we pick up through routine patrols."

"You could ask for reinforcements," Elena suggested.

"I won't get them. And anyway, where would we put them?" her husband said sardonically. "Besides, it's a question of shutting stable doors. Rosas claims that the dynamite was always under lock and key or heavily guarded. But it disappeared over a Sunday, and I'll bet Rosas wasn't in to check then. And probably those clowns in the Policía Armada took the day off, too."

"The prisoners hear mass Sunday, don't they?" Elena pointed out. "So if the dynamite disappeared then, they have an alibi for part of the day."

Tejada nodded, and took a thoughtful drag on the cigarette. "There's a chaplain who comes down from the monastery to hear confessions and then give the service. But it's over by four. And so is the mass at San Vicente, in town."

"You think someone from town made contact with a prisoner Sunday afternoon then?" Elena asked.

"No." Tejada shook his head. "The prisoners are all from other provinces. They don't have local visitors. And according to Rosas's assistant none of them had any visits that Sunday." He made an annoyed noise. "None of them even went *out* that Sunday. It was cold, and they kept to their rooms."

Elena reflected that the prisoners' barracks were probably cold in the best of circumstances. "Then you don't think they helped steal the dynamite," she said, glad that the guardias would not have a chance to vent their frustration on a captive.

"No. I think the key time is Sunday morning, when everyone is in church. If they knew what they were looking for, a small group of men could have easily gotten into the Devastated Regions compound, taken what they wanted, and been up in the hills before anyone knew they'd been there."

"Wouldn't they have been missed in church?" Elena asked.

Tejada smiled. "Not if they've been up in the hills for the last six months. I went through the files with Márquez. We have a number of local boys playing hide-and-seek."

"For six months?" Elena protested.

"Longer than that, in some cases. A couple are going on two years now. And then there are the more recent ones. Our landlord, for instance." Elena's knitting needles froze in midair. The lieutenant looked at her with concern. "What's the matter?"

Elena paused before replying, and deliberately resumed her work. "You think Anselmo Montalbán has taken to the hills then?"

Tejada shrugged. "Face the facts, Elena. He's not here. It's been a week since we asked that he report to the post. He's a wanted man."

"And you think we should still stay here?" Elena's voice was troubled.

Tejada considered his sense of well-being. "I don't think we're in any danger from Montalbán. The contrary, actually, since he'd be doubly responsible if anything happened to us here. And I'm sick of moving. Aren't you? Once we get furniture we'll be nicely settled."

Elena came to the end of a row. "What about Montalbán's wife?" She pretended to count stitches so that she could look down.

Tejada sighed. "I'm sorry if she's been giving you the cold shoulder. But you mustn't let her bother you."

"What about *us* bothering *her*?" Elena demanded, furious. "How do you think she feels about having a guardia in her home?"

"We're paying her," Tejada said. "And times are hard. I'd think she'd be glad of the extra cash. And I don't think we're difficult tenants."

"But how do you think she'll feel about having to share her house with a man who's declared her husband a bandit?" To her dismay, Elena heard a treacherous crack in her voice. "How do you think it feels to see the uniform of the Guardia every day and be reminded of the man who murdered her son?"

Tejada sat up straight. When Elena sounded on the verge of tears, there was usually a reason. "Her son was tried and executed by a military court in Santander," he said, curious to see if he would be contradicted.

"But he was denounced by a guardia!"

"Back up," the lieutenant commanded. "I don't know any details. Tell the story from the beginning."

Elena drew a hiccuping breath, and then poured out what she had learned that afternoon about Lieutenant Calero and Jesulín Montalbán. Tejada was frowning heavily by the time she finished. "You don't know that's true," he said.

"Why would they lie to me?"

Tejada drew his chair next to hers and put one arm around

her shoulders. "I didn't mean they were lying," he said gently. "But they live in Tama, not Potes. Suppose it was just a story that they'd heard reported thirdhand. They might have *believed* it was true."

Elena shrugged his arm away. "They live twenty minutes' walk from here. They're probably here for the market every week."

"All right then," Tejada sighed. "Suppose that Calero was in love with this Laura. Even supposing he knew the Montalbán kid was too, he might still have genuinely believed Montalbán was a Red. What was he supposed to do? Keep silent for the girl's sake and risk his own career? Give Young Montalbán a chance to take to the hills and pick him off like a sitting duck?"

Elena looked at him, skeptical. "And threatening the girl's brother?" she demanded. "That was a coincidence?"

Tejada opened his mouth to say that no guardia could let his personal feelings interfere with his job, considered the hideous possibility of his Red brother-in-law returning from Mexico, forcing him to do just that, and shut it again. "You've just given Anselmo Montalbán a lovely motive for murder," he pointed out, hoping to change the subject.

"I know." Elena sounded unhappy. "I thought of that, too. But surely you can't blame him."

Tejada considered. "I can understand why he did it," he said honestly. "If he did do it. But I don't think he was justified, if that's what you mean. And if we catch him and it turns out he killed Calero, I'll still turn him over for trial."

Elena made a despairing noise. "And keep living here, all the while?"

"Let's blow up that bridge when we come to it, shall we?" Tejada grimaced, his mind once more running on saboteurs. "At the moment, we don't even know why Calero was killed. It could have been because he found something out about the missing dynamite, and the Reds didn't want him to have a chance to pass it on."

Elena nodded, and finished another row. "That's true. And I suppose you're right, but . . ."

"But?"

Elena folded her knitting and smiled ruefully. "Sometimes I really hate it that you're a guardia."

The lieutenant brushed her cheek. "Only sometimes?"

"Well, all the time actually," she admitted.

Tejada stood up and held out his hands to her, wrists crossed. "Sometimes I wish you were a different person, too," he said, thinking of Sergeant Márquez's unfinished comment. "But we're stuck with each other. Come on." She grasped his hands and he pulled her to her feet. "Time for the baby to be in bed."

Elena had a hard time falling asleep. The weight of the baby made her back ache, and her sleeping husband's encircling arm was smotheringly heavy. *Carlos is a decent man,* she thought, shaping the words of an imaginary dialogue with Marta Santos, and carefully inching her way out from under his arm. *Really, he is. It's just that he only talks to the guardias, so he doesn't know your side of the story. But if you talked to him . . . well, maybe that wouldn't work, but we have to try. He has to try. I don't think he's spoken to anyone in Potes about anything that wasn't strictly related to Guardia business. Of course, no one wants to talk to him, but if he wasn't being pigheaded he would make the effort. And I think he'd listen to people here. I'm pretty sure. I wish he'd try.* She did not remember the end of the dialogue, but when she woke up sunlight and cold air were streaming through the windows, and Carlos was bending over her fully dressed, saying, "Good morning, Sleeping Beauty. I have a surprise for you."

Elena sat up and rubbed sleep out of her eyes. "Give me a minute to get up and dressed."

"Of course. It will wait for breakfast." He was looking so pleased with himself that Elena hurried more than she would have otherwise.

She discovered that two mugs were already sitting on the

table, along with a loaf of bread, and turned to her husband, smiling. "You got breakfast? Thank you."

"Not *just* breakfast," Tejada said, enjoying watching her face. "I meant to do this yesterday, but then I overslept. Look!" He produced a tin from behind his back with a flourish.

Elena took the tin and inspected it, bewildered. "Milk?"

"We're in dairy country." Tejada looked smug. "I talked to one of the farmers at the fair on Monday. Of course, technically, he shouldn't be selling anything above the ration price, but it's only a liter a day, and since we're neighbors—"

"A liter a *day?*" Elena interrupted, stupefied. "What on earth for?"

"For you." The lieutenant looked wounded. "To drink," he amplified, since she was still staring at him openmouthed.

"You can't have gotten involved in the black market for this!"

"It's not *really* the black market." Tejada shifted, uncomfortable. "I told you, it's practically extra. And it's good for you. For the baby, I mean."

"But I don't *like* milk," Elena protested.

Tejada, who had been disappointed by her reaction, suddenly remembered his wife's lamentable upbringing. "This is *fresh* milk," he said encouragingly. "It's not like what you get in the city. Trust me. Just try it."

Elena sat down, gingerly poured the foamy white liquid into a mug, and raised it dubiously, with an expression of distaste. Then she sipped. It was as cool as the morning air, and tasted almost as thick as honey. She waited, her mouth braced for the faint sour aftertaste that she remembered from the milk of her childhood. The taste did not change. She drank again, more deeply.

"If you're not going to finish that, I'll drink it," Tejada said.

Elena glared at him. "*You're* not having a baby," she pointed out.

He grinned. "I told you you'd like it."

Elena did not bother replying. She drank and was content.

Carlos *had* spoken to someone. It was a start. Tejada watched her in silence for a few minutes, pleased that his gift had worked as planned. "What are you doing today?" he asked finally.

"I thought I'd try to find Father Bernardo, and talk to him about Simón Álvarez."

"You think the kid is bright enough for a scholarship?" Tejada asked.

She shrugged. "I don't know. But I think it's a shame there's no school in Potes. There are enough children. Señora Santos said she felt the same way. I wanted to talk to him about it. Maybe if he sent a letter to Devastated Regions . . ."

Tejada laughed and stood up. "For God's sake don't confuse them," he advised. "Rosas has enough on his plate right now with that fairy-tale plaza."

"You want the baby to go to school?"

"You want the baby to have a permanent place to live?"

Elena frowned. "You think I shouldn't then?"

"No." Tejada was putting on his cloak. "I think it's a good idea. But why not ask the good father if the diocese has any plans for a school before you go pestering the civil authorities." He kissed Elena on the cheek and hurried out before she could begin one of their endless debates about secular education.

Márquez greeted him at the post with the news that the post at Santander had called to say that intelligence reports about recent guerrilla activity were on their way, that the Devastated Regions engineer was expected back within the hour, and that Guardia Torres had the flu and was unable to go out on a two-day patrol. Tejada sighed. "Great. Put Ortíz with Battista. One of us will have to go with Carvallo." He hesitated. "I'd rather stick close to the phone in case something comes up. Would you mind patrol duty?"

"Of course not. If I hurry I should be able to interview the prisoners Rosas has put in charge of work crews before I leave. Then if you talk to what's-his-name—the engineer—we'll have covered everyone, and—" The sergeant stopped suddenly. "I mean, at your orders, Lieutenant."

Tejada smiled at him. "Relax, Márquez. You weren't out of line. It's a good idea. Go talk to the prisoners and I'll interview Señor—" he glanced at the folder—"Señor Ladislao Oquendo as soon as he returns."

"Yes, sir." The sergeant saluted and disappeared.

Tejada walked over to the Torre del Infantado and announced that he intended to wait for the chief engineer. He was in luck. Ladislao Oquendo arrived within fifteen minutes. Their interview was brief and to the point. Yes, the engineer had keys to all the offices in the tower and also to the storage areas of the barracks. Yes, he carried them on his person at all times. No, he lent them to no one. If one of the skilled prisoners needed materials, he went with the man to the storeroom and unlocked the door for him. Yes, he was aware of the possibility of theft and had been very annoyed by the disappearance of the dynamite. Oquendo was careful not to criticize Señor Rosas directly, but his tone of voice was eloquent as he said, "*I* have always believed in an *organized* construction site." Tejada, listening to the precise and almost obsessional answers, mentally absolved the engineer of carelessness. The lieutenant wondered, with a flicker of amusement, how the pragmatic engineer got along with the ideologue Martín. Of course, it was possible that the precise Ladislao was also precisely stealing from his organization. Tejada turned to a fresh page in his notebook. "How long have you worked for Devastated Regions, Señor Oquendo?"

"Since the winter of 1938, shortly after it was founded."

"And before that?"

"I worked for a private firm in Bilbao until the war broke out. Then I slipped across the Red lines to Vitoria in August of 1936."

"Quick work," Tejada commented.

Oquendo's face showed distaste. "I had some . . . family experience with the Reds."

Tejada glanced at the beginning of his notes, where he had written the engineer's full name: Ladislao Oquendo Pavlov. "Your mother was a White Russian?" he suggested.

"That is correct, Lieutenant." Oquendo pursed his lips and then added, "My father is a Spaniard. And I was born in this country. I consider myself thoroughly Spanish."

"There's no need to be defensive," Tejada said mildly. "You've devoted your career to rebuilding our country."

The engineer smiled slightly. "I'm sorry, Lieutenant. I find that many people automatically associate Russia with the Reds. And since my given name is somewhat conspicuous—"

"Understood," Tejada said, mentally crossing Ladislao Oquendo off his list of suspects for the theft of dynamite. "It must be doubly irritating to be suspected of being a Red, and to have suffered at their hands."

He ended the interview and returned to the post to find Sergeant Márquez just on the verge of starting off on patrol with Guardia Carvallo. "The reports on the interviews are on your desk sir," Márquez said as he saddled one of the Guardia's mounts. "I was in a hurry, so they're not formal, but if there's anything you don't understand, jot it down, and I'll answer it as soon as I get back. And the intelligence reports from Santander came today, too."

"Good." Tejada nodded, satisfied. "Anything interesting come up in your interviews with the prisoners?"

"They all deny everything, of course," Márquez snorted. "What did you expect?"

Tejada laughed. "Well, it's what I expected, but I was *hoping* for something a little more useful."

Guardia Carvallo led his horse out into the plaza and swung himself into the saddle. Márquez checked to be sure that the packs on his mount were secure, and then prepared to follow. "See you in two days, sir."

Tejada nodded, and then, against his better judgment, said quickly, "Márquez?"

"Sir?" The sergeant half-turned.

"What did you think would be awkward?" Tejada asked, wishing that he had raised the subject in a more casual and graceful way.

Márquez looked blank. "Awkward?" he repeated.

"You said yesterday, 'It could be awkward if—'" Tejada prompted. Then, seeing that the sergeant still looked puzzled, "We were discussing Madrid."

The sergeant thought for a moment and then he laughed. "Oh, I was only going to say that it would be a bit awkward if Devastated Regions transferred Herrera here," he said cheerfully. "But I don't think we need to worry about that. I think he's in a crew in Valencia somewhere."

Tejada, who had been half-worried that Márquez had discovered something utterly damning in Elena's file, was relieved but also puzzled. "Who's Herrera?" he asked.

Márquez had already mounted. He raised his eyebrows and looked down at his commander. "You didn't know about him?" he asked. "I assumed your wife had told you about her connection with him during the war. But, as I say, I don't think it's anything to worry about now." He waited a moment for Tejada to reply and then said, "Tell Torres I hope he feels better so that I don't have to freeze my tail off for another two days. And have fun with the reports from Santander, sir. Come on, Carvallo."

The two guardias spurred their horses and started out of town. Tejada watched them with a certain sympathy for Márquez's light bay. He felt rather as if the sergeant had just kicked him in the stomach as well.

Chapter 8

Like much of Potes, the church of San Vicente was in poor repair. But unlike much of the town, the church had a stone roof, so it had been undamaged by fire. The oldest part of the church dated from the fourteenth century, and had been built without wide and smashable windows, so its exterior had been largely spared by the war. Everything breakable or burnable had been broken or burned at the outbreak of the war, however, so the inside was a dark, cavernous space.

There were no signs outside the building to state the hours of mass and confession, much less where the priest was to be found. Elena pushed open the heavy door a little hesitantly. She had never seen the church in the middle of the week before. It was unlit, except for a few guttering candles, and, coming from the bright daylight outside, her eyes took a few moments to adjust. The smell was an odd mixture of old fires and new incense. She took a few steps forward, her shoes echoing in the dark silence. "Hello? Is anyone there?" No one answered, and she turned to leave.

Her hand was already on the door when she heard a clunk in the darkness behind her. She froze, heart pounding with irrational terror for a moment, and then a reassuringly normal voice said, "Sorry, I was in the sacristy. Were you looking for me?"

Elena spun around and saw that the voice was attached to a shadowy figure who appeared to be holding an electric flashlight.

The figure moved toward her, and she made out the swish of a priest's cassock. "Father Bernardo?"

"That's right." The priest reached her and held out his right hand, the flashlight in his left. "Do you wish to confess, daughter?"

"N-no, thank you." Elena shook his hand. "I wanted to speak to you about an issue I was told you were interested in."

"Then we had better go over to the parish house," said Father Bernardo, opening the door and holding it for her. "It's warmer, and better lit."

Elena inspected the priest as they emerged into the sunlight. He was a fair, thin man, a few years shy of forty. He peered with frank curiosity at his guest through wire-rimmed glasses. "Forgive me. I believe you must be the new lieutenant's wife but I'm afraid I don't know your name."

Elena introduced herself. "And I'm Bernardo Peña," the priest said, bending his neck in a way that suggested a full bow. "A pleasure."

He led her along the riverbank to a long, low-lying building with smoke coming from the chimney. "I work here in the winters," he explained, unlocking the door and ushering her across the hall. "Most of the parish knows to search for me here if I'm not in the church. But I should put a sign up for newcomers. Please, sit down. Would you like something to drink? Coffee?"

Elena sat down in the armchair he was indicating, and inspected her surroundings. She was in a square, low-ceilinged room, with a woodstove against one wall. The room was furnished as a study, with a desk near the stove and a semicircle of chairs arranged around a rug on which stood a reading table. Lead-paned windows looked out on the river, and there were bookcases with glass doors opposite the fireplace. Elena fought the urge to get up and inspect the books. She had always believed that a person's library was a sure index to character. As far as she could tell from her seat, the books were mostly full series: encyclopedias, and Alianza's Castilian Classics and World Classics. The complete works of Augustine and Aquinas.

Father Bernardo took the seat behind the desk and opened a drawer. "If you'll just wait a moment." He drew out a diary, made an extended note, and then closed it and put it away again. "I'm at your disposal, Señora."

Elena had been considering the best way to broach the subject. "I understand that you have been teaching the local children, in the absence of a regular school in Potes," she said, and waited for his response.

He nodded. "Yes. Of course, most of the children here are shepherds' or farmers' sons. They don't have the time or the need for real schooling. But I do my best to teach them to read and write and the simple arithmetic they need for business. These days even a shepherd needs to know how to sign his name. And when the boys go away to do their military service they can write home. It's wonderful what a comfort that is to them and to their families. And then of course there's . . . ," he paused, looking a little embarrassed. "There are several advantages, I believe," he finished. "But I shouldn't bore you with this, Señora."

"Oh, no," Elena spoke eagerly. "No, I think you're absolutely right. It would be wonderful to have a school in Potes."

Father Bernardo sighed. "I have taken the matter up with my superiors," he confided. "But we're not a wealthy parish, and many people don't see the need. Of course, if we were to have a larger force of guardias stationed here, and *they* brought children, it would be a different story." He looked hopefully at Elena. "The government might take an interest then, you see."

"My husband told me that I shouldn't pester the government to take on the church's responsibility." Elena laughed, and the priest laughed with her, guessing the end of her sentence before she finished it.

"It *should* be the church's responsibility," Father Bernardo said, still smiling, but serious. "But unfortunately none of the teaching orders are here. And in these times no one thinks of the young."

"But there's still legislation mandating compulsory primary education, isn't there?" Elena protested. "Surely someone *has* to take an interest?"

"You're the first person who has," the priest said. "That is, if this was what you wished to speak to me about?"

Elena nodded vigorously. "Yes. I thought it was a shame that there was no school here, and someone suggested that I take it up with you. But I don't quite understand. There was a school here before the war, wasn't there?"

Father Bernardo frowned and nodded. "Yes. Unfortunately, the teacher was tried as a Red in '38. There was no one to fill the post afterward."

Elena gulped, remembering that in 1938 she had been teaching in a school that undoubtedly would have been categorized as Red. "I can see where that might discourage applicants!"

"Señor Benigno had a proper trial!" the priest reassured her a little defensively. "He wasn't–er–removed from prison by militias, or anything like that. Lieutenant Calero made sure everything was legal."

"I'm sure that was a comfort to him." Elena was unable to keep her voice completely free of sarcasm.

The priest took her seriously. "I believe it was. I was with him at the end and he seemed calm. And, of course, that way his family was able to give him a decent burial, which was a blessing to the whole town, really. The Románs were well liked, even though they weren't from around here."

Elena felt her throat muscles working as she fought nausea. She knew that the Regime regarded teachers as automatically suspect, but she had managed to ignore what might have happened to her if she had not met Carlos. She wondered how many of her former colleagues were dead or in prison, and if the ones who were dead had been "lucky" enough to have legal trials. "It's a shame there's a shortage of qualified teachers," she said, keeping her voice soft so that it would not scream an accusation.

"Yes." The priest turned a pen around in his hands. "Of course, entrusting the instruction of the young to anyone without the proper moral qualifications is . . . well, a risk, if not actually a sin. But it's been extremely difficult to find someone of good moral and political character who is able to teach school here. And willing to, on what my esteemed cousin will pay," he finished with a touch of acid.

"Your cousin?" Elena asked, momentarily bewildered.

"The mayor is my aunt's son," Father Bernardo explained. "I have spoken to him repeatedly about the desirability of a school in Potes. But he insists the town's finances will not permit it."

Elena remembered her husband's not always printable comments about the mayor, and felt some sympathy for Father Bernardo. But if the mayor had based his major opposition to the school on the expense of a salary, she could outwit him. "How many children do you have?" she asked, already thinking about how to get around the lack of materials, and wondering whether reasonable classroom space could be prepared by the following autumn.

"Anywhere between twenty and thirty-five. It varies. At the moment I'm working only with this spring's communicants. Then in the summer the kids are needed at home. I expect I'll have about twenty-five in the fall."

"And how old are they?"

"Usually between six and twelve." Gratified by the unexpected interest, Father Bernardo added, "Sometimes I have a little class for girls, too. Of course, that means only doing the morning session for the boys."

Elena's jaw dropped. '*A little class for girls,* too!' she thought, stunned. *So that's all Teresa and Nita have. Just a few odds and ends! And he'd have* room *for girls in the regular session if he tried!* Father Bernardo misread her horrified expression and shifted a little uncomfortably in his chair. "I know a woman would be better fitted for the job. But there's no one in the Liébana who could teach the girls. They need to learn doctrine and catechism anyway. And I don't believe it corrupts their essential natures. I'm sure you yourself learned to read, Señora. . . ."

"I have a degree from the Madrid Complutense," Elena said in a strangled voice. "And I taught primary school for five years. That was why I wanted to see you."

"Oh!" The priest relaxed visibly. "How wonderful! I take it you would be interested in any efforts to start a regular primary school in Potes, then?"

"With girls equally included," Elena said firmly.

"Ideally, yes," Father Bernardo agreed cautiously. "I've thought for a while that the best thing would be to have an advisory committee made up of parishioners, who could petition the diocese for the necessary resources, and perhaps oversee the hiring of teachers. I'd spoken to the secretary of the Falange in Cillorigo, and the head of the Women's Auxiliary, but they weren't very interested. Given your qualifications, I'd be extremely grateful if you chaired the committee. Would you be willing?"

"To chair a committee?" Elena said, disbelieving.

Father Bernardo turned his pen in his hands again, and blinked behind his glasses. "I'm sorry." He sounded embarrassed. "I shouldn't have phrased it like that. Of course, you'd have to discuss it with Lieutenant Tejada. But would you consider the position provided he didn't object?"

It was on the tip of Elena's tongue to say that Carlos could put up with her profession as she put up with his, but she had the sense to suppress this retort. "I don't see the need for a committee, Father," she said carefully. "I'm fully qualified to teach all primary subjects. If the diocese can provide space, it would be my pleasure to take the open position at whatever salary the municipality sees fit to provide."

"B-but . . ." The priest's blush was faint but widespread. He was pale pink from forehead to collar. "You couldn't possibly *teach*. I-I mean, you're . . . obviously a married woman."

"I imagine no arrangements would be made until the following autumn at the earliest," Elena said. "And by then I'll be . . . less obvious, I suppose."

"But your child—," Father Bernardo protested. "You couldn't *leave* it."

"Only for a few hours a day," Elena argued, "no more than I would if I was expected to pay morning visits or lunch with friends. I'm sure that I could arrange for a babysitter."

Father Bernardo shook his head. "You can't have considered this sufficiently. What would your husband say to this scheme? And what kind of example do you suppose it would set for the girls? It would hardly prepare them for marriage and motherhood!"

Elena sighed, and fought down disappointment. She had known that the priest would disapprove of her idea, and she had a reluctant suspicion that Carlos would as well. But her afternoon with the Álvarez children had thrown her boredom and loneliness and sheer misery in Potes into stark contrast. For a few moments Father Bernardo's unexpected sympathy had made her hope that she would be able to shrug off the stifling burden of being the lieutenant's wife, and be simply herself: Elena Fernández, teacher. "You're right, of course," she conceded, folding her hands over her stomach, and absently tapping her wedding ring with one finger. "I'm sorry. I don't know what I was thinking."

"You were happy as a teacher," Father Bernardo said, shrewdly but not unkindly.

"Yes." Elena avoided his eyes and wondered if she had irreparably damaged her chances of teaching again or if her tactical error could be overcome, given time and strategy.

"It's perfectly understandable." Father Bernardo's voice was professionally soothing now, the voice of a priest discussing a matter of conscience with a parishioner. "I was happy as a seminarian. We all look back on times when we were young with fondness or regret. But we can't let this sort of nostalgia make us avoid our responsibilities."

"No, Father."

The priest judged her sufficiently subdued. "You will ask the lieutenant if you can chair this committee?" he urged. "I would be most grateful for your help."

"Yes, Father." Elena raised her head. "I don't think Carlos will object. He has always believed in—" she smiled sardonically, "working for the good of the community." Father Bernardo saw her smile but read it as pride in her husband's good qualities, and honored her for her loyalty.

"Good," he said. "I'll speak to the mayor, then. And I have a few colleagues at Santo Toribio who might also be interested."

Elena nodded. It was not the same as actually teaching. But it was something to do. The priest had drawn out a pad, and was jotting notes with enthusiasm. She felt superfluity creeping up on her again, and said quickly, "Also, there was one other thing."

"Yes?"

"Simón Álvarez," Elena said. "The carpenter's son. He mentioned that you know him—that is, he mentioned that you were his teacher, and his parents were the ones who suggested I speak to you."

"Oh, yes." Father Bernardo spoke warmly, his attention caught. "A fine boy. With some real gift for mathematics. He was one of my brightest students."

"You don't think he might like to study more?" Elena suggested.

"He's nearly twelve." Father Bernardo was thoughtful. "And he already knows more than is taught in most primary schools. I thought for a little while that he might have a vocation but that seems not to be the case. A shame, in a way. He seems to enjoy studying."

"I understand he's his father's apprentice," Elena said.

"Yes, that's correct. And Quico has always said that the boy has a feel for carpentry, and is quick to learn. So perhaps it's for the best that he follows his father and helps the family."

"Señor Álvarez has never been opposed to his schooling, though?" Elena asked experimentally.

"Oh, no. Quico wanted Simón to start working with him nearly two years ago, but I'd just gotten classes organized then— it was right after the war—and the boy begged to be allowed to stay on. The Álvarezes have always been indulgent parents," Father Bernardo added, with mild disapproval.

"He could study for the baccalaureate?" Elena knew the answer to the question as she spoke. Simón was perfectly capable. But there was no way he could leave his home to study.

Father Bernardo was already shaking his head. "If he felt a calling for the priesthood it might be different. But there's no question of that. If I had time, I might try to give him some extra tutoring, and then arrange to have him sit for exams when he's a little older. But I'm afraid I can't devote the necessary time and effort to it. And neither will he be able to, as Quico starts to depend on him more."

Elena mentally reviewed the necessary preparation for baccalaureate exams. She was fairly sure that she knew the material, although teaching it—especially without textbooks—would be a challenge. She considered asking if one of the monks at Santo Toribio who had taken an interest in the school might be persuaded to tutor Simón. Then she decided that further consultation with Simón and his parents would be necessary first. If Simón could convince a few of his friends to study for the baccalaureate, Potes's hypothetical school might be able to offer more advanced classes as well. She nodded, and rose to leave. "I suppose you're right. Thank you so much for seeing me."

"Thank you for coming." The priest stood as well. "I suppose . . . if you and your husband have a few hours free sometime I would be happy to take you up to Santo Toribio. Some of my colleagues there are also interested in starting a school, and I think you should meet them."

"My husband has been busy lately," Elena said honestly. "Although I'm sure he'd be interested in seeing the monastery. But I can come whenever is convenient. And I understand the monastery has considerable architectural interest."

"Yes." Father Bernardo nodded. "Although it was heavily damaged during the war. It should be very beautiful when it's restored. I thought the lieutenant might be able to arrange transportation so that you would be more comfortable."

"Transportation?" Elena was startled. "How far away is the monastery?"

"Oh, only a few kilometers. Forty-five minutes' walk if there's no snow. But given the weather, and your . . . your condition." Father Bernardo went pink again. "I thought a cart might be advisable."

Elena laughed although she was more than a little annoyed. "I've never felt better in my life, Father. I'm sure I could manage the walk. And if I wait for my husband to be free to do it, I may never get there."

"Well . . . if you're sure . . ." The priest appeared to be pondering a decision. "I was planning to walk up to Santo Toribio tomorrow morning. Would you like to come?"

"What time?" Elena asked promptly.

"Ten o'clock?"

"I'll meet you here," Elena said with satisfaction. She thanked Father Bernardo again, and went home, still hammering out plans for a primary school, and for Simón Álvarez's further education in her head.

Chapter 9

Elena had expected that Carlos would be pleased that she had made a new friend in Potes, and with such a respectable person as a priest. That evening she recounted her interview with Father Bernardo and announced her engagement with him for the following day with considerable pride. To her surprise, Tejada scowled. "Honestly, Elena, what's the matter with you? It's bad enough to go wandering off on your own, but to hike all the way up to Santo Toribio with some stranger? What will people say?"

The unexpected attack left Elena speechless. "You mean . . . you don't want me to go?" she faltered.

She looked so hurt that the lieutenant regretted his words. "No," he said, more gently. "No, it's fine if you go. I just worry about you."

"Father Bernardo's as bad as you are," Elena reassured him. "He didn't think I should walk because of the baby."

Tejada nodded, and his frown returned. He could not think of any reason why his wife should not spend a few hours unchaperoned in the company of a parish priest of (as far as he knew) unblemished reputation, but he was not happy. Elena questioned him about his day with every appearance of cheerful sympathy. She exclaimed over the inconvenience of Torres's illness, and added Father Bernardo's comments on his cousin's intractability when Tejada mentioned another interview with the mayor. She was politely interested in the news that the Guardia was receiving new weapons from Santander, and she laughed when Tejada told a funny story about a farmer who had come to complain to the Guardia about a stolen sheep. Tejada would have thought the evening perfect had it not been for the shadow that Márquez's last words had cast. There was, Tejada thought, no point in asking Elena about the mysterious Herrera. The simplest thing would be to simply wait until Márquez was not present, and read through Elena's file. Although it was unlikely the file would contain anything of interest. Doubtless, Herrera had been an acquaintance of Elena's during the war. Perhaps even a friend. Certainly nothing more. It would be an insult to ask her exactly what their relationship had been. Furthermore, his Elena was a brave, generous soul, who did not forget her friends, and if she learned that some probably totally forgotten casual acquaintance was doing penance in a work camp somewhere, she would undoubtedly waste sympathy on him.

Tejada woke early the next morning by an effort of will. He slipped out of bed and dressed without shaving, to go and get Elena's milk. It was amazing, he thought as he left her sleeping, the discomforts that a man would endure for a woman he loved. The morning was clear and bright, although clouds were massed above the peaks. As he climbed toward the village of Rases he saw the work crews moving out along the highway toward Espinama to clear the ground for a new highway, and looked at the gaunt figures with dislike. Somewhere in Valencia the unknown Herrera was probably starting his work as well. Tejada wondered if the Red ever thought about Elena Fernández during his imprisonment. Herrera would have no way of knowing that she was married, of course. Perhaps he cherished hopes of finding her again when he was released. Unless he was serving a life sentence. Tejada was momentarily cheered by this thought, and then reflected that if this were the case Herrera might never suffer the disillusionment of learning of Elena's marriage.

He reached the farm perhaps half an hour after sunrise. The girl milking the cows had been told to expect him, and she handed over the milk without comment, although she managed a timid smile when he paid her. They exchanged a few words about the weather and roads, and the lieutenant was momentarily distracted. He cradled the milk in one arm on the way back, fondly remembering Elena's reaction the previous day. What did Márquez's snide malice matter? She loved *him*, and he was quite sure that she had never been in love with this Herrera. Of course, Herrera might have been in love with *her*. That was perfectly understandable, and even acceptable, provided that he never thought about her anymore. Although *that* didn't seem too likely. Tejada suffered a flash of rage, imagining some pathetically filthy, skeletal Red prisoner (probably crawling with lice) having lustful fantasies about *his* Elena. He told himself sternly that he was being silly. Herrera was probably dead, or close to it. Márquez was an ass. And to prove that the sergeant was an ass, he would check the files when he reached the post, and find out exactly how trifling Elena's acquaintance with Herrera had been.

Somewhat cheered by these reflections, he quickened as he reached the end of one switchback and turned around a hairpin bend, squinting into the glittering dawn. The blinding light irresistibly suggested the Falange's anthem, and he began to sing. "Onward, with faces turned toward sunrise—"

Bang. Tejada recognized the report of a shotgun, and doubled over, cursing himself for going out unarmed. *Bang. Bang.* There was a spray of dirt on the road a few yards ahead of him, and a stone skimmed across the path like shrapnel. He ran for the relative cover of the ditch by the side of the road and dropped into it, the milk sloshing out of its tin. He counted three more shots, calculating furiously whether it would be more or less risky to take to the woods. When he starts shooting again, the lieutenant thought, I'll try to guess where it's coming from, and head away from there the next time he reloads. Unless there's more than one of them. He waited for more gunfire, pulse thudding. There was nothing.

Finally, after five minutes that felt like twenty, Tejada remembered Ortíz's insistence that the maquis frequently shot merely to get the attention of the guardias, without actually trying to kill. Feeling somewhat like a mouse that a well-fed house cat has forgotten in the pursuit of some other amusement, the lieutenant cautiously pushed himself to his feet and brushed off his clothing as best he could. He retrieved the milk tin, and started back to Potes as quickly as possible, feeling considerably less like singing.

Elena was already awake and dressed when he reached home, and she greeted him with a smile. "Oh, Carlos. Milk again? You're sweet."

"I'm afraid some of it got spilled," he said, apologetic. "I . . . fell. That's why I'm all muddy."

"You poor thing!" She kissed him, instantly sympathetic. "Careful," she added a bit breathlessly, as he gave her a hug. "You'll crush the baby."

"I wouldn't do that." Tejada drew back and gave her stomach a proprietary pat. "Give the kid a drink."

They breakfasted quickly. Tejada had reluctantly decided to go on a foot patrol through the town on his own, if Torres was still not mobile, and Elena did not want to be late for her appointment with Father Bernardo. He walked her as far as the parish house, where he met Father Bernardo and exchanged a few courtesies, then he headed on to the post alone.

Corporal Battista met him at the door with the news that Torres was still in bed. Tejada thanked him, told him to take Guardia Ortíz and begin a patrol toward Tama, and then went to see the sick guardia. Torres was huddled in quilts. An empty mug and several dirty handkerchiefs were strewn around his bed. He groaned slightly as the door opened. "Good morning, Torres." Tejada surveyed his subordinate with distaste.

"Good morning, Lieutenant." Torres sketched a salute with one hand, and then drew it under the quilt again. His voice was a hoarse whisper.

"Can you sit up?"

"Yes, sir." Torres obligingly struggled to a sitting position, his back propped against the wall. Beads of sweat popped out on his forehead, and his face was flushed dark red, but he shivered uncontrollably. "I think I'll be fine by this afternoon, Lieutenant," Torres added optimistically, drawing his knees to his chest and leaning on them for support. "I just have a bit of a headache."

The words banished Tejada's faint hope that the guardia was malingering. Torn between annoyance at the scheduling problems caused by Torres's unexpected illness and real pity for his discomfort, Tejada said simply, "I'm going out on patrol this afternoon. Do you think you'll be well enough to do desk duty then?"

"Yes, sir."

"Good. Get some sleep."

Tejada left, reflecting that, with his voice in its current state, Torres would be useless answering the telephone, but that it was unlikely anyone would call anyway. He settled into his office, did some nonessential paperwork to satisfy his conscience, and then moved almost stealthily toward the filing cabinets. There was no need for caution. He was the only able-bodied man at the post, and he had a perfect right to look at the files in any case. Still, he pulled open the drawer labeled PERSONNEL with a furtive feeling.

His own record was in an accordion file at the back of the drawer. He flipped through it hastily, until he found the slim manila folder labeled FERNÁNDEZ RÍOS DE TEJADA, ELENA (WIFE). He opened the folder and looked down at a poor carbon copy of the standard information form, undoubtedly forwarded by the Guardia in Salamanca. There was a small rectangle in the upper right-hand corner of the form, with Elena's identity number printed below it, where the original had a copy of Elena's photo. Tejada hastily skimmed his wife's personal data, marveling how little information was conveyed by so much detail.

DOB: 12 March 1913 Place of Birth: Salamanca (Salamanca)
Hair: Black Eyes: Black Height: 155 cm Weight: 52 kilos

The physical description was foolish, Tejada thought. The file could have been describing any tall, slender young woman. It made no mention of the way her hair tangled into curls when she fell asleep with it unbraided, or the way her eyes could become lightless, depthless pools, like water in a deep well, when she was thoughtful or troubled.

Married: Carlos Tejada Alonso y León (Lt. Gª Civil file #854-948-213) 28 July 1940
Father: Guillermo Fernández Ochoa (see file #293-394-098 Salamanca)
Mother: María Pilar Ríos de Fernández
Siblings: Hipólito Fernández Ríos (exiled)
Children: None

There was no mention of the baby, Tejada thought, and then reflected comfortably that he would probably be the one to update the file to include his offspring. He continued reading:

Education: Graduated Madrid Complutense 1934, degree in education
Colegio Santa Rosa (Salamanca) 1930, baccalaureate
Occupation: None (1939–present) Primary School Teacher (Madrid) 1934–1939

Tejada frowned, and began to pay more attention, knowing that the date and place of Elena's former occupation would have attracted Márquez's attention, and fairly sure that the information he was looking for would come in the next few lines. He was not disappointed. Membership in the Women's Auxiliary of the Falange and the National Movement's Association of Teachers was conspicuously absent from the lines marked "affiliations." In their place was the curt but damning notation: Syndicate of Primary Schoolteachers (PSOE) 1934–1939 Membership #2493. A handwritten asterisk followed the typed entry, leading to a note at the bottom of the page in nearly illegible script: Records seized 17/4/39 show E. Fernández recruited by J. Herrera (arrested 16/4/39, currently doing penance in Ronda (Málaga)).

Tejada sat back, relieved. Of course Elena had belonged to a teachers' union in Madrid. Given the aggressively socialist climate of the capital during and before the war, she would have had no choice. Herrera was simply the man who had recruited her. There was no reason to think that there had been any personal connection. Tejada shook his head at his own stupidity, and then uncomfortably remembered Márquez saying, *"I assumed your wife had told you about her connection with him."* Elena liked talking about teaching. She had frequently told him stories of her days as a teacher before the war. But she had never mentioned Herrera. That was odd. *Probably she never spoke about him because they were barely more than casual acquaintances,* Tejada told himself. *She probably lost touch with him before the war ever started.* Although he was a little relieved by this logical explanation, he put his file back in the filing cabinet with a vague feeling of unease. He worked steadily and conscientiously through the pile of papers on his desk to avoid thinking any more about his wife or the mysterious Herrera.

Shortly before noon a call came through from Colonel Súarez in Santander. "Just a heads-up, Lieutenant," the colonel said, once he had identified himself. "The Policía Armada is sending a force of fifty men to the Liébana, to combat banditry. They'll be under their own command, and you're not responsible for them. But you're expected to cooperate fully with them if they ask."

"*We're* expected to cooperate with *them*?" Tejada said pointedly.

Colonel Súarez made an exasperated noise. "I'm sorry, Tejada. I know you asked for reinforcements. But frankly, the Liébana's a trouble spot, and our record there's not so great. No one's going to gain glory from this campaign. So let the Policía Armada get the blame. *And* the casualty lists. We don't need more Caleros."

"We don't need more missing shipments of dynamite, either," Tejada retorted. "And that was the Policía Armada's responsibilty."

The colonel laughed. "That's why you're there, Lieutenant. To sort out details like that. I have every confidence in you."

"I'm sure fifty of the Policía Armada are going to be helpful," said the lieutenant sourly.

"Look, Tejada," Súarez lowered his voice. "This comes from Madrid. So just make sure if there are any screwups it's not the Guardia who makes them, understood?"

"Yes, Colonel." Tejada ended the conversation and took a certain satisfaction in banging the phone down.

Ortíz and Battista returned from their patrol without incident. Tejada ate lunch with his men and announced his intention of doing the afternoon patrol himself. He added that Torres had agreed to do desk duty. The guardias were finishing their meal, and Battista had just said that he thought Torres should stay in bed for the rest of the day and volunteered to stay in the office for the afternoon when the sound of galloping hooves outside drew their attention. "Someone's in a hurry," Ortíz commented. Tejada opened his mouth to reply, and then the door of the post slammed, and they heard running footsteps in the hallway. The three men exchanged glances, and silently stood. Tejada's pistol was ready before he was on his feet, and he approvingly noted that the other men followed his example.

"Corporal Battista! Lieutenant!" The guardias relaxed as they recognized Carvallo's breathless voice.

"In here." Tejada lowered his weapon, but did not put it away. "What's happened?" he asked, as Carvallo entered, gasping for breath.

"Sergeant Márquez, sir." Carvallo saluted, gulping a few breaths to steady himself. "He's been hurt. And he says we should start a patrol toward Espinama, and do a house-to-house to try to find Montalbán's accomplices."

"Hurt how? How badly?" demanded Battista.

"Accomplices?" Tejada asked at the same time.

"We ran into Montalbán. There was a shoot-out. He's dead. Neither of us were hit but the sergeant was riding ahead of me and he took a bad fall when the shooting started. I think his arm's broken." Carvallo managed to answer both questions with admirable speed.

"Where is he now?" Tejada demanded.

As if in answer to his question there was a faint shout. "Carvallo!"

Tejada headed for the main entrance to the post, his men at his heels. Sergeant Márquez was sitting on his light bay. The left side of his cloak had been awkwardly looped under to make a crude sling. The odd drape did nothing to disguise the fact that the cloak was smeared with mud and grit, and had been torn in several places. His right hand clutched the pommel of his saddle. The left side of his face was badly scraped, and his lips were white. "Sir." He attempted to salute at the sight of Tejada, and then swayed in the saddle and clutched the pommel again. "Sorry to bother you. Spot me while I dismount, Carvallo. I don't want to make this worse by falling again."

"Here." Tejada stepped forward, arms outstretched. "Why did Carvallo leave you?"

"He didn't until we reached the outskirts of town." Safely on the ground, Márquez heaved a sigh of relief. "Then I sent him ahead to alert you. I didn't feel up to anything more than a walk."

"I heard you ran into Montalbán," Tejada said, ushering the sergeant into the building. "Carvallo," he added over his shoulder, "get on the phone to Unquera and tell them we need a doctor. Then get the sergeant a drink." Carvallo headed for the office, and Tejada turned his attention back to Sergeant Márquez. "You said we need a house-to-house search?"

"Yes." Once again, Tejada was struck by how much better Márquez reacted to a crisis than to the minor irritations of routine policing. The man was obviously in pain, but he was calm, lucid, and almost eerily focused on his work. "But not for Montalbán. He's half in the Río Deva with a hole in his chest. I think he was traveling with friends, though. And if we hurry we may be able to pick up a few. Take the truck as far as you can toward Espinama, and then head for Treviño and Cosgaya, along the track to Fuente Dé."

Tejada frowned. "I don't know that area at all." He turned to Battista. "Have you been there, Corporal?"

"Yes, sir." Battista nodded. "All of us have done that patrol route before. But—" He stopped.

Tejada raised his eyebrows. "But?"

"But with Torres sick and Sergeant Márquez wounded we don't have much manpower."

Carvallo returned, carrying a cup and bottle. "The doctor's on his way, Lieutenant. Would you like a drink, Sergeant Márquez?"

"Thanks." Márquez held out his good hand. "Don't waste time fussing over me. Battista's right that we don't have enough men. Our only chance is to move fast."

Tejada hesitated for a moment, remembering the morning's phone call. "We could ask for help from the Policía Armada. Do you think they'd lend us men?"

The other guardias exchanged glances. Then Battista said, "I'd rather just worry about the bandits, sir."

"Understood." Tejada stood. "Tell Torres what's happened if he's awake, Sergeant. Then rest until the doctor arrives. And tell him to stay until we get back, in case there are others wounded. Oh, and if you can send a message to Rosas, let him know that we may be bringing in prisoners and he should have cells available, just in case."

The guardias were ready quickly, although not as quickly as Tejada would have liked. The two horses had to be unsaddled and stabled, and the lieutenant wasted a few precious minutes looking for a detailed map of the country they were going through, knowing that he was the only one of the guardias who would need it, but unwilling to set off without this basic preparation. Finally, however, the four men piled into the Guardia's single vehicle, and roared down the half-built road to Espinama.

They covered the first ten kilometers within ten minutes. "Pull off here, Lieutenant," Battista advised. "We want to head up that path to the left."

Tejada slammed on the brakes and looked dubiously at the track the corporal was pointing toward. "I don't think the truck will handle it."

"No, it won't." Battista was laconic. "We'll have to leave it."

"Come on then." Tejada pulled off the road and yanked the keys out of the ignition as the guardias climbed out. "Speed counts. Battista!"

"Sir?"

Tejada was already moving up the path at a fair pace. "You know the terrain and you know the men we're looking for. I don't. So you're in charge. If you have to give orders, give them. Understood?"

"Yes, sir." Battista caught up with the lieutenant. "You'd better stay back then. Carvallo, stick with the lieutenant. Ortíz, come with me."

They did not speak for a few minutes after that. The path they traveled was wet and rocky, streaked with water running down to the Deva. Piles of broken rock along the side of the road signaled Devastated Regions' plans for a highway, but at the moment the path was little better than a drainage ditch. The road climbed through open country, broken only by a few bushes. Tejada wished that they were less exposed. He strained to hear behind the birdsong, the murmur of the distant river, and the sighing wind, listening for the sound of a man, or men. All the guardias carried their rifles across their chests, ready for use.

If Montalbán was with other bandits, Tejada thought, then they already know that the guardias who killed him got away. They'll be expecting us. But not so soon, I hope. He was eager to reach the first village. They were too good a target along the unfinished highway. Of course, the bandits might well be holed up in one of the houses. But they would announce their position with the first shot they fired. *And they're local,* Tejada thought. *They're probably in the houses of family. So they won't want to hit civilians in the crossfire. Whereas out here we're practically the only thing they* can *hit.*

The path had sloped steeply upward at first, but now it leveled out and curved around the side of the mountain. Corporal Battista stopped short as they came around one curve and signaled the others to be still as well. Tejada saw that they were approaching a dry, steeply sloping field and a stone farmhouse and barn. "That's the Robles place," the corporal said in a low voice. "You and Carvallo had better loop around and cover the far side of the barn, sir. I'll talk to Pepe. He knows me."

"Should we go through the barn?" Tejada asked quietly.

"Let Carvallo do it. He's been here before," Battista advised.

"Right. Let's go."

The guardias fanned out. As Tejada came around the far side of the barn, he saw that there was a dark jagged hole in the stones under the roof on one side, obviously a hayloft. A ladder was leaning negligently against the side of the building,

providing easy access to the hole. The lieutenant tapped
Carvallo's arm and pointed upward. "Any others?" he mouthed
silently. Carvallo shook his head, and the two guardias moved
toward the ladder, hugging the wall to make themselves more
difficult targets.

Carvallo made a face as he reached the ladder. Then, with a
faintly rueful glance at the lieutenant, he began to climb. Tejada
waited below, tense. He could faintly hear voices from the
house: Corporal Battista, sounding sharp and official; a
woman's voice, expostulating. Carvallo reached the top of the
ladder and disappeared into the hayloft. There was no sound
from within. The distant voices became more distinct, and
Tejada heard footsteps. Then he was able to make out Corporal
Battista saying, "You know the rules, Angela; we have to check
the barn, too."

"We've never had anything to do with bandits!" That was the
woman's voice. Tejada heard the barn door creak open.

"Just making sure it stays that way." Battista's voice was calm.

There was noise and movement in the barn for a few minutes, and then Battista said loudly, "All clear, Carvallo?"

"Yes, sir."

"Good. Go around the back, and then meet us back at the
road." An instant later Carvallo reappeared and Tejada heard
the retreating corporal say, "Sorry for the inconvenience,
Angela. Say hello to Pepe and tell him to keep out of trouble."

The guardias met back at the road, and began rapidly heading for the next house in Treviño. "That was practically a courtesy call," Tejada remarked.

Battista smiled. "Pepe Robles is an old fox. We've never
caught him at anything, but that's just because he's too sharp.
We'll have to move fast now or he'll have the whole town alerted
ahead of us."

The rest of the searches in Cosgaya were without incident.
Whether this was because the Robles family had in fact succeeded

in sending warning or because the bandits were not in the town was unclear. The searches were exhausting and discouraging. As they headed back toward the truck, Tejada sighed. "Have we ever caught anyone this way?"

"Once in a while you can panic someone into opening fire," Battista explained. "And then we've got them dead to rights."

Tejada restrained the urge to say that painting a bull's-eye on his forehead seemed like an expensive way to track bandits. "How much further do we have to go?"

"Las Ilces is only a few kilometers," Battista reassured him. "And Espinama's just beyond that. We can take the truck a little ways, but it would be better to leave it at Las Ilces, because we really should make a loop through the forest, and that road's not passable."

"Whatever you think is best," the lieutenant said, resigned.

Las Ilces, Espinama, and Pido were equally discouraging. The farmhouses began to blur together for Tejada. They all seemed to have the same angry, fearful inhabitants; the same furniture; the same dark, musty barns. Even the hysterically barking guard dogs that met them seemed to blend into a single barking dog. By the time they left Pido and headed along the heavily forested track Corporal Battista had picked out, the sun was nearing the top of the mountain in front of them.

Tejada squinted into the sun and then glanced at his watch. "How long is this loop?" he demanded.

"A few hours' walk, Lieutenant." Battista sounded tired, too.

"Will we be done by dark?"

"Yes, sir. If we hurry. We're at the farthest point now."

"Let's move it then." Tejada unconsciously increased his speed, and the men with him began to walk faster, too. No one wanted to be in the mountains after dark.

The path was buried in sweet brown pine needles now, and sprinkled with dead leaves that crunched loudly underfoot. Tejada wished that there were more pines and fewer deciduous trees. He was acutely aware of the noise they made, but he knew it was futile to be more furtive. Their uniforms showed up clearly against the dark wood and the occasional patches of snow that glimmered between the trees. *When we get back,* Tejada thought, *I have to ask Márquez about exactly what happened with Anselmo. And we'll have to go get his body as well.* He considered asking Carvallo for details as they walked, but the path climbed steeply through a series of switchbacks, and he did not want to waste the breath. Besides, he thought, talking makes noise, and we're trying not to attact attention. It occurred to him that his predecessor had died on a mountain patrol like this one. He wondered whether Calero's last moments had been like this, slightly sweaty from exercise in spite of the cold, with the scent of pine needles and the sound of wind in the trees creating a falsely idyllic scene.

They reached a crest, and the path began to go downhill. The noise of running water got louder, and Tejada realized that they were walking beside another of the innumerable streams that fed the Deva. He was next to Battista. The two guardias had fallen a few steps behind. Suddenly, the lieutenant stopped. Up ahead, where the trees thinned out, there was a small cabin by the side of the river. He tapped Battista, pointed toward the cabin, and raised his eyebrows. The corporal nodded.

The routine was so familiar by now that it required no thought. Tejada and Carvallo cut through the trees, heading for the back of the building. It was far easier here, where they could remain under cover. Tejada noted absently that Carvallo moved quickly and quietly in the woods, even when he was off the path, and approved. He did not know it, but Carvallo was silently thinking the same thing about him. Battista and Ortíz marched on along the road, toward the entrance to the lone building. The inevitable dog barked at them.

Battista called a greeting. Tejada and Carvallo waited, unable to hear anything over the animal's frenzied yapping. The barking went on, longer than it should have. The owners of the house were not calling off their dog. Then they heard Battista yell a curse, sounding considerably less calm and sure of himself. Then sudden silence.

Carvallo turned a frightened face toward Tejada, and the lieutenant remembered that the young man had already seen Márquez injured and another man killed in the course of the day. "Don't break cover yet," he murmured.

Carvallo looked dubious, but his fears were allayed a moment later as Battista's voice rang out again, clearly uninjured. "Open up!"

There was a series of thuds, and then silence again. Tejada and Carvallo waited a few minutes, and then Ortíz came around the side of the house at a run. "Lieutenant!"

Tejada was already on his way to meet the guardia, Carvallo at his heels. "What have we got?"

"It's a barn, sir, not a proper house," Ortíz explained as they reached the front of the building. "And it's deserted. Someone must have sent word up from Cosgaya we were coming."

"Why wouldn't it be deserted?" Tejada asked as they reached the door. "They left a dog to guard it."

He stepped inside and found a bare-walled single room, piled high with hay. Corporal Battista stepped forward, grinning. "They certainly left a dog! Thank God I clubbed the poor brute."

"He was that vicious?" Tejada asked.

"No." Battista laughed. "I meant thank God I didn't pull a weapon anywhere around here." He gestured toward a fallen bale. "I knocked this one over checking for someone behind the pile. Take a look."

Tejada's eyes were growing accustomed to the dim light that leaked in between the cracks in the boards. He squinted and saw that what he had taken for a smaller bale of hay was in fact a metal crate, stamped with the words DANGER. FLAMMABLE. Battista was still grinning. "I think we've found our missing dynamite, sir."

Chapter 10

The Monastery of Santo Toribio was only a few kilometers' walk, but much of the road was steeply uphill. Elena was reluctantly grateful for Father Bernardo's gentle assumption that she was too weak to do any real walking, although it had irritated her earlier. He was quite willing to go as slowly as she wished, and to stop whenever she asked for a rest.

Elena found the priest an easy companion in other ways as well. He clearly knew and loved the route, and he was eager to signal points of exceptional beauty or historical interest. Perhaps because of his experiences with the Liébana's children, he was a skilled lecturer. Doubtless the Señora already knew that Santo Toribio was the home of the *lignum crucis*, one of the fragments of the True Cross, and thus a renowned pilgrimage site, but did she know that the monastery also sat near pre-Romanesque ruins? Yes, indeed, pre-Romanesque, probably tenth century, and well preserved. According to the tradition, Toribio himself had used the spot as a hermitage, for prayer and meditation. That was why it was called the Cueva Santa. Although it had earned its name again when the monks had hidden the *lignum crucis* there to protect it from Napoleon's invading troops.

Elena listened to her guide quite contentedly. When they reached the monastery itself, she admired its mixture of Gothic and Romanesque architecture and agreed politely that the cloister was charming and that it was a shame that there was no money to properly restore the convent. The conversation then returned to the problems of schooling in Potes. Elena met various colleagues of Father Bernardo, who all agreed that it was the church's responsibility to found a proper primary school, and expressed satisfaction at Elena's interest. It annoyed her somewhat to be treated as a prospective parent rather than as a fellow professional, but she swallowed her discomfort and tried to focus the discussion on the practical difficulties of finding space, materials, and a qualified teacher.

She had lunch at the monastery and then agreed to Father Bernardo's suggestion that she might like to look at some of the interesting ruins around the building. There were old hermitages and chapels, sadly damaged by time, but still quite beautiful. San Miguel was an easy walk, and if she was feeling strong they might even be able to make it up to Santa Catalina, which held a very interesting set of bells.

"What about the Cueva Santa?" Elena asked hopefully, intrigued by the idea of pre-Romanesque ruins.

Father Bernardo coughed. "The Cueva Santa is quite close also," he admitted. "Perhaps forty minutes' walk. But it's up the mountain, and the trail is rather difficult. You might find it easier at some other time."

"Some other time then." Elena submitted with good grace. "But I would love to see San Miguel and Santa Catalina."

The walk was pleasant, although the path was muddy with melting snow in the afternoon sunshine. San Miguel sat at the same level as Santo Toribio, but the ruins of Santa Catalina were perhaps one hundred meters above the monastery, on the edge of a flat, table-like ridge that jutted out from Monte Viorna. The land around the ruins was open and provided a majestic view, not only of Santo Toribio, but of the valley below, all the way to the unmistakable silhouette of the Torre del Infantado in Potes. The trees, lulled by the brief break in the weather, had put forth a few hesitant new leaves, and from above the valley looked as if it were coated with green fuzz, interrupted by the brilliantly white chestnut blooms. The work crews moved along the highway to Espinama like ants. Looking down, it was easy to feel at the top of the world, but a glance upward showed peaks rearing far above on the opposite side of the valley, and Elena was confronted with the bulk of Monte Viorna when she turned away from the valley. She was uninterested in the bells of Santa Catalina, but she had to admit that the location was impressive.

The path was reasonably wide, but it ran along the edge of the cliff, bounded by a wooden fence that enclosed a field cleared for grazing. The priest insisted that Elena walk on the inside, next to the fence. "If we were to continue along here in the other direction, we'd reach the path to the Cueva Santa," Father Bernardo explained, as they picked their way back along the ridge.

"Toward where the house is, you mean?" Elena asked, pointing to the right, where a stone building with a tiled roof sat on the edge of the forest, looking out over the sheep-dotted field they were passing.

"No, straight ahead. It goes up into the woods, and then practically ends. The last bit is barely marked. There's probably still some snow on it at this time of year."

"I'd love to see it in the summer then," Elena commented.

Father Bernardo nodded. "Perhaps the lieutenant could come then as well."

Perhaps in a few summers we'll be able to come with the baby, Elena thought. *Except it won't be a baby anymore then.* "I'm sure he'd be interested," she said aloud.

They stopped briefly at the monastery when they returned, to thank their hosts, and then began their trek down into the valley. Elena had enjoyed the excursion, but her feet hurt, the baby was kicking vigorously, and she was looking forward to getting home and taking a nap. Perhaps after that she would write a letter home, and tell her parents about Father Bernardo, and Santo Toribio, and the school. And then Carlos would come home. It had been a good day. Life in Potes was definitely getting easier.

They reached the valley highway and crossed it, to walk along above the river, chatting desultorily. "Is Lieutenant Tejada a fisherman?" Father Bernardo asked as they passed under a clump of trees clinging precariously to the steep riverbank. "The Deva is a good place to catch salmon. Although the best runs are in the gorge, further down, of course."

"I don't think so," Elena said, concealing a smile as she remembered her husband's answer to a similar question on their honeymoon. *No, darling, I hunt and fish for a living. I prefer to do other things in my leisure time.*

"I like to fish," the priest admitted, turning his head a little away from her, perhaps in embarrassment or perhaps merely to inspect the river better. "It teaches you patience, and you learn to observe. You look at a ripple on the surface. Is it a fish? Is it a current? White water becomes—" He stopped suddenly and hastily raised his eyes from the Deva and fixed them on Elena. "I'm sorry. You shouldn't let me run on like this about my favorite hobby. It's terribly boring really. I shouldn't have brought you this way, the damp is bad for you." He took Elena's arm, his eyes still fixed on her face, and his voice loud and fast. "Let's go back to the highway. It's drier and more direct—"

Father Bernardo tugged at Elena's arm, but it was like trying to move a statue. She had already followed his gaze down to the briars that trailed in the water and seen the torso grotesquely protruding from them, head and forearms dangling in the rapid stream. Her eyes widened, going round with horror, and the priest wondered if she was about to faint. Then he saw the telltale flicker of her throat muscles and quickly stepped to one side as she clumsily leaned over and retched.

Elena emptied the contents of her stomach. Then she spat the taste from her mouth, wiped her watering eyes, and began looking for a way down to the stream. "You said you fish for salmon here? What's the nearest path to the water?"

Father Bernardo stared. "There's one just a little ways back. But why—" He hurried after her as she began retracing their steps. "Señora! You can't think . . . He's dead, Señora. There's nothing you—"

"Isn't your business with the dead, Father?" Elena spoke grimly.

"I . . ." Father Bernardo blinked. "Yes. I give you my word I'll make sure that poor unfortunate is taken out of there, and buried like a Christian. But there's no need for you to get involved. I'll take you home and then I can get men and come back."

Elena had reached the path down to the river. It was steep and fairly muddy, and her thighs were already tired of going downhill. *The last thing the baby needs is for me to fall,* she thought. She grabbed hold of a tree branch to steady herself, and placed her feet sideways, cautiously. "The Guardia are short-staffed, Father. All able-bodied men are on patrol this afternoon. And the townspeople will still be at work. It could be hours before you get a party together to come back here. We can at least pull him out of the river."

Father Bernardo followed her reluctantly. "It's not fitting for you—"

"He's someone's husband probably," Elena interrupted, her voice harsh. "Maybe someone's father. Do you want him to be totally unrecognizable to his family?"

"I'm sorry you had to see this, Señora." Father Bernardo sighed, and capitulated as they reached the water's edge.

There was perhaps a meter of semidry ground between the water and the sharp cliff they had just descended, most of it covered in prickly bushes. Elena fought her way through the bushes, noting as she did so that they seemed to be undisturbed. She wondered how the dead man had reached the water's edge.

Perhaps he had taken a different route. Or perhaps the man had been standing above, and had been knocked off the road and into the water. The fall would have stunned him, and if he had landed face-first in the water, he might have drowned without being able to save himself. But that was impossible. If he had fallen from above, his whole body would have been visible from the road. He was lying *under* the bushes, partly concealed by them. So he must have either crawled under them, or been put under them by someone.

It did not occur to Elena that the man might have died of natural causes. Or rather, years of war and fear had made her consider death by shooting, shelling, or bombing as seminatural causes. She reached the corpse, and forced herself to look down at him. His hair was gray and long, and he was wearing a sheepskin coat. There was a fist-sized hole in his back. She averted her gaze from the wound and said to Father Bernardo, "Do you think if we each take a shoulder we can pull him out?"

He nodded and silently stepped over the dead man. "On three? One, two, *three.*"

Pulling the corpse was more difficult than Elena had expected, and her back ached sharply, but they succeeded in removing him from the water. Father Bernardo knelt, and heaved the body onto its back. "Holy Mother of God," he murmured.

"What is it?" Elena glanced down at the white, swollen face, and then quickly looked at the priest again.

"Anselmo Montalbán." Father Bernardo swallowed. "I heard he'd taken to the hills but . . ." He tugged at the corpse's arms. They bent reluctantly, and the priest crossed them over the hole in Anselmo's chest. Then he glanced up at Elena. "Excuse me." He lightly touched the dead man's forehead, and Elena instinctively turned away as the priest began to give the body last rites.

"Let me take you home." Father Bernardo rose and put an arm around her shoulders. "This has been a horrible experience for you. And . . . I have to tell Montalbán's wife anyway."

Elena allowed the priest to guide her back to the highway without replying. She walked back toward Potes wearily, aware of her aching feet and back, and frightened of the reception they would receive from Bárbara de Montalbán. *We should stop at the post,* she thought, although the last thing she felt like doing was confronting her husband's colleagues in his absence. *Someone has to tell the guardias. Unless they already know.* She wondered with sudden fear if Carlos had killed Montalbán, and if she would have the courage to ask him. *He'll tell me,* she thought. *He won't lie to me. But he's been looking for Montalbán. He wouldn't kill him when he has questions to ask him. Unless he'd already gotten the answers he wanted.* No. *He wouldn't kill him out of hand. I don't think.*

It was nearly seven when they arrived, and a number of Elena's neighbors were drifting into the *fonda* for evening drinks and snacks. Bárbara Nuñez de Montalbán was behind the counter. The men at the bar nodded respectfully to Elena, and several of them greeted her companion. Father Bernardo acknowledged the greetings, but made his way deliberately to the bar. Bárbara Nuñez greeted him courteously. "What can I do for you, Father?"

"If we could speak for a moment in private?"

The woman's eyes widened, but all she said was, "Why don't you head up to the living room. I'll be there in a moment."

Father Bernardo nodded and guided Elena out of the bar and up the stairs. He stopped at the first landing and turned into the Montalbáns' apartment with a familiarity that Elena, who had never crossed the threshold, envied a little. The living room was directly over the bar, and warmed by the same chimney. A few chairs sat around the fireplace, and a table against the shuttered window held a photograph of a younger version of their hostess, against the background of the mountains, her arm linked with that of the man they had just pulled out of the river, two boys of perhaps twelve and fourteen grinning on either side of them.

Elena, too tired to be courteous, sank into one of the chairs. She stood up again a few minutes later as the door opened and Anselmo Montalbán's widow stepped toward them. "Now, Father, what—" She saw Elena and stopped, frowning.

"I'm afraid I have bad news," Father Bernardo said gently. "Señora de Tejada and I were coming back along the Deva this afternoon and we found your husband."

Bárbara Nuñez stared into the ashes of the fireplace for a long moment. Then she said tonelessly, "Anselmo's dead, isn't he?"

"I'm so sorry." Father Bernardo held out his hands to her but she avoided him and sat in one of the chairs, her expression still stony. "I'll get the men downstairs to bring him home now. But I wanted to tell you."

"Thank you, Father." The words were a whisper.

"Señora Fernández will stay with you," the priest said comfortingly, oblivious of the startled glares of both women.

He let himself out, leaving a tense silence behind. Bárbara Montalbán sat in her chair and stared straight ahead, without moving or speaking. Elena took a few steps toward her, uncertain what to say. "I am so sorry for your loss, Señora Nuñez." No response. "Is there anything I can do?"

"Leave me alone."

Elena hesitated, and then sat down beside the widow and leaned toward her. "Would you like to know what happened?"

The older woman laughed harshly, a sound more bitter than a sob. "A bullet to the head is what happened, isn't it? That's usually how you people operate."

Elena winced. "I don't know if it was the Guardia," she said, praying that it had not been. "But even if it was, I'm sorry. I don't think the Guardia is always right. And I'd like to help if I can."

Bárbara Nuñez turned to face her unwelcome guest. "Conscience money?" she asked, her voice suddenly ferocious. "You think a few apologies make up for Anselmo? And Jesulín?

Get out of here, Señora. I'm sure your husband will be wanting to speak to me soon, and I'd rather have a little rest before he shows up."

Elena left silently, knowing that anything she said would sound hypocritical or moralizing or both. She went upstairs to her apartment and lay down, fulling expecting to start crying. Instead, her eyes closed and she fell asleep. When she woke up, the room was dark, and someone was pounding on the outer door. "Coming!" Elena fumbled for her shoes and hurried to the door without turning on a light. She wondered what time it was, and then, with sudden unease, why Carlos had not returned.

A uniformed guardia stood outside the door with a lantern in one hand. She blinked for a moment, and then recognized him as Corporal Battista. "The lieutenant asked me to give you a message, Señora," he said. "Something's come up in the mountains, and he'll be out late this evening. He said not to wait up."

Elena's eyes widened. "Does this have to do with Anselmo Montalbán?" she demanded, before she could stop herself.

Corporal Battista hesitated. Then he said slowly, "May I ask how you know about that, Señora?"

Elena quickly explained the afternoon's events. Battista nodded slowly. "So his widow's telling the truth."

"You haven't answered my question," Elena pointed out sharply.

"I'm afraid the best I can do is, 'Not directly,'" the corporal said apologetically. "We were all called out this evening in response to the run-in with Montalbán, and then we found some other interesting developments."

"Run-in?" Elena demanded, instantly worried by the corporal's reassuring tone. "Then Montalbán *was* killed by the Guardia?"

"In self-defense." Battista looked reproachful.

Elena's eyes widened. "Is the lieutenant all right?"

"Yes, yes, he's fine." The corporal was once more reassuring. "I'm afraid I can't explain more at the moment. I'm in a hurry. But your husband should be back safe and sound within a few hours. Don't worry."

He left and Elena was faced with the unpleasant prospect of eating dinner alone and wondering where Carlos was, or going back to bed. She opted for the latter, although it took her a long time to fall asleep again. *The corporal said Carlos was fine,* she reminded herself. *He knows how to take care of himself, even if he did fall this morning getting milk.* The reflection comforted her a little, and she smiled drowsily. *I wonder why he fell. He's not clumsy generally, even on slippery roads. Unless someone distracted him. I wonder if he knows about Anselmo. Anselmo couldn't have fallen before he was shot, though. Maybe he tried to take cover under the bushes. The way we always told the kids in Madrid: If you hear gunfire, fall and take cover.* The half-remembered injunction jolted her awake. *Did he fall this morning to take cover? The maquis only shoot over the guardias' heads here. Corporal Battista said Carlos was fine. He would have told me if he was hurt. Why isn't he home?* She wriggled in bed, telling herself it was only the weight of the baby that prevented her from finding a comfortable position. She finally dozed, and dreamed of a woman staring into the ashes of a dead fireplace, as Corporal Battista's voice said, "He should be home in a few hours . . . we were coming back along the river . . . we wanted to tell you." And Elena was not sure if the woman in the rocking chair was herself or Bárbara Nuñez, but she knew that the woman had a terrible ache in her rib cage and was holding back a wail of terror and grief.

She was roused at an uncertain hour by soft footsteps in her room. Someone had turned on the hallway light, and yellow glowed under the edge of the door, giving her a dim view of a figure moving toward her. "Carlos?"

"Sorry to wake you." He sounded tired.

"Are you all right? What happened? Why are you so late?"

"I'm fine. It's a long story."

"Father Bernardo and I found Anselmo Montalbán," Elena said, anxious to hear his voice again.

"I know. I heard." Tejada sighed. "Why don't we talk in the morning? I'm dead on my feet."

"You're not on your feet," Elena pointed out as he lay down.

"I'm not awake either."

Elena lay still for a few moments and then sat up. "What is it?" Tejada demanded.

"You left the light on."

"Oh. Damn. Stay there. I'll get it."

There was a creak as Tejada swung himself out of bed. Then the glow under the door was extinguished, and he returned in total blackness. He stretched out with relief, glad to be home and safe and horizontal. Then he heard his wife's voice again. "Carlos."

"Yes?" He heard the troubled note in her voice and rolled onto one side to put an arm around her. "What's the matter?"

"Did you kill him?"

"Montalbán? No."

"Really?"

"Word of honor. I never laid eyes on the wretched man."

"Anyone else, then?"

Tejada laughed. "I haven't so much as swatted a fly today Elena. Honestly."

"Good." Elena hugged him as fiercely as she could, given the baby. "I'm glad."

"I'm glad you're happy."

Elena heard the edge in his voice, and felt a sudden surge of pity for his exhaustion. "I'm sorry, dear," she murmured soothingly. "Get some sleep. We'll talk in the morning."

"Good idea." Tejada smiled in the darkness. A proper wife, he knew, would have meekly gone to sleep without debate. A proper wife certainly would not have reproached him with questions. But her approbation would have been worth less than his Elena's firm "I'm glad." Tejada had heard the story of Anselmo Montalbán's removal from the river thirdhand from Corporal Battista, who had heard it from Father Bernardo. Battista had been rather struck by the priest's version of Señora Fernández's role, and had repeated it a little dubiously to the lieutenant. *That's my Elena,* Tejada thought, imagining the fragile figure in his arms leading the way down to the river. *Wait until she hears how we got the dynamite back!* He realized that the first thing she had said to him when he returned was "Are you all right?" and almost felt disinterested pity for the unknown Herrera as he remembered the concern in her voice. He fell asleep smiling.

Chapter 11

"Lieutenant, I can't thank you and your men enough." Señor Rosas emerged from his office the following morning beaming with satisfaction even before Martin announced Tejada. "If there is *anything* Devastated Regions can do for the Guardia, you only have to give the word. Would you like to look at the plans for the new barracks and make any amendments?"

"It's our job," Tejada said modestly, amused at the architect's form of goodwill. "And it was mostly just luck."

"Well, your luck is our good fortune," the director of Devastated Regions said. "We'll be able to finish the highway on schedule now, and that means we can move on to the plaza before we lose our workforce."

"Maybe you could move on to the construction of new quarters for the Guardia?" Tejada suggested. "And a prison?"

"Oh, yes, that too, of course," Rosas agreed expansively. "You deserve a commendation, Lieutenant. And of course, poor Sergeant Márquez, too. How is he doing, by the way?"

"He was a bit banged up by the fall, but the doctor says his wrist is only sprained. He should be fine in a few weeks," Tejada said.

Señor Rosas had been somewhat less gracious the night before, when an annoyed Corporal Battista had gotten him out of bed at one thirty in the morning and curtly told him that the Policía Armada's officers were being uncooperative, and that if he wanted his missing dynamite back he should tell them to place themselves and one of the Devastated Regions trucks at the disposal of the Guardia. He had, however, finally submitted to the corporal's urgent demand for men and materials, and had been rewarded a few hours later by the return of his crates of dynamite. Tejada, who had spent several tense hours waiting at the abandoned barn with Guardia Carvallo, wondering if Battista and Ortíz had made it back to Potes without being ambushed and if the guardias would return with reinforcements before the guerrillas did, accepted Señor Rosas's compliments somewhat sardonically. But he was genuinely pleased that the operation had gone so smoothly.

In fact, Tejada sailed through the next several days feeling satisfied with himself. Everything seemed to be going well. He received polite congratulations from the mayor, relieved ones from Colonel Suárez, and surly ones from his counterparts at the Policía Armada. The weather warmed slowly but steadily, and wildflowers began to bloom in the pastures. Guardia Torres's fever went down and became a sniffly head cold that no longer prevented him from taking on his share of the post's work. Sergeant Márquez's sprained wrist prevented him from doing patrols but not from desk duty or errands, and the sergeant promptly made himself useful by locating the owner of the barn where the dynamite had been found. The property was registered to one Miguel Cruz, a dairy farmer in Cosgaya. Tejada sent two guardias to arrest Cruz, who stoutly denied any knowledge of the theft and maintained that since the barn was barred only from the outside to prevent livestock from escaping, it would have been possible for anyone to place the stolen goods there without his knowledge. The lieutenant did not believe a word of Cruz's story, but he released the man and promptly put him under surveillance. Then he alerted the post office to forward all mail addressed to Miguel Cruz to the

Guardia Civil for inspection. Tejada fully expected Cruz to be careful for a while but he was sure that the farmer would eventually let his guard down, and when he did, the Guardia would be waiting to capture him and his confederates. The lieutenant was content to wait.

Tejada's main worry over the next few days was his wife. Elena was nervous and irritable. When Tejada asked encouragingly about her plans for a school she only shrugged listlessly and said that Father Bernardo had everything in hand and that she was useless to everyone. When he told her what had happened with Cruz she snapped at him, and then, to his horror, nearly began to cry. He suspected that finding Anselmo Montalbán's body had been more of a shock than she was willing to admit. But any mention of Montalbán made her so bitterly sarcastic that he avoided the subject. On Friday night she announced, a little defiantly, that she intended to attend the innkeeper's funeral the next day. "It's the right thing to do," she finished, her eyes daring him to contradict her. "We were neighbors."

Tejada sighed. He knew Elena was still upset about Montalbán's death, and he suspected the ritual would comfort her, but he was afraid she would be more upset by the reactions of the dead man's family and friends and he did not want to leave her to face their hostility alone. "I wish you'd told me earlier," he said. "I can't go with you tomorrow morning. I have to work."

"I didn't expect *you* to come," she retorted.

The lieutenant frowned. Elena was right that he would never have dreamed of attending Anselmo's funeral under normal circumstances but her calm assumption that she had some sort of relationship with their neighbors that he was denied irked him. "You'll give my respects to Señora Nuñez?" he said, staking his claim as a member of the community.

"If she'll take them," Elena answered dryly.

Tejada was forced to be content with that. He left for work the next morning with the uncomfortable feeling that he was leaving Elena vulnerable to an unpleasant task.

Anselmo Montalbán had been well known in the Liébana Valley, and his funeral was widely attended. All of the mourners knew Guardia Ortíz, and if some of them thought his presence was hypocritical, none of them were startled by the fact that a Lebeño had turned out to bury one of his own. The presence of the new lieutenant's wife, on the other hand, caused considerable surreptitious comment. Most of the town knew that she and Father Bernardo had found Anselmo's body, and that she and her husband were living with Anselmo's wife. Public opinion was divided as to whether her presence at the grave was an expression of goodwill or an intolerable intrusion. But everyone was curious to see whether Bárbara would invite her back to the *fonda* with the other mourners after the burial, and how she would manage to make her way back separately if she was not invited.

Bárbara Nuñez had pointedly not invited Elena to the gathering, and that fact, along with her husband's reaction, had made Elena wonder if attending the funeral at all was wise. But a useless sense of honor had driven her to the little cemetery, where patches of dirty snow still glistened in the spring sunshine. She had seen Anselmo's body lying in the river and had seen his widow's face when she received the news. To shut her eyes to his death now seemed like hypocrisy. She stood quietly at the back of the crowd as Father Bernardo gave the deceased a warm and unspecific eulogy. He did not say how Anselmo had died and Elena was grateful for his reticence. Telling the truth would have been impossible, and to label the death a cardiac arrest—the standard euphemism for cases like Montalbán's—seemed obscene in light of the hole in the innkeeper's chest.

When the service was over, Elena silently moved out of the

way as the mourners left the cemetery, talking in low voices. Ortíz saw her, and nodded amicably, but did not approach. Father Bernardo, who had been talking to Bárbara Nuñez, saw her as well and came over to speak to her. "It was good of you to come," he said quietly, as they shook hands.

Elena shrugged. "The least I could do."

"You will come back to the *fonda*, of course, and give Bárbara your support."

"I don't think I'm invited."

Father Bernardo smiled at her. "Bárbara is a good woman," he said. "She is struggling now with bitterness. You might help her greatly."

Elena nodded, but was too polite to say that she thought the priest was mouthing platitudes. He turned and looked over at the widow, a little pleadingly. Her face was stony, and she did not move toward them. "You had better go and comfort her," Elena said dryly. "I'll be along in a little while. And if she needs anything this evening I'll be there."

The priest accepted his dismissal, disappointed but not surprised. He escorted Bárbara from the cemetery while Elena watched from a distance. Elena waited until the last of the funeral procession had left, then went up to the grave. It was a family plot, a long flat slab, with the names of many Montalbáns engraved on it. The freshly chipped letters at the end of the list were still a powdery gray, paler than the rest of the slab:

Anselmo Montalbán Soroll
December 1, 1882–March 13, 1941
Husband, Father, and Friend -
We will remember you.
Rest in Peace

Immediately above them, obviously recent but not new, were the words:

Jesús Montalbán Nuñez
January 4, 1913–September 15, 1937
Beloved son of Bárbara and Anselmo
"I cry to the Lord, that he may answer me. . . ."—Psalm 120
Rest in Peace

Elena looked at the names for a while, the birdsong and the bubbling music of the river loud in her ears. She wondered a little at the inscription for Jesulín. It was odd that a young man in sympathy with the maquis should have a Bible verse carved on his tomb. None of the other Montalbáns did. She wondered if Father Bernardo had insisted, and then decided against the idea. The priest of Potes was free from that sort of petty cruelty.

She wandered around the cemetery to give Anselmo's friends and family time to get back to the *fonda* without being disturbed by her presence, still idly wondering about the quote from the Psalms. Few of the other family tombs had citations carved on them. She was about to leave when she saw a flat, simple headstone, placed a little apart from the other graves. *Benigno Román Márquez,* she read.

April 2, 1908–February 4, 1938
Our teacher and our friend
Your students and sister will remember you always.
"I am for peace. . . ."—Psalm 120

Jesús Montalbán's epitaph had apparently inspired another. There were no other Románs in the cemetery. Elena remembered Father Bernardo saying that the teacher had been well liked, although not local. *They gave him a decent funeral,* she thought. *Even though he was a Red, and it was wartime.* She turned away, her eyes stinging with tears, and wondered what had become of Señor Benigno's sister. Was she in prison? In exile? Had she joined the maquis?

Then she remembered Marta Santos saying, *"Poor Señorita Laura."* Elena had wondered at the time what young woman among these farmers would earn the courtesy title *"Señorita."* *The teacher's sister,* Elena thought, with a wave of nausea. *She came to the mountains as a foreigner, and the lieutenant of the Guardia fell in love with her and killed her brother and her lover when she refused him. That's why the two epitaphs are similar. That's why Potes doesn't have a school.* She shivered and began to make her way home as swiftly as possible, forgetting that she wished to avoid the gathering at the *fonda.* She managed to sneak upstairs without running into anyone when she reached home.

When Tejada came home that evening he found her on her knees, going through cartons of books. "Do we have a Spanish Bible?" she asked, in response to his astonished demand to know what she was doing.

"I think so." He knelt beside her and removed a stack of books from her hands, instantly concerned. "Be careful, will you? Why do you want the Bible?"

"I wanted to read the Psalms." Elena got clumsily to her feet and sank into a chair, content to let him search.

Tejada's vague unease grew into alarm. "Are you feeling all right? Did something happen at the funeral?"

"No, nothing." Elena sighed. "But there was a line on a tombstone that interested me."

"I don't think you should be reading tombstones in your condition," Tejada said. "It's morbid. Here, it was at the bottom of the pile." He held out a black volume, one of the few books that had been his rather than hers.

Elena found the 120th psalm and read aloud: "In my distress I cry to the Lord, that he may answer me: 'Deliver me, O Lord, from lying lips, from a deceitful tongue.'" She smiled faintly.

"That settles it. Jesulín Montalbán was killed for a purely personal grudge."

"Elena, for goodness' sake, this isn't good for the baby," her husband protested. "And I don't have the faintest clue what you're talking about."

"Jesulín's epitaph," Elena explained.

She summarized her morning in the cemetery, leaving Tejada with the uneasy suspicion that the funeral had been as upsetting as he had feared and that her anxious interest in death and decay would do some obscure harm to the baby. He regretted letting her go but she had been so fragile lately that he hated to remonstrate with her. "Were your friends the Álvarezes there?" he asked, for the sake of saying something more cheerful.

It was a mistake. Elena's face fell as he spoke. "I saw them. But they didn't talk to me."

"It's always hard to make small talk at a funeral," Tejada said comfortingly. "Maybe you'll get a chance to see them tomorrow."

"Maybe," Elena agreed softly, although the thought of facing Marta and Quico Álvarez after seeing the graves of the Guardia Civil's victims was not totally appealing. She allowed her husband to change the subject, hoping that he would forget about his absurd plans to have her making social calls by the following day.

Unfortunately, Sunday afternoon was beautiful, clear, and sunny, with a hint of spring in the air, and Tejada renewed his efforts to be solicitous. "Would you like to go for a walk?" he asked after lunch. "You should get some fresh air."

"To where?" Elena shrugged one shoulder, hoping that he would take her apathy for exhaustion.

"How about to Tama? To visit your friends there?" Tejada suggested, pleased that he could suggest a route that did not offer excessive climbing or transverse the path where she had found Anselmo Montalbán's body.

"I don't really want to go so far alone."

Tejada smiled at her. "I do have the afternoon off, Elena."

"I can't take *you* to the Álvarezes."

"Why not?" he demanded, stung by her tone. She gave him a look that clearly said that such a stupid question did not deserve an answer. He was annoyed. "Damn it, Elena, you have to get over this nonsense about the Guardia being some sort of plague. We are *not* lepers, we are *not* an occupying army, and—"

"Aren't you?" she interrupted.

"No! And if we are it's because of people with *your* attitude," Tejada retorted, too irritated to be logical. "I've been a guardia for almost ten years now, and I promise you I've socialized with my neighbors off duty everywhere." He heard the anger in his own voice and spoke more quietly, trying to sound reasonable. "It makes you look silly, you know, this going off on your own always. As if you were ashamed of your own husband."

"I'm not ashamed of you." Elena smiled at him a little ruefully. "But the Álvarezes were friends of Anselmo Montalbán."

Tejada frowned. A small part of his mind longed to know why Elena was incapable of making friends with the mayor's wife, or the head of the Women's Auxiliary, or any number of people who would have proven his point that the guardias were perfectly socially acceptable. *Because she wouldn't be Elena then,* he thought. *Because she always picks the hardest route.* Aloud, he said slowly, "I'm sorry about that. But Montalbán was killed almost accidentally. Márquez returned fire practically as his horse bolted. It's hard to hit anything you aim at under those circumstances. And Montalbán was wanted. Márquez was within his rights."

"Anselmo couldn't have fired at Márquez," Elena protested. "He didn't have a weapon." She swallowed. "Father Bernardo and I would have seen it."

"According to Márquez and Carvallo, there were several men down by the river," Tejada said gently. "Márquez fell, and

Carvallo stopped to help him. By the time Márquez told him to go after the others, they were gone. And they probably took Montalbán's weapon. They always have a use for guns."

Elena still looked unhappy. "You can't ask Marta and Quico Álvarez to believe that."

Tejada sighed. "The man was a terrorist. He probably killed Lieutenant Calero."

"He had good reason to!"

"There are no good reasons for shooting an officer of the Guardia Civil."

Elena's expression was stormy, but all she said was, "So it's a closed case for you, then? The word of two guardias against a dead man's, and his family and friends are just supposed to bury him and be grateful?"

Although this actually was more or less Tejada's opinion, he did his best to be diplomatic. "I'm not claiming that Montalbán's death was the best possible outcome. I'm just saying that you can't blame an officer who's attacked while on duty by a known criminal."

Elena's face was still drawn, but her tone was sad rather than angry as she said, "A shame they didn't just hide in the bushes until the patrol went past. There's heavy cover there, and I'm sure Márquez and Carvallo wouldn't have noticed them if they hadn't attracted attention somehow."

One part of Tejada's mind indignantly protested that if Montalbán and his confederates had not attracted attention, his recovery of the missing dynamite and the subsequent triumphs would never have taken place. But he was glad that Elena seemed to be calming down, and he had to admit that her point was well taken. *They couldn't have known who the guardias on patrol would be,* he thought. *But Elena's right; if they* were *looking for specific men, all they had to do was stay hidden and no one would have known they were there.* "I wonder if they had any special reason to ambush Márquez and Carvallo?" he said aloud.

Elena blinked, and her haze of depression lifted slightly as she saw that Carlos was actually listening to her. "Maybe one of them turned someone in during the war, like Calero did," she offered, a little afraid that her husband would be annoyed by the reference.

Tejada heard her hesitance and smiled at her, recognizing that she was trying to make peace. "It seems far-fetched," he said. "But you're right; it's odd they should have taken a risk for no reason. I'll check the files tomorrow."

He was rewarded by a real smile. "Thank you. I guess we could go for a walk now. But I'd still rather not visit the Álvarezes."

"Then we won't." Tejada stood, relieved that Elena seemed to be more relaxed. *Maybe she still needs to talk more about Montalbán to help her get over finding him,* he thought as they headed outside. *If I find anything in the files tomorrow I can tell her. It will make her feel better if she thinks that Montalbán and his friends had some kind of "just cause."*

Chapter 12

Tejada was not able to check the files the next day. Monday morning was market day in Potes, and all the guardias except Sergeant Márquez were out on patrol. The absence of a proper plaza meant that the market spilled into the little winding streets away from the river, and the open space between San Vicente and the Torre del Infantado was roped off to create makeshift pens for the herds of cows driven down from the hills. The town was crowded with people and animals, and the guardias' presence was a necessity. Tejada was unsure how he felt about markets. Patrolling them was stressful, and the concentration of people always meant that there was an opportunity for conspiracy or rabble-rousing. On the other hand, Potes was a rather sadly dull little town when it emptied out, and the market lent it a certain liveliness.

He returned to the post around one o'clock, as the herds were beginning to leave the town, and found Sergeant Márquez waiting for him at the door. "I was on the point of going to look for you." The sergeant greeted him in a low voice. "There's someone waiting to see you."

"He couldn't talk to you?" Tejada asked, following the sergeant into the building.

"He wouldn't." Márquez made a face and then lowered his voice even farther. "He says it's something to do with the bandits."

"Where is he?"

"I put him in the office. But he's nervous as a cat."

"Informers usually are." Tejada lengthened his stride with the happy conviction that one victory was about to lead to another. People liked being on the winning side. *If he can tell us something about who stole the dynamite in the first place,* he thought, *we'll be getting somewhere.*

When Tejada opened the door to his office the man standing by Sergeant Márquez's desk started. He was short and rosy-cheeked, with wispy hair the color of corn silk. He blinked near-sightedly at the lieutenant, and turned his cap in his hands. It was worn gray felt, and like his clothing, suggested a shepherd or farm laborer.

"How do you do?" Tejada hung up his cloak and spoke in a carefully neutral voice. "I'm the commander of the post here. I understand you wanted to speak to me."

"Y-yes, sir," the little man gulped. "I know where they are. The maquis. I mean the bandits. I mean, I know where they'll be, tomorrow night. You could capture them."

"Go on." Tejada sat down without taking his eyes from the man's face.

"Up past Argüébanes." The man spoke jerkily. "You take the bridge over the Mancorbo, and head into the chestnut grove. There's an old shepherd's hut there that no one goes to anymore. They'll be meeting there tomorrow evening."

Tejada mentally located Argüébanes. It was only a few kilometers northwest of Potes, and mostly interesting for a very pretty ruined church. He had the vague feeling that he knew something else about Argüébanes but had no time to track down the memory. "How do you know this?" he asked.

The lieutenant's guest shifted from foot to foot. "I was taking the flock down to the Mancorbo for water, and I saw them yesterday," he explained. "They were getting water. I'm not one of them," he added hastily. Márquez, standing behind the man, met the lieutenant's eyes with a look of pure amusement, and for a moment Tejada found himself in perfect sympathy with his colleague.

"And they invited you to a meeting?" Tejada was politely incredulous.

"N-no, sir! It's just—well, they saw I'd seen them, and Rafa and I went to school together and you can't very well pretend you don't recognize someone you've known all your life. So he said hello and I said hello and then he asked me if I was going to Potes on Monday and if I'd bring him back a carton of ciga-rettes and some stationery and a few other things if I was. And I told him I couldn't because I didn't want any trouble, and he said—" The man gulped. "He said not to worry about it, that he could make it worth my while, and that if I brought the stuff up to Marcial's old cabin on Tuesday night we'd have a real party, because all the old crowd was going to be there."

Tejada took a pen from the container on the desk and began to doodle thoughtfully. "They'll be expecting you Tuesday?" he said.

"Y-yes, sir. I-I came to town today to buy the things he sent me for and then I came to see you but I have to go quickly or they'll be wondering why I'm back late."

"You'll have to go to this party then, so they don't get suspi-cious," Tejada said. "Make sure you wait until they're all inside, and then make some sort of excuse to get out."

Tejada's informer coughed anxiously. "H-how will you know it's me outside, sir, instead of one of the others, before you move in?"

The lieutenant considered. "Take off your cap and wave it around your face as if you were beating off mosquitoes," he said.

"Like this?" The little man flapped his free arm and hit him-self in the face several times with his cap with the enthusiasm of a penitent.

"Fine. We'll see you tomorrow night, Señor—?" Tejada raised his eyebrows.

"Santiago Roldán. Domingo Santiago Roldán." The man filled in the pause quickly, as if he was eager to give his name.

"Señor Santiago." Tejada opened his desk drawer and looked regretfully at the unopened pack of cigarettes lying on top of various pads and pens. "Here." He tossed the pack onto his desk. "If you want to give that to your friends I'll reclaim it tomorrow evening. Or you can keep it for yourself. Consider it a thank-you present."

Santiago's hands were shaking as he took the cigarettes. "Thank you, sir. Also, I—I wondered—"

"Yes?" Tejada had been trying to figure out why Santiago had turned traitor, and he was genuinely interested in what the man was going to ask for as a reward.

"M-my brother's in the Tabacalera." The man's fair skin colored painfully as he named one of Santander's more notorious prisons. "A thirty-five-year sentence. I thought maybe a good word from the Guardia—"

"Also Santiago Roldán?"

"Yes, sir. José María."

"José María Santiago Roldán." Tejada leaned forward to make a note on the pad. "It'll depend on what he's in for. And how this operation goes. But I'll see what we can do. I assume you'd be willing to do more jobs like this in the future, provided all goes well?"

Domingo Santiago looked haunted. "I-I guess."

"Good." Tejada stood and held out his hand. "It's a bargain."

The informer's handshake was limp, and his eyes watered slightly at Tejada's firm grasp, although the lieutenant's grip was hardly tight enough to be painful. He left furtively, as he had come. Tejada was already flipping through the filing cabinet when Márquez returned from seeing off their guest. "Do you know anything about Santiago?"

The sergeant shook his head. "No. He's probably never been in trouble before."

"Do you believe his story?"

"It's plausible." Márquez was neutral.

"It sounded good to me," Tejada admitted. "We'll have to organize a stakeout. You're out of it, with that wrist. Do you think we can take Torres?"

"If you can trust him not to sneeze at the wrong moment," Márquez said dryly.

Tejada snorted. "We'll risk it. If this place is near the stream we shouldn't have to worry too much about silence. I wish we had more men. Do you think we could call for reinforcements from Panes or Unquera?"

Márquez nodded. "I'll phone them this afternoon, sir. But I don't know how many they'd be able to send."

"The problem is that it makes it too obvious we're going to move if they arrive in a bunch," Tejada said slowly. "Of course, there's always the Invincible Armada."

Márquez laughed and reached for the telephone. "Good one, sir. I'll call Unquera first."

The rest of the day and much of the following one were spent in preparations for the raid. Tejada warned his wife Tuesday morning that he might have to work late. "Why?" she demanded.

"It's paperwork about the dynamite," Tejada lied. "The colonel wants it by the twentieth and—" He saw her face and stopped. "I'm sorry, Elena. It's not that. But . . . I can't tell you about it yet. Do you mind?"

"Yes," Elena said. "But I mind more if you lie to me."

Tejada dropped his eyes. "Don't wait up for me," he said quietly. He left, wondering if he had avoided telling her about the raid because he did not want her to worry about his possible danger or because he was afraid of her disapproval. *I'll tell her everything tomorrow morning,* he promised himself.

Two pairs of guardias from Unquera and one pair from Panes arrived on Tuesday afternoon. Tejada went over the operation with them, and showed them maps of the area, although the success of the raid would depend on the actual knowledge of the terrain by the Potes guardias. They ate an early dinner together at the post, and then set off for Argüébanes. They parked in front of the church and started through the town on foot. Tejada hoped that their presence would not be remarked on by the residents of Argüébanes since he strongly suspected that they were in sympathy with the bandits. A fat wedge of moon lit their way making the flashlight Battista was carrying unnecessary. The corporal switched it off, glad to avoid advertising their presence.

The climb up into the hills above the village took about half an hour. The path through the forest was lit by muffled moonlight, which dappled the leaves of the trees. It was after eleven when the faintly sweet smell of the night breeze in the chestnuts gave way to the sharper scent of wood smoke, and the sound of singing floated through the chilly air. The trees thinned and gave way to meadow, and patches of yellow light spilled out of the windows of an ancient adobe structure.

Battista, Ortíz, and the guardias from Unquera circled through the woods to take up positions behind the cabin. Tejada took the remaining guardias and crept out into the open meadow, carefully avoiding the puddles of light. He dropped to his stomach in the high grass, and inched forward on his elbows. The guardias fanned out and followed his example. When they had arranged themselves in a semicircle, they lay still, weapons cocked.

"Shit," the guardia next to him exclaimed softly.

"What's the matter?" Tejada murmured, without turning his head.

"Sheep shit, sir." The guardia sounded embarrassed. "I'm lying in it."

Tejada smiled, but gestured the man to silence. Talking was an unnecessary risk. They settled down to wait. The ground was damp, and the breeze was cold, although it was a relatively mild evening. Tejada reminded himself grimly that he had been in more uncomfortable places. Still, he resented the snatches of song and laughter that reached the guardias in their hiding places, along with the scent of roasting meat. He wondered if Domingo Santiago was inside enjoying the meal and the warmth. And *my* cigarettes, he thought. Oh, well, let them have one last fling. They won't be so cheerful in a few hours.

It was after eleven when the door in front of Tejada opened. A figure emerged, silhouetted against the light. He turned back to wave, and someone inside called a good-natured farewell. Tejada strained his eyes, trying to recognize Domingo Santiago. The door closed behind the lone figure. The man took a few unsteady steps and then shook his head, as if trying to clear it. He stood still for a moment, and then half-turned back in the direction he had come. Tejada tensed. The man had not given the signal Domingo had agreed on, and he was behaving oddly. *If he's seen us,* the lieutenant thought, *we'll have to attack right away. And Santiago's still in there. Damn.*

He was about to give the signal when the figure in the moonlight resolutely turned his back to the house, raised one hand to his head, and took off his cap. He flapped it slowly back and forth, as if fanning away mosquitoes, a ridiculous gesture in the cold darkness. The man seemed to grow tired of fanning himself. He pressed the cap against his face for a moment, as if holding back a scream. Then, almost too quickly for Tejada to follow the motion in the dim light, he tapped his chest and shoulders in rapid succession and hurried down the path without looking back, almost at a run.

The grass beside Tejada rustled. "Wait!" he hissed. "Give them five minutes, so they don't identify us with Santiago's leaving."

Someone in the cabin began to sing, a light tenor loud with wine, but not unpleasant. "You are tall and slender, like your dark-eyed mother." Other voices chimed in and the words became clearer. "I've spent all night thinking of you, my darling." It was an old folk song that Tejada remembered as a lullaby from his childhood. He had sung it once, teasingly, to Elena, because he thought that the words were apt. *When the music stops,* he thought, *we move in.*

The song ended in a round of applause, then there was a moment of stillness. Tejada wondered if the people in the cabin had been dancing, and were now catching their breath, perhaps even sweating a little from the exercise. The fire must have warmed the small cabin thoroughly by now, and they had eaten and drunk heavily. Or perhaps they were simply quiet and staring into the heart of the flames, wondering whether the next singer would pick a love song or a war song. They were probably happy. Relaxed. Off guard. "Now," he said.

The quiet of the mountains was shattered by a burst of machine-gun fire that pockmarked the adobe and shattered the windows of the cabin. Inside, someone screamed. As the echoes died away, Tejada raised his voice. "Guardia Civil! The house is surrounded. Throw out your weapons, and come out with your hands over your heads!"

For a few tense moments there was silence. Then the lights went out in the cabin, and there was a burst of return fire. Tejada flattened himself against the earth as bullets rained around him. "You're making it worse for yourselves!" he called, as soon as there was a pause. There was another round of firing. The shots came considerably nearer this time. They were aiming at his voice. Tejada edged himself a little farther out of range, and spoke up again. "If you give yourselves up peacefully now, I give you my word it will weigh in your favor at trial."

The cabin's inhabitants fired again, and Tejada heard a grunt to his right. Then one of the guardias from Panes said softly, "I'm hit in the shoulder, sir."

"Get out of range," the lieutenant ordered. "And stay low. We'll take care of them."

"Yes, sir." There was a sob in the man's voice, but he began dragging himself backward.

"Last chance," Tejada yelled. "Come out now, or we come in shooting."

He waited thirty seconds, and then started firing. The echoes of the guns multiplied, as Corporal Battista and the guardias on the other side of the house began shooting as well. After perhaps five minutes, the door to the darkened cabin opened, and a figure emerged, crouched, and running in a wild zigzag. He seemed to have the Devil's own luck in dodging bullets, and he made it almost twenty meters down the path. Tejada wasn't sure which of the guardias finally hit him. The guardias crawled forward, still firing rapidly. The return shots became more infrequent, and finally stopped. There were no more casualties among the Guardia, and after a few more minutes, Tejada called a halt. "Had enough?" he shouted. There was no answer. Cautiously, he pushed himself to his knees. "Anyone still alive in there?"

Again, the only answer was the whistling of the breeze. "All right," the lieutenant said in a low voice. "Carvallo, you and I will take the door. The rest of you, cover the windows. Be prepared for a trap."

They reached the walls of the cabin without incident. It was designed for housing sheep, and the door opened outward. Cautiously, Carvallo reached over to the handle and pulled the door open. No one emerged. The unwounded guardia from Panes and one of the guardias from Unquera were flattened on either side of the windows. Tejada took a deep breath, and then stepped into the black hole of the cabin's doorway, strafing the floor as he did so. He was rewarded by a sudden cry. "Light!" he yelled.

The faint beams of Battista's flashlight helpfully flickered through a window on the other side of the cabin. The firelight on the hearth was brighter. It illuminated a bare room with an earth floor, empty except for two long wooden benches and several bales of hay stacked along one wall. Empty bottles of wine lay on the floor, along with a confusion of tin plates holding cheese rinds and the bones of well-gnawed lamb chops. Two men were lying dead beside the windows. One of them still clutched his machine gun. A third was obviously the one who had cried out at Tejada's entrance. He had been crouched at one side of the door, probably holding the hunting knife that now lay beside him. He was now clutching a wound in his thigh.

The guardias quickly occupied the little space. "The magazines are empty, sir," Carvallo reported after checking the guns. "They must have come without spare ammunition."

Tejada relit the lamp that the bandits had blown out when they were attacked. The unwounded guardia from Panes jerked the wounded man's hands away from his leg and handcuffed them. "The others are dead, sir, right?" he said. "So it's just this one."

The harmony of the voices raised in song came back to the lieutenant and he shook his head. "Search," he said briefly. "There should be a woman as well."

They found her hiding behind the bales of hay, with mud on her dress and straw in her hair. Her eyes were enormous, and in the flickering light she looked very young. "Pedro!" She jerked her elbow out of Carvallo's grasp and flung herself at the wounded man with a cry.

"Stand away from him!" one of the guardias said sharply.

"It's all right." The man she had called Pedro spoke at the same time. His teeth were clenched and he was sweating, but his voice was soothing. "It's just a scratch. I'm fine."

She began to cry, still kneeling by him. "I said stand away!" The guardia cocked his pistol.

"Put that away!" Tejada snapped, and moved to stand in front of the girl. He took her by the shoulders and dragged her to her feet. "Come on, Señorita. Perhaps you can identify these men for us?" He turned the girl toward the first of the dead men as he spoke, and felt her sway in his grip, racked by dry sobs. "Stop bawling. You obviously know who he is. We just need a name."

"Rafa-Rafael," she choked, twisting away from the sight of the corpse. "Rafael Campos."

"Thank you. And this one?"

"Oh, no," she whispered. "Oh, no. No, no, no, please, God, no."

Tejada frowned, wondering why she refused to name the dead man and also why the man's face looked vaguely familiar. "That's Luis Severino," the voice came from behind him. It was the wounded Pedro. "And you might spare his daughter the chore of identifying him."

Tejada stared at the corpse and suddenly remembered Bárbara Nuñez saying, "Good night, Luis," as the wagon that had brought him to Potes drove off into the night. Another piece of the puzzle fell into place as he remembered his first encounter with Luis Severino at the railway station in Unquera. "To Argüébanes, sir. I live there. See, here are my papers." *No wonder he hadn't wanted to take a pair of guardias as passengers,* Tejada thought, grimly amused. Ortíz was already going through Severino's pockets, while one of the guardias from Unquera did the same to Campos's body, under Corporal Battista's direction. Another guardia from Unquera was searching Pedro. The wounded man's eyes were closed, and his face was drawn in pain. His leg was still bleeding heavily. Tejada handcuffed the girl, but left her wrists in front of her so she would be less uncomfortable, speaking as he did so. "Carvallo, Guardia Riera—from Panes—was hit. Take his partner and get him back to the post as quickly as possible. Take one of the trucks. The rest of you, move it. Make sure you take the weapons with you when we go."

They left the cabin quickly, two guardias dragging the

semi-conscious Pedro, and Tejada still escorting Severino's daughter. The town was dark and still, and Tejada wondered if any of the neighbors had heard the gunfire in the forest, and what they had thought of it if they had. Everyone was keeping their windows shuttered. "What are we going to do with the girl, sir?" Battista asked as they reached the remaining truck.

"Put her in one of the cells for the night," Tejada said. "We have an extra one. And they have facilities for female prisoners in Santander."

The guardia who had searched their other prisoner laughed. "No need to worry about the little lady's virtue, Lieutenant," he said. "Her friend Pedro had condoms in his pocket."

"Interesting." Tejada raised his eyebrows and turned to look at Pedro's slumped form. "You've been over the border recently then?" The wounded man did not reply.

"You won't get anything out of him now. He's out like a light," a guardia said. "You're sure we shouldn't question the girl? Find out what such a cute little thing was doing unprotected up there in the mountains?" He gave their prisoner an appraising glance that made her shrink back against the seat.

Ortíz saw the glance, opened his mouth, and then closed it again, looking unhappy. Half-buried memories of wartime slithered out of the muck like crocodiles, making Tejada's stomach clench. "No," he said. "Put her in one of the cells. And don't touch her."

"Yes, Lieutenant. At your orders." The guardia shrugged, philosophical. Ortíz and the girl both heaved silent sighs of relief as Tejada turned the key in the ignition, and the little convoy rolled out of Argüébanes, and back to the post.

Chapter 13

"How late did you get in last night?" Elena kept her eyes on the flow of coffee into the cup and her voice neutral.

"Not late. A little after one." Tejada hesitated, and then added, "I'll tell you about it, if you like. But I wonder if you'd do me a favor?"

Elena had expected him to be reluctant, or even ashamed, but she had not imagined he would ask for her help. She looked up, forgetting her reservations. "Of course. Why? What's the matter?"

Tejada hastily summarized the night's adventures. Elena was frowning heavily by the time he finished, but when he said, "So I thought, maybe—Severino's daughter doesn't look more than eighteen, and we have no female wardens," she instantly understood him.

"Of course I'll visit the poor girl," Elena interrupted.

"I thought you might be willing to search her," Tejada explained, embarrassed. "I don't mean a strip search or anything," he added quickly, seeing that she was about to object. "Just go through her pockets. It's really a formality. But I thought she might prefer having another woman do it. In case she's carrying—how should I know?—something private. And of course you could stay and talk to her a little. I'm sure she'd be grateful for the company. The poor kid's just lost her father, after all."

Elena scoffed. "Delicate attention from someone who's just blown him away! Oh, you don't need to worry," she said impatiently. "I'll do it. I'll do it."

"You're a woman in a million."

"I know," Elena retorted. "The other nine hundred ninety-nine thousand, nine hundred ninety-nine wouldn't put up with you."

That was why after breakfast Elena found herself retracing the steps of her first day in Potes, over the ancient stone bridge to the Guardia's makeshift headquarters and up the stairs to the long hallway where two of the doors stood locked, with Guardia Torres on guard outside. Tejada had remained downstairs in his office, but had obviously informed the rest of the post about Elena's errand. The guardia saluted when he saw her. "Good morning, Señora. You're here to see the prisoner?"

Elena nodded. "How is she doing this morning?"

Torres shrugged and sneezed. "How you'd expect, I suppose. I'll let you in." He unlocked one of the doors and pushed it open, saying cheerfully but not unkindly, "Morning, sweetheart. You've got company. Call if you need me," he added to Elena as she stepped through the door and it swung shut.

The cell was bare except for a cot and a basin and pitcher in the far corner. The cot had no sheets, but someone had left a pillow and a folded blanket across one end. The girl had been curled up on the cot, her face buried in the pillow, but she sat up as the cell door opened, and watched Elena, wide-eyed. Unruly ringlets of hair escaped from the knot at the back of her neck and frizzed wildly over her head. Her face was smudged with dirt and tears, and the fingernails clenched in the pillow she was clutching to her stomach were grimy. Her skirt was an ankle-length plaid, the clothing of a schoolgirl, not a grown woman. She stood up, a little clumsily, as Elena approached. "You—are you a prisoner, too?"

Elena felt a surge of pity for the girl's grief and confusion, and thought that Carlos had probably overestimated her age. "No," she said gently, putting one arm around the girl's shoulders. "My name is Elena Fernández. I'm the lieutenant's wife. My husband thought you might like company."

The girl shivered. "I have to go home." Her voice was pleading. "I'm the oldest. Concha can't get breakfast for the boys without me. And they'll be up by now, and see that I'm not there. Or Papa." Her voice died.

"I'm sure your mother . . . " Elena began.

"My mother died three years ago. I *have* to go home!"

"I'm sorry," Elena said quietly, sitting down and drawing the girl down beside her. "I'm sure the neighbors will take care of your little siblings for today. But I'll take them a message if you like. What should I say?"

The girl screwed up her face. "Tell Concha that Juan and Avelino should stay with Marcial and keep working, and that she should take the babies to Uncle Nino in San Vicente until I can send word. And tell them I love them."

"I will," Elena promised. "What's your name?"

"Dolores. Dolores Severino." The girl took a deep breath. "Señora Fernández?"

"Yes?"

"What's going to happen to me?"

"I don't know," Elena said honestly. "I think you'll be taken to Santander for trial. You might go to prison. But from what I heard, you didn't participate in the shooting and—how old are you?"

"I'll be sixteen in April."

"I don't think anyone would consider you a dangerous criminal," Elena said encouragingly.

Dolores gulped. "Papa told me not to go," she whispered. "He said he'd bring a message for me if I wanted to say hello to—if I wanted to say hello. But I wanted to see everyone so badly. I baked bread for them." Her voice warbled around a sob.

"They all said they liked my bread. And then when Rafa was hit, Papa yelled at me to get down behind the hay and hide." She was crying openly now. "I was so scared. I put my head down and put my fingers in my ears and I didn't help them! I didn't help them." The rest of her sentence was unintelligible.

Elena put both arms around the girl and rocked her back and forth as if she were a much younger child. *I'm damned if I'll search her,* she thought. *She can go to Santander without a search, and Carlos will just have to live with it.* She waited until Dolores's sobs had subsided somewhat, and then pulled out a handkerchief. "Blow," she commanded, still using a voice appropriate to a child.

Dolores hiccuped, sniffed, and blew. Elena stood up and went over to the basin. It was empty. She picked it up and rapped on the door. "Get some water," she ordered Torres. "And a sponge, if you can find one."

He hurried down the hall and returned a few minutes later with the basin three-quarters full. The water was icy cold, but the guardia had brought clean and reasonably soft towels, and a small chunk of soap. Elena thanked him and turned her attention back to Dolores. By the time the girl had washed her face and hands and run her fingers through her hair, she was calm enough that Elena thought she might like breakfast. "The guard brought some before," Dolores admitted. "But I said I wasn't hungry so he took it away again."

"Maybe he'll bring it back," Elena suggested. "And I could go and see about getting word to your little sister."

Dolores nodded. "Yes, please."

Elena called Torres to the door. "Señorita Severino wants her breakfast now," she said. "And I'll be back to see her in a little while."

As Elena left the cell, Dolores raised her voice. "Señora Fernández!"

"Yes?"

The girl gave her a timid smile. "Thank you."

Elena found her husband alone in his office. "How can I get to Argüébanes?" she demanded. "I need to take a message for Dolores."

Tejada raised his eyebrows. "I didn't mean for you to transform yourself into her personal servant."

"Carlos, do you have any idea what that poor child has gone through?"

"The poor child was involved in a shoot-out that left Guardia Riera seriously injured," Tejada retorted. She began a furious retort but he held up one hand and cut her off. "I know. She wasn't the ringleader. I'll drive you over to Argüébanes this afternoon. I'd like to see Severino's family anyway."

"Dolores says he was a widower," Elena said. "She's the oldest child."

Tejada looked quizzical. "Is that what she says? How interesting."

"Why?"

The lieutenant tapped the papers on his desk. "I pulled the civil register on Severino. According to this, Dolores has an older brother, Luis Gil, born in '22. I'm wondering where he is."

"Maybe he died young."

"It's not recorded." Tejada made a wry face. "Unless, of course, you think he's the one who panicked and headed out under fire last night, in which case, yes, he did die young. We still haven't identified him, but Dolores was in no state to tell us more last night."

"You wouldn't ask her to do that!"

"Not if I can get Father Bernardo or a reliable neighbor to do it instead," Tejada said pragmatically. "I don't want to have to drag her out to the morgue and back."

Elena frowned. "At any rate, she's responsible for her little brothers and sister. She wants to know what's going to happen to them."

"That would have been a good question to ask before she decided to play queen of the bandits," Tejada said.

Elena stared at him, unable to believe what she was hearing. "You don't care at all?"

"Her father and his friends tried to kill me last night," the lieutenant reminded his wife. "I admit that lessens my sympathy." He eyed the civil register thoughtfully. "Although Severino passed up a chance to kill us both when he picked us up in Unquera. So maybe I owe his daughter something for that."

"All we did was ask for a ride!" Elena protested.

"I was in uniform," Tejada reminded her. "And he could have caught me off guard easily."

"Maybe he was unarmed," Elena said grimly, disliking her husband's logic. "He probably didn't take a machine gun along when he went to visit his brother in San Vicente."

"How do you know he has a brother in San Vicente?"

"Dolores said she wanted to send the younger children to her uncle there, and I assumed . . ." Elena heard what she was saying and stopped. "Where else could he have been traveling?" she asked, but her voice lacked conviction.

"That was a very unpleasant experience," Tejada said, again tapping his pen on the desk. "Waiting for so long at the station, remember?"

"Because the guardias didn't arrive to pick us up," Elena said slowly.

"Because they were searching for the Valencians who had just escaped," Tejada finished, beginning to smile. "And along came an old peasant making a seventy-kilometer trip in a snowstorm and I was so cold and tired and impatient I didn't even think to ask where he'd been and why!" He began to laugh. "Jesus, poor man! Here he takes the Valencians down to the coast, where they'll have a shot at a boat to France, or a train south, or God knows what, and he trundles along home congratulating himself on a job well done and then out of nowhere up pops a guardia civil demanding to know who he is and where he's going. I must have given him a heart attack!"

"And then you asked for a ride," Elena said, smiling a little reluctantly as she recognized the grisly humor of the situation.

"And damn near made him pull up in front of the post." Tejada was still grinning. "No wonder he said he thought I was on duty!"

The door opened as he was speaking. "Who was on duty?" Sergeant Márquez asked.

"Nothing. I think we've just figured something out about the Valencians." Tejada sobered in the presence of his subordinate, but his voice was still good-humored. "Luis Severino was the man Elena and I rode with on our way to Potes, and it seems he has a brother in San Vicente. We were just considering the possibility that he'd taken the runaways to the coast."

"It's a good thought," Márquez agreed, moving toward his desk.

Elena, who had unthinkingly taken his chair because it was available, stood up. "I'm sorry to intrude. I'll see you this afternoon then?"

"I'll pick you up at home," Tejada agreed.

Elena nodded and left. When the door had closed behind her, Márquez turned toward his commander. "You and Señora de Tejada have plans for this afternoon?"

Tejada was uncomfortable as he said, "Elena wants to visit Severino's family. I thought I'd drive her over this afternoon and ask about the brother as well."

"Are you sure that's wise?" the sergeant asked. "I mean, given her sympathies, I think any contact with the maquis—"

"I'll be the judge of that," Tejada interrupted shortly. "Have you finished the patrol schedules, Sergeant?"

Márquez still looked disapproving, but there was nothing more he could say. It was perhaps just as well that paperwork kept him in the office all morning, so he missed Elena's second visit to the prison. This time, she came carrying a package with an extra blouse, a sewing kit, and a hairbrush. She found Guardia Torres, and demanded to see Dolores Severino again.

The girl was sitting on her cot looking rather forlorn, but she brightened at the sight of Elena. "Did you find Concha?"

"No. I'm going this afternoon." Elena explained the reason for her delay, and then held out the package she had brought. "I thought you might like a change of clothes. The blouse will need to be altered, but it will give you something to do, and then you can rinse out the one you have on. It's pretty badly stained, but maybe I can see about hot water for washing."

Dolores smiled ruefully. "No need. I think that's mostly blood. When I saw Pedro was hurt, I went over to him and—" She lifted her elbows and inspected the stains on her sleeves. With a stronger voice she went on. "You're very kind, though, Señora Fernández. Especially about the hairbrush." She pulled her hair free of its pins and managed a shaky laugh. "I've been feeling itchy and messy all morning, but I didn't want to just attack it with my fingers."

"Should I leave you alone?" Elena asked as Dolores picked up the hairbrush and began to yank it through her knotted curls.

"No, please. It's nice to have someone to talk to."

Elena knew exactly how Dolores felt, and her strong sympathy for the girl made her unsure whether her next words would be kindness or cruelty. Dolores was still barely more than a child, though, and Elena's conscience made her say as she sat on the cot beside the girl, "I'm happy to stay and talk. But you'll remember that I'm the lieutenant's wife before you say anything?"

"Yes." Dolores's face was obscured by her hair. "I didn't mean to talk about that. I just meant, well, it's hard being alone because you don't get any news or know what's happening or even what time it is, and you start imagining all sorts of terrible things."

"It's just before noon," Elena said, amused. "And so far as I know nothing has happened of note today."

Dolores brushed silently for a few moments, picking at a recalcitrant knot. Then she said abruptly, "How is Pedro, do you know?"

Elena had heard the brief pause before the word "Pedro" and guessed that Dolores's casual tone had cost her dearly. "I'm not sure," she said. "I know he's alive. And I don't think he's been interrogated. But I don't know how badly he was wounded."

"He was unconscious when we arrived last night." Dolores was still straining to sound offhand. "But I know the lieutenant said the doctor would see to him after the wounded guardia. I hope he's all right. He—he's a friend of the family."

Elena, unsure what to say, thought of repeating her warning that she was the lieutenant's wife. But she had remained silent for too long, and Dolores, brushing hair out of her eyes, began to speak again. "One of the guardias said last night that he was my . . . that we were . . . well, friends." She blushed painfully. "We're not. I mean, I think he's a wonderful man, of course, but he's like an older brother. I mean, I didn't want you to think, just because I asked about him—"

"He's a comrade?" Elena suggested gently, remembering her own unreciprocated adoration of one of her father's younger colleagues fifteen years earlier.

"Yes, that's right." Dolores nodded eagerly. "A comrade. A good friend."

Elena could see that Dolores was aching to talk about Pedro, but she knew that the wounded guerrilla was probably a topic of considerable interest to Carlos, and she also knew that Dolores would never forgive herself if she inadvertently betrayed anything about her "comrade" to his enemies. "You said you were the oldest at home," Elena said, determined to give the girl another gentle hint. "But the lieutenant says that according to the records, you have an older brother?"

Dolores's face clouded and she nodded. "Yes, Luis. But he hasn't lived with us for a while now."

"He took to the hills?" Elena said.

The girl nodded. "Last year," she admitted. "Papa didn't like it. He said Luis was too young. But all his friends . . ." She stopped, resolute. "He wasn't there last night at least," she said firmly.

Elena nodded, pleased that Dolores seemed to be in control of herself once more. They chatted for a few more minutes, and then the lieutenant's wife excused herself and went home. Tejada picked her up a few hours later, as he had promised, and they drove together to the Severinos' home in Argüébanes. As Elena had expected, a neighbor was comforting a flock of frightened children. Tejada quietly took the neighbor aside and demanded information about of the late Luis Severino's recent activities. Elena, left to supervise the children, gently asked to speak to Concha.

"I'm Concha." A gaunt thirteen-year-old with the eyes of an old woman stepped forward, speaking with a quiet self-possession beyond her years. "I've heard my father's dead. Did the sergeant send you?"

"No," Elena said, a little disconcerted by the question. Then she remembered that Sergeant Márquez had been the commander of the post before Carlos's arrival, and that Concha might even be using the term "sergeant" generically. "No, I came from your sister."

"What's happened to Dolores?"

"I'm afraid she was arrested last night." Elena felt the cowardice of saying "was arrested" but she had already found it difficult enough to meet Concha's eyes. "She asked me to give you a message." She repeated what Dolores had said. The child gravely thanked Elena and politely accepted her awkward condolences with an expression that gave nothing away. The Señora was very kind. No, she and the children did not need any help. Their uncle would take them in. No, there would be no difficulty in getting to San Vicente. She had bus fare.

Elena's last sight of Concha Severino was of the little girl gathering her siblings together to give them Dolores's message. Tejada was finishing with the Severinos' neighbor. It was time to go. Elena leaned against the side of the truck and tugged at her shoe to dislodge a pebble. As she straightened, she saw her husband coming toward her. His back was to the Severino house, and beyond him Elena glimpsed one of Luis Severino's older sons, a boy of about ten with tousled, dirty-blond curls that gave him the look of a Renaissance cherub. The boy did not see her. He was focusing on Tejada's retreating back, his face twisted with hatred. Suddenly, he spat ferociously and then turned and fled into the house.

"What's the matter?" Tejada asked as he reached the truck. "You look like you've seen a ghost."

Elena looked at him. He was smiling a little anxiously, the look he had when he was concerned for her welfare and afraid she would resent it. He reached out one hand to her, and Elena knew that if she started to cry he would embrace her and murmur endearments and not ask questions until she stopped. "Nothing," she said softly. "I'm fine. Let's go."

They drove down to the valley in silence. Then Tejada said carefully, "Did you deliver Dolores's message?"

"Yes. Her sister asked if the sergeant had sent me."

"I have to remember to tell Márquez," Tejada said, amused. "He didn't think you should go at all."

Elena shuddered, remembering Concha's firm politeness and her too-old manners. "Well, you can tell him that I hope I never have to do anything like that again. It was pretty unpleasant."

Tejada heard the agony in her voice, and spoke more seriously. "You didn't have to this time, you know. I would have taken the message to Concha."

Elena knew that he was speaking the truth, and that he saw no incongruity in the errand. "Dolores asked me to do it."

"Yes." Tejada kept his eyes on the road. "But you shouldn't sacrifice your own peace of mind for Dolores."

"You think I would have more peace of mind if I didn't know anything about your job?" Elena asked a little bitterly. "That I'd sleep better at night thinking you were staying up late doing paperwork?"

They had reached home. Tejada sighed, and drew up to a careful stop. "I'm only trying to protect you."

"By pretending that some things don't exist?"

Tejada climbed out of the truck, slammed the door a little harder than necessary, and then came around to the passenger side to help her down. "They exist," he said flatly. "But they're not your business. You don't have to get involved."

Elena drew her elbow out of his grasp and turned to face him. "Then why are you involved?" she demanded.

Tejada thought that he recognized the beginning of a familiar argument, and drew her inside, unwilling to argue in the street. "Because I'm a guardia. That's my job."

Elena knowing his reluctance to speak further in public, waited until they had climbed the stairs to their apartment. "*Why* is it your job?" she demanded then, derailing the argument from its standard lines. "You could have peace of mind, too, if you wanted it. You could be Señor Tejada Alonso y León, and live on your family's estates in Granada. Or if you wanted to be independent of them you could have a law office in the city, or work for an import-export firm or something, and sit behind a big desk from ten to six. And if you said you were staying late to catch up on paperwork I'd only have to lie awake and worry that you were having an affair with your secretary, not that someone was going to knock on my door and tell me that you were dead."

Tejada had been frowning uncomfortably, and even Elena's idea of an affair with a hypothetical secretary did not lighten his expression. As her voice caught on her last words, he turned away from her and said, in a slightly strangled voice, "Is that what you want?"

Elena, who had been trying to make a point, and had somewhat lost the thread of her argument, was confused for a moment. "Is *what* what I want?"

"Do you want me to retire?" The set of Tejada's shoulders was tense. He could feel blood pounding in his temples, and an internal voice nagged at him. *But why have you never considered retiring before? Suppose you'd died last night? Or at the barn where you found the dynamite? You should think about the baby. And anyway, with Elena's background you'll never advance in the Guardia.*

"No!" Elena's cry of denial was instant and convincing.

He relaxed and turned toward her with a smile, almost dizzy with relief. "I somehow had the impression you disapproved of my work."

"I do." Elena took his hands. "But all the things I disapprove of wouldn't stop happening just because you weren't a guardia. They would just be happening where we couldn't see them. So we could close our eyes and pretend they didn't exist, and . . . have peace of mind. But you don't *want* that kind of peace of mind! At least I don't think you do. Wouldn't you rather know the worst and try to prevent it than just bury your head in the sand?"

"Yes," Tejada said seriously. "I . . . being a guardia has always been important to me, but . . . I was never able to put it quite so well before."

"Well, that's why I had to take Dolores's message," Elena said, suddenly feeling very tired. "Do you understand?"

"Yes." Tejada touched her cheek, more grateful than he could say that she was not offering him logical reasons to leave the Guardia. "I love you, and I would be more protective of your peace if you would let me, but I understand." He smiled mischievously. "You're very persuasive. Do you think you could explain all those reasons to my mother the next time she starts harping on my career?"

Elena laughed. "I couldn't explain a recipe for fish soup to your mother, and well you know it. She wouldn't sit still long enough to listen to the dangerous Red slut who entrapped her baby."

"I guess you couldn't," the lieutenant admitted. "But I'm sure she never actually said slut."

"It was implied."

Tejada laughed and watched Elena settle herself into her armchair with a feeling of infinite satisfaction. Suddenly relaxed, and very sure of the answer, he said, "Elena, who's Herrera?"

"Herrera?" Elena was puzzled. "The only Herrera I knew was in Madrid."

"Yes, that one," Tejada said eagerly. "Was he—were you close to him?"

"I wouldn't say close," Elena said, wondering why on earth her husband was interested. "We worked together for five years."

"He's a teacher then?"

Elena stared. "Carlos, he was the director of my school. You *met* him, remember?"

A vivid memory of a fussy little man with square-rimmed glasses and a yellow complexion, terrified of the Guardia and quite willing to sacrifice any of his employees to them to ensure his own safety, came back to Tejada. He had asked to speak to Elena Fernández regarding a murder, and the director had practically begged him to arrest her and spare the rest of the school. Tejada laughed in sheer relief. "The sneaky little coward who fired you? *That* Herrera?"

Elena pursed her lips. "He wasn't really a sneaky little coward. And I resigned."

"Much good it did him." Tejada wiped away tears of mirth. "*That's* the Herrera Márquez was talking about!"

"Márquez?" Elena looked startled, and not at all pleased. "What does Márquez know about him?"

"Your file mentions what you did in Madrid," Tejada explained rapidly. "Márquez said something about how it would be a problem if Devastated Regions ever transferred Herrera here, given your connection with him, and I thought . . ." he trailed off, embarrassed.

Elena ignored his embarrassment. "Señor Herrera is in prison then? Poor man. I can't think why."

"Neither can I," Tejada said frankly. "He struck me as expert at wriggling out of tight spots."

His wife's eyes narrowed suddenly. "*What* did you think about him and me?" she demanded.

"I . . . " Tejada flushed. "Márquez only said there was a connection, and I thought maybe . . . well, I knew that you'd lived alone in Madrid and, after all, you're a beautiful woman and with so many soldiers . . . I didn't really imagine—"

Elena shook her head, but she was smiling. "You are a jealous pig," she said affectionately. "Thank God you don't like Golden Age drama."

"I didn't really believe—" Tejada protested.

"Leave it alone," Elena interrupted, laughing. "You'll only make it worse."

"I'm sorry. How can I make it up to you?" Tejada smiled, then spoiled his contrition by adding hopefully, "I could sock Márquez in the jaw if you like."

"No, it's bad enough for you to have a sergeant with a sprained wrist," Elena said kindly. "Suppose you come up to Santo Toribio with me one afternoon this week? Father Bernardo invited both of us on a tour, and even if he can't come, the walk is lovely, and the monastery is really beautiful."

"I would love to," Tejada said. "How about Saturday?"

"I'll be at home," Elena said with a twinkle. "And I'll leave the butler orders to admit you."

Chapter 14

Tejada had assumed that his prisoners would be taken to Santander for further questioning and then trial and sentencing within a day. But by Thursday afternoon, although Guardia Riera had been taken to the hospital at Unquera, where he was recovering, and the other guardias had returned to their posts, no transport and no word regarding the prisoners had arrived. Tejada finished typing his report on the raid on Marcial's cabin, deposited one copy in the filing cabinet, put the other in the outgoing mail, and then called his commander. There was so much static on the line that he was barely able to make himself understood, and the secretary at the other end was disposed to be officious. Tejada argued politely, and doodled rude words on a piece of scrap paper while he waited to make his request to the commander.

"Sorry, Tejada, but we can't pick them up this week," Súarez said when Tejada finally managed to get through to him. "The road's washed out just past Unquera, and with all this rain we've been having there's no way it will be passable until Tuesday at the earliest. And God knows what it's like in the gorge."

"What rain?" the lieutenant asked, bewildered. "It's been dry as a bone here."

"Lucky you," snapped the colonel. "Santander's a sponge. Two bridges are out, and I just got a call from the commander in Torrelavega saying that the barracks basement there has three inches of water in it."

"I'll expect transport Tuesday or Wednesday then," Tejada said, steering a diplomatic course between sympathy and insistence.

"Look, Tejada, I've got ten thousand homeless living in *tents* here in the rain." Súarez was not noticeably pacified. "Devastated Regions is telling me that the *blueprints* for the new city won't be ready for another six months, and the only thing standing between us and bread riots is a shipment of humanitarian aid from the Germans, which may or may not be repeated. I'll send someone for the prisoners as soon as I can. In the meantime, *you're* the one dealing with the bandits. *You* keep the prisoners and question them."

"Yes, sir." Tejada made a final attempt. "Could you give me a rough estimate of how long we'll be out of touch, sir? One week? Two weeks?"

"It had better be less than two weeks." Súarez sighed noisily into the phone. "Otherwise we'll get into Holy Week, and I'll lose half my force for Good Friday. Just what I don't need."

"I'm sorry, Colonel. But there was one other thing, speaking of personnel."

"If it's another request for reinforcements, Tejada, forget it."

"No, sir," Tejada said. "It's about a prisoner in the Tabacalera, one José María Santiago Roldán. Native of Argüébanes."

"If you want us to look at his mail, we don't have the manpower," Súarez refused automatically.

"No, sir. His brother's information led to the operation in Argüébanes. The brother's indicated willingness to continue as an informant, but he's asked for word on Santiago Roldán."

"I'll tell someone to check what he's in for when I get a chance," the colonel said, slightly mollified. "If it's another one of these war tribunal sentences for shying a rock at a stained-glass window, we can spring him. I'd rather have the mountains secure. And one less warm body to look after can only help."

"Thank you, sir," Tejada said, satisfied. "The only other thing was the consignment of new arms and ammunition that was on its way. I assume it's been delayed?"

"Unavoidably. Sorry, Tejada. Stay in phone contact if you can, Lieutenant. *Arriba España.*"

"*Arriba España.*" Tejada hung up and sighed. *The next thing that's going to happen,* he thought *is that we're going to be left like Severino and Campos, holed up with guns but no bullets. I wonder what the Policía Armada's supplies are like. I should send word to them, too, if the road is washed out.* He wrote a quick memo to his counterpart at the Policía Armada, informing him of the possible delay in supplies. Then he sent for Guardia Torres, who had been alternating with Márquez on guard duty. "How are the prisoners?" he asked when the young man arrived in the office.

"Dolores seems to be doing well, sir," the guardia reported. "She's stopped crying all the time, anyway. Your wife visited her again today."

"And the other?"

Torres shook his head. "Not so good. He tore some strips off his shirt to change the bandages on his leg, but I don't know if that's going to help him. He's been running a fever, I think, saying he's cold even though he's wrapped up and sweating."

"You think he's malingering?" Tejada asked.

The guardia considered the question. "No, sir. He had diarrhea in the night, and that's hard to fake."

"Indeed." Tejada made a face. "Well, it looks like he's going to be staying with us for a little while. You might want to try to find out his full name, and a bit about him. Be friendly, for the moment. Get him cleaned up, offer him a drink, and see if he lets anything interesting slip."

"Yes, sir." Torres hesitated. Then he said, "I still have some aspirin. Maybe I could give him one?"

"Sure." The lieutenant nodded approvingly. "Tell him you've been sick too so you have some fellow feeling for him. And say you wouldn't turn over a sick dog to the lieutenant. You're on his side for now, got it?"

"Yes, sir. Should I tell him you're a tyrant and all of us are terrified of you?"

"Good idea. Or—no, better—" Tejada shuffled through the papers on his desk, searching for a duty roster; Guardia Carvallo was scheduled for guard duty that night, "tell him Carvallo's a sadistic bastard. The type who saw a lot of action during the war, but wasn't decorated because of a few things with a funny smell. And then find Carvallo and tell him to report to me before he goes on duty tonight."

"Got it, Lieutenant." Torres saluted and left, looking amused.

Tejada watched the guardia depart with contentment. Torres was young, but his instincts were good, and he could be trained. The lieutenant spoke to Battista about the possible delays in supplies due to flooding and had the satisfaction of having the corporal provide an instant and detailed inventory of the post's current munitions. Battista was a solid officer, Tejada thought. Torres and Carvallo were still relatively inexperienced, but they were conscientious and teachable. And Ortíz, born and raised in the mountains, with fifteen years in the Guardia, was a valuable addition to the post. Sergeant Márquez was not easy to work with, but he was reasonably intelligent, and he had been less hostile since his injury. Remembering Colonel Súarez's harassed tones and his former captain's rank incompetence, Tejada congratulated himself on the men under his command.

He spent much of the following days on patrol with Battista, familiarizing himself further with the outlying villages. There were no serious incidents although the lieutenant quickly learned that the maquis were keeping a watchful eye on the Guardia's activities. Tejada had been initially concerned by his men's nonchalance about being fired at during routine patrols but he had come to be grateful for their good sense. The maquis aimed high or wide so consistently that he could not attribute it simply to poor marksmanship. They liked to announce their presence, and sometimes test a guardia's horsemanship over a patch of rough terrain, but unless a man provoked them—by rudeness to local famers or by loudly singing the Fascist anthem, for example—they shot almost playfully. The guardias took cover, returned fire when they could, and continued on their way.

In spite of the lack of crises it had been a busy week, and by Saturday afternoon the entire post was ready for a brief break. Ortíz disappeared to visit his family, Torres went to lunch with a friend who shared his passion for checkers, and Márquez retired to his quarters to fiddle with the nearly new shortwave radio that was his pride and joy and that consumed most of his leisure hours. Tejada left a somewhat sulky Battista and Carvallo on duty, and kept his promise to Elena to escort her to Santo Toribio.

She had arranged to meet Father Bernardo at the parish house. He was leaving as they arrived. "I'm terribly sorry," he apologized. "I left a note. I've been called to a deathbed. I'm afraid I can't go with you today."

"It happens when you're always on call," Tejada said, sympathetic. "We'd love your company some other time, Father."

"Thank you. If you're walking toward the Deva I can go with you. It's on my way."

Tejada agreed, and as they fell into step together the priest sighed. "I'm sorry. I was looking forward to showing you the monastery. And I did want to show you the path as well, although I'm sure there will be time soon. Speaking of which, I assume you'll be taking the Virgin this year, or are you leaving that to your men?"

"I beg your pardon?" Tejada said.

"Our Santuca, the Virgin of the Light," Father Bernardo explained. "She always visits all the major towns of the valley on her feast day, and then a pair of guardias from Potes escorts her to the monastery on the day of the festival. Lieutenant Calero usually formed part of her guard."

"If you don't feel having a stranger would be an imposition, I will gladly," Tejada said. "When is the festival?"

"May second. We're assured of good weather by then, even up at the monastery."

"We seem to be having better weather than at the coast already," Tejada commented, and mentioned his conversation with Colonel Súarez.

"Not surprising," the priest said. "It always rains less in Liébana."

The conversation explored the topic of the weather, and a few minutes later the priest turned off to make his visit. Tejada and Elena continued along the river alone. The silence between them was companionable until Tejada noticed that she was staring down into the white water of the river. "A penny for your thoughts?" he said, although he suspected he knew what she was ruminating about.

"We found Anselmo Montalbán down there." Elena gestured.

The lieutenant put an arm around her shoulders. "It must have been a nasty shock."

"It was. The thing is—" Elena stopped abruptly and looked pleadingly at him.

Neither of us wants easy peace of mind, Tejada thought, reading her desire to keep talking and her worry that he would be angry if she did. "The thing is?"

"He was lying facedown under the bushes, Carlos, as if he'd been hidden. Now even supposing he had a weapon and it was taken away when his companions fled, how could he have shot at Márquez and Carvallo from that position?"

"Maybe he didn't have a weapon at all," Tejada said, considering. "Maybe one of the others shot first, and Montalbán was just unlucky enough to get hit."

"In the back?" Elena demanded. The large hole in his chest had been an exit wound.

There was a vicious cracking noise as Tejada absently snapped a dead branch off a pine tree as they passed. "What's your point?"

"Did you ever check the files on Márquez and Carvallo?"

"No, the raid in Argüébanes came up and I forgot," Tejada admitted. "Why? Do you think someone had a specific grudge against them? You sound as if you believe it's the other way around!"

"I didn't mean that," Elena protested, a little absently. An idea had surfaced like the vague shape of a whale in the distant sea when her husband had said, " Argüébanes," and she was trying to pinpoint it.

"You practically just said you thought Márquez had deliberately shot an unarmed man in the back who was trying to hide from him!" Tejada said, annoyed because although Elena's scenario made sense, he could see no logic to it, and no way to pursue it even if it was true. Everyone knew that a certain amount of latitude was allowed in reports detailing casualties in "self-defense," and there was no way that Colonel Súarez would appreciate an investigation into Sergeant Márquez's actions, unless the motives for investigating were clear and compelling. "Even granted that that was the case, what am I supposed to do? Márquez had standing orders to find Montalbán for questioning; perhaps he shot when he saw him and aimed badly."

"He had orders to ask him about the Valencians!" Elena interrupted suddenly. The idea had surfaced again, and this time its silhouette was clear. "Remember, I told you Montalbán had been missing since before we came to Potes. Since before the Valencians escaped. And you thought he might have something to do with Calero's murder."

"And you provided a motive for him," Tejada pointed out.

"Yes, but remember, Luis Severino thought he was at home when we arrived in Potes. So he hadn't made contact with the maquis." Elena saw her husband's frown and corrected herself.

"With the bandits, I mean. And if he hadn't met up with them, where would he get the weapon to kill Calero?"

"This is bear country," Tejada pointed out. "Most people probably have hunting rifles."

"No, but listen." Elena frowned, concentrating on presenting her points logically. "Let's say Anselmo killed Lieutenant Calero. That was when?"

"October eighth," Tejada supplied promptly.

"So Anselmo was missing for nearly six months before he was shot," Elena proceeded. "But we know that he didn't make contact with the–the bandits right away, because we know they were looking for him. They were people whom he knew. And someone like Luis Severino would have been able to find them. So why did Anselmo wait to make contact with them?"

"You have a theory?" Tejada asked, intrigued.

Elena shook her head. "No. It just seems odd. As if Montalbán wanted to disappear *completely*, so that neither side knew where he was."

"He must have changed his mind," Tejada said out.

"And as soon as he did, he ended up dead," Elena retorted.

The lieutenant sighed. "All right. Who do you think wanted him dead then? Us or them?"

"I'm thinking out loud," Elena apologized. "I haven't gotten that far yet."

"It's a fanciful scenario." Tejada began to methodically snap the dead branch he had been carrying in half, and in half again.

"But it works either way," Elena pointed out. "Márquez or Carvallo wanted to kill him so they hunted him down and shot him in the back, and made it look like self-defense. Or the maquis wanted to kill him, so they deliberately drew fire from the Guardia, knowing he was unarmed and likely to get hit."

"He trusted the maquis," Tejada said, forgetting to refer to them as bandits.

"So much that he hid from them?" Elena retorted.

Tejada began throwing broken sticks into the river. "I can't think of any reason anyone would want Montalbán dead."

"Check the files," Elena said dryly. "If there's no reason there, then maybe you can start thinking about why he shouldn't have trusted the maquis."

"It would be interesting if he was on anybody's payroll," Tejada agreed, thinking of his recent informant, Domingo Santiago. "The only thing is, if he took to the hills for his own reasons, then we're back to square one about Calero's killers."

"Not necessarily," Elena said. "Maybe he took to the hills for other reasons, but when he saw a chance to even the score with Calero, he took it."

"It's possible," Tejada said neutrally. He had no wish to end up like Lieutenant Calero, and he planned to have a heart-to-heart talk with his prisoners about Calero's other possible murderers, but he knew that his wife was touchy about prisoner interrogation, and he saw no need to share this information with her. "You know where we're going. Shouldn't we be turning off soon?" he asked, to change the subject.

Elena noticed her surroundings, and laughed. "We've missed the road. We'll have to go back."

Tejada laughed also as they turned around. "I've only gone this way when I was driving. Funny how that changes your sense of scale. The monastery really is fairly close to Potes, isn't it?"

"Yes. It's my own stupidity," Elena said. "At least we'll get exercise."

Tejada frowned. "Are you sure—?"

"I feel *fine*," Elena interrupted hastily.

Tejada was unconvinced, but he knew that Elena was stubborn to the point of foolishness when she thought that he was being overprotective. He contented himself with stealthily slowing his steps and forcing his wife to match his pace, and suggesting that they turn off the highway a little early onto what looked like a shortcut. Elena, who was happy to leave the grim memories of the river, readily agreed, and they headed up a dirt path that was momentarily so steep Tejada regretted his impulse. He was about to propose turning back when the track suddenly leveled out and began run smoothly along the mountainside, gaining altitude so gradually that it almost would have been suitable for a railroad grade. Elena, who had been panting from the climb, took a few deep breaths as they slowed at the crest. "It smells good," she said with a smile.

"Pines," Tejada agreed.

They continued along the path single file, Elena in front, moving in what both of them were fairly sure was the correct direction. Elena was just thinking that it was time for the path to rejoin the main road to the monastery when the road suddenly forked. She stopped, dismayed. The lieutenant leaned over her shoulder and made an annoyed noise. "Good shortcut," Elena said wryly.

Tejada inspected the two paths. "It should be that one," he said, pointing to the right-hand branch.

Elena frowned. "Why? I would have said the left. And you haven't been to the monastery before."

"Because that one has a blaze like the ones along the path," Tejada sounded smug.

"What ones?"

Smiling at the ignorance of city-bred women, Tejada pointed. "There, the cut on the birch. We passed another one like it about twenty-five meters back. And another before that. The right-hand branch is clearly part of the same path."

"We don't know that the same path goes where we want it to," Elena argued. "And that path looks like it heads up into the woods. The left-hand one should join up with the road at any moment."

Tejada looked dubiously in the direction his wife was point-ing. "The problem with following an unmarked trail is that it's hard to retrace your steps," he said cautiously.

"I'll bet it's less than a hundred meters." Elena was insistent.

Tejada knew that she was probably right, but he was annoyed with himself for proposing a shortcut that had turned out to be ambiguous, and a little disappointed that she had not been more impressed with his woodcraft. Seized with a desire both to prove himself right and to show off, he shrugged off his cloak. "Hold this," he said, moving toward a pine tree that stood at the division of the path. The broken remnants of dead branches hung low to the ground and formed an inviting ladder. "I should be able to get enough of a view to see where both paths lead for a little ways."

"You'll break your neck!" Elena protested.

If she had been concerned for his welfare, Tejada would probably have given up the idea. Since she sounded faintly amused, he grabbed two branches as handholds, and tested his weight on two lower ones. "I was always good at climbing trees," he retorted, censoring the thought that he had not climbed a tree since he was seventeen, and that this was a ridiculously undignified pastime for a man of his age.

He was at least able to make good the boast. His hands were rapidly stained with sap, and flecks of bark rained downward and caught in his clothing, but he managed to gain a decent height within a few minutes. Elena, watching his progress, smiled and unthinkingly began to sing. "I climbed a green pine tree to see if——" She choked. "If I could glimpse her," she fin-ished rapidly, embarrassed.

The lieutenant, alarmed by her song, shifted his weight care-lessly, and almost missed his footing among the branches. "Jesus, Elena, don't do that when anyone else is around!" he implored.

"It's just an old love song," Elena called back, glad that he could not see her burning face.

Tejada's laugh floated down to her along with dislodged pine needles. "It's "Anda, jaleo," dear, and you know it."

Elena fell silent, abashed, the newly adapted words of the song echoing in her head. "When the whistle blows, we'll see how Franco runs." She wondered how Carlos had learned the Republican version of the song. From prisoners during the war, perhaps. "Can you see anything?" she asked, hoping to change the subject.

"Not much." Tejada grunted. "There's a sort of nest of branches above that blocks everything. I'm going to see if I can get around it."

"Be careful." This time the concern in Elena's voice was real.

Tejada was too absorbed to reply. The trunk of the pine was still thick and steady, but the spreading branches of neighboring trees tugged at him from behind, and he was unable to see a way around the nest of branches. It was an odd thing, he thought, as he edged sideways, looking for a free space. The weaving didn't look typical of a bird's nest, and it would have to have been a large bird, an eagle or something even bigger. But the branches were too solidly interlocked to be random. It was almost as if someone had started to build a child's tree house. "Stand back, Elena!" he yelled, suddenly tense. "Move! As fast as you can!"

"Which path?"

"Doesn't matter."

Worried by the grim note in his voice, Elena hurried down the left-hand path. It curved slightly and then descended to the road to the monastery, as she had expected. She hesitated a moment, and then turned and headed back toward her husband. Tejada was still clinging to the big pine. Little branches were falling to the forest floor. Heart in her mouth, Elena suddenly wondered if he was about to fall. Then she heard a yell.

Several larger branches crashed to the ground, and something cloth-covered bounced downward and hung suspended, apparently caught on a crook in the tree. For a heart-stopping moment Elena thought that her husband had fallen, and then she realized that the dangling object was a cloth-covered bag on some kind of rope, and that Tejada was still gripping the trunk. He half-slid, half-fell down the pine. The cloth bag bounced down below him, and Elena saw that his movements were hampered because he was clinging to the rope that held the bag.

He let go of it only after the bag had safely reached the ground, and then tumbled the last few feet to the forest floor, landing on his knees. "What happened?" Elena demanded, as she came up behind him.

He turned his head and looked up at her. "I told you to get out of the way."

"Yes, but I couldn't *leave* you," Elena protested.

Tejada was working at the knot that closed the bag. "Damn it, Elena. Suppose this is some kind of explosive? Suppose I'd dropped it? You have to think about the baby."

"What about you?" Elena demanded as the knot finally gave way and the lieutenant gingerly folded back the edges of the sack. "You could have been—oh." She backed up a step as Tejada turned toward her, cradling his booty.

"This," the lieutenant said flatly, "is not good."

"No. Could you point that somewhere else?" Elena said nervously, inspecting the gun he was holding.

Tejada set the weapon down and rummaged further. "There are three more here. And ammunition. Shit." He picked up the gun again, ignoring his wife's discomfort. "Do you know what this *is?*"

"It looks a lot like a carbine." Elena attempted to speak lightly, not entirely successfully.

"Looks like," Tejada agreed. "But it's a Thompson machine gun."

"How is that worse?" Elena asked, puzzled by his tone.

"You've never seen one of these," Tejada said.

"They do a lot of damage?"

"That, too, yes. Quite the dream of the machine gunner, to quote the song you claimed you weren't singing just now. But the main point is you've never seen one before."

Elena made an exasperated noise. "Carlos, don't be irritating."

Tejada laughed, although he did not feel particularly cheerful. "If this was a Breda or a Maxim, it would be bad but no big deal. The Reds had teams of guerrillas operating throughout Nationalist zones, and I'm sure a number of former soldiers hid their old weapons before capture. If these were old Soviet arms I'd know how the bandits got ahold of them. But Thompsons are English, I think. Or maybe American. You've never seen any because there weren't any in Madrid. *I've* only seen a few because we took some off international prisoners once. And these look like a new model."

"Expensive?" Elena guessed.

"Very." Tejada had been fiddling with one of the magazines. Now he succeeded in clipping it to the barrel. "And right now, I'd bet English armament manufacturers have more contracts than they can handle from their own government. Their Ministry of Defense is probably controlling production by now. To make and ship these guns without the English government's knowledge . . . an arms dealer could name his price. Where the hell are the bandits getting that kind of money?" Elena opened her mouth to reply and then closed it again as Tejada began to rapidly repack the bag of arms. He retied the bag's neck and then scrambled to his feet, catching her distressed look as he did so. "What?"

"The English have a new prime minister, don't they?" Elena said in a small voice. "I mean, since the end of the war. I-I've heard he's very interventionist."

Tejada stared at her with a sinking feeling in the pit of his stomach. "You've just changed this from a phone call to

Santander to a phone call to Madrid," he said quietly, slinging the sack over one shoulder. "Can you loop the rope around to make a pack? I want to have my hands free."

"If you put that one back in the bag you'd have a hand free," Elena pointed out, gesturing to the Thompson he was still holding.

"I want it *out*," Tejada said. "That's why I want both hands free. Come on. I don't like having you here. If we run into any trouble, get down, and when the coast's clear get away as quickly as possible."

"It's the left-hand path," Elena said, shaken. "I went a little ways along it when you said to get out of the way."

"Fine." Tejada was in no mood to argue.

They walked quickly and quietly. Elena relaxed when they reached the road to the monastery and turned down it toward Potes, but Tejada remained tense until the flag in front of the post waved cheerfully in front of them. "Go home," he said in Elena's ear. "Don't mention this to anyone. I'll join you as soon as I can."

"Be careful." Elena smiled faintly. "I'm sorry we didn't just take the road up to Santo Toribio."

"Next Saturday, I promise," Tejada said automatically and headed for the post.

Chapter 15

Tejada spent Monday morning writing a long report to his superiors about the discovery of the cache of arms on Monte Viorna. Serendipity played a much smaller role in the report than strict honesty demanded, but the lieutenant felt that results were more important than motivation, as far as his commanders were concerned. He then spent a long time rehashing the possible sources for the bandits' arms with Márquez and Battista. Neither of them had any good ideas, although Battista cursed sharply at the idea of the maquis being supplied by English Intelligence, and Márquez said that the way things were going it might help to have Reds in the family soon. Tejada chose to ignore the significant glance in his direction that accompanied the sergeant's comment. "Let Madrid worry about that," he said. "Let's suppose they're paying for weapons. Where are they getting the money? Are there any local landowners who support them? Do any of them have family in the Americas who could be sending back money?"

Neither of his subordinates provided any new information, and by the time Battista said, "But you never know, sir. Reds turn up in the oddest places," Tejada could only grit his teeth and hope devoutly that the remark had been a chance one, spoken without ulterior motive, and that Elena was doing something completely innocent and uncontroversial.

Elena's day was taken up by a visit from Federico and Simón

Álvarez, who had brought over the first installment of furniture. The carpenter had done a good job with the bookshelves, and they fit perfectly in the places Elena had measured for them. Elena thanked both father and son with warmth, and mentioned that she planned to spend the rest of the day unpacking cartons onto the shelves. The carpenter expressed concern at the bending this would involve, and on impulse Elena asked Simón to stay and help. Quico Álvarez gave his permission, and Simón energetically stocked the bookshelves he had helped to build. Elena offered the boy lunch, and he spent a happy two hours munching absently, his elbows propped on the table and his nose buried in an old Sherlock Holmes volume that the lieutenant had received as a gift from his brother, who sometimes showed unexpected glimmerings of a sense of humor.

Elena found Simón congenial company, although most of his conversation was limited to exclamations about the book. After answering a few questions about forensic science to the best of her ability, and pleading ignorance to a good many more, Elena gently raised the topic of Simón's schooling. He eagerly and somewhat wistfully expressed a desire to study for the baccalaureate examinations, and added that he would like to study engineering. Or possibly medicine. Or mathematics. Elena mentally recorded the conversation to be repeated to Father Bernardo at the earliest opportunity, and invited Simón to borrow whatever books he wished. Simón went home with a volume of Hernán Cortés's letters under one arm and Elena's promise that he could come and use the library again whenever he wished.

Tejada was both relieved and amused when he heard the story of his wife's day. He was even willing to forgive the presence of a number of crumbs inside the spine of his collected Sherlock Holmes. He accepted Elena's determination to visit Dolores Severino the following day as a further tribute to her maternal instincts, and made no objections.

Elena set out for the prison the following morning in a good mood. Dolores greeted the lieutenant's wife almost warmly. The girl looked far better than she had during Elena's first visit. Her hair was combed, her face was washed, and her clothes, though wrinkled, were reasonably clean. She stood to greet her guest and held out her hand. "Thank you for coming again, Señora. Do you have news from my brothers?"

"I'm afraid not," Elena apologized. "I know Concha took the boys to San Vicente, but I haven't heard any news since."

"That's all right." Dolores smiled ruefully. "It's just that there's nothing else to think about here. I never thought I'd *miss* doing housework but, well, it's boring." She hesitated. "Is there any chance of anything happening soon?"

Elena, who had discussed the visit with her husband the night before, decided that there was nothing to be lost by honesty. "You'll probably go to Santander at the end of the week," she said. "But I don't know exactly when."

"It will be a change." Dolores spoke bravely but she looked forlorn. "I've never been so far from home before."

Elena was silent, embarrassed. She had asked the lieutenant, with some urgency, whether Dolores was likely to be interrogated in Santander. "Probably not," Tejada had said. "I don't think she knows anything. But now that we've found those weapons, we can't take any chances. It might be worth something if she could even give us names." Now, facing Dolores's terrible uncertainty, Elena found the ambiguous words cold comfort. She murmured something reassuring, and tried to change the subject.

The two women chatted for a few minutes. Then Dolores said, "I don't suppose you know how Pedro is doing?"

Elena looked at her hands. "No," she said quietly, and waited for Dolores to take the hint, as she had in previous conversations.

But Dolores's preoccupation was too strong to let the subject rest. "I suppose when we go to Santander we'll be separated?"

"Yes."

"H-he hasn't been well, you know." Dolores stammered a little, but her voice was admirably level. "I've heard him, in the
night sometimes. I hope he's all better before we go to
Santander."

Elena said nothing, but Dolores suddenly leaned toward her
and said in a rush, "You've been so kind to come and visit me,
Señora. And to take messages to Concha and everything. I don't
know what I would have done without you. And poor Pedro has-
n't had anyone. Do you suppose you could go see him? Just to
tell me how he's doing? And to give him my . . . my best wishes?"
Unconsciously, Dolores reached out and clasped the older
woman's hand.

Elena sighed, knowing that the kindest thing to do would be
to squeeze the girl's hand in silent sympathy. "I don't know if I'll
be able to," she said quietly. "But I'll try."

"Thank you." The words were a whisper.

The rest of the visit was awkward. Dolores clearly wanted
Elena to leave immediately, and Elena was dreading the visit's
end. After a few stilted minutes, she rose and walked to the door
of the cell. "I'll come back when I can," she said.

Guardia Torres was on duty again. He nodded to her as he let
her out of Dolores's cell. Elena took a deep breath, knowing
that Dolores could clearly hear what went on in the corridor.
"Do you suppose I could see your other prisoner as well?"

She was expecting a flat denial, or at best more questions. So
she was surprised when Torres said easily, "Of course, Señora.
This way."

Her surprise became flat astonishment when Torres opened
the door at the other end of the hall with the words, "Hello,
Pedro. Good news. I've managed to swing a visitor for you."

"Not another priest, I hope." The voice was light and mocking.

"Don't worry," Torres laughed, exuding genial good humor,
and Elena wondered a little if she had stepped into some alter-
nate reality. "I wouldn't push that crap on you on a weekday."

The guardia turned to Elena. "Here you are, Señora. Try to cheer the poor man up a little." Then the cell door swung shut, and Elena was alone with Dolores's Pedro.

His cell was the twin of the one in which Dolores was imprisoned, but where the girl's room was scrupulously clean, its starkness softened by the hairbrush and clothes Elena had brought, this cell stank faintly of blood and urine. The prisoner was stretched full length on his cot, with the blanket that Dolores always folded neatly across the foot of her bed wrapped around his shoulders. He was wearing shorts, and a bandage rusty with dried blood was wound around one knee and thigh. He shrugged off the blanket as he saw Elena, and flung it awkwardly over his bare legs. "Forgive me, Señora. If I'd had more notice that you were coming I would have made myself decent. I'm afraid standing to greet you is out of the question."

Elena was too unnerved to do more than stare for a moment. The man was unshaven, hollow-cheeked, and badly in need of a haircut. His shirt was torn, and he had a cut above his right eye and a bruise across his left cheekbone that looked like the result of a determined and experienced backhand. His nose had been recently broken. But his voice was cheerful and faintly amused; a voice that defied pity, equally ready to laugh at himself or at others. It was really his voice, and his calm, appraising look, that made Elena understand Dolores's ill-concealed infatuation. Both voice and look would have been caressing, under other circumstances. Since Elena was only tangentially aware of these things, her conscious thought was that he had probably been quite handsome before his encounter with the Guardia. "Don't trouble yourself," she said, straining to match his tone. "I'm here on behalf of Dolores Severino, Señor—?" She paused as she realized that Dolores had only called him Pedro.

"Surely she told you my name?" He was amused. "Señora—?"

"Fernández," Elena said. And then, in the interest of honesty,

"Fernández de Tejada. She didn't tell me your surnames. And it seems rude to call you Pedro."

"I could only be flattered to have a beautiful woman use my first name." He spoke the exaggerated compliment with a touch of malice, and she knew that he had recognized Tejada's name. "And I think we ought to honor little Dolores's discretion, don't you?"

"She didn't tell me because I didn't ask," Elena said, irritated by his mockery. "I'm not a spy, even though I am the lieutenant's wife." She stressed the word *wife* a little more than necessary, and then flushed because she had emphasized it.

"You mean to say *no one* has asked Dolores about me?" Pedro was still smiling, but his voice was suspiciously intense.

"No," Elena said firmly. "And I doubt she'd say anything about you, even under torture."

"Is that what you came to tell me?" Pedro's voice was politely interested, but his body was rigid with tension. "That she will be tortured if I don't provide the necessary information?"

"No," Elena snapped, glad that he had stopped pretending gallantry. "She asked me to see how you were doing, and tell her, and she said to send you her best wishes. You're both being taken to Santander later this week, and she wants to have news of you before you're separated. If you have an ounce of humanity, you'll send her your love."

Pedro raised his eyebrows. "I will?"

Elena snorted. "You'd have to be blind not to see that she's in love with you!"

There was a pause, and when Pedro spoke his voice was serious. "Dolores is a good, sweet, capable girl. Pretty, too. I respected her father greatly. But I'm not in love with her."

"I said that *she* was in love with *you!*" Elena retorted. "And that she would be happy to hear the message, no matter how casual."

"Especially since it's unlikely she'll ever see me alive again?" Pedro smiled crookedly, a real smile this time. "I suppose you're right. Give her my love if that will make her happy. But really, Señora, I'm twice her age. You make me feel like Don Giovanni."

Elena smiled wickedly, suddenly glad of an opportunity to return his mocking humor. *"Don Giovanni?* How unpatriotic to pick an Italian opera when there are Spanish plays available!"

Pedro laughed. "But *Don Giovanni* epitomizes your Spain! A German and Italian collaboration on Spanish themes!"

Elena laughed also, amazed by his courage. "Whereas Spain should be epitomized by *La vida es sueño?* Russian in costume but Spanish in essentials?"

"Exactly." Pedro nodded appreciatively. There was a slight pause and then he said, "Forgive me, Señora, but you're not exactly what I would have expected of Lieutenant Tejada."

"A lot of people say that," Elena said dryly. "Especially his colleagues."

"I'll bet!" He grinned. "Why are you really here, chatting with a man who tried to stab your husband?"

Elena blinked. Tejada had given few details of the raid on the cabin. "You tried to stab my husband?"

"Only after I ran out of ammunition."

Elena swallowed, remembering the wounded Guardia Riera. *Carlos would never have seen the baby,* she thought. And then, confused, *But the maquis are fighting for freedom. For what I believed in, during the war, at least.* "I'm here in Potes because I love my husband," she said slowly. "And I'm here talking to you because I don't believe in everything he does."

"That is somewhat difficult to comprehend," he admitted.

"Why?" Elena demanded, annoyed. "I thought one of the things the Republic stood for was equality between the sexes. Do you find it so difficult to believe a woman has a mind of her own?"

His faintly mocking smile disappeared, and he thought a moment before replying. When he spoke, his voice was serious.

"I beg your pardon, Señora. I only thought that the lieutenant might not appreciate an independent mind in his wife."

"And what business is that of yours?" Elena snapped.

"None whatsoever." He smiled with disarming charm. "I seem to have underestimated your husband a second time." He gestured to his wounded leg and added sardonically, "Although perhaps with less grievous results. In any case, Señora, I do thank you for the visit, and be sure to send Dolores my love."

"I will." Elena knew that the visit had been a success. She could return to Dolores with a clear conscience now, having done the girl a kindness. But she hesitated. "Is there anything I can bring you? Food? Tobacco?"

"No, thank you. Guardia Torres has been cultivating my acquaintance, and has spent a fair amount of cigarettes and treats doing so." Pedro smiled. "He even offered me a shave, but I distrust guardias with razors in their hands."

"You're being well treated then?" Elena spoke with some relief.

"By Guardia Torres. Guardia Carvallo is responsible for this little souvenir." He indicated the bruise along his cheek. "And a few others." Seeing Elena's frown, he added, "I have no doubt that your husband has mandated both forms of treatment, Señora, so if you were planning to inform him, save both your breath and your illusions."

Elena would have liked to defend the lieutenant, but she had the uncomfortable suspicion that the guerrilla was right, so she only said, "Would you like newspapers then? Or books? Dolores has been saying that she's bored."

"That would be very kind of you." Pedro spoke with grave courtesy. "Guardia Torres is generally on duty starting at ten o'clock."

"Newspapers then?" Elena asked as she knocked on the door of the cell.

The prisoner smiled. "Novels, if you have them. I prefer fiction without the pretense of truth."

Guardia Torres promptly opened the door for Elena and escorted her to the foot of the stairs. "Did you find anything out?" he asked in a low voice when they were out of earshot.

Elena reflected that Pedro's paranoia was absolutely justified. "No," she said.

"What about his accent?" Torres asked, interested. "He's not from around here. Or from the south, either. I'd know an Andaluz, for all that he tries to use those fancy words. Castilian, you think?"

Elena unwillingly considered the guardia's question. "Probably," she said slowly, although, thinking about it, Pedro's crystalline consonants had the hypercorrect quality of a radio broadcaster or a movie star. *He disguised his voice,* she thought. *But he's not Salmantino. Nor Madrileño.* "Maybe New Castile, or Extremadura."

"Far from home either way," Torres said. "I've got to go. Nice to see you, Señora."

Elena was thoughtful on her way home. She had no desire to betray Dolores's Pedro to the Guardia, and she was rather relieved that he had been so careful not to give her any information. But their conversation had made her curious, and Torres's question about his origin had done nothing to quiet her curiosity. Why, she wondered, had such an obviously cultured man taken to the mountains? He had probably fought for the Republic. Had he simply gone underground to flee prison? Was he working his way north, hoping to cross the border? But no, if Dolores had known him for a long time, he was settled in Cantabria. *Your* Spain, he had said, as if there were two, and of course there were, whatever Carlos might say. Still pensive, Elena dragged out a box of stationery and sat down at the kitchen table to write a letter, wishing mildly for a proper writing desk. She wrote for a long time, unable to keep a lid on her thoughts any longer. Then, after spilling words out onto three pages, she neatly blacked out the lines that she knew would be censored anyway.

She was making dinner when the lieutenant arrived home. "I'm sorry," she apologized. "The table needs to be cleared still. I was writing a letter and I lost track of time."

"I'll go and mail it for you, if you like," Tejada offered. "If it will help to be out of your way."

"Thanks. Everything should be ready when you get back."

Tejada picked up the letter and headed outside again in the twilight. The envelope was stamped with the flag and the likeness of General Franco, partially obscured by stamps. He frowned slightly. Elena had plastered the letter with far more postage than was necessary to send a letter to Salamanca, even for such a fat composition. He glanced down at the address:

> *Hipólito Fernández Ríos*
> *Calle Cinco de Mayo, 12*
> *Veracruz, México*

Tejada was suddenly aware of the chill in the evening air. *He's her brother*, the lieutenant thought. *It's only natural that she should write to him. She's loyal to her family. Her brother. And my brother-in-law.* Absently, he went through his pockets and came up with a pencil. Then he changed *México* to *Méjico*. He carried the letter by one corner, as if it would soil his hands, although he had forgotten his gloves, and his fingers began to suffer from the cold. *We'll have to send him photographs of the baby*, Tejada mused. *Or maybe someday he'll be able to come back and see it. The war's over, after all.* He dropped the letter in the mailbox, and blew on his cold hands. *I hate the mountains,* he thought. *You'd think it would stay warm in the evenings by now. Spring never seems to come up here.*

Chapter 16

The next day, Simón Álvarez presented himself at the Tejadas' apartment as they were finishing lunch and announced that he had come to return the book. Elena, who doubted that he could have read all the *Cartas de relación* in two days, received him kindly but with some disappointment. It was magically dispelled when, after politely thanking her for the loan, Simón said, "I didn't know there were pyramids outside of Egypt. Do you have any other books about America? Any novels? Histories are fine, but I like novels."

Elena directed him to the bookshelves, where he browsed for half an hour. "Those are girls' books," he proclaimed disapprovingly, surveying the top shelf.

"Yes, they were mine when I was a child," Elena said.

Simón sighed and shook his head. Then he turned a little timidly to the lieutenant. "I don't suppose you have any books from when *you* were a child?"

"I'm afraid most of mine went to my nephew," Tejada said, amused.

"Oh, well." Simón returned his attention to the shelves, discouraged.

Tejada took pity on him. "I kept a few of my favorites," he admitted. "You can borrow them if you promise to take good care of them."

Simón promised enthusiastically, and went home with Zane

Grey's *El espiritú de la pradera* and *Al último hombre* under his arm. At Elena's gentle suggestion he also took one of her despised girls' novels for his sisters. Tejada, who had liked the boy, approved of his wife's plan to provide reading matter for the carpenter's son, and thereafter assumed that the gaps in their bookshelves were the result of Simón's research. This was largely true, but he only learned many years afterward that Elena had loaned several volumes of Unamuno not to Simón but to Pedro.

Elena had not intended to visit Pedro again, but when she dropped off the books, he thanked her gravely and then said, "I expect I'll be done with these by tomorrow. Friday at the latest. Be sure to reclaim them before I'm taken to Santander." Trapped by the casual assumption that she would return, Elena visited him again the next day. He greeted her cheerfully, spoke of his reading, and asked her opinion. He listened to her answer with interest, and then began an argument. Had she read Ortega y Gasset? Américo Castro? Did she think of Unamuno more as a novelist or more as a philosopher?

Elena watched him gesture animatedly, her back propped against the wall of the cell, and felt that she had come home. His arguments were solidly conventional, and though his opinions were well expressed, she sometimes found them trite. But he spoke a language that she understood, and spoke it fluently with flawless grammar. She answered eagerly, with the relief of a well-assimilated traveler who finds a compatriot in a foreign land. The conversation ranged wider, and he became more unguarded, perhaps for the same reason. He was fond of opera, but also of the theater, and he had an encyclopedic knowledge of specific performances. Had she seen Margarita Xirgu's Mariana Pineda? What had she thought of Dalí's sets? And what about that George Bernard Shaw play—the name would come to him in a second—about a patriot being hanged for treason? Elena reflected that a careful review of old newspapers' culture pages would give the Guardia fairly accurate dates of his stays in Madrid and Barcelona. He was an enthusiastic admirer of "la Xirgu," and his pronunciation of the name made Elena wonder a little if he was actually a Catalan. Although perhaps he merely took the trouble to say the actress's name correctly, just as he enunciated the English playwright's name precisely.

"See you tomorrow, Señora Fernández," he said easily, when Elena finally excused herself.

"Until tomorrow, Señor—um—Pedro," Elena answered automatically, and then flushed as his namelessness slid the invisible barrier between them back into place.

He smiled at her. "You really are welcome to use my name, Señora. But as I would never dare to use yours, you can call me, oh, say . . . Vargas. Pedro Vargas."

"It isn't your real name?" Elena said, still anxious.

He laughed. "It is now. Tell your husband you wormed it out of me with feminine wiles. Or better still, tell Guardia Torres. Your husband would be jealous."

"Don't be ridiculous," Elena snapped, aware that she had not told Carlos of her visits to the wounded guerrilla, and annoyed with herself for not telling him earlier.

"It's not ridiculous. I would be, in his place."

Elena left annoyed, resolved to tell Carlos what she had learned and wash her hands of the guerrilla. But that evening the lieutenant told her in a somewhat put-upon voice that he had received orders from Santander to hold the prisoners until their trial date, which would almost certainly be after Easter. "At least they're sending us reinforcements finally," Tejada said. "Although they'll probably want them all on patrol all the time."

"Surely no one will be overseeing how you deploy them that closely?" Elena said.

Tejada snorted. "Don't bet on it. Thanks to your happy idea about English arms, Suárez told me he was getting phone calls from some civilian in the Ministry of Foreign Affairs. Madrid's jumpy. A lot of people are going to be looking very closely at what these guardias do."

"How many are there?" Elena asked.

"Twenty. Arriving next week. And since the barracks won't hold them we'll have to quarter them in town, which will be another headache."

Elena smiled. "Am I supposed to feel sorry for you?"

"Don't strain your sympathies." Tejada laughed. "But you should know that I'll be busy over the next week or so."

"Unlike most of the time?"

"More busy," Tejada amended. "I don't want to neglect you, but . . ."

"It's all right. I understand."

Tejada was as occupied as he had predicted. Elena, left to her own devices, ended up visiting the prison on a daily basis. Dolores was always eager to see her, and after the first few days of Dolores's requests to give messages to various friends and family, Elena started simply bringing the girl other visitors. The news spread quickly through Potes that the lieutenant's wife had been kind to the Severino girl, and that it was easy to visit the prison with her. Elena ended up escorting a friend or relative of Dolores's to the prison nearly every morning. She spent a few minutes each day gossiping with Dolores and the girl's other guests. In the process, she began to form a picture of the varying strata of society in the Liébana. The subjects of Dolores's conversations with her well-wishers taught Elena a good deal about Potes. She learned, for example, that the pharmacist's daughter Celia was engaged to a boy who had emigrated to Argentina and had promised to bring her over as soon as he had the money, but the way Celia made eyes at all the boys in Potes was scandalous; that the reason Lame Francisco, who worked in the stationery store, was so gloomy all the time was because his mother hated his wife and made their lives a living hell; and that there was lively betting at the bar on whether the reason Miguel Sandino kept hanging around Lucita Vega without ever coming to the point was that he had been wounded in the war or that the engineer Señor Oquendo had been taking Lucita out too and Miguel stood a little in awe of him. In spite of their chatter, the people of Potes said nothing about Dolores's brother or about the other people who had taken to the hills or those helping them. Elena enjoyed speaking with them, but it was something of a relief to say good-bye to Dolores every day and turn to the cell at the other end of the hall, where the conversation was less relentlessly focused on the youth of Potes.

Vargas was not local, and in spite of Señora Fernández's sympathy, no one was willing to commit themselves by calling on him, so Elena remained his only visitor. She continued to bring him books, but their discussions did become less confined to art and literature. Both of them meticulously avoided politics. They shared anecdotes of urban childhoods, Elena freely naming the streets of Salamanca, and Pedro speaking only of "plazas" and "avenues" without giving hints of a specific city. Elena, judging from a few comments he let slip about the size of his home, guessed that he had to be from Madrid or Barcelona. Judging from his hypercorrect pronunciation of Castilian, she eliminated the former. Guardia Torres, who continued to show an interest in her conversations with the prisoner, was impressed by her logic, but pointed out gloomily that finding a needle in a haystack was probably easier than running a check on a Red from Barcelona with only one surname, and that probably an alias. Elena agreed and pretended to commiserate, although she had in fact only given away the information because she was sure that it would not hurt Pedro. Torres comfortingly told her not to worry, and encouraged her to keep visiting the prisoners.

"How on earth did you come to marry the lieutenant?" Vargas asked the following Thursday, his voice teasing but genuinely curious.

"How did you come to be a maquis?" Elena retorted.

"Sorry. I wasn't meaning to pry. Is why you're in Potes a secret?"

"My husband was promoted to his own command," Elena said, suppressing extraneous details.

"A dangerous sort of promotion, from Salamanca!"

"More so for you!" Elena retorted loyally.

"For me, personally," Vargas agreed. "But your Carvallo isn't just giving me a nightly working over out of spite. And I'm not keeping my mouth shut to protect corpses. Guardias die up here in the mountains."

"Like Calero, you mean?" Elena asked, smiling slightly.

"What do you know about Calero?" He sounded amused, and almost contemptuous.

"Something very like one of Dolores's histories," Elena admitted, and summarized the tale she had heard from the carpenter's wife. "I thought perhaps Anselmo Montalbán had killed him in revenge," she finished.

"That sounds about right," Vargas agreed. "You have good sources of information."

"Then I won't worry about my husband," Elena said. "He hasn't made any personal enemies like that."

"That's a very feminine position," the maquis said. "The idea that personal grudges are more important than political issues."

"It seems to be true as far as Montalbán and Calero were concerned," Elena replied.

"Only because Montalbán was an idiot." Vargas spoke without heat.

"So now feminine and idiotic are synonyms? Thank you."

The maquis smiled. "I didn't mean that. I only meant that Montalbán had a good relationship with the Guardia. He'd never been in trouble, in spite of that business with his son. He was . . . oh, not a spy, but a man who was very well placed to find out what was happening in Potes and tell his friends. A man like that is rare for us. Necessary. To suddenly go haywire and shoot the lieutenant for the sake of some personal vengeance is pure idiocy. Not what we expect of a man who has responsibilities."

"We?" Elena asked.

Vargas laughed. "Sorry, Señora. No comment. I've never believed that feminine and idiotic are synonyms. But I do believe that loyalty to loved ones is a feminine trait, and that you possess it."

Elena fought down her irritation at being dismissed as "feminine" and said coolly, "Leave aside specific examples then. You believe that humanity has no place in politics?"

"I might have said it did before the war. Time in the mountains gets rid of illusions like that."

"And you think it's worse to kill someone who has hurt you than to shoot someone out of pure political expedience?"

Vargas shifted to find a more comfortable position to think over the question. "Put that way it sounds brutal, but yes, I do. That's the difference between the government's executing a murderer and the victim's family starting a blood feud. The state acts without personal malice. It's what separates the twentieth century from the seventeenth."

Elena laughed. "That's a funny argument to hear from a prisoner of the state."

"Not the legally constituted state," Vargas said firmly. "I represent the Republic, the *legal* government of Spain."

"So you have the right to kill on the Republic's behalf?"

"Yes." The maquis nodded. "And if I killed for personal reasons I'd be no better than a bandit or highwayman. Which is why that is precisely what your husband and his kind call me."

Elena considered for a moment. "So the fact that Calero was a despicable human being would have made no difference if he had been useful to the Republic?"

"None, if the risk involved in killing him outweighed Anselmo's benefit to the cause," the guerrilla agreed.

"And the fact that my husband is a decent man would make no difference to someone planning to execute him?"

"Theoretically. In practice I don't know that it arises." Pedro gestured toward his wound. "If I were you, I wouldn't question the Severino kids too closely about his decency."

Elena winced, remembering Dolores's hopeless sobbing. "What if you make mistakes?" she asked softly, remembering what she knew of Carlos's career.

He snorted. "I don't think Luis and Rafa were errors, Señora."

Elena shook her head. "No, I mean what if *you* make mistakes? Anselmo *knew* something about the lieutenant. But suppose you're sent off to kill someone who you don't know? Who you've only been told is a danger? It doesn't really matter that you're killing without malice then, does it?"

Vargas looked impatient. "That's a condition of wartime, Señora. Sometimes good men die."

"And women, as well," Elena agreed, still thinking of her husband. "But the state kills without malice even when it's not at war."

He laughed. "Make no mistake, we are at war, Señora. And France as well, for all the propaganda they print in the newspapers."

"And after the war?" Elena demanded. "Since we're still speaking theoretically, there has to be an afterward."

"After the war," Vargas repeated slowly, his sparkling cynicism dulled for a moment. "After the war?" His shoulders slumped, and suddenly he looked both younger and sadder. Then they straightened, and he regained his mischievous smile. "Afterwards I sincerely hope there will be time for malice. I would like someone to avenge me, and Luis and Rafa."

Elena made a gesture of frustration. "I don't know why I'm talking to you!"

"I haven't the faintest idea, Señora." Vargas shrugged. "Human nature never ceases to puzzle me."

"At least you didn't say 'women's' nature," Elena said, a little bitterly.

"That's because I'm equally puzzled by Anselmo," the maquis replied. "He was a good man for years. An innkeeper's job is to get along with everyone, and Anselmo did that and well. He picked up a lot of information, too, and passed it on faithfully—mostly to Luis, I believe, which is why I don't mind telling you. Then, the next thing we hear, Calero is dead on patrol, and Anselmo's disappeared to God knows where. He knew that the best revenge he could have on Calero was to stick with what he was doing."

"Maybe he didn't feel that way," Elena said, noting absently that Pedro seemed to assume that Anselmo was guilty of the lieutenant's death.

The maquis looked sardonic. "I would bet a fair sum of money that if Anselmo had stayed where he was, Dolores and I would not be enjoying the pleasure of your company. You'll forgive me if I find that more important than some private vengeance."

"Because he endangered representatives of the legally constituted state?" Elena asked sweetly.

He laughed, acknowledging a hit. "Of course. Personal feeling doesn't enter into it at all."

Elena laughed also, and stood up. "I have to go. I hope you continue to mend."

"Not too quickly," the guerrilla said. "The sooner I'm fully recovered, the sooner your Lieutenant Tejada can begin a real interrogation."

Elena chewed her lip, unable to deny the truth of his words. "Until tomorrow," she said, eyes on the ground.

"Until tomorrow. Give Dolores my love."

As usual, Guardia Torres escorted her to the bottom of the stairs. "Vargas say anything interesting?" he asked.

Elena reviewed their conversation with her customary twinge of guilt. "I don't think so. Mostly we just argued about ethical theory."

Torres patted her shoulder comfortingly. "Don't feel bad. You got a surname and birthplace out of him, and that's better than we could do. He's read everything under the sun, and when he gets to quoting things he gives me a headache. How about Dolores?"

Elena shrugged. "She asked me to find out if Marisol's made up with her boyfriend yet."

"She hasn't." The guardia spoke with authority. "I saw his cousin last night. He says the whole family's been trying to talk sense to them, but it's no use."

"You could let her know," Elena suggested. "It sounds like you know more details than I do."

Torres flushed. "Well, Eliseo and I play checkers sometimes, and he tells me things. But Dolores doesn't like me."

Elena refrained from pointing out that the girl had well-founded reasons for her dislike, then said good-bye to the guardia. She was thoughtful on the way home. A visit from Simón after lunch distracted her a little, but that evening after dinner she said hesitantly, "Carlos?"

"Mmm?" Newspapers and mail had arrived that morning, and Tejada was diligently plowing through a week's worth of old news. "It says our pilots are giving the Russians hell."

"Carlos, pay attention. Did you ever check the files to find out if there was any reason anyone would want to kill Anselmo?"

"Montalbán?" Tejada folded the paper. "Yes, a couple of days ago. There was nothing there."

"He wasn't a spy or anything?"

"The term is informant. And no, not according to our records. We had nothing against him either, except the business with his sons, but most of the young men around here were more or less on the left, so that wasn't damning."

"Do you think he was in contact with the maquis?"

Tejada snorted. "Bandits. And around here, I'd say every second household is in contact with them. Why?"

"Well," Elena paused, "suppose he was in contact with them. And suppose he did kill Lieutenant Calero, but he wasn't acting under orders, so to speak. Do you think he might hide from them afterward?"

Tejada looked down at the newspaper and thought about what it had to say about the Communist chain of command. "I sure as hell wouldn't cross them in his position," he said consideringly. "You think he acted on his own, because of his son? And then fled because he knew that the Reds would come after him just as surely as we would?"

"Does that make sense?" Elena asked, still timid.

"Of course. He found an opportunity to go after Calero, and then he realized that he was in major trouble and took to the hills. But he couldn't make it on his own, so after a few months he hooked up with the bandits and they disposed of him, using Márquez. Very neat." The lieutenant smiled briefly. "This is why I like talking to you about my work."

"The only question is why he went after Calero *then*," Elena said slowly. "I mean, he'd been nursing a grudge since '37. Why this fall?"

Tejada shrugged. "Who knows? Maybe he'd just picked up a new weapon. Why is this on your mind?"

Elena shook her head, embarrassed. "I don't know. I suppose I'm worried about you."

Tejada smiled at her. "We're all prepared against attack, Elena. The new men help. And the shipment we've been waiting for finally arrived today, thank God."

"The shipment?" Elena asked, willing to change the subject.

"Eight hundred rounds of ammunition. And a new set of carbines." Tejada laughed. "The carbines are nice, but the ammunition was necessary. I wasn't looking forward to going cap in hand to the Policía Armada."

"So the roads are back to normal?" Elena said, reflecting that the Guardia had to worry about logistical problems, though never about financial ones. A rag waved at the edge of her mental field of vision, but she was unable to focus on it.

"Yes. With any luck we should be rid of your friend Dolores right after Easter. And the mysterious Vargas. It's a pain having to divert so many resources to guard duty."

Tejada was glancing at the newspaper again, so he did not see Elena's guilty look as she said, "Yes. I suppose it must be."

There was a brief silence and then Tejada said, "Looks like the Germans will finish with Russia before England."

"Maybe." Elena was neutral. "The English are rich. The Russians don't have much to bargain with."

"Except Spanish gold," Tejada said, thinking of the national reserves that the Republicans had sent to Russia during the war. *Expensive English guns,* he thought. *And Spanish gold to bargain with.* "They traded for those weapons!" he exclaimed, enlightened.

"Yes, that was what I meant," Elena said, puzzled.

"No." Tejada shook his head. "The maquis. That was why they wanted material from Devastated Regions. I couldn't figure out the logic of what they'd taken! The only common denominator was that it was portable! They've been selling Devastated Regions materials and buying weapons. Or maybe just bartering one for the other."

"Would the cash value of what they took be enough for those guns you found in the forest?" Elena asked.

"I hope so!" Tejada said fervently. He frowned. "They probably bartered directly. It would be hard to find buyers with that much ready cash."

"That still means contacts with England," Elena pointed out.

"Arms dealers will take barter sometimes," Tejada said.

"Luis Severino," Elena said suddenly. "That cart to San Vicente. To the border."

"Our helpful chauffeur!" Tejada snorted. "I hope I never have to explain to the colonel that I blithely hitched a ride with a maquis who was dropping off escaped prisoners, and possibly stolen goods."

"He wouldn't let you get the suitcases," Elena remembered. "He didn't want you near the back of the cart. Suppose he was not only dropping off the Valencians, but also picking something up."

Tejada made a noise somewhere between a laugh and a groan. "Elena, you are brilliant, and you are the joy of my life, but for goodness' sake don't have any more insights this evening. I would hate to have to court-martial your husband for incompetence."

Chapter 17

Tejada had hoped to be able to spend that Saturday with Elena, to make up for their previously aborted trip to Santo Toribio, but the rest of his week was absorbed in administrative tasks. The new guardias created almost more problems than they solved, not least because of the resentment the natives of Potes felt at the influx of armed strangers. (Two days after their arrival, Torres was stopped on the street by Fermín the grocer, and asked frankly how he could understand what "those foreigners" were saying. Himself a native of Sevilla, Torres was more amused than irritated by the comment, but he made no friends when he repeated it in the barracks.) Three of the newcomers were married, and one had children, and Tejada was forced to hastily find rooms for them with local residents, who were less than enthusiastic about their presence. Several of the guardias themselves grumbled about their new posting.

Their complaints became more pronounced as the maquis learned of the Guardia Civil's increased numbers, and expressed their disapproval. The warning shots that the Potes guardias had learned to expect as a routine part of patrol became more frequent, and less benign. Four days after the arrival of reinforcements, Guardia Ortíz returned from a patrol with one of the new guardias, indignant. "Pablo Roldán took a potshot at me!" he exclaimed. "And the bastard wasn't even aiming to miss! I winged one of his friends, at least. I'd expect it of a foreigner like Vargas! But Pablo! I never would've believed it! We went to school together!" The next day one of the new guardias was hit in the arm while on patrol. Then a group of four was ambushed near Camaleño. The shooting that followed left one maquis dead and three of the four guardias injured, one of them critically. The wounded men had been hit in the stomach and shoulder, and a bullet had grazed the head of the third. The maquis were shooting to kill.

Knowing that his force was rapidly being reduced to its original size, Tejada wondered with alarm if he had done the right thing in asking for reinforcements. He communicated his theory to Madrid about how the maquis had been financing their purchases of arms, and received no reply. When he asked if there was any suggestion whatsoever that the maquis had received arms from a foreign government, he was told that the Ministry of Foreign Affairs would communicate with the Ministry of Defense as soon as any definite information was known. Colonel Suárez, displeased with Tejada's casualties, began to hint that there had been no problem in the Liébana until his arrival there. The lieutenant's only comfort was that the Policía Armada's force was being similarly preyed on, and that they, too, were suffering casualties.

Preoccupied with these worries, Tejada also suffered from a vague feeling that he was neglecting Elena. He had hoped that she would make friends with some of the other guardias' wives, but although she dutifully visited them, she did not show any enthusiasm for pursuing the acquaintances. She walked less, and spent a good deal of time napping, and Tejada was torn between the conviction that this was good for her health and the fear that it meant she was depressed. When he hesitantly apologized about not being able to walk to Santo Toribio with her on Saturday, she rolled her eyes. "I doubt I could make the walk anyway now," she snapped. "My back is killing me." Tejada hastily expressed sympathy, and escaped to the post, unwilling to listen to a detailed review of his wife's symptoms. When he arrived, he was greeted by a detailed review of the wounded Guardia Moreno's symptoms, which failed to improve his mood.

Monday morning, the lieutenant met with Márquez and Battista to review the post's duties during Holy Week, and to try to come up with possible ways of minimizing injury to the force. He also summarized his theory about ways the maquis were obtaining arms. "If you're right, sir, why not have more men guarding Devastated Regions?" Battista suggested. "That should cut off the maquis' piggy bank. Don't send out any pairs of new men without at least one experienced guardia. That'll get them used to the countryside."

"And the countryside used to them," Tejada agreed. "It's not a bad idea. But I feel like I have to justify the reinforcements to the colonel."

"And it's stepping on the Policía Armada's toes," Márquez objected. "Besides, with all due respect, sir, what if your idea about them bartering construction materials for arms is wrong? I don't think the stuff they took would buy the kind of guns they have, unless the English or somebody were helping them out."

Tejada snorted. "I'd rather not be the man who didn't notice an invasion," he said. "But it's hard to start beating the hills for English spies when the maquis are getting so much local help, and I don't know where to start. The colonel's stonewalling me, and Madrid is stonewalling, too."

"They probably don't know anything about it," the sergeant pointed out.

"That or it's not politically expedient to tell me," Tejada sighed. "Either way, it doesn't help."

"We need information," Márquez summarized.

"And the only question is where we can get it," Tejada finished.

There was a short silence. All three officers looked glum. Then Battista said, "Our best bet is Vargas."

The lieutenant nodded, and opened the filing cabinet

behind his desk. He flipped through it, pulled out the folder with Torres's and Carvallo's reports on the prisoners, and read silently for a moment. "As far as I can tell from this," he said slowly, "we've learned that the prisoner is one Pedro Vargas, presumed Catalan, university educated, veteran of the Red army. Worked closely in the mountains with Luis Severino and Rafael Campos, both deceased. In other words, damn all."

"How did he end up with a name like Pedro Vargas if he's Catalan?" Battista demanded.

"Phone book, probably," the lieutenant said dryly. "Get Torres down here, and see if he has anything to add."

Torres, when he appeared, was unable to add much more. "He's a slippery one, sir," he apologized, in response to Tejada's questions. "He talks pleasantly enough, seems to enjoy it even, but if you ask a specific question he'll just turn it off with a joke, or quote some philosopher and spin you a long speech about something totally different. Hard to pin down."

"If the carrot's not working maybe we should just go with the stick," Tejada said. "What's Carvallo picked up?"

"Nothing, sir." Torres shook his head. "He's a bloody mess after Carvallo's through with him, but he won't say a word if he's beaten."

"We could try him in the bathtub," Tejada suggested.

"Carvallo did, three nights running. Didn't get anywhere. He finally overestimated the timing and nearly drowned him."

Sergeant Márquez whistled. "Tough one. Electric shocks?"

"We could, I suppose." The guardia looked dubious. "But"—he hesitated and looked at Tejada. The lieutenant nodded encouragingly and Torres continued. "I don't think he'll crack. Everything we've gotten so far has been from being nice to him."

Tejada sighed. "Well, it's not much, but I guess we don't have much choice." Then, because the guardia looked downcast, he added, "You're doing a good job, Torres. Just keep it up."

"Thank you, sir." Honesty compelled Torres to add, "Really, your wife has done better than all of us, though."

"What?" Tejada said.

"She was the one who figured out he was a Catalan," the guardia explained, generously giving credit where it was due. "And she's read some of those books so she can follow him when he starts trying to spin some tale."

"I see." The lieutenant spoke quietly. There was a faint crackle of paper as the report in his hand wrinkled in his grip. "I hadn't realized she visited Vargas so frequently."

"Oh, yes, sir. Practically every day. I think he relaxes around women," Torres added sagely. "Flirts a bit, you know."

"I can imagine." Tejada was acutely conscious that Márquez and Battista as well as Torres were watching him closely. He turned the discussion to other ways of finding information about the bandits, and took notes on his colleagues' suggestions automatically. Eventually, Torres and Battista left to go on patrol. Márquez, whose wrist had just emerged from a bandage, began to type a requisition. Tejada stayed at his desk, ostensibly making notes on the Vargas file, but actually doodling, barely noticing his surroundings.

She lied to me, he thought. *She knows what's been happening, and she lied to me. If she'd asked me in advance I wouldn't have minded. She's always wandering off on her own—to the carpenter's and to Father Bernardo and I don't mind. I'm not jealous. I trust her. I haven't put any limits on her freedom. But Vargas is different. He's a guerrilla, an enemy soldier. He's dangerous. She's only seen him caged and pathetic and she feels sorry for him, but she doesn't know what he's done.* Tejada was unable to crush the appalling thought that Elena might know considerably more than he did about Vargas's activities in the mountains. No. *She would have told Torres. She would have told me. She wouldn't betray me. But if she's talked to him frequently, what do they find to talk about if not that? He can't have that much in common with her. He's a Catalan. It's not as if they know the*

*same places or people. Unless he did university in Madrid. They
would have been there around the same time. But she would have mentioned that. She would have told me. Why didn't she tell me? Why did
she visit him? She can't be in sympathy with the maquis. Not knowing
what happened to Calero. Not after everything that's happened in the
last week. Not after all I've told her. But she can't see anything in
Vargas personally. Torres said he flirts. Elena's never flirted. She's not
the eyelash-batting type, thank God. So why did she visit him? And
why didn't she tell me?*

Márquez finished his typing, pulled the sheet free, and scav-
enged for an envelope in his desk. Then he glanced at his watch.
It was almost two. "You're staying for lunch, sir?" he asked easily.

Tejada looked up. "What? No. I promised Elena I'd be home
today."

"All right. I'll hold the patrols until you get back then. We
should have someone here, just in case."

Tejada escaped from his office with relief. It had been cloudy
all day, and it started to rain as he walked home. The wind drove
the cold droplets viciously against his cloak. He hurried along with
his head bent against the weather. His neighbors in Potes had
never been overly friendly, so he did not notice how the few people on the streets slid away from him as they saw his expression.

The apartment was warm, and smelled of soup. Elena levered
herself out of the armchair as she heard the door slam, and
came to meet him. "Good, you're here. I'm sorry it's just left-
overs. I don't know why I've been so tired—" She broke off as
she saw his face. "What's the matter? What happened?"

"Why didn't you tell me?"

Elena backed up instinctively, and sank into a chair. "Tell
you? About visiting Vargas, you mean?" she faltered.

"Yes, about visiting Vargas!" Tejada's numbed sense of
betrayal finally gave way to fury. "Why do I find out from
Torres—from *Torres*—that my wife has been having cozy chats
with a dangerous criminal?"

Elena gulped. "Dolores asked me to visit him," she said softly. "To find out if he was all right. I didn't even think I'd be able to . . . only then Torres seemed to think it was all right."

"*Who the hell is Torres to be telling you what's all right?*"

"It wasn't planned!" Elena cried. "It just happened the first time. And then. . . and then I felt sorry for him."

"Sorry for him?" Tejada echoed disbelievingly, beginning to pace back and forth. "The bastard tried to kill me!"

"And you tried to kill him!" Elena retorted, relieved from the pressure of his eyes on her face. "And he's tortured on your orders! So, yes, I felt sorry for him. Besides, I liked talking to him. He was easy to talk to. It was like being at home again."

Tejada froze, staring at the floor. "At home in Salamanca, or at home in Madrid?" he asked softly, terrified of the answer.

"Either! Both!" Elena choked on a sob, and all of the misery of her life in Potes bubbled out of her. "Somewhere where people read and write and where there are theaters and concerts and things to *do!* Where the educated people aren't all priests and Fascists! I can't talk to anyone here!"

"That's ridiculous. What about the Álvarez kid?" Tejada protested. "What about Dolores Severino, for God's sake?"

"They're children!" Elena cried. "And neither of them has ever even seen a movie! Or ridden a streetcar! I wanted to talk to an adult! Someone who's read and traveled and . . . and is from my world. The world that used to be my world. I hate it here, Carlos! You have your work, it's easy for you—"

"Easy!" Tejada swung around to face her, and squatted in front of her chair, placing his hands on the arms. "Easy? Elena, we're practically in a state of war! I've had six guardias under my command wounded in skirmishes in barely a month! One of them may still die as a result. I am damn near out of contact with headquarters, and I've been told in no uncertain terms to forget about further reinforcements and handle anything from petty thievery to armed invasion without making a fuss. So don't talk to me about easy!"

"You wanted the promotion!"

Tejada laughed without humor. "Oh, yes, my wonderful promotion! You think I'm here because I requested a posting to the back of beyond? I'm here because of *you*, Elena! Because someone in Madrid thought this would be a great way to get rid of an officer who married a Red. Park him in the Picos de Europa, where he can't get into too much trouble. It won't be much of a loss if the bandits wipe him out."

"Don't blame me." Elena was crying openly now. "I told you this would happen if you married a Red!"

"You did," Tejada agreed savagely. "But I stupidly thought that if we started over somewhere else, and if I did a good job, it wouldn't matter. How was I to know that you couldn't be trusted not to get mixed up with that kind of scum again?" Seeing that he had given her pause, he went on with bitter sarcasm, "Márquez has already been giving me hints. That business with Herrera. Little solicitous comments about how you're adjusting from Madrid. He's read your file, you know. I do my best to protect you but what can I do? Charge him with insubordination for telling the truth? And then you go and provide him with ammunition like daily meetings with Vargas!"

Elena put her head in her hands. "I always told Torres what we talked about. There was never anything clandestine about those meetings."

"Why didn't you tell me then?"

"At first because it didn't seem important. He was going to Santander in a few days." Elena's voice was weary. "And then I didn't say anything because I thought Torres already had. And because I thought you'd get upset for no reason."

"On what planet is a man not supposed to get upset when his wife meets privately with another man without telling him?" Tejada demanded.

"Most of this one!" Elena retorted. "Spain is backward!"

"Don't start that shit now!"

Elena hissed, a long in-drawn breath, and then lashed out, no longer arguing rationally, but only seeking to hurt. "Has it ever occurred to you that maybe that was why I enjoyed talking to Vargas? Because he doesn't see why Spain *should* be backward?"

"And looking forward means what?" Tejada snapped. "The freedom to sink to Vargas's level?"

Elena made a derisive noise. "You mean the level of a man who has the taste to appreciate literature and the strength to withstand torture? Someone who's brave and intelligent and funny and actually *cares* about his fellow creatures? I doubt you could reach that level if you tried!"

Tejada gritted his teeth, unwilling to give her the satisfaction of hearing him curse. "You won't see him again," he said softly.

Elena's eyes narrowed. "I'm not one of the men under your command."

"You're my wife."

"And that means that I have no more freedom than a . . . a prize of war?" Elena choked.

"It means you'll obey me."

There was a pain in Elena's rib cage, and her temples were throbbing, but her voice only shook a little as she answered. "Not in something that goes against my own conscience or judgment."

Tejada's fists clenched. "And you think visiting a Red prisoner is one of those things?"

"If I've promised to, yes."

For a few seconds, the only sounds in the room were the soft crackle of the wood in the stove, and two sets of harsh breathing. Then Tejada stood up and said, very quietly, "I won't have my child raised by a woman who feels that way. As soon as the baby is weaned, I'm sending him to my parents in Granada." He had the satisfaction of seeing her shrink back in her chair, clasping her hands over her belly. "You can stay here with me, if you choose," he continued, merciless. "Or go back to your parents in Salamanca. But you won't be allowed to see the baby."

"You can't," she whispered. "You have no right."

Tejada smiled bitterly. "Thank God Spain is 'backward,'" he said. "I have every right. I'll see you this evening." He turned on his heel. A moment later, the door slammed.

Elena began to tremble. She wanted desperately to break something, but everything in the room was either a treasured possession or something that would make Carlos angry if she broke it. *Make him angrier*, she amended. She stuffed her handkerchief into her mouth to stifle sobs. She would go, flee, slip away and hide, and never let him find the baby. The thought died even as it was born. She had no money and no family besides her parents who could take her in. A woman could not legally travel without her husband's permission. She could not take to the hills like the maquis with an infant. *He can't take the baby*. She shuddered, willing the thought to be true. But she knew that he was absolutely within his rights. He could and he would, unless, she choked on another sob, unless he forgave her. Unless she begged his pardon and promised to obey him.

Elena's pride and her reason rebelled equally against a groveling apology. She had done nothing wrong—except possibly not telling him about meeting with Vargas earlier. Everyone had *known* she was meeting with Vargas. No one at the post had objected. Torres had been *glad* of her help. She had defended Carlos from the maquis' accusations. She had kept quiet when he described his torture, and had not interfered, even though every instinct had screamed at her to reproach her husband. She had borne Bárbara Nuñez's malice and Quico Álvarez's obscene deference, and the cold shoulders of her neighbors without complaint. The smell of the stew began to nauseate her and she took the pot off the stove, without bothering to eat. She had agreed to come to this hateful place, hemmed in by peaks and cut off from civilization because she loved him. She hiccuped and almost retched. She had tried to be happy here, had tried to drink the revolting milk that he insisted on pressing on her every morning and to make friends he would approve of and to furnish their miserable apartment comfortably. He couldn't take the baby away for no reason. It wasn't fair.

It was not fair, but it was more than probable if she didn't apologize, she acknowledged drearily, after an hour of furious crying. He might apologize as well, eventually, but she knew the limits of his tolerance, and knew it was up to her to make the first move. She washed her face, blew her nose, and then washed her face again. Her head was throbbing and her back was in spasm and all she wanted to do was lie down. But she went back to the kitchen, covered the soup, and put away the bowls that they had not used for lunch, grimly determined to be as good a wife as possible, so that he would have no more cause for complaint.

She allowed herself to fall asleep a little before four o'clock. Carlos would not be home for another three hours, and it would not be hard to prepare dinner quickly. She woke a few hours later because someone was pounding on the door. Afraid that her husband had returned early, Elena hurried to open the door, worried that he might interpret the delay as a further sign of defiance. She was relieved as she reached the foyer to hear a voice calling, "Lieutenant! Lieutenant Tejada!"

She straightened her shoulders, glad that she would have an opportunity to speak to a neutral third party before talking to Carlos again. A faint, sickly sweet smell made her wrinkle her nose and hope that the odor did not reflect on her housekeeping. "I'm sorry," she began politely, pulling open the door, "my husband isn't here now. You could try at the post or—"

Everything happened so quickly that Elena had no time to side-step, much less struggle. She identified the smell as chloroform as a soaked rag was clasped firmly over her nose and mouth. She twisted her neck wildly, trying to break free of the gag without inhaling, but the grasp on her head was implacable, and a second man had pinioned her arms. Finally, she gasped, choked, and then gasped again. Her last conscious thought was that they could as easily have knocked her out with a club, and that perhaps this unexpected gentleness meant that they would not harm the baby.

Chapter 18

Tejada left the fonda without knowing where he was going. He had left Elena because he knew that if he stayed longer he would do something unforgivable, and some small part of him knew that if he so much as raised a hand against her he would regret it for the rest of his life. But the satisfaction of having the last word was insufficient consolation for the inability to continue fighting with somebody. She should have stayed in Salamanca, he thought, as he paced the empty, rain-slickened streets. I could have come back to her then and none of this would have happened. The sound of knives rattling on plates and the hum of conversation behind shutters mocked his thoughts. On the other side of the dirty adobe walls that loomed over the street, people were warm and dry and enjoying a hot meal. He looked up as a sudden shout of laughter on the second floor mingled with the clinking of glasses, and water ran down the back of his neck. He had wanted Elena to come so that he could live like the people behind the walls. So that he could laugh with her over meals, instead of bolting down food in a barracks, listening to endless work-related conversations about patrols and requisitions, or—he scoffed mentally—maudlin reminiscences of loved ones. He had wanted her to come because for the first time in his life, the idea of family had meant something besides an obligation to be fulfilled.

Idiot, the lieutenant thought bitterly. Better to have said goodbye to Elena in Salamanca, and promised to write to her. Stupid to have forgotten that his place was with the Guardia, outside the warm circle of light and laughter, waiting, guarding, as he had waited in the dark and cold that night in the woods above Argüébanes to capture Vargas and his companions. He had been a fool to take Elena to the mountains; to drag her from the warmth and domesticity where she belonged into the darkness with him like a child clutching a teddy bear for reassurance. *If I hadn't told her to visit Dolores,* he thought, *none of this would have happened. And if Vargas hadn't been such a plausible bastard, damn him.*

It was easier to think about Vargas than about Elena's anger and contempt, or about what might have been behind the dawning horror in her eyes at his last words. *It's* his *fault,* Tejada told himself violently. *She would still be in love with you if he hadn't corrupted her somehow. And if you hadn't said that to her about the baby.* Firmly quashing this last thought, the lieutenant headed for the post, his free-ranging rage focused on a specific point. He was going to find out what Vargas had said or done to Elena, or make the maquis die in the attempt. Tejada did not really doubt that he would be successful. Carvallo had interrogated the prisoner under orders, without personal malice. The lieutenant was fairly sure that Carvallo's efforts had been halfhearted.

The other guardias were still at lunch in the barracks attached to the main building. The prison was deserted. Tejada shoved open the door of Vargas' cell with so much force that it flew against the wall. The prisoner had already finished his lunch. He looked up as the door slammed with an expression of mild inquiry. "Hello," he said. "You're new. Are you Torres's replacement or Carvallo's?"

The nonchalant tone was a bad mistake. Tejada crossed the cell in a few strides, grabbed the prisoner by his collar, and dragged him upright, slamming him against the wall. Vargas gasped in pain. "Listen, smart-ass," the lieutenant said quietly.

"I've been trying to keep you alive in case you have information. But after what you've done to my wife, I'm not sure that I care."

Vargas managed to catch his breath. "Your wife? Señora Fernández?"

"Have you seduced anyone else lately?"

Amusement flickered in the guerrilla's eyes. "Be reasonable, Lieutenant. Aside from the fact that I'm hardly in the ideal position for a seducer, your wife isn't really a candidate for seduction in her present condition."

"You talked to her," Tejada hissed, infuriated by the man's flippancy. "You with your damn 'man of the world' pose! What the hell did you say to her?"

"Nothing that couldn't be repeated to you," Vargas said. "In fact, I rather assumed that it *would* be repeated to you."

Tejada backhanded the lingering smile off the guerrilla's face. "She visited you out of kindness!" he spat. "And you . . . you suborned her! You took advantage of her! You made her lie to me! To *me*, her husband!"

At least Vargas had stopped being amused. When he spoke, his voice was serious. "I seem to have underestimated the lady. I hope she won't suffer for this."

"What business is it of yours if she does?" Tejada demanded, suddenly terrified that Vargas had more than a political interest in Elena.

"None." The maquis' voice was soothing. "But I will tell you again: Nothing that we said could not have been said in front of you or anyone."

"You're *worried* about her!" Tejada accused. "You think that *I* would hurt her?"

Vargas shrugged. "The thought does occur."

Tejada's pistol came out of its holster almost of its own accord. "Give me one good reason why I shouldn't kill you," he said, his voice shaking.

The maquis had instinctively turned his head to avoid the

gun, but his back was to the wall, and the barrel remained firmly pressed just below his ear. He sighed and turned back to meet the lieutenant's eyes, with the sad resignation of a man who has accepted his own death. His voice was quiet. "Whether you kill me now or later won't make any difference in the long run. But your wife believes you're a decent man, Lieutenant."

Vargas felt the pistol trembling under his chin. He closed his eyes. He was therefore unprepared when Tejada seized his shirt again and flung him at the corner of the cell as hard as he could. He fell against the stones heavily, unable to suppress a gasp of pain.

"Damn you," the lieutenant whispered. He spat at the prone form, and then fled the cell, his hands shaking. As he went downstairs, he heard Dolores Severino crying. *Why couldn't he have stuck with the Severino chit?* Tejada wondered angrily. *She loves him. Why* my *Elena?*

Márquez was waiting for him in his office when he arrived. "Good, you're back," the sergeant said. "I'm sending out the patrols, and if you don't mind, sir, I'd like to go over to Lebeña this afternoon. Ortíz says there's a man selling a motorcycle there, and I thought I'd take a look and see how much he wants."

"Fine," Tejada said automatically. He was more than happy to not have to talk to Márquez all afternoon, and if the sergeant was actually doing something useful, so much the better.

Left alone at the post, his thoughts began inexorably to circle around Elena. She would try to see Vargas again. She had never broken her word, once given. He could give orders that would bar her from the prisoners, or that would allow no one access to Vargas. *And announce to the entire post that you can't control your own wife?* asked a cynical voice in his head. *How long do you think it will take before the whole town knows it as well as the post?* He could not lock her in the *fonda.* She would see the maquis again, and see the bruise across his face. Tejada knew it was futile to hope that Vargas would not tell her who was responsible for his latest injury. He could practically see the maquis' smirk and hear the mocking voice pronouncing his name. He could send her away. For her own safety, until the child was born. Everyone would expect her to give birth in Unquera, near a doctor anyway. No one would think it was unusual after that for her to return to her parents' home with an infant. The best thing was to send her away.

Tejada received a certain amount of bitter pleasure from imagining speeches to his wife, explaining why their separation was in everyone's best interest. He also came up with a number of cutting remarks he had been too upset to think of at lunchtime. In his various mental scenarios, he was always perfectly calm and collected, and replied to imprecations and entreaties with detached and witty sarcasm. However, as the afternoon lengthened into evening, he was by no means enthusiastic about returning home to actually confront Elena. He did a number of nonurgent chores, read and wrote several reports, and thoroughly organized his desk. The routine tasks helped clear his mind, but his resentment simmered away on a back burner, steaming gently, and casting a mist of rage over his brain. Several pencils broke instead of sharpening, and his attempt to refill a fountain pen resulted in ink all over his hands and the blotter. He mopped up the spilled ink, muttering curses, and decided he had done enough desk work for one day.

Márquez returned a little after seven, and the pairs on patrol began drifting back over the next half hour. Three sets of men would not be back until the following day. Unwilling to socialize, Tejada excused himself and said good night. The rain had stopped, but the clouds were blocking the sunset, enveloping the town in premature grayness and obliterating the mountains. Tejada hurried away from the post, but slowed as he reached the river, disliking the prospect that lay ahead of him.

He stopped completely at the Torre del Infantado, and then,

with sudden decision, turned along the Quiviesa and began to head away from the town. He needed a walk. And if Elena was worried that he was late, it was too bad for her. *I won't go far,* he thought, though he knew that wandering in the mist was stupid in the extreme, and that the weather was not cold enough to make the bandits lie low.

He avoided the road parallel to the river, picking his way along the riverbank instead. Fighting his way through bushes was something of a relief. The rain and the relatively warm weather had swollen the stream, and the water rushed steadily along, many of the rocks that created white water later in the year fully submerged. Tejada came around a bend, and then froze as he saw a dark figure silhouetted against the gray, with a long stick in its hands. Then the stick took on the shape of a fishing pole, and Tejada relaxed. It was just some lone peasant with a taste for salmon, wrapped in a greatcoat against the rain. He was starting to see bandits hidden behind every tree. He started forward again silently, knowing that no fisherman would thank him for a sudden loud hail.

He stepped carelessly, and a piece of the bank nearly gave way under him. He grabbed at a nearby tree to steady himself. He regained his footing, but the dead branch snapped loudly, and the fisherman turned toward him. "Good evening."

Tejada saw as he came closer that what he had taken for a greatcoat was actually a cassock. "Good evening, Father."

"How are you?" the priest asked.

"Fine. And you?" Tejada moved to go around the priest.

"Well enough." Father Bernardo watched the lieutenant with narrowed eyes for a moment and then said, "May I ask what you are doing on the river at this hour?"

"I wanted a walk."

"Your wife informed me that you were not a sportsman."

Tejada's mouth tightened. "That's correct. I'm sorry if I've spoiled your fishing for this evening, though. I was just leaving."

"Lieutenant!" The priest spoke with authority, and Tejada paused, unwillingly.

"Yes, Father?"

"I come here most evenings," the priest said simply. "This is the first time I have seen you. If your walk was to settle some matter of conscience, perhaps I could be of service?"

"That's kind of you, Father, but unnecessary." Tejada was annoyed that his preoccupation was so obvious, and his annoyance showed in his tone. "But *my* conscience is clear, thank you."

"You are perhaps worried about your wife's?"

Tejada turned back to the priest and stared. "How did you know?"

"I've been a parish priest for more than fifteen years," said Father Bernardo, keeping his tone neutral. "I find that among married parishioners, disturbances of the spirit frequently involve the spouse."

Tejada gave a harsh bark of laughter. "Do I display the typical attributes of a cuckolded peasant, then?"

Father Bernardo took a few moments to wind his line and cast it again before replying. His eyes scanned the darkening water as he spoke. "Is that your fear?"

"That Elena's been unfaithful? No! Or . . . well, nothing that simple."

Pause. Wind. Cast. "Do you want to tell me about it?"

Tejada took a deep breath, and the story tumbled out without a pause: the raid on the cabin, his suggestion that Elena visit Dolores Severino, the visits to Vargas, how he had found out about them, his confrontation with Elena, and his meeting with the captured guerrilla. The priest stood like a statue, the water swirling around his ankles. He was silent for a little while after Tejada had talked himself to a standstill. Then he nodded slowly and said, "She should not have met with this unfortunate without your knowledge."

"That was what I told her!" Tejada agreed. "That's what bothers me most! It's dishonest."

"Do you think there was anything else . . . dishonest about these meetings?"

Tejada scowled. "I suppose not. But that's not the point!"

Pause. Wind. Cast. "When is your child due, Lieutenant?"

"The end of this month." Tejada's voice sounded sulky in his own ears. "But I don't see what that has to do with anything."

"You've been married long?"

"Eight months."

The priest sighed. "Your wife," he said slowly, "struck me as a highly intelligent woman. She mentioned to me that she had graduated from university, and had worked to support herself for several years. That would have been during the Republic?"

Tejada braced himself for the familiar pinprick hostility. "Yes," he snapped.

Pause. Wind. Cast. "So she has acquired a habit of independence, which is unfortunate," Father Bernardo said. "But it seems to me that she is trying to break this habit. Often women who marry late and have experience of self-sufficiency have difficulty adjusting to marriage. And your wife is adjusting to marriage, to motherhood, and to a new home all at once. I'm sure she's making an effort. But she may need you to be tolerant of any lapses."

"I am tolerant," Tejada protested. "But this is something that could affect my career. Something that's important."

"And how does she feel about your career?" Father Bernardo asked shrewdly.

Tejada opened his mouth to complain, and then remembered Elena saying gently, *We neither of us want peace of mind.* "She understands what it means to me," he admitted softly.

"That's a rare blessing," Father Bernardo cast again, and added encouragingly, "Also, remember, she's in her last month of pregnancy. Women at that time are always beset with doubts, fears, terrors even. When the baby comes she'll settle down to taking care of it, and you'll have to worry less about all this."

Tejada stared at the muddy ground, and flushed. "I told her I'd take the baby away if she didn't give way about Vargas," he muttered, embarrassed.

"That," said the priest briskly, "would be the worst thing you could do. Aside from being inhumanly cruel to a woman of warm heart and fondness for children, as Señora Fernández obviously is, it would be precisely the thing most likely to push her into more defiance. Think about it: If you crush her maternal feelings, a woman of her intelligence and education is likely to take refuge in exactly the sort of unfeminine intellectualism that you're trying to avoid."

Tejada stopped listening shortly after hearing the words "inhumanly cruel," and started remembering Elena's face as he had last seen it, drawn with misery. "I didn't mean it," he said guiltily. "I'll apologize to her. I . . . is there anything you think I could bring her? Wine? Roses? Chocolate?"

"The gold of El Dorado?" Father Bernardo suggested, teasing but not unkind. "It's early in the season for roses, and Fermín hasn't had a delivery of chocolate in six months, but I have a bottle of a nice local vintage that you're welcome to, if you think it's necessary."

"I couldn't—" Tejada began.

"It would give me great pleasure to see a husband and wife reconciled," Father Bernardo interrupted gently. He drew in his line a final time, and stepped out of the water. "It will soon be too dark to stay anyway. Come along."

Tejada was impatient to set things right with his wife, and he was afraid that the priest would delay him. But Father Bernardo moved along the bank with the speed of long familiarity, and they reached the parish house within a few minutes. "Give my respects to Señora Fernández," said Father Bernardo, smiling, as he handed over the bottle of wine.

Tejada thanked him briefly but fervently, and set off for home as rapidly as possible. The streetlights were just beginning to come on, and house windows glowed through the gathering dark. Tejada rehearsed the scene in his mind. Elena would probably be very quiet at first. She always was when she was frightened or upset. But he was optimistic that she would forgive him. She always had forgiven him before. He anxiously replayed their last conversation, wondering if he had said or done anything unpardonable. He thought not. All the same, he entered the *fonda* and headed up to his apartment with a certain sense of foreboding. The lights were all out when he entered. He wondered if she had taken refuge in bed. He headed for the bedroom. Perhaps she had fallen asleep. He imagined creeping across the room and leaning over to kiss her on the cheek and murmur endearments as she woke up. That would not be the worst way of apologizing.

He was still gripping the wine bottle by its neck. Smiling slightly, he went to the kitchen to put it down, flipping the light switch as he went. The kitchen was spotlessly clean. He wondered what had happened to the soup he had not eaten for lunch, and felt pleasantly hungry. They could have a late supper together, with the wine. He headed back toward the bedroom. The door creaked as he pushed it open. "Elena?" He crossed the room and turned on the lamp beside the bed. It was unmade, but empty.

Tejada frowned, worried, and retraced his steps. "Elena?" In spite of himself he spoke a little more sharply. *It's nothing serious,* he told himself, fighting down irrational panic. *She's not here. She probably went to see a friend. So she'll gossip about our fight. Damn. Well, I suppose I did the same thing. With luck it won't be all over Potes before the end of the week.* He passed the dining-room table and saw that a folded note with his own name on the outside was propped up against a book. He picked it up, a little relieved. At least she had told him where she was going. She could not have left in a state of total anger then. He unfolded the note.

Lieutenant, he read, shocked first by the cold salutation, and then by the realization that it was not in Elena's handwriting. *Your wife and her child are safe. If you wish them to remain so, bring the shipment of carbines you received from Santander and the eight hundred rounds of ammunition that accompany them to the pine where you found a cache of arms two weeks ago and leave them there within the next forty-eight hours. If you comply with these conditions Señora de Tejada will be released unharmed within a day of the delivery of the arms. If you do not deliver them, or if the Guardia or the Policía Armada initiate any house-to-house search, her body will be returned to you. Sincerely, the Republican Army of Liberation.*

Tejada sat down, mouth open, eyes staring at nothing. "Elena," he whispered, half-hoping that if he managed to say her name aloud he would feel her arms around him and hear her saying gently, *Carlos! Carlos, wake up! I'm here, it's all right. It was just a dream.* He repeated her name, willing himself to wake up, to discover that the whole day, the whole time they had spent in Potes leading up to this day, had been only a dream. Desperate, he slammed his fist into the table.

His knuckles bruised, the pain brutally forced him to admit that he was awake. He reread the note, trying to focus on the details beyond the fact of his wife's absence, but his only coherent thought was that his Elena was being held prisoner somewhere in the mountains, cold and frightened, and perhaps wounded, and still believing that he hated her.

Chapter 19

The sound of horses in the street brought Tejada out of his daze. Perhaps one of the patrols was returning late. The cold thought struck him that Elena's kidnappers might mistake the end of a routine patrol for a house-to-house search. He grabbed the note and headed for the post at a run. His men were at dinner when he arrived. He found Márquez and Battista eating together, their heads bent over the sergeant's radio, which had nearly miraculously managed to pick up a program from Radio Cantabria, in spite of the mountains. Tejada reached over and switched off the radio. "We've got a problem," he said.

The two officers looked up at the lieutenant, and then exchanged glances. Then they stood up. "The office?" Márquez suggested.

Tejada nodded, and the three men left the cafeteria in silence. When they reached the office, Márquez took a seat at his desk, and Battista stood behind him. Tejada paced back and forth, ignoring his chair. It was the corporal who finally broke the silence. "So what's the matter?"

Tejada took a deep breath and found that he was unwilling to say the words aloud. Telling someone else what had happened made it somehow more real and irrevocable. "I found this when I got home," he said finally, and held out the note.

Márquez leaned forward to take the piece of paper from the lieutenant. He read it silently, considerately holding it up so that

Battista could read over his shoulder. Tejada was looking at the ground, so he did not see their faces as they read, but he heard Battista's breath hiss between his teeth, and heard Márquez mutter softly, "Pigs."

Battista looked up at his commander. "I'm so sorry, sir."

The sympathetic words almost broke Tejada's self-control. He sank into a chair, one hand over his eyes. "I don't know what to do," he said. "If I could think of any way of finding her . . . but I can't." His voice was shaking, and he stopped, unwilling to betray any more weakness.

Márquez took a deep breath, and seemed to be speaking very cautiously. "Lieutenant, the maquis have been wasting ammunition lately. Their supplies are running low. They can't buy it here, and the Germans may be blocking their supplies in France. All we have to do is wait them out. But if we *give* them enough ammunition for the next six months—"

"I know that," Tejada snapped. "We can't give them the ammunition."

"Good." The sergeant looked relieved. "And let me say how much I admire your heroism, sir." He turned in his chair, speaking more rapidly now. "We do have a chance. You were home for lunch, so this can be only a few hours old at the most. We'll send out patrols in all directions right away. Battista, get the register for each of the villages, so the men who haven't gone on patrols yet will know how many houses they have to search."

"We can't. They'll kill her," Tejada interrupted. "You know word travels faster than we do for the house-to-houses, and we don't even have a clue which direction to start."

"I know it's a slim chance, sir," Márquez said. "But we have no choice."

Tejada had been frantically revolving plans, and now he put forward the best of a flawed lot. "I thought maybe we could stake out the arms drop. Use dummy arms, even. If they'd only given us a little more *time* it would be easier. But even as it is . . ."

He stopped; the sergeant was shaking his head and looking disapproving. "This is *terrorism*, Lieutenant. You can't give in to their demands."

"Leave them the guns without ammunition then," Tejada pleaded. "We could have the whole area surrounded."

"It's too much of a risk." Márquez was firm. "Besides, what kind of precedent would it set? No. We have to show them that we can't be bargained with. You have to order a house-to-house search *now*."

Tejada stared the sergeant, understanding dimly that Márquez was worried about the ammunition, about keeping order in the Liébana, about everything except Elena. *He's never liked Elena,* Tejada thought despairingly. *He thinks she's a Red. Oh, God, if they'd only known that before they'd taken her. This is all my fault.* "No," he said, barely above a whisper. "I can't do that to her."

"Lieutenant, if we allow them to take hostages the entire valley will become unsafe," Márquez said. "Order the house-to-house, or I will."

"I . . . can't." Tejada looked past Márquez to Battista, and saw sympathy in the corporal's face, but not support.

Márquez looked grim. "I understand from your file that you were in Toledo in '36, Lieutenant."

Tejada blinked, confused. "Yes. So what?"

"So you were privileged to witness the example of Colonel Moscardó's heroism."

For a moment, Tejada did not understand what Márquez was talking about. Then the part of his brain that understood why the maquis could not be given the ammunition in exchange for Elena's safety gave him a sharp mental kick. All of Spain knew of Colonel Moscardó's heroism: The Reds besieging the Alcázar de Toledo had called the Colonel and told him that if the Alcázar was not surrendered within the hour his son would be shot. Moscardó had given his son his blessing, and said farewell to him in a brief telephone call. Tejada closed his eyes, and tried to remember the months he had spent in the Alcázar, under Moscardó's command. He remembered the exhilaration that something was finally *happening*; that the die had been cast, and the Falange was finally sounding the call across the nation. He remembered excitement and well-suppressed nervousness about how he would perform in combat for the first time. He remembered fear and overwhelming hunger and remembered the first time he had seen a man shot at close range. He remembered grim nights passed in darkness because the Reds had cut off electricity and water to the fortress. He had an odd, anomalous memory of the phone lines being cut as well, but surely that was a mistake, one of the mind's treacherous tricks. For the life of him he could not remember anything about Moscardó's son, or about the phone call that had since become famous throughout Spain, but he was sure it had happened. He knew that the death of the colonel's son had been confirmed that autumn when the siege was lifted. But he couldn't remember hearing the colonel refer to his son during the siege. *Heroism*, Tejada thought dully. *Heroism is making the ultimate sacrifice for your country. But I never thought the ultimate sacrifice would be* someone else.

"Moscardó's son was a grown man," he said hoarsely. "My . . . my child hasn't even had a chance to live yet." *And Moscardó had a telephone call*, he added silently. *Or . . . well, he must have had one. He was able to make things right with his son. But if I never see Elena again I won't be able to tell her how sorry I am. She'll keep thinking I'm angry with her until she . . . she'll keep thinking I'm angry. Suppose they tell her about the house-to-house before they . . . Suppose they tell her? Taunt her with my inhumanity? She'll believe them.*

"That makes their crime more despicable," Márquez said quietly. "But it doesn't change the only honorable course."

Tejada propped his elbows on his desk, holding his temples. "No," he whispered.

The sergeant stood and put one hand on his commander's

shoulder. "I'll give the order, sir," he said soothingly. "And Battista and I can arrange everything. You won't have to ride with the patrols. The men will understand." He picked up the duty roster and gestured to Battista, who went over to the filing cabinet to pull out a census of the villages in the Liébana.

Tejada raised his head as the two men headed for the door. "I said no. A house-to-house is useless without more directions. We'll spend the next two days gathering intelligence, paying for informants, everything we can. And then we'll stake out the arms drop."

Márquez's lips thinned. "With all due respect, sir, I don't think your judgment is trustworthy in this case. It's quite understandable. But we'll do a house-to-house."

Tejada stood up. "That was an order, Sergeant."

Márquez froze. Then he said softly, "I'm sorry, sir. I believe that course is not in the best interests of the corps or the security of this region. I'm sure that after a little reflection you'll agree with me."

"The hell I will!" Tejada retorted, incensed. "Where do you—?" He stopped suddenly. Márquez had drawn his pistol.

"I think," the sergeant said deliberately, "that you will reconsider when you've had time to think it over, Lieutenant. I'm going to take you upstairs, and then Battista and I will organize a house-to-house. As soon as the guardias return and whatever news they have is communicated to Santander, you'll be released to perform your regular duties. Come on, and quickly. The faster we go the better chance we have of recovering your lady."

Tejada stared at the pistol, uncomprehending. "You're mutinying?"

"No, sir. I'm authorized to act as commander of the post if the lieutenant is rendered unfit for any reason. You're clearly too distressed to act competently. As soon as you recover, I'll cede command, with the greatest of pleasure." He jerked the pistol. "Let's go."

The lieutenant turned to Battista. "You're going to allow this, Corporal?"

Battista looked unhappy. "I . . . I'm sorry, sir. But I think Sergeant Márquez might be right."

Tejada was again struck by the odd sense that he was dreaming as the sergeant advanced toward him, gun leveled, and gestured him around the desk. "Battista will take care of your pistol for now, sir," Márquez said quietly.

Tejada felt as if he were watching a film of himself as the corporal stepped forward and disarmed him with an apologetic expression. Except he was not quite sure which of the three figures in the silent movie he was as they left the office, Márquez behind him, and Battista at his elbow. He had seen prisoners escorted a thousand times, without ever noticing his own perspective before. "Should I put my hands on my head?" he asked without sarcasm, merely curious to see how far this strange excursion into a mirror image of his world would go.

"I don't think that's necessary, sir." The sergeant was reassuring.

Tejada was almost sorry for the response. Márquez was being so reasonable, so deferential, that he began to doubt his own sanity. *I should do something*, he thought, as they climbed the stairs. *Márquez wouldn't dare use the gun, really. He'd have to explain it to the colonel if he did.* They reached the cells, and Battista stepped forward to unlock the empty one. In retrospect, Tejada found it funny that he had worried so much about space to put prisoners. As the corporal gestured him inside, he did not see anything amusing. He knew that he was faster than most men. He was fairly sure that he was faster than Márquez, and he suspected that both of his captors would hesitate an instant before using a pistol on a superior officer. There was a good chance he could knock the sergeant's arm out of the way without injury, and he might well be able to make a dash down the stairs before either of them reacted.

What kept him from resisting was not so much the possibility of being shot as the nagging suspicion that Márquez and Battista were right, and that he was in fact temporarily insane. He was not reassured when Sergeant Márquez said gently, "I'm sure when you think it over you'll agree this is for the best, Lieutenant."

"We'll tell you as soon as there's any news," Battista added. "And we'll leave someone on duty here, so you can call if you need anything."

"And you don't need to worry about what the colonel will say," Márquez finished. "When we write the reports, you'll have full credit for the operation. Your . . . temporary mental disturbance can remain between us."

The cell door swung shut, leaving Tejada alone in darkness. *How many times have I left someone like this?* he wondered. But they understood why they were there. *I understand why I'm here, I suppose. Márquez thinks I've gone crazy. Maybe I have gone crazy. I wouldn't be locked up by my own officers otherwise. I don't feel crazy. But do madmen even know that they're insane? Maybe, if they lose their minds after being normal for a long time. God, how terrible, like a cripple who knows that other people can walk, to know that you can't trust your own mind where normal people can. Am I like that? I wouldn't have fought with Elena over a stupid nothing if I'd been in my right mind. But it's not a hallucination that she's been kidnapped. It's not a hallucination that the maquis will kill her if they get word of the house-to-house.*

He took a deep breath, and tried to think calmly and logically. Perhaps Márquez was right, and the patrols would find Elena. But that was a faint hope. And in the meantime he would have to wait here, impotent, until the patrols returned. Waiting was unbearable. *All right,* he told himself firmly. *Slow and steady. Worry about getting out of here first, and then about stopping the house-to-house.* The tramp of horses' hooves and the jingle of bridles outside his window nearly drove him to despair again. The house-to-house was starting already; it would be impossible to recall the patrols now. He gritted his teeth and forced himself to ignore what he could not control. Battista had said to call if he needed anything. He yelled for the corporal. There was no response, and he yelled again, his faint embarrassment at raising his voice expanding into outright humiliation at this ritual of pleading with the empty air.

Finally, after what seemed like a long time, Battista opened the door. "The patrols have gone out, sir."

Tejada inspected the corporal in the light that filtered in from the hallway. Battista's stance was cautious, but he had not drawn his weapon. The lieutenant spoke carefully. "I haven't eaten anything today, Battista. Would you get me a tray?"

"Of course, sir." The corporal's voice was sympathetic. "You'll feel better after you eat."

"I hope so," Tejada said. "Send one of the men with the tray, and spare yourself the stairs," he added casually, as the corporal withdrew.

"We're the only ones left at the post, sir. The sergeant thought it would be better if no one else knew about . . . your situation."

"Tactful of him," Tejada said. His mind was clearing the way it did in combat, picking up details of Battista's stance, gauging distances and timing. *If the maquis are smart,* he thought, *they'll attack the post now. They could pick up the ammunition and there's no way Battista and I could hold them off. My God, suppose the kidnapping is a decoy. They might return Elena once they have what they need, and then Márquez will have quite a bit of explaining to do about leaving the post unguarded!*

Cheered by these thoughts, Tejada waited impatiently for Battista's return. He considered telling the corporal of his worries about the post's vulnerability. He doubted that Battista would release or rearm him. Still, it seemed worthwhile to say cautiously as the corporal opened the door a second time, "Have you thought about what will happen if the maquis try to attack here?"

"Yes." Battista nodded, pleased that the lieutenant appeared to be recovering his sense of responsibility. "I thought of that. I've locked the stuff in the cellar for the night. And I've stored the key separately, so if anything happens to me they won't get it, even if they think of looking there."

"Good work," Tejada said, sincerely pleased. He sat quietly on the cot as far as possible from the door, his hands dangling between his knees. "That smells good," he added sociably, as the corporal turned his back.

"*Favada asturiana*," Battista said cheerfully, over his shoulder.

Tejada knew that he would not have more than a few seconds. Battista had brought a tray with bread and a heavy bowl up the stairs, but he was no waiter. The tray had occupied both his hands. There was no place to set it down in the hallway, and the heavy bolts on the cell door were unoiled so that it was easier to open with two hands. Even so, Tejada had hardly dared to hope that Battista would set the tray on the floor before opening the door. But the lieutenant was lucky. Battista stooped, half-facing away from his commander, and picked up the heavy tray. The corporal heard a faint creak, and something flickered in his peripheral vision, but his instinct was to not move too quickly to avoid spilling the hot *favada*. Before he could straighten to see what had happened, a weight landed on his back and his hands were jerked behind him. The tray crashed to the floor, the *favada* spraying along the wall.

Battista stumbled and lost his footing, landing heavily on his knees. He was lowered inexorably onto his face, and the weight behind him resolved itself into a knee in his back. "Didn't they teach you at the academy never to turn your back on prisoners?" Tejada said, slightly breathless, as he reached for the pistol in Battista's holster.

"Yes, sir. I'm sorry, sir."

"This is grounds for court-martial," Tejada said dryly, standing up but keeping his weapon trained on the prone guardia. "But thanks to Sergeant Márquez, you're the only person available to make sure the post isn't raided by maquis tonight. Try not to screw that up."

Battista pushed himself to his knees and felt the barrel of his own pistol against his shoulder blades. He froze. "What about you, sir?"

"I'm going to find my wife," Tejada said grimly. "Before this damn house-to-house kills her."

"B-but, sir!"

"Lie down and put your hands on your head," Tejada interrupted. "And pray that the maquis don't make off with so much as a teaspoon from the post while I'm gone. I may overlook insubordination, but not incompetence. Have a good night, Corporal."

He stepped over Battista, and hurried down the stairs. He headed for his office at a run, unsure how long Battista would remain cowed. His cloak was there, along with his own pistol. He tossed Battista's weapon onto the table, grabbed his own, and left the post, thinking rapidly.

It was nearly eleven, and low-moving clouds scudded across the sky in a heavy wind. Tejada could see lights in the houses high above the river and hear the angry residents arguing with guardias who were making their way through the town. He sprinted for the parish house, and pounded on the door. It seemed like a long time before he saw a light go on in the hall, and heard the bolt being drawn back. Father Bernardo's eyes widened at the sight of the lieutenant. "Good evening, my son. Come in. What happened?"

Tejada stepped inside, gasping for breath. "I need to find the maquis," he said.

The priest's eyebrows shot up. "That is your job, yes. But why this urgency?"

"I don't mean find them to stop them," Tejada explained. "I need to find one of their leaders. To speak to him. Just for a few minutes. That's all. I'll go anywhere within reason. You know the people here. You must know who has sons or brothers in the mountains. Vouch for me to them." As the priest opened his mouth to reply, Tejada added, "If it's something you only know under seal of confession, I won't ask for names. We can meet anonymously. They can be masked, if they like. But I have to give them a message, and it has to be tonight."

Father Bernardo frowned. "There are one or two families who might talk to me," he admitted. "But in the middle of the night? And while the guardias are doing a house-to-house search?"

"That's the problem," Tejada interrupted, in agony. "I have to tell them that I didn't order the house-to-house. That they can't hurt Elena because of it. Tell them I'll give them what they want, but they can't hurt Elena."

"Why would they hurt your wife?" Father Bernardo asked, frowning. "What do they want?"

Tejada hastily summarized the contents of the note he had received, and his encounter with Sergeant Márquez. "You understand why I have to find her," he finished desperately. "I never got a chance to tell her I was sorry after all those things I told you about, and if . . . if anything happens to her now she'll think that it's because I didn't care enough to protect her."

"Yes." Father Bernardo took the lieutenant's arm and led him into the study. "I don't like to mix in Guardia business," he said. "But Señora Fernández and her child shouldn't be endangered like this. Sit down and wait here. I can't promise you anything, but I'll try to pay some calls."

"Bless you!" Tejada leaned on the chair Father Bernardo had indicated, too nervous to sit down.

At the door to the study, the priest turned. "I won't ask whether you really intend to comply with the maquis' demands," he said quietly, "because I don't like to bargain in bad faith. But I suggest you have the answer clear in your own mind."

He left, and Tejada paced back and forth, trying to crush the hope that Father Bernardo would be helpful before it became too strong. *If I can just have a* clue *where to start looking for her,* he thought. *Just a* clue *and a little more time. We've been lucky so far.*

Lucky with Santiago telling us about Argüébanes, and lucky about finding those Thompsons, and about recovering the dynamite. Hard to believe how lucky. Almost divinely guided. We just have to stay lucky a little longer. Just one more miracle, please, God, just one more small miracle and I'll never ask for anything else.

Tejada had hoped that Father Bernardo would return quickly, but the little clock on the mantelpiece ticked quietly past eleven thirty and chimed midnight, and there was no sign of the priest. *Hurry, hurry, hurry,* Tejada willed silently. *It can't be too late yet. But hurry.* At twelve thirty, Tejada began to wonder whether he should strike out randomly searching for Elena, or risk walking to Tama to find the Álvarezes and see if they had any information. At one o'clock, he began to worry that Elena might already be dead. Finally, a little before one thirty, the door opened and Father Bernardo came in, looking grave. Tejada, who had finally sunk into a chair, shot to his feet. "Well?"

"The whole town is up because of the house-to-house," the priest said. "So I was able to talk to a few people."

"And?"

"Check around Monte Viorna," Father Bernardo said quietly.

Tejada seized the priest's hand. "Thank you."

"Wait a moment," Father Bernardo said as Tejada headed for the door. "Do you have a flashlight?"

"No."

They were already in the hallway. The priest turned and disappeared up the stairs, leaving Tejada shifting from foot to foot with impatience. He was back within a few minutes, holding out an electric flashlight. "I find this useful in the sacristy. Don't wear out the batteries," he said quietly.

"I'll replace them," Tejada promised.

"Go with God," Father Bernardo said as he opened the door for his guest. Tejada thanked him again, and set off into the night.

Chapter 20

A spasm of back pain jolted Elena awake. For a moment she was conscious only of her discomfort and a cold terror that the baby had been hurt. Then she understood that she was uncomfortable partly because she was lying on her back—which had been an uncomfortable position for the last several months—and partly because her hands were tied behind her, digging into the small of her back. The baby was utterly still, but its by-now-familiar weight was still there. Slowly, her panic receded, and, to her relief, the pain followed it. She was still uncomfortable and frightened, but terror and agony no longer made it impossible for her to think.

She was lying on damp and uneven stone, in near-total blackness. The cellar—or cell or vault or whatever it was—was wet and probably not overly clean. She wriggled onto her side in an attempt to make herself more comfortable, and felt grit when she turned her cheek against the damp rock. A breeze made her shiver, and brought the incongruously pleasant smell of pines. Elena craned her neck sideways and upward, and saw that her prison was equipped with an open doorway. Although "doorway" was perhaps a grandiose term for the long rectangular opening, gray against the blackness and measuring perhaps five feet by one, which rose just beyond her feet. She inhaled the sweet chilly wind, trying to shake off the last traces of chloroform. It was too dark to tell what lay beyond the gray opening, but the temperature and wind suggested that she was in some sort of structure that was open to the outdoors. Judging from the darkness, she had been unconscious for several hours. It was not an overly cold night, but Elena had no coat, and now that she was awake she was shivering uncontrollably. The baby was still not moving, and Elena's first thought was to reassure it.

"Don't worry," she whispered to her stomach. "We'll get out of this."

No friendly squirm or kick greeted her reassurance, and Elena began to worry again about the baby's health. *He was probably kicking a lot when I was unconscious, and I didn't feel it,* she told herself. *He's asleep now, that's all. Come on, baby. Come on, move, move. Let me know you're all right.* The only answer to her plea was an intense cramp that did not ease her fears at all.

She took a few sobbing breaths, trying to calm herself, and realized that her movements must be clearly audible to her guards. There was no use in feigning unconsciousness, and her pain and fear made even the company of enemies preferable to loneliness. She raised her voice. "Hello? Where are we? Why have you done this to me?"

There was no response. She could not even hear the sighing wind or the distant hoot of an owl, only a terrible overwhelming silence, and her own harsh breathing. She had never been anywhere so completely quiet before. "Hello?" Elena called a little louder, and her voice cracked. "Hello? Answer me, please!"

She listened hard enough to hear her own pulse thudding in her ears, and almost hard enough to hear the baby's heartbeat as well. But no one answered her. She tried again, her voice shaking. "You don't have to tell me where we are. Or why we're here. Or anything. But please say something! Anything!"

It slowly dawned on Elena that no guards could be so totally silent. Curiously, the thought that she had been left unguarded did not raise her hopes for escape. Rather, it plunged her into an irrational panic. "Come back!" she cried uselessly. "Don't leave me here!" *There are bears up here,* she thought, light-headed. *And wolves. I've been left in a bear's den. And they'll come back to the cave and eat me and no one will ever find my body so no one will ever know what's happened. But Carlos will look for me. Unless he's still angry with me.* It struck her that Carlos might have no idea what had happened. *He'll think I've run off and left him,* she thought. *That I've taken the baby and hidden from him on purpose. He won't know that it wasn't my fault.*

The growing certainty that her kidnappers could no longer hear her broke Elena's self-control. Perhaps even the baby could no longer hear her. "Help me! Don't leave me alone!" she sobbed. And then, more than half way to hysteria, "Carlos!" She wept until the pain in her back took her breath away again. The need to alleviate her discomfort cleared her mind, and she awkwardly rubbed her bound wrists against the sore place as best she could. *Carlos wouldn't expect you to cry like a baby,* she told herself sternly. *And if you don't get out of here he'll never know that you didn't leave him voluntarily. It's good that this place is unguarded. If you could get your hands free, all you'd have to do would be to find your way home.* Forcing herself to think logically in small steps, she considered ways to free her hands. They were bound with rope that felt coarse against her wrists. So if she could find something sharp to rub the ropes against they would part. Where could she find something sharp? Perhaps on the floor of the cave there was a sharp stone.

She inched along her side until her forehead brushed one wall of her prison. A little more inching put her in place to wriggle her way into a semisitting position. Her elbows were scraped and the back of her head was sore by the time she finished, but she was leaning against one wall, relatively comfortably. It was definitely a wall. She could feel irregularities in the stones, and something that felt like mortar crumbled behind her fingers. Not a cave then. Experimentally, she slid her arms up the wall, palms outward, feeling for jagged rocks that might cut her loose. There were none. With a sigh, Elena began to move sideways along the wall, searching for a sharp and convenient stone. "It's all right," she whispered, half to herself and half to the baby, who remained ominously still. "Don't worry. I'll find a way to get us out of this."

She reached the corner of her prison without finding a stone that would suit her purposes, and stopped to rest, temporarily overwhelmed by pain and exhaustion. Her entire body seemed to hurt, either from various scratches, bruises, and cramps, or from general weariness. She took a few deep breaths and began to scoot her way along the next wall, blocking out the thought that the structure might have been too smoothly built to harbor the cutting edge she needed.

The walls were smoothly built, but she found a sharp stone halfway along her second wall by the expedient of sitting on it painfully. For a moment she was afraid that the jagged shard had escaped from her in the darkness, or that it would be too difficult to pick up, but by bracing her shoulders against the wall and scrabbling with her fingers, she managed to pick it up. She dropped it three times before she was able to force it into a workable position to saw at the ropes binding her hands, and each time it clattered in the darkness her heart leapt into her mouth for fear that its edge had been dulled.

The cutting was painfully slow, and her fingers were sticky with blood long before the first strand parted. She stopped often, panting to clear her mind, and a few times she nearly despaired of ever making progress, but finally the first loop separated. The extra play made it easier for her to grip her chosen tool, although her impatience made it seem as if the final cutting took twice as long as it actually did. The moment of bringing her hands in front of her was ecstasy. She massaged her wrists, sucked her bleeding fingers, and gave the baby a comforting pat.

Fortunately, her exertions had warmed her up. Elena rubbed sweat from her forehead, glorying in the ability to freely use her hands, and stood up, cautiously clinging to one wall. She promptly doubled over again, nauseous and slightly dizzy, her back throbbing. Even this setback did not dim her sense of triumph. She sank to the floor again, afraid that light-headedness might mean a fall dangerous to the baby, and then stood up in stages and tottered toward the gray outline of the doorway of the room she was in, half-expecting a guard to confront her.

She reached the doorway and stepped out into what seemed to be a tiny grassy clearing, surrounded by woods. Clouds blotted out the moon and stars, but the sky was a ghostly gray, far lighter than it would have been on a clear but moonless night. The night air on her face felt like a victory. *Now all I have to do is find my way home*, she thought joyfully.

She turned around to see what lay behind the structure she had just emerged from, and felt her optimism dim a little. The place where she had been left was clearly not a typical shepherd's hut or barn. It was too small, and too well concealed. It looked as if it had been built into the side of a mountain, and the slope rose above it, far too sheer to climb. If she had not felt the stone walls herself, she would almost have believed it was a natural cave. A ledge extended a few feet on the other side of the cave like building, but the drop below it was steep as well. Elena worked her way along the ledge, hoping that the cave blocked an obvious path in the other direction. *If there were stars, I could tell which way was north*, she thought. *Or, I think I could.* She was slightly depressed by the thought that knowing which direction was north was a useless piece of information since she did not know in which direction she wanted to go.

Her hopes for an easy path on the far side of the cave were dashed as soon as she reached the end of the stone wall. The ledge ended abruptly, merging seamlessly with the mountain-side. Far below her, in the distance, she could see pinpoints of light from what must be a village. Elena looked at the lights hun-grily, knowing that they would be impossible to reach from her current position. With a sigh, she turned and headed back along the ledge toward the front of the cave, to look for another path. *I know what direction to head in now*, she thought. *If I can just find a village, I'm sure someone will take me in for the night.*

She was walking with one hand along the edge of the cave for support, so when she was attacked by another intense pain she had something to lean on. *This is all I need*, she thought grimly. *It feels like I'm going into labor. Oh, my God! Not labor! Not here! Not now!* With some alarm, Elena mentally checked her physical condition against all the friendly advice and anecdotes she had heard since she had known of her pregnancy. Everything fit.

"Oh, no." Elena spoke the words aloud as she hurried toward the boundary of trees that hemmed in the clearing. "No, baby, this is a mistake. You're not due for another two weeks. Just stay quiet now, and I'll drink a nice glass of milk for you when we get home."

She was answered by another contraction.

"I can't deal with this right now!" Elena spoke aloud, because words seemed more dignified than a moan.

No friendly and obvious road opened between the trees, but Elena knew that logically the men who had brought her here—wherever *here* was—must have followed some path. She strained her eyes through the darkness, and finally made out what looked like a definite gap between the trees. At any rate, there was no underbrush there, and although it was hard to tell in the dim light, the ground looked as if it had been trampled recently. Naturally, the trail—if it could be called that—ran almost directly down the steepest part of the slope, at an angle that she would have found difficult to scramble down under the best of circumstances.

"Why does everything have to be halfway up a cliff in this country?" Elena murmured, disgusted. Then her brain started working. Her kidnappers had taken some trouble to get her here without serious injury. Obviously, they did not want her to escape. But they did not want her dead either. So she must be a hostage for something. If she was a hostage then they had told Carlos, and he would not be angry with her for disappearing. He was probably looking for her already. Elena's wave of relief was abruptly dammed by another contraction. When it had passed, she continued thinking rapidly. The men had not posted guards around the cave. Either they did not have the manpower, or they trusted that she would be unable to escape on her own. Or they had posted guards *somewhere else.* At the bottom of the only path leading away from the cave perhaps? That was a clever way, if they knew the guardias were searching. Even if the guards were found, they would not lead directly to Elena.

She peered dubiously through the gloom of the forest, trying to make out the end of the track. A man could be hidden within a few yards of the path in the darkness, and she would never know. And making a rapid escape was impossible. Elena considered what her kidnappers might do to her if they caught her escaping. Another contraction decided her. She was a hostage, and they wanted her alive. Besides, she couldn't think of anything much worse than being in labor alone on a mountaintop. Cautiously, she sat down and began to lever herself down the path. If her guards attempted to stop her, she would take the opportunity to tell them that they had better find a midwife if they wanted their hostages to remain healthy.

It was almost pitch-black in the forest, and her progress was hampered by increasingly frequent pauses to deal with labor pains. She had little sense of time, and she began to hope that she would encounter her captors soon, if only because of the protection they could provide from wild animals and the simple danger of losing the path. She was vaguely aware that the trail became less steep and more definitely a path as she progressed. Then, quite suddenly, after what felt like forever and was probably between one and two hours, the trees opened, and she was in another clearing, this time with a wide, level road fit for a horseman, and almost for a truck, leading out of it in one direction. Unfortunately, as far as Elena could tell, it was heading away from the lights she had seen from her prison.

A road has to go somewhere, she thought fuzzily, too tired to wonder why her kidnappers had gone to the trouble of imprisoning her and then left her apparently totally unguarded. *A road has to go somewhere. And it looks like it's flat enough to walk, thank God. So follow the road, slow and steady.*

Getting to her feet was difficult, and she had a splitting headache by the time she was upright, but standing up on a clearly marked road made her feel slightly more human. For a few minutes, walking upright was sheer joy. Then she found that it was making the contractions worse. Although it was not steep, the road was heading steadily down, and Elena hoped that this meant it led toward civilization. She stopped thinking and focused on forcing herself to go on in an endless pattern: Walk, rest through contraction. Wipe forehead. Walk again. Sometimes it seemed as if she progressed no more than a few steps between rests.

She stopped expecting to meet guards, and began instead to have the irrational feeling that she was completely alone in the valley. Somewhere an eternity ahead, the road ended where there were people, but here there was only the rustling of the wind in the trees, and the stones underfoot, and the brambles by the edge of the path. She cried out freely now when she was in pain, because there was no one to hear. *What will happen if the baby is born here with no one else around? The two of us will be alone in the valley, in the night. Don't think about that.* Walk. Rest. Walk. *The sun will come up before then.* Walk. Rest. Walk. *You'll reach the end of the road before then.* Walk. Rest. Walk.

Then, miraculously, the trees fell away on her left hand, and she was next to an open field, dotted with dark shapes that were oddly familiar. She stumbled forward, paused as another contraction shook her, and realized she was leaning against a fencepost. She bent over and pillowed her forehead with her hands on top of the post, crying with relief. A fence post meant people. A fence post meant civilization. She remained that way for several minutes, unable to force herself to move farther, and so shaken by her own sobs that she didn't notice a dark shape that suddenly loomed over her and said sharply, "Hey! What are you doing here?"

Elena turned her head and made out the bulky silhouette of a man carrying a rifle. The rifle hardly gave her pause. "I'm in labor," she said simply. "I need a midwife."

At the time it seemed a perfectly logical thing to say, although afterward Elena could hardly blame the man for being taken aback. "Er . . . why are you in labor *here?*" he ventured.

"It wasn't by choice," Elena said, indignant. "Is this your land?"

"These are my herds," he explained. "The land is common grazing pastures. I heard you and thought maybe one of the ewes was in trouble."

"I am not a ewe," Elena snapped.

"You sound a bit like one having trouble with a lamb." His voice was amused, but he added, "Can you walk a little ways? There's a shelter near here, and I can go for my wife, if you don't mind being left alone."

The idea of walking farther was suddenly almost unbearable, but Elena agreed. It was far easier to walk with someone to lean on and without having to worry about which direction to go. Ten minutes' walk along the edge of the forest brought them to a windowless wood-roofed hut with a hole near the top of the stone walls for smoke to escape. An oil lamp sat in one corner of the hut, along with a blanket and an empty bowl with the remnants of stew clinging to the inside. A bale of straw lay along the opposite wall. The floor of the hut was earth, but the whole place smelled of clean straw, and stew, and to Elena it looked like a haven of safety. She gratefully sank down beside the straw, to test her theory that lying down would be a lot more comfortable. It was not more comfortable, but getting up took an energy she discovered she did not have.

"Will you be all right alone?" the man asked again. "My wife is in Congarna. I could get her. She'd know what to do."

Elena managed a smile. "I'll be all right," she said. "I've been on my own so far."

In spite of the words, Elena was sorry when the shepherd left. The human contact had seemed like a link to sanity. Now, lying alone and vulnerable and in increasing pain, she began to fear that her rescuer would never return. He would forget about her, or be caught by the maquis or the Guardia, or an avalanche. How far away was Congarna? It was horrible to have no way of knowing what time it was, or how much time had passed. She had never thought she would have to have the baby alone. She did not know what to do. She would die here and the baby would die before he returned, before she was able to tell him her name and give him a message to send to Carlos in case she died.

She was near hysteria when the door to the cabin opened again, and two figures entered. Elena recognized the first as the shepherd who had guided her. The second one was a woman wrapped in shawls, carrying what looked like a bundle of blankets in her arms. "Now then," the woman said, casting an experienced eye over Elena. "There's no need to be crying yet, dear. When did you start having pains?"

"I don't know," Elena admitted.

"Is this your first?" The woman knelt by her, unwrapping the bundle as she spoke.

"Yes."

The woman clicked her tongue. "And at your age. Well you just lie comfortable, and do what I tell you, and everything will be fine. How did you ever get into this mess?"

Elena smiled faintly. "It's a long story."

"Well, if this is your first, we probably have time for it," the woman said briskly. "Go ahead and talk, dear. It'll take your mind off the pain."

Chapter 21

Tejada set off along the highway toward Espinama on foot, regardless of the risk. Going back to the post to take his horse would have taken too much time, and would have involved another encounter with Corporal Battista. Besides, more mounted men tonight could only endanger Elena. He walked quickly, restraining himself from running only by force of will and the knowledge that if he exhausted himself too quickly he would be of no help to Elena.

He did not bother to turn on the flashlight. He knew the road well by now, although he had never walked it in the dark before. The distance seemed blessedly short at night. Only a few minutes brought him to the turnoff to Santo Toribio. "Check around Monte Viorna," Father Bernardo had said. He turned left sharply, and began to head up the hill, his blood pounding in his ears. The maquis had hidden their arms along Monte Viorna. It was logical to hope that they had hidden Elena there as well. He would have liked to follow the path he had taken with Elena when he had found the hidden arms, but he was not at all sure that he could find it in the dark, and he was afraid of getting lost. Gaining as much altitude as possible and then working downward seemed like a logical plan. *I never took Elena up here*, he thought grimly, as the road wound up the mountain in long lazy curves. *I promised to take her to the monastery and then I never went with her. If I hadn't found the arms that time we would have gone. If I hadn't found them, the maquis wouldn't need replacements now. We shouldn't have taken that shortcut. If I hadn't made her talk about Montalbán we would have come this way, and I wouldn't be here now. Oh, God, why did we have to pass the spot where Montalbán was killed on our way to the monastery? Why did it have to upset her?*

Somewhere an owl hooted. Tejada hoped it was an owl and not a man signaling to someone. He took off his tricorn, since he knew the silhouette made him instantly recognizable, even by night. But the wind blew cold, and he disliked having his hands occupied, so after a few steps he put it on again. *We've been lucky so far,* he told himself. *We just have to keep being lucky.* He tried to concentrate on his good fortune, instead of feeling guilty about taking Elena past the site of Anselmo Montalbán's death, but it was difficult. Suddenly, the subterranean stream of thought gushed to the surface, and mingled with his over-counted blessings. A murky pattern began to emerge in the depths of his mind. *Divine guidance,* he denied desperately frightened by his conclusion. *Father Bernardo would say it was divine guidance. Every time we've been on the verge of disaster something has happened to save us because God is on our side. That was why we found the dynamite. That's why there have been no more thefts from Devastated Regions. Because we're blessed. It's a lack of faith to think otherwise.*

It was a lack of faith, but alone in the darkness before dawn, with Elena still a prisoner of the maquis, and his own officers in open rebellion against him, Tejada could not help thinking of a secular explanation. He walked faster as his mind worked, occasionally breaking into a jog trot without noticing it, until the road opened out before the looming bulk of the monastery. Then he stopped. He had no proof, and nothing more than a series of coincidences that seemed logical at two in the morning but would probably look as insubstantial as mist in the sunshine. And none of them helped him find Elena.

Santo Toribio was dark and silent. It had apparently been undisturbed by patrols. Who, after all, would suspect the guardians of the *lignum crucis* of protecting the maquis? Tejada stood in the shadows of the trees by the side of the road and inspected the building. Turned in on its cloister, it had the unfortunately fortresslike quality of many secluded religious communities. The chances of finding Elena there were slim, and the time it would take to rouse the inhabitants, explain his errand, and search the building would kill the rest of the hours before dawn, even if the monks were cooperative. Remembering Elena's narration of her day at Santo Toribio with Father Bernardo, Tejada kept to the edge of the woods, giving the buildings a wide berth and searching for a path that led into the forest.

There was a grassy hill that sloped down to the monastery's grounds and what seemed to be an opening between the trees. Tejada thought a moment, and then decided that the flashlight was worth the risk. He switched it on and held it out toward where he thought the path might be. It was definitely a path, and definitely recently used. The rain had made it muddy, and there were traces of footprints. He inspected the grass. It was a meadow, probably used for grazing, with no apparent tracks. He turned off the light, allowed his eyes to adjust once more to the night, and then started up the path.

It led steadily upward, curling around the back of the monastery into Monte Viorna. Then, quite suddenly, the path ended along with the forest, and he was in an open field, with a trail running perpendicular in both directions to the path he had followed. *Shit*, the lieutenant thought. *Which way now?* His own instinct was to keep to the woods. The maquis would want cover. Both they and their prisoner would be too exposed on the tableland opening ahead of him and to his right. He turned left and continued up the mountain until he was well into the trees again. Then he took a deep breath and flicked on the light, prepared to turn it off and dive for cover. *The time it takes three men to light a cigarette is the time it takes to aim*, he thought. He flashed the beam along the path, feverishly looking for further signs of use, and mentally extending a match toward a cigarette. Let it catch, pass the match to the next man, let it catch. There were footprints here, too, and where the road curved suddenly—Tejada forgot about the three-match rule and trained the flashlight on the brambles by the side of the path, fascinated. They were wicked-looking spiked blackberries that had curved around a nearly dead tree branch that stuck out into the bend in the path a little above waist height, ready to treacherously catch at any unwary traveler. Suspended among them, sparkling in the faint electric light like dew in a spider's web, was a single diamond, set in a tiny gold cross.

Tejada reached out and gently untangled the necklace from the brambles. The fragile chain had snapped, and it fell into his hand like a dead thing. He knew now that he was looking in the right place. Elena had been here, perhaps had stumbled carelessly from weariness and lost the chain. Or perhaps she had been dragged unconscious or—*unconscious,* the lieutenant decided, refusing to consider other options—and her captors had not noticed that her necklace had snagged here, betraying them. He pocketed the necklace and switched off the flashlight, uncomfortably sure that he had left it on for far too long.

He waited a few minutes for his eyes to readjust to the dark before going on, straining his ears for the sounds of anything unusual in the forest. There was no sound. He was about to start up the path again when he heard a faint moan. He froze. *It's a sheep*, he thought. *They always sound human. The meadow I passed must be grazing grounds. It's* only *a sheep.* The moan was repeated. He crept back down the path in the direction he had come. It would do no harm to check that it was in fact some lonely and wakeful sheep.

He turned off the path before he reached open ground, and worked his way through the woods. There were definitely dark shapes outlined against the meadow that were the right size for sheep. There was also—he sniffed the air—the smell of wood smoke. Someone human had built a fire nearby. The clouds were clearing, leaving a faint glimpse of the moon. He could see a house silhouetted against the meadow. That had to be where the smoke was coming from. Tejada took a deep breath. *It isn't illegal to pasture sheep,* he reminded himself. *They could just be there with the spring flock.* He crept closer, expecting to hear the sharp bark of a guard dog. A lamb bleated, sounding eerily like a child crying, and the lieutenant relaxed. He had heard a sheep, and nothing more. A shape stepped out of the shadow of the house and became a man. Tejada felt his pulse speed up. The man was carrying a rifle.

Then Tejada heard the moan again, much closer, and his doubts vanished. No sheep made noise like that. He pushed away the thought that the only humans he had ever heard make noises like that had been under interrogation for several hours, and crept toward the house. *One outside,* he thought. *With a rifle. And at least one inside. Probably armed as well. I suppose a rifle's better than a machine gun. I could take him out from here. But that would alert them, and if they decided to hurt her—hurt her more—they'd have too much time before I could get inside. I have to get them all together.*

The man with the rifle was watching the path along the woods, not the woods themselves. He paced back and forth and then walked into the shadow of the building. Tejada made his way to the edge of the trees, holding his breath. A match flared, and a moment later there was a pinpoint glow of a pipe. The sentry made no effort to cover the glow with his hand. He was inexperienced, or self-assured, or both.

There was another semihuman groan. Tejada was close enough now to hear it die away into quiet sobbing. This time he recognized his wife's voice definitely, distorted as it was by agony. For a moment he was glad she was still alive and conscious. Then his stomach knotted with rage at the indifference of the smoking sentry. *They'll get back everything they've done to her,* he promised himself fiercely.

The man walked restlessly out toward the perimeter of the woods again. Tejada forced himself to wait until the sentry turned his back. Then he sprang forward. His plan was to yoke the sentry's neck with one arm, and subdue his arms with the other. If the lieutenant had been less exhausted and fearful and furious it might have worked. It might have worked anyway if his cloak had not billowed behind him in the breeze at the last second, slowing him down infinitesimally and making a soft flapping noise that alerted his prey.

The sentry spun around just as Tejada brushed his shoulder. The lieutenant realized his miscalculation at the last minute and was able to knock the rifle out of his opponent's hands, but before he could draw his own weapon the watchman's fingers closed on his throat. Tejada fought desperately to break his enemy's grip, cursing himself for missing his opportunity to catch his foe off guard, for coming without reinforcements, and for failing Elena at the last minute. He managed to break the choke hold, but the sentry was an experienced wrestler, and he was fighting on his home ground. Tejada gained a hold for a moment, and then the sentry stepped sharply backward and sideways, and the lieutenant sprawled over a half-buried stone, losing his grip on his enemy and falling forward heavily. By the time he righted himself, a rifle was pointing at him. "Don't move!"

Tejada knelt and brought his hands away from his sides, palms outward. He had lost his tricorn in the struggle. *He'll be able to say he thought I was a bandit,* the lieutenant thought dully. *He didn't see the uniform by moonlight and I didn't say who I was. They won't believe him, but he'll be able to say it.* He heard Elena cry out again, and some inner core of self-control melted and gave way. "Stop hurting her," he said hoarsely. "You won't get the arms through her. She's not a valuable enough hostage. I am. Take me instead. But stop hurting her."

"And who are you?" The words were suspicious.

Tejada closed his eyes. "I'm the commander of the Guardia

Civil post in Potes." He choked. "Please. The Guardia will care more about one of their own officers than about her. She . . . she's always been one of you anyway."

"And where's your partner, then?"

"I came alone."

There was a pause of several heartbeats. Then the sentry said quietly, "Stand up, and keep your hands where I can see them." Tejada obeyed. "Walk forward," the man said, backing toward the shelter of the house.

Tejada walked toward the house with him, reflecting bitterly that the maquis were considerably more competent in their handling of prisoners than his own men. *At least I'll get to see her*, he thought, as the maquis reached the wall, never taking his eyes off his prisoner. *I'll get to say good-bye to her.*

"Inside." The sentry flattened himself against the wall, and swung the rifle sideways. "I'll be behind you."

Pride kept Tejada's footsteps steady as he walked toward the door and opened it. Then he stopped. A small lantern flickered over the inside of a shepherd's hut. A kettle was set on a fire in one corner. His wife was lying in a mass of blankets. A woman was kneeling beside her. No one else was there. Befuddled, Tejada looked for instruments of torture. Elena saw him and held out her hands. "Carlos!"

He dropped to his knees beside her, giving her one of his hands and wiping off the curls plastered against her forehead with the other, speaking so quickly he was almost incomprehensible. "Elenita-precious-darling-love-I'm-sorry-forgive-me-what-have-they-done-to-you-I'm-sorry-I'm-sorry."

"Carlos." Elena's voice was a thin whisper, but her grip on his hand was almost painfully tight.

"Yes, beloved?"

"Shut up. I need to concentrate."

Tejada stared, his relief at finding Elena alive suddenly giving way to another fear. He took in the woman on the other side of

Elena for the first time. She looked at him with calm amusement. "You're a midwife?" he demanded, with sharp anxiety.

She snorted contemptuously. "I've had eight of my own. I know about bringing babies into the world." Taking pity on him, she added, "My husband found your lady out in the pasture, and called me because she seemed to be having trouble."

"I'm sorry, sir." The lieutenant recognized the voice from the doorway as belonging to the man who had wrestled with him. "Your lady's told us a bit about what happened to her, and Milagros thought I should be out on guard. I thought it would be best if I didn't let you out of range until we knew you were really who you said."

"What happened to her?" Tejada said.

"They're not the ones who took me," Elena interjected. "I got away. But then the baby came and I couldn't get home."

Tejada's jaw dropped. "You escaped?"

"It wasn't difficult. They didn't even have the cave guarded. The hardest thing was the baby."

"That's my Elena." The lieutenant stroked her forehead, and suddenly remembered that he had a good deal more to apologize for. He leaned over her, ignoring Milagros's annoyed look. "I'm sorry for this afternoon," he whispered. "I didn't mean it. Any of it. I . . . when I thought I wouldn't be able to tell you . . ." She squeezed his hand, and he stopped, relieved.

Elena said nothing but she smiled and thought that it was easier not to cry now that Carlos was here. Because Tejada had not seen her earlier, he did not realize how much calmer she was, and he was stunned by the way she suffered in the following hours. *This isn't fair*, he thought, squeezing her hand, and listening to Milagros' calm instructions. *In sorrow thou shalt bring forth children, all right, but this is too much. They have drugs for this. In France and England women don't go through this. If I could have taken her to Unquera she wouldn't have had to go through this.* Because he could not bear the thought that he might have found Elena only to lose her again, he began to mentally review the pattern he had started to see on his way up the mountain. More details fell into place, but it was hard to put them in their correct order in the face of Elena's distress.

The growing light in the hut was an aid to his anxious scanning of Elena's face for the signs of exhaustion. Her eyes were frequently closed now, and he wondered if she even saw him when they were open. He was so absorbed that he hardly heard Milagros's instructions, and the thin, angry cry of an infant startled him.

"Congratulations," said the midwife. "It's a boy."

Elena dropped her husband's hand and held out both arms. "Let me see him," she commanded.

Tejada closed his eyes. He had not slept all night, he could not remember the last time he had eaten, and he did not care. He sat with his head bent as Milagros busily washed the baby and swaddled him, and then placed him in his mother's arms. The sound of Elena's voice interrupted the lieutenant's fervent prayer of gratitude. "Hi, there!" she cooed. "Hello, pretty baby! Hello good, clever baby."

Tejada looked at his wife. There were circles under her eyes and smudges on her forehead. She was cradling a tiny thing that seemed to be mostly blankets. He shifted position so that he could see the baby, and brushed back the blanket from the top of its head. A tiny hand waved as his finger slid over downy hair. "Look," the lieutenant said in an awed whisper. "He's got fingernails and everything."

"What are you going to call him?" Milagros interjected matter-of-factly.

Elena looked up at her husband and smiled. "Carlos?"

He shook his head, remembering that he had threatened to take away the minute, perfect person nestled against her, and unwilling to do anything that would lessen her triumph. "Your choice."

Elena laughed faintly. "No. I meant, what do you think of Carlos?"

Tejada hesitated, flattered, unnerved, and secretly a little fearful of giving up too much of himself to the newcomer. "It's a good name," said Milagros. "But if he's named for his father you'll want to give him a middle name as well, to tell them apart."

Tejada looked up as she spoke and saw that her husband had come to stand in the doorway. He was outlined against full daylight now. It looked like it was going to be a sunny day. "What is your name?" the lieutenant asked.

The shepherd started. "Me, sir? I'm Antonio, for my saint's day."

Tejada looked at his wife. "Carlos Antonio?" he suggested.

She smiled and nodded. The shepherd cleared his throat, embarrassed, but obviously pleased. "That's kind of you, sir. But—" He broke off, raising his head. "Someone's coming," he said in a different tone of voice.

Tejada had already heard the rhythmic drumming of hoofbeats. "More than one, would you say?" he asked, getting to his feet. "I'll be right back, Elena," he added.

Antonio stepped out of the house and looked along the line of the woods. Tejada followed him and saw that the heads of the figures riding up the path he had walked the previous night were already coming into view above the ridge. Antonio spat into the dirt. "Tricorns," he said in a fatalistic tone. "Perhaps you'd better talk to them, sir."

Chapter 22

The two riders came forward silhouetted against the rising sun. "You there!" one of them shouted to Antonio as they came above the crest, "stay where you are!"

"Oh, damn," the shepherd murmured, almost too softly for Tejada to hear.

"Don't worry," the lieutenant said quietly. He stayed in the shadow of the doorway until the pair of guardias arrived and dismounted. One of them was one of the new men. Tejada recognized him after a moment as a Galician named Ferreira. The other was Sergeant Márquez.

Márquez left the guardia to hold the horses and stepped toward Antonio. "You own this property?"

"These are common grazing lands, sir. It was my turn to take the flock up here."

"We're doing a register of all houses," the sergeant said shortly. "We'll have to check the hut."

Tejada stepped out of the doorway. "I don't think that's necessary, Sergeant. We've found what we're looking for."

Márquez's jaw dropped. "Sir!" he exclaimed. "But what are you . . . ? How . . . ?"

Tejada looked at his fellow officer with dislike. "I seem to recall telling you that a house-to-house would be useless without information, Márquez," he said dryly. "I left Battista in charge of the post, and went to find information."

The sergeant looked like he had swallowed a very large piece of meat without chewing it. His eyes were bulging slightly. "You . . . found information, sir?"

"Yes. You and Ferreira had better go back to the post, to relieve Battista. I'll join you as soon as possible, but I'd like to make sure that my wife is comfortable first." Tejada absent-mindedly took out his pistol. He was not exactly aiming it at the sergeant, but it was not pointing toward the ground either.

Guardia Ferreira cleared his throat. "Excuse me, Lieutenant, but is your wife all right?"

Tejada smiled. "She's fine, thank you."

Sergeant Márquez moved toward the lieutenant. "Are you sure you don't need help with the prisoners, sir?"

"What prisoners?" Tejada asked. Antonio backed up a step.

Márquez stared. "Why . . . this one, sir. And his confederates. Your wife's kidnappers."

Tejada shook his head. "These aren't my wife's kidnappers," he said. "They helped her and sheltered her when she got away."

Ferreira and Márquez wore identical looks of disbelief. Then Márquez said slowly, "She got *away* from her kidnappers?"

Tejada smiled, foolishly proud. "She's an exceptional woman."

"Granted," the sergeant nodded. "But . . . well, have you considered that she might be . . . a bit confused, sir? After all, for a woman in her condition under heavy guard to escape from the maquis? It's a piece of almost incredible good luck."

Luck that's too good to be true, the lieutenant thought fuzzily. *Luck or divine guidance or human intervention. It all made sense last night. Better not to say anything to Márquez until I have proof. If I can find proof.* "We've had a lot of incredible good luck," he said aloud.

Perhaps because he, too, had been up all night, Márquez did not notice the faint undercurrent in the lieutenant's voice. He coughed. "Of course, if you're *sure* that they have nothing to do with it, that's fine, sir," he said. "But I'd bring them along for questioning, at least. After all, suppose they were involved with taking her, and then they showed her some kindness and your wife didn't want to get them in trouble. Her sympathies . . . her sympathetic nature is well known." The full force of Tejada's glare hit the sergeant and he continued hastily. "Or suppose she was simply mistaken. They could have told her anything, even that they'd rescued her. She woke up confused, still a little befuddled with chloroform. . . ."

Márquez had no opportunity to finish his sentence. Tejada moved like lightning, reaching out and spinning the sergeant up against the wall of the building, his arms twisted behind him. Ferreira made a noise of protest. Tejada pulled the sergeant's pistol from its holster and held it out to Antonio. "Keep Guardia Ferreira covered," he ordered.

The shepherd gasped, but he obeyed with a competence and speed that Ferreira later found highly suspicious. (At the time he merely found it unnerving.) Tejada handcuffed his sergeant. "That was stupid, Márquez," he said quietly. "I was willing to let it go. All I had was a series of coincidences that could have just been very good luck. But you had to try to pin it on someone. Was she supposed to be kept under guard, Márquez? Was your arrival going to be the signal to kill her?"

"Sir, are you out of your mind?" Márquez spoke breathlessly, partly because Tejada had punctuated his sentences by slamming his prisoner against the wall.

"*How did you know she was chloroformed, Márquez?*" Tejada demanded.

"I didn't!"

Tejada slammed Márquez against the wall again, and the prisoner gasped. "I just guessed. After all, logically she had to be unconscious to be taken up here, and you said she was unharmed so I guessed she hadn't been hit on the head."

"Good guess," Tejada said. "But you make a lot of good guesses, don't you? You know, last night on the way up here, I started thinking that Elena's ransom must be a replacement for the arms I found when I was taking her up to the monastery. And I started thinking about how I'd found those guns. It was luck, really. We were on the wrong path. You see, Elena found Anselmo Montalbán's body, and when we walked along the river it reminded her. She pointed out the spot to me. She was upset, so we went on talking and missed the turnoff to Santo Toribio. And last night I remembered passing the spot where Elena told me she'd found Montalbán's body *before the road to Santo Toribio*. And then I wondered: You came back from that patrol injured and told us to do a house-to-house *toward Espinama and Fuente Dé*. But Montalbán was killed practically on the outskirts of Potes, and if his companions had fled away from the town, they could have taken any one of a hundred roads before Espinama. They could have gone up to Argüébanes, or up Monte Viorna, or even to Mogrovejo. We were all so pleased about finding that missing dynamite that none of us stopped to wonder how your intuition had been so good."

Márquez made a disbelieving noise. "I'm in trouble for having good intuition, sir? We've had a lot of reports of bandit activity around Espinama. Ask Battista, if you like. That seemed like a logical direction."

"Very true," Tejada agreed reasonably, letting the sergeant turn away from the wall, but keeping a grip on his collar. "And of course you could have just said that you *think* of that road as the road to Espinama. You weren't thinking about the side roads. You just make fortunate guesses. But you're fortunate in other ways, too, aren't you?" The lieutenant had the giddy feeling of running on pure adrenaline, and he spoke quickly, to keep Márquez from interrupting his fragile chain of thought. He continued speaking rapidly, too tired to judge whether his conjectures made sense. "That shortwave radio of yours. That's a nice expensive little toy. And you're very generous about letting other people use it, aren't you? And yesterday when you wanted the afternoon off to go and look at a motorbike. You said you wanted to see how much the man was asking, but you didn't ask how much I'd authorize. That wasn't a motorbike for the Guardia, it was for you personally, wasn't it? Another nice expensive toy. I know how much a sergeant earns, Márquez. The thing is, I even have a pretty good idea how much allowance a señorito from a well-off family gets in addition. And it doesn't run to your toys. In a city I'd say you were funneling goods to the black market. But there aren't enough customers with ready cash here in Potes. Now you might be smuggling, but we're pretty far inland. But that little operation the maquis had set up: Steal the supplies from Devastated Regions and trade them for weapons. *That* might be a really profitable business. Oh, I don't know if they gave you a percentage of the cash value, or if they just paid you a lump sum to keep your mouth shut and make sure the Guardia didn't stumble too close, but either way, it would be a nice explanation of your extra income."

"That's ridiculous," Márquez said calmly. "I would never help purchase arms to be used against the Guardia. It would be digging my own grave."

Tejada hesitated. He had not planned to accuse Márquez, but the sergeant's injudicious reference to Elena had made him angry. He had been positive that Márquez was mixed up with the guerrillas, but he could figure out no motive. Tejada was sure that the sergeant's contempt for Elena's left-wing sympathies was genuine. In fact, he was almost ready to believe that distaste for her politics had played a role in her kidnapping. But a man of such staunch Fascist loyalty was unlikely to aid the maquis for the sake of pure greed. "You wouldn't like helping them," he admitted slowly. "Because you do believe in the Regime, don't you? But I bet they had something on you. Maybe they tricked you into helping them at first. Put you in a position where you could have been accused of bribery or corruption. And then they came back to you and said, 'Sorry, Sergeant, we need a small favor from you,' and they had you over a barrel. Maybe they just asked you to turn a blind eye to the thefts from Devastated Regions. If they were smart, they made you help them with the smuggling so you were pulled in deeper. I do believe you wanted to stop them. That was why you tipped us off to the dynamite, wasn't it? You didn't want them to have material for sabotage, and you were trying to bankrupt them. But it was a little late for that. And then I found that cache of Thompsons, and they said, 'We need help financing a replacement' and you came up with a nice scheme: 'The lieutenant's a fool for his wife,' you told them. 'And on top of that she's expecting a child. Get her and use her as a hostage, and he'll hand over just what you need.' And then you told them exactly where and when they could do it and helped them work out the details like chloroforming. But you were planning to double-cross them, weren't you? You put that little item about the house-to-house search in the ransom note, and then made damn sure that we did a house-to-house, to make it clear that we wouldn't cooperate. And it was all going to be on my orders." Tejada heard his voice starting to shake. "You were going to tell them that you'd tried to stop me, weren't you? That you didn't know I'd been in Toledo with Moscardó, that you didn't realize I'd insist on being a hero. I was going to be your excuse to stop working for them."

Márquez shrugged, as eloquently as it is possible to do while handcuffed. "I don't quite know what to say, except that it isn't true, sir," he said. "Obviously, you've been under a lot of strain lately—"

"The Severino girl!" Tejada interrupted. More and more pieces were falling into place as he talked, and he was thinking out loud as much as accusing now. The pieces of the jigsaw puzzle were all there except one, and he stared the shape of the hole, willing the missing part of the picture to come clear.

"Who, Dolores?" Márquez looked puzzled.

"Not Dolores, her little sister. Elena will remember her name. Dolores asked Elena to take her a message. And the kid asked Elena if the sergeant had sent her. Elena thought it was just a general term for the commander of the post, but it was you, wasn't it? Luis Severino was the maquis' contact with the coast. He ran the smuggling part of the operation. When he was killed, they thought you would get in contact to propose another method."

"No, Lieutenant."

"Makes sense to me." All three guardias turned to stare at Antonio, who had spoken in a slow, thoughtful tone, without taking his eyes or his weapon off Guardia Ferreira. The shepherd spoke as if weighing his words. "Lieutenant, I might as well tell you, because you could find it out if you asked the right people anyway. I usually take a dog up here to guard the flocks with me, not a rifle. I took the rifle and not a dog last night because there was a rumor in town that there'd be something going on up at the Cueva Santa that honest men should keep their noses out of, and I didn't want a dog barking at the wrong time. And then, when your lady told me what had happened, I thought maybe the gossip was wrong. But now I'm not so sure."

"Kidnapping and extortion aren't things honest men should keep their noses out of?" Guardia Ferreira said sarcastically.

"It seems to me that this man knows a good deal more than I do about the bandits' activities," Márquez said at the same moment.

"What gossip?" Tejada asked.

Antonio looked evenly at Guardia Ferreira. "The gossip was that what was going on up at the Cueva Santa was Guardia business."

"I don't suppose this gossip gave any particular information or originated with any particular person?" Tejada asked, but good-humoredly.

Antonio shook his head, smiling faintly. "No, Lieutenant. Just gossip. You know how it is. It's hard to remember who you first hear something from."

"We do find a lot of people have fatally flawed memories," the lieutenant agreed. He smiled. "Sometimes their amnesia is fatal, too."

The shepherd nodded, completely unmoved. "Yes, sir. So I've heard."

"And this is what you intend to put in your report?" Márquez demanded, disgusted. "That a lot of subversive gossip and a series of coincidences that have only resulted in the Guardia's benefit led you to make outrageous accusations of kidnapping?"

For a moment, Tejada was taken aback. Then he laughed. "Oh, I don't think Colonel Súarez would believe a word of this," he said cheerfully. "Or, even if he did, he wouldn't be able to prove it. I might be able to get you transferred on the grounds that I couldn't work with you, but it would take time, and I wouldn't sleep too well at night while the paperwork was going through."

"Then what do you intend to do?" Márquez was unnerved by the lieutenant's laughter, and his voice was a little uncertain. "Ferreira here is a witness—"

Tejada laughed again. "Well, no, actually, he isn't," he said. "But Corporal Battista is. Since you mention it, though, it may interest you to know, Ferreira, that not only did I *not* order the house-to-house last night, it was done against my explicit orders. Furthermore, Sergeant Márquez drew a weapon on me, and I was locked into one of the cells like a criminal. If it hadn't been for Battista's incompetence, I'm quite sure you would be escorting your prisoners back to the post in triumph by now."

Guardia Ferreira looked uncertain. Tejada smiled kindly. "Sergeant Márquez was guilty of gross insubordination," he explained. "I think you might want to take charge of him now, Guardia."

Ferreira gulped. "Umm . . . sir . . ." He gestured toward Antonio.

"Oh, yes, I'm sorry, Ferreira. I just didn't want you making any sudden moves until you understood the situation." He took the gun from Antonio, and pointed it downward. Ferreira moved forward and took his place at Sergeant Márquez's elbow.

The sergeant raised his head. "I stand by what I did," he said stiffly. "You were clearly unfit, sir. And with all due respect, your behavior now leads me to think that you are deranged."

Tejada had to admire the sergeant's nerve. "That's an interesting defense," he said. "But I think Battista was a little unhappy about such open insubordination. Otherwise he wouldn't have been so careless. I don't think I'll have trouble persuading him to testify that it was originally your idea, in exchange for my overlooking his participation."

The last shot hit home. Márquez's shoulders sagged, and he said nothing. Tejada turned to Antonio. "I'm afraid I have to go back with them," he said. "Would you please tell my wife what's happened, and tell her that I'll be back as soon as possible. I'm sorry for the inconvenience."

"Yes, Lieutenant."

It was a long walk back to the post, and Tejada was shaky with exhaustion by the time they arrived. Ferreira showed no signs of doing anything other than obeying the lieutenant, but Tejada was taking no chances, and he insisted on having the guardia lead the horses while he led Sergeant Márquez. His anxiety and sleeplessness were catching up with him, and if it had not been downhill all the way he doubted that he would have been able to make the walk back. Márquez said nothing, and Ferreira tactfully studied the ground, so he was spared the further effort of talking.

The first of the patrols had already returned when they arrived, and the post was open. Tejada dismissed Ferreira with the suggestion that he catch up on some sleep, and then quietly locked the sergeant in the empty cell between Dolores and Pedro, and pocketed the key. Then he went to his office, sank into his desk chair with intense relief, and sent for Corporal Battista. "No attacks on the post last night, Battista?" he said, when the corporal arrived.

"N-no, sir," Battista gulped. "The ammunition's fine. D-did you find Señora de Tejada, sir?"

"Yes."

"Is she all right?"

"Yes."

"Er . . . Lieutenant?"

"Yes?"

"I . . . I didn't know you had a plan, sir. That is . . . I . . . I knew you wouldn't give in to terrorism but . . . well, Sergeant Márquez seemed so sure, and . . ."

"Sergeant Márquez is under arrest for insubordination," Tejada said gently. "He'll be court-martialed, and I intend to press for the full penalty. But I understand it must have been a difficult position for you. After all, Márquez was your superior officer for longer than I was. Naturally, you obeyed your immediate superior."

Battista looked unsure whether to be relieved or alarmed. "Y–yes, Lieutenant."

"I think if you explained the whole situation to Colonel Súarez in your own words, he'd understand and agree to leniency," the lieutenant said. "A signed statement, maybe? Explaining the sergeant's actions exactly, and your own position with regard to them?"

The corporal nodded, definitely relieved now. "Yes, sir."

Tejada jerked his head toward the typewriter. "The carbon paper's in the box on the right," he said. "Date it and show it to me when you're done."

He stayed in the office to supervise Battista, and delegated one of the guardias to tell the returning patrols that the search had been successful and that normal duties should be resumed. It was early afternoon by the time all the patrols returned, and Tejada thankfully ate a huge meal along with his men. He felt much better after eating, but he was hardly able to keep his eyes open. He read and approved Battista's confession, and then left the post, hoping the fresh air would clear his head.

He walked through the afternoon sunshine to the Devastated Regions barracks, hailed the policía on guard, and asked to speak to the commander of the Policía Armada's force. The commander, Sergeant Villamán, met him with every appearance of surly hostility. "I need your men to guard a prisoner until he's taken to Santander tomorrow," Tejada said without preamble.

"That's usually the Guardia's province," Villamán said. "We don't like to interfere."

Tejada grimaced. "Look, this man is one of my own officers. He was insubordinate. I have a largely new force, and I don't trust them to guard him."

Villamán's rocky face broke into a grin of malicious amusement. "That's terrible, Lieutenant. Of course we can take him for as long as you want."

"Thanks." Tejada left, annoyed at holding the Guardia up to ridicule by the Policía Armada, but satisfied that the Policía would do their best to humiliate a member of the rival corps. He took Márquez to the Devastated Regions barracks, left him under the care of the guards there, and went home to take a well-deserved nap.

He woke up a few hours before sunset with a strong desire to shave, bathe, and go back to sleep. He settled for a quick shave and a change of shirts, and went back to the post, where all of the guardias were by now assembled. He called them together and announced that Sergeant Márquez was under arrest for insubordination, and had been relieved of his duties, and that all of his normal authority would temporarily be transferred to

Corporal Battista. Battista, glowing with relief, strained every nerve to prove his loyalty to the lieutenant.

Tejada made sure that someone would be awake for night guard duty at the post, and that everything appeared to be running smoothly. Then he rode up to Antonio's shelter to see how Elena was doing. The shepherd greeted him at the edge of the pasture with an outstretched tricorn. "You lost this last night, Lieutenant," he said as Tejada dismounted.

"So I did." Tejada took the battered hat and brushed it with his hand. Then he put it on. "Thanks. Is Elena all right?"

"Yes, sir. She's nursing the little one. My wife went home a few hours ago."

"You've been very good to her," the lieutenant said, a little awkwardly.

Antonio shrugged. "We couldn't do less, really."

"If there's any way we can repay you . . ."

The shepherd laughed. "Well, now, sir, you're a guardia. It never hurts to have a guardia for a friend."

Tejada snorted, but made no reply. It was going to be difficult to clear the Guardia of the complications Márquez's corruption had created. He reached the shepherd's shelter and entered. Elena was leaning against one wall, her legs stretched out in front of her, cradling the baby at one breast. She glanced up as he entered, smiled at him, and returned her attention to the infant. Tejada squatted beside her without saying anything.

Carlos Antonio nursed and then slept with the ferocious concentration that newborns devote to their few accomplishments. His parents watched him in silence. "He looks happy," Tejada said finally, with some envy.

Elena nodded. "Milagros says it's too early, but I think he recognizes me now," she said.

"That's good."

The two of them sat peaceably for a few more minutes. Elena slumped against his shoulder, and he put one arm around her and the baby. Then she said quietly, "Antonio told me what happened with Márquez. What are you going to do with him?"

"Court-martial for insubordination. And tell the colonel off the record what I suspect about the smuggling, to make sure he gets the maximum penalty."

"How about murder?" Elena's head was a heavy weight against his shoulder. Her voice sounded sleepy.

Tejada sighed. "I can't charge him with Montalbán's murder, even if he was dealing with the maquis. You know that."

"I meant Calero," Elena mumbled. "I was thinking about it earlier." She yawned. "Suppose the maquis were blackmailing Márquez because they knew he'd murdered a superior officer. He might"—she yawned again—"have killed Anselmo because Anselmo was the only person who knew he was involved in Calero's death. And Anselmo had a good motive for killing Calero, too. So it helped to have him on the run and then dead."

"Why on earth would *Márquez* kill Calero?" Tejada demanded, stunned.

"Pretty much the same reason Anselmo would. Good baby," she added absently, as Carlos Antonio blew a bubble.

"What?" Tejada was certain that strain and exhaustion had derailed someone's sanity. He was reasonably sure that his wife was the delirious one, but he would not have staked large sums of money on it.

Elena sighed. "The teacher's sister. Laura Román. Anselmo's son Jesulín and Lieutenant Calero had fought over her, so Calero arrested Jesulín as a Red. But when I went to Anselmo's funeral, I saw the grave of Laura's brother as well. Their name was Román *Márquez*."

"You think they're related?" Tejada was shaken.

"I don't know. It's a common name. But Father Bernardo said the Románs weren't from around here." Her voice was barely above a murmur, and her eyes were at half-mast.

Tejada shook his head. "I don't like the man," he said softly. "But I don't think he'd kill a member of the Guardia for personal—family—reasons."

"That's because you're naive." Elena peacefully closed her eyes. Tejada considered answering, and then decided that she needed to sleep.

The baby was resting in her lap and was in no real danger, but Tejada gently eased the bundle of blankets out of her arms. After a little experimenting that made Carlos Antonio grumble perilously in his sleep, the lieutenant discovered that he could hold the baby along one arm, with its head propped in his elbow. He looked down at the sleeping face of this alien creature no longer than his forearm who shared his name and his blood. *And she says* I'm *naive!* he thought. "Son," he whispered, testing the word the way he might have slipped into a newly tailored jacket, amazed and slightly disbelieving at how well it fit. "Your mother is a good, brave, intelligent woman. But she's a born troublemaker."

Chapter 23

Tejada called Colonel Súarez the next morning and announced that he needed to bring a prisoner to Santander. "We've been through this." The colonel sounded annoyed. "Hold them until after Easter."

"I'm not holding an insubordinate officer for that long," Tejada said flatly. "I want to start proceedings for a court-martial as soon as possible."

"A court-martial!" Súarez was shaken. "Are you sure that's necessary, Lieutenant?"

"Positive."

The colonel sighed noisily. "All right. What for? Cowardice under fire?"

"No, sir. Mutiny. I'd prefer to discuss the details in person, but we may be talking about a capital offense."

"Jesus, Tejada! I know this is your first command, but I sent you reinforcements on the understanding that you'd be able to handle them."

"This wasn't one of the reinforcements, sir," Tejada said grimly. "I'd really rather not talk about it over the telephone."

"All right, you can bring them all in tomorrow."

"Today, sir."

Súarez groaned. "Fine, I'll expect you this afternoon. But there had better be a *really* good reason."

Tejada agreed and ended the call without justifying himself

further. Then he went to see Señor Rosas, and borrowed one of Devastated Regions' trucks for the afternoon. He set off for Santander with Guardia Ortíz, a pair of the new guardias, and the Guardia's three prisoners: Márquez, Vargas, and Dolores Severino. No one shot at the truck as they passed through the Liébana and into the gorge that led north to the coast.

No one talked much. The prisoners swayed as Guardia Ortíz navigated the curves of the gorge, and Pedro Vargas, made clumsy by his wound and unable to right himself in handcuffs, landed nearly in Dolores's lap. He murmured an apology, and then leaned over and whispered something to her. Dolores flushed, coughed, and then said hesitantly, "Is Señora Fernández well, Lieutenant? I'd hoped to say good-bye to her. And thank her."

"She had her baby yesterday," Tejada explained. "But she's fine." He caught Vargas's eye and added sardonically, "I'll tell her you both sent your regards."

Dolores looked embarrassed. "Thank you," she said. "Boy or girl?"

"Boy."

"Congratulations."

"Thank you."

They rode in silence for a few more minutes. Then Vargas began to whistle under his breath. Tejada turned to inspect him. The maquis' face, hard to read under any circumstances, was made completely incomprehensible by bruises. After a moment, Tejada recognized the "Toreador Song" from *Carmen. Arrogant bastard!* the lieutenant thought, remembering his last conversation with Vargas. "She's recovering well," he said, still looking at the maquis. "And she's in *no danger.*"

Márquez snorted. Vargas said nothing, but he stopped whistling. They reached the coast without speaking further. Dolores broke the tense silence again as they approached San Vicente de la Barquera. "I expect Concha and the babies are here already," she said wistfully.

The window to the driver's cab was open, and Guardia Ortíz heard her. He spoke without taking his eyes from the road. "Yes, I overheard someone in Fermín's yesterday saying they were fine."

"How long do you think they'll have to stay there?" Dolores asked.

"I think they can go home whenever they like, right, Lieutenant?"

Dolores flushed. "No. I meant how long do you think . . . I'll be away for?"

Tejada shrugged. "You'll be all right unless the tribunal finds you involved in anything besides that night in Argüébanes. You shouldn't get more than a few months as long as Guardia Riera recovers all right."

"And if he doesn't?" Dolores asked, white-faced.

"Don't worry. He should be fine. But even if the wound gets infected—" The lieutenant looked at Vargas. "Any act of banditry that results in someone's death is automatically a capital offense. But I assume you'll have a witness to testify that you weren't using any weapons, Señorita Severino?"

The maquis nodded, and Dolores turned her head toward him with a little cry. "The lieutenant's right," Vargas said. "You shouldn't worry. I'm sure Riera will be fine."

The girl nodded and hunched her shoulders, withdrawing into some private nightmare. Vargas closed his eyes and either slept or pretended to sleep. No one said anything else until they rolled into Santander. Tejada deposited Vargas and Dolores at the Tabacalera, and left the pair of new guardias to deal with the formalities of registering them with the prison authorities. "I'll make sure your sister knows where you are and what happens to you," he said to Dolores as he climbed back into the truck. She thanked him, barely audibly.

Ortíz and Tejada drove with Sergeant Márquez to the provincial headquarters of the Guardia in Santander. The presence of a guardia in handcuffs created a mild sensation and they were shown into Colonel Súarez's office rather quickly. The colonel greeted them looking unhappy. "You have formal charges?" he asked when Tejada had introduced Ortíz and explained their errand.

Tejada held out the folder with Battista's statement and his own account of Márquez's actions. Súarez opened it and scanned the first page quickly. Then he closed the folder, walked to the door, and opened it. "Guardia," he said, beckoning to his secretary.

"Colonel?"

"See that this gentleman is escorted to a private cell," Súarez said, indicating Márquez. "And then pull the file on"—he glanced down at the folder in his hand again—"Alfonso Márquez Delgado. Guardia Ortíz will help you."

"Yes, Colonel." The secretary saluted.

When the door had closed behind the prisoner and his guards, Colonel Súarez sat down behind his desk. "All right, Tejada," he said quietly. "This is a nice report. You've got a witness, and even a good lawyer couldn't poke a hole in it. Now tell me why it happened."

"I have no proof about Sergeant Márquez's motives, Colonel," Tejada said.

"Speculate, Lieutenant. And make this good."

Tejada hesitated. Súarez had not been overly friendly so far, and Tejada feared his suspicions about the sergeant were so far-fetched that they would give credence to Márquez's claim that he was deranged. "Sergeant Márquez is several years my senior, sir," he said slowly, sticking to the facts and trying to decide how much he should tell the colonel. "And he was the interim commander. He's . . . never been easy to work with. It's occurred to me several times that he might resent the authority of someone younger."

He was saved from continuing by a knock at the door. A moment later the colonel's secretary entered, holding a folder. "This is the Márquez file, Colonel," he said.

"Thank you." Súarez took the file and opened it. When the door had closed, he said, "You were saying Márquez was resentful of the authority of a younger man?"

"Yes, sir."

Súarez read silently for a moment. "That's possible," he said. "But Lieutenant Calero was the same age as Márquez. And it seems that he had difficulties with the good sergeant, too. Why do you think that might be?"

Tejada thought of his last conversation with his wife. *Am I naive?* he wondered. *Oh, shit.* "What sort of difficulties did Calero report?" he asked, tense.

"Doesn't say. Just that the fifth of October Calero requested that Márquez be transferred due to incompatibility."

Calero died October eighth, Tejada thought. *Suppose Márquez had confronted him first. Threatened him?* "You did nothing about this report?" Tejada asked.

The colonel raised his eyebrows at Tejada's tone. "It was filed posthumously," he pointed out. "And Márquez was the most senior officer at the post. What should we have done?"

Tejada took a deep breath. "I'd like to look at an inactive file, sir," he said quietly. "For one Benigno Román Márquez. Teacher. Executed in '38."

"Román Márquez?" Suárez was surprised. "The sergeant was a relative?"

"I'm not sure, sir," Tejada admitted. "But I have a theory. If I could just check the files I could confirm it."

The colonel frowned. Then he picked up the phone on his desk and spoke into it. "Check the archives for 1938 for any proceedings relating to Benigno Román Márquez. If you lay your hands on a file I want to see it. Right away." He hung up the phone. "All right, Lieutenant. Even if they are related, so what? Probably half my force have family members who are Reds. That doesn't make them all guilty of insubordination."

"No, Colonel." Tejada's agreement was heartfelt. "But

Román had a sister and there are rumors in the valley that Calero was," he hesitated, "pestering her. If Márquez found out that Calero was responsible for the death of one of his cousins, for example, and was bothering another, he might have confronted Calero. And if the confrontation turned violent—"

"You think he killed Lieutenant Calero and then blamed bandits?" Suárez demanded.

"I don't have any proof," Tejada said honestly. "But if he did, it would explain a good deal about the thefts from Devastated Regions, and about his current insubordination." Slowly, Tejada sketched his suspicions of how Anselmo had discovered Márquez's involvement in Calero's death, and had blackmailed him into helping the maquis steal materials from Devastated Regions to trade for arms. He explained how Anselmo Montalbán's death had been convenient for the sergeant and why he thought Márquez had suggested holding Elena hostage. "That was why he was so desperate to have us do a house-to-house right away," he finished. "He wanted the maquis to see that he'd done his best, but that the Guardia couldn't be bargained with. He didn't want them to get the arms. He's not a traitor, sir."

"According to you, he's a murderer, a thief, and a kidnapper," Suárez pointed out. "And also an idiot, for letting the maquis get a handle on him for blackmail."

"Well, yes, Colonel. But not a Red." Tejada was scrupulously fair.

There was a tap at the door. It opened in response to the colonel's command and the secretary deposited two files on the desk. "Here they are, sir. There's the regular file and one devoted to trial proceedings."

"Thanks, dismissed." Suárez picked up one file as the door closed again and gestured to Tejada to look at the other.

The lieutenant opened it and found himself looking at the proceedings against Benigno Román Márquez, accused of subversion and treason. With a sinking heart, he saw that the

primary witness against the teacher had been Lieutenant Juan
Calero of the Guardia Civil.

"Oh, dear," the colonel sighed. Tejada looked up and saw
that Suárez had both the Márquez and Román folders open and
was comparing them. "Looks like you were right, Lieutenant.
Benigno Román was the only son of Desiderio Román and
Graciela Márquez Delgado, both deceased. He was born in
Teruel. And our Sergeant Márquez Delgado was born just south
of Teruel, and his eldest sister is listed as Graciela."

"Nephew and niece," Tejada said quietly. "Do you suppose
they knew him, growing up?"

The colonel shook his head. "No. Graciela was ten years
older than her brother, and she moved to Zaragoza with her
husband when Benigno was only four. Márquez joined the
Guardia five years later, and he never served in the same area as
the Románs until '38, when he was transferred to Potes."

"And he arrived to discover his nephew had been shot for
treason," Tejada said.

"It still doesn't prove anything," Suárez pointed out.

"Probably only Márquez himself could confirm everything,"
Tejada argued.

The colonel nodded. "And possibly Laura Román. Do we
know what's happened to her, by the way?"

Tejada shook his head. "She's not in the valley, and no one
talks about her. Which may mean she's with the maquis. Or
dead. Or just that she entered a brothel after she left."

"Hard to believe Sergeant Márquez would commit murder
for her and her brother and then let her support herself like
that," the colonel commented.

"She might not have known he was involved. Or she might
not have wanted to be indebted to him," Tejada said thoughtfully. "She can't have very kind feelings toward the Guardia."

"I suppose not." The colonel made an annoyed noise. "You do
know how this is going to look if it goes to trial, Tejada? One

officer who abused his position to get some girl into bed, and another who murdered his commander and then helped smuggle arms to the Reds." He lowered his voice. "There've been rumors that the Generalissimo wants to disband the Guardia altogether and fold us into the Policía Armada. Have one national police force, under his own command. Do you have any idea what kind of ammunition a scandal like this could provide?"

"With all due respect, Colonel, I didn't condone any of these activities," Tejada reminded his commander.

Súarez considered. "Do you think anyone else at the post is involved with the maquis, besides Márquez?"

Tejada blinked, horrified by the idea that he might have overlooked another conspirator. "I don't think so," he said, after thinking for a moment. "Ortíz is local, of course, so he probably knows some of them from before the war. And Torres would play checkers with the Devil himself if the Devil entered a tournament. But I don't think they're either of them a security risk."

"What about this Battista? Your report says that he disarmed you?"

Tejada shook his head. "I honestly think he was just caught off guard by Sergeant Márquez, and tried to use his best judgment to obey orders."

Súarez steepled his fingers. "Well, that's a relief to hear, Lieutenant, but it brings us to another interesting question: *Would* you have given the maquis the arms in exchange for your wife's safety?"

Tejada stared straight ahead. "That would have been a gross violation of the Guardia's guidelines for dealing with hostage situations, sir."

"I'm glad you're aware of that," Súarez said dryly. He closed both folders. "If you can find any proof about the murder or about smuggling, pass it along, Tejada. But in the meantime, I think we'll proceed with a very quiet court-martial for gross insubordination. Your testimony and Corporal Battista's should be enough to insure a lengthy prison term."

"Yes, Colonel," Tejada said with relief.

"We'll have to proceed against Battista, too, but we can make it a slap on the wrist, if you like."

Tejada thought a moment. "Demotion?" he suggested. "Ortíz is well known in the mountains, and pretty well liked. I think he'd be a good interim corporal."

Súarez nodded. "Demotion and transfer, I think. And that's a good idea about Ortíz." He sighed. "I don't know what it is about the Potes station. First Calero, now you and Márquez. Everyone who gets sent up there somehow manages to get into trouble."

"I think it's who we're working with, sir," Tejada said.

"Maybe," the colonel admitted. "If you're right about the way the maquis are getting arms we can cross off the foreign angle, and I can get Madrid off my back." He stood up. "Thanks for the report, Tejada. If it turns out you're right about this it will look good in your file."

"Thank you, sir."

Súarez saluted. "Have a good trip back, Lieutenant. *Arriba España.*"

Tejada collected Ortíz, and the two guardias headed back to Potes. The sky was orange and pink by the time they reached the town. "Make a report to Battista," Tejada ordered, as they climbed out of the truck. "I'm going to ride up to see how my wife's doing."

"Yes, sir." Ortíz coughed. "It will be dark by the time you come back, sir."

Tejada snorted. "I can ride in the dark, Guardia."

"I know, sir. Only," the guardia hesitated. "if you wait a bit I could go with you. I know it's not a guarantee, the way the maquis have been behaving lately, but it's something."

"Thanks, Ortíz." Tejada smiled, touched. "But the corporal should have that report as soon as possible, and I don't want to wait. I'll be careful, though."

The guardia's concern turned out to be unfounded. Tejada rode up to Antonio's pasture without incident, and found his wife in the process of changing a dirty diaper. "Milagros showed me how," she explained, in response to his question. "But they need to be washed, and we're running awfully low. Do you think we could find someone who would do the washing for a few weeks?"

"I'll talk to the women who do the Guardia's laundry," Tejada promised. He told her about his trip to Santander, and dutifully conveyed Dolores's message. He considered telling her that Vargas had also expressed concern for her well-being, but decided against it. Then he told her about his meeting with the colonel, and about Márquez's imprisonment. She was interested, and genuinely pleased on his behalf, but she did not grow really animated until she was able to explain how many times Toño had been up in the night, and how well he had eaten that morning, and about his brief fussiness later in the afternoon before he settled down to nap. After a few minutes holding his son, Tejada decided that her day really had been more interesting than his own.

Elena was impatient to be home, and Tejada was feeling increasingly guilty about imposing on Antonio, so they decided that the lieutenant would borrow a cart the following day and take it up to the hut to bring Elena and the baby back to the *fonda*. Tejada reluctantly said good-bye to his family and went back to Potes, happy in the knowledge that the following day he would not have to leave them halfway up Monte Viorna. He returned his horse to its stable at the post without meeting anyone, but when he reached the *fonda* Ortíz was waiting for him at the bar. "I'm glad you're back, sir," the guardia said in a low voice. "Go on up to Bárbara's apartment. She wants to talk to you."

Tejada raised his eyebrows, but he made no comment. He climbed the stairs at the back of the restaurant, and then paused on the landing, uncertain whether to knock or to wait for some signal from within. He was still hesitating when Ortíz joined him. "Bárbara." The guardia knocked confidently. "It's us. I've brought the lieutenant."

The door opened, and Bárbara Nuñez de Montalbán gestured them silently into her living room. Tejada stood, waiting to be offered a seat. Ortíz settled himself comfortably on the couch. The widow returned to her rocking chair and did not speak. "You had something you wanted to tell us?" Ortíz prompted.

The woman looked up at Tejada. "I've heard Sergeant Márquez was arrested yesterday."

Tejada nodded, neutral. "That's correct."

"They say he wasn't following your orders."

"Yes."

"And that he was mixed up with kidnapping your lady?"

Ferreira must have talked, Tejada thought. *Or else Antonio and Milagros spread the word. Damn.* "We have several charges against Sergeant Márquez at the moment," he said aloud.

Bárbara met his eyes with an expression of concentrated hatred. "Do you want to get him?"

Tejada was unsettled by the intensity of her gaze. He gambled on honesty. "Yes."

Bárbara Nuñez laughed bitterly. "Well, I can tell you that Márquez was as crooked as a snake. He used to drop in for a drink quite a bit, and didn't he always have news for Anselmo! My husband learned about every shipment that was coming to Devastated Regions through him. And every now and then Anselmo would slip the sergeant a little something, a gift on the house, he used to call it. Oh, yes, Márquez knew that materials were being stolen from Devastated Regions. He was running the whole show and he got a nice cut in return! And I'll swear to that in court, if you need me to, Lieutenant."

Tejada blinked. *Such good luck it's almost divine providence,* he

thought. And then, cynically, *And what's the catch this time?*
"Why?" he asked aloud.

Bárbara misunderstood the question. "Because he didn't
have any choice except to smile and shut up about it! Anselmo
told me he had something on Márquez that was as much as
Márquez's life was worth."

"Why are you suddenly willing to swear to this now?" Tejada
amplified.

Bárbara's smile was unsettling to see. "Because Anselmo
knew when he took to the hills that Márquez was going to try to
kill him. He said he couldn't make contact with anyone because
the sergeant might find out where he was. But it didn't do any
good. Márquez still killed him. And guardias don't go to prison
for murder. But you put them in prison for double-crossing
their own, don't you, Lieutenant? I'll testify that Márquez was
helping us steal from Devastated Regions if it will punish him
for killing Anselmo."

"You didn't come forward with this information before,"
Ortíz said, a little reproachfully.

"The lieutenant wouldn't have believed me," Bárbara
pointed out, turning to the other guardia. "Even you wouldn't
have believed me."

There was a small silence while Tejada considered. Then he
said quietly, "If I found out that Márquez had—for example—
killed a member of the Guardia, a superior officer maybe, I
could guarantee a firing squad."

Bárbara dropped her eyes. "I don't know anything about that
sort of thing, Lieutenant."

Tejada had a sudden vision of Elena cradling Toño and coo-
ing to him. He imagined the woman in front of him cradling a
child. "Your son, Jesulín," he said. "He was your youngest,
wasn't he?" A tremor of emotion crossed her face, but she said
nothing. "Your baby," Tejada continued, relentless. "Would your

husband have killed for him? I know that *I* would see any man dead who harmed my son."

Bárbara put one hand to her mouth, and Ortíz made a protesting noise. "What did your husband know about the sergeant that was 'as much as his life was worth'?" Tejada demanded.

Bárbara stood up rapidly, without speaking, and left the living room. Tejada took a few steps after her automatically, and then stopped as he realized that she had only gone toward her bedroom. "She won't try to get away, sir," Ortíz mumured. Abashed, Tejada took a seat on the sofa beside him and waited.

The innkeeper's wife returned a moment later, carrying a much-creased envelope. She held it out to the lieutenant, but addressed herself to Ortíz. "Pepe, explain to the lieutenant about Laura."

The guardia coughed and shifted uncomfortably as Bárbara resumed her seat. "Señorita Laura? I-I don't really know what to say about her. I tried never to listen to gossip—"

Tejada cut him off. "Laura Román Márquez," he said, reading the return address on the envelope. "The teacher's sister. I already know." He ignored Ortíz's amazed embarrassment, and inspected the envelope. It had been mailed from the *zone libre* of France, the preceding summer. Someone had slit open the top. He pinched the ends between his fingers and slid out two sheets of paper, both covered with neat, tiny handwriting. He unfolded both, and read the larger one first.

23 August 1940
Sare (France)

Dear Bárbara and Anselmo,

I hope you and all our friends are well, and that you have had good news of Baldo. Please give my respects to everyone, especially Maya and Paco.

I hope things are well in Spain. Jesusa and I are both in good health, thank God. She is walking very well on her own now, and she can say "mama" and "hello."

I am actually writing on her behalf. It has been a little difficult here, especially since June, and I am afraid of her going hungry. You and my other friends in Potes have already been too kind to me, and I would not dream of asking for more. So I have decided to ask you for something that I hoped I would not have to. Would you please take the enclosed letter to Sergeant Márquez? Forgive me a thousand times for the request.

Love,
Laura

Hardly knowing what to think, Tejada turned to the second sheet of paper. It, too, had been written from Sare at the end of August. It was brief but every word tasted bitter on the tongue:

Dear Uncle,

Forgive the imposition, but I have no one else to turn to, and no honest way left of making a living. Can you wire money to the post office in Sare? I hate to ask the favor, but I will do whatever I must to keep my daughter from starving, and the Guardia Civil owes me that much at least.

Your niece,
Laura Román Márquez

Tejada shut his eyes for a moment, and then handed the letters to Ortíz without speaking. He remembered Márquez's shortwave radio again, and wondered if the sergeant had answered Laura Román's plea. Ortíz read, and swore softly. "Did your husband show these letters to Sergeant Márquez?" Tejada asked.

Bárbara's face was bitter. "He did. The sergeant threw the letter back in his face and told him that he wanted nothing to do with a niece who was Red. He said he'd kill Anselmo if he ever told anybody that there was a family connection. And then"—her laughter was a cruel sound—"then he asked Anselmo if Jesulín and Laura had ever been married, and asked what concern a Red whore's bastard was of his!"

"But"—Ortíz looked up from the letters, hesitant—"Jesulín was tried in the fall of '37. And Señorita Laura didn't leave Potes until the following spring. And she wasn't pregnant when she left, or not that anyone could see. So this little girl she talks about . . ."

"She knew she was expecting," Bárbara said. "But she made the mistake of telling the lieutenant. He was pressuring her to have an abortion and she was scared. That was why she left. And that was what Anselmo told Márquez." For a moment her voice was proud, and she smiled, remembering a moment of her husband's strength. "He told the sergeant to his face that if anyone had made Laura a whore, it was the Guardia. *That* shut him up."

"He hadn't known about Calero," Tejada suggested.

"No, not until Anselmo told him," Bárbara agreed. "And then he thanked Anselmo, and told him he would take care of it."

"And a few weeks later Calero was dead?"

"That's right." Bárbara nodded. "But he didn't send a red cent to Laura. Anselmo knew the postmaster and he checked it. He waited two months, and then decided that if the sergeant wasn't going to pay for his niece it was time to make him pay for the people who were trying to make it safe for her to come home."

"And that's when the thefts from Devastated Regions started?"

"That's right, Lieutenant."

Tejada considered. He could not condemn Márquez for his role in Calero's death. Even Anselmo had not objected to that, initially. Of course, Bárbara Montalbán might well be lying about the purity of her husband's motives. Perhaps he had decided to blackmail Márquez from the moment Laura had placed the two letters in his hands. Perhaps she had given him the letters with the knowledge that he would. But Márquez had left his niece to starve rather than acknowledge a family tie to a Red, and had kidnapped Elena to extricate himself from a compromising position. He was guilty of that. "Would you still be willing to swear to this in court?" Tejada asked.

Bárbara thought for a moment. Then she nodded. "Yes. If you want me to."

"You'd implicate yourself," Tejada reminded her, neutral.

She shrugged. "So what? Anselmo's dead. Jesulín's dead. Baldo's in prison in Málaga and I can't help him. What more can you do to me, Lieutenant?"

Some faint memory of Vargas and Elena held Tejada still for a moment. Then he said slowly, "And what if you implicated other people?"

"I could only name Anselmo and Luis Severino and Rafa Campos."

"And we can't ask any of them anything." Tejada smiled briefly. "I suppose that takes care of Calero and the arms thefts. But—you have my word it won't go past this room—do you know how Márquez was mixed up with Elena's kidnapping?"

Bárbara hesitated. "I don't know the ins and outs," she said. "But Márquez stopped in here for a drink last week, with a few people I don't really know. They had something to eat, and they looked like they were having a nice cozy conversation. Then, when he was leaving, he stopped off at the bar and told me I'd better stay closed up that afternoon and not be too nosy about who was coming and going. So I stayed in the apartment all afternoon. But I heard them come in and come upstairs yelling for you, and knocking on your door. Then a few minutes later they came downstairs again." Bárbara closed her eyes, remembering. "They must have known the sergeant had fixed it with me. They weren't trying to be quiet. One of them said some-thing like, 'Damn, she's heavy. Why don't we just dump her at your place like Márquez said?' And then the other said, 'And what if he double-crosses us? I'm not taking a chance on the Guardia finding her there. We'll leave her where we agreed.'"

Tejada inhaled sharply. "You wouldn't recognize their voices or their faces if you saw them again?"

Bárbara shook her head. "No, Lieutenant. Not a chance." She saw his face working and added gently, "They're good boys, Lieutenant. They wouldn't harm Señora Fernández, no matter what the sergeant told them."

Tejada frowned. *Márquez meant for her to be found,* he thought. *He meant for her to be found right in town, and for us to get the maquis who took her. But they might still have panicked and killed her and Toño when the house-to-house started. Just as well they decided to leave her up at the Cueva Santa unguarded.* He nodded, accepting Bárbara's omission. "All right. You can come down to the post tomorrow and make a formal statement."

She stood up. "Will I go to prison, Lieutenant?"

"Anselmo was the one involved in Calero's murder, and in blackmailing Márquez," Tejada said, standing also. "And I don't see how a wife could have gone against her husband under the circumstances."

"Thank you, Lieutenant." She shook hands with him, and then closed the door behind them.

In the stairwell, Ortíz coughed nervously. "Do you believe her, sir?"

Tejada laughed. "Believe? She's the answer to a prayer! I'd give a hundred pesetas to see Súarez's face when he gets the news."

The guardia bowed his head. "I went over to tell her that you were going up to see your wife," he admitted. "I thought it might make your trip a little safer. She . . . she has a lot of contacts."

"Obviously," Tejada said, as they reached the crowded bar and stepped out into the night.

Ortíz looked embarrassed. "H-how did you know about Lieutenant Calero and Jesulín, sir?"

Tejada shrugged and quoted Antonio. "Just gossip."

"You haven't really seen the good side of the valley, Lieutenant." Ortíz spoke apologetically. "But . . . well, we're not all bad people. And it used to be very nice here. Very tranquil, before the war."

They had strolled out of the ruined arcade, toward the footbridge. Tejada looked up at the stars. "It's still tranquil here," he said, thinking of the Sierra Nevada, where he had spent his summers as a child, fascinated by the stories of the bandits who haunted the peaks. He had wanted to play the outlaws as a child, but his older brother had always taken all the best parts, and made him be the guardia civil. He thought about his brother and the local peasant boys swooping down on him in a thousand intricate ambushes, and about his brother saying to him the last time he had visited home, in a voice half-joking, half-querulous, "Honestly, Carlos, when are you people going to *do* something about the bandits in the hills? They're a bunch of ragtag peasants. It can't be that difficult." He spoke partly to Ortíz and partly to himself. "The mountains are beautiful. And I think people are pretty much the same all over."

Chapter 24

"Your attention, ladies and gentlemen, your attention, please. The seven-fifteen express to Madrid from Zamora now arriving on track two."

The crackling announcement broke the peace of the summer afternoon. Women furled their fans, calling to errant children, and men hastily folded their newspapers. Porters sprang into action as the train crawled to a halt. The crowd surged forward, eager to board as quickly as possible and to greet those arriving.

Their enthusiasm left little space for the elderly couple who had been sitting under the station clock. The lady walked with a stick. The white-haired man beside her was anxious to shield her from the hurrying passengers, and so did not have the arms and energy to devote to clearing a path to the train. They would have been pushed to the outskirts of the crowd had they not had the presence of mind to place themselves directly behind the pair of guardias civiles who had strolled through the station five times since seven o'clock, apparently on patrol, and were now hurrying toward the incoming train. The guardias had no difficulty making their way through the crowd, and they managed almost without effort to secure a place at the left side of the exit of the final coach.

The train stopped, and the conductor jumped down and pulled down the steps with a cry. "Salamanca! Station stop, Salamanca!"

Travelers poured down the steep steps to the platform, the men hopping down with the energy of schoolboys, and women in heels picking their way. Those waiting to greet the train began to wave and call to passengers. "Eulalia! Eulalia, *hija*, over here!" "Papa! Papa!" "Hey, Primo!" The steady flow of people bottlenecked as porters lugged trunks off the train, and disembarking passengers stopped abruptly in the middle of traffic to be embraced by friends and relatives.

The shape of a tricorn appeared in the door of the last car, and the crowd around the steps fell silent for a moment, apprehensive. Then the older of the guardias waiting by the side of the train raised a hand in greeting. "Lieutenant!"

The lieutenant turned his head rapidly at the hail, saw the pair of guardias, and grinned. He waved and then turned sideways on the steps, flattening himself against the narrow opening to help a young woman carrying an enormous bundle of blankets that presumably had a baby somewhere inside them. The white-haired man behind the guardias peered over their shoulders, and then touched his wife's arm. "There she is! Elena! Elenita!"

Tejada saw his wife safely down the steps and into her parents' arms and then turned to his colleagues with pleasure. "Hernández! Jiménez! How are you? I didn't expect an honor guard! What's happened?"

The younger guardia flushed. "Sergeant Hernández arranged the patrol schedules so we could meet you, Lieutenant."

Tejada held out both his hands to Hernández, remembering a little wistfully what it had been like to work with men he trusted and who trusted him. "Thanks. Sorry the train was late."

Hernández vigorously shook his former partner's hand. "No problem. We're always delayed on the Plaza de España route. Sorry I couldn't bring a truck for your luggage."

Tejada laughed. "We'll manage. But you haven't met the most important piece yet." He put an arm around his wife, drawing her away from her parents. Elena's father, uncomfortable in the presence of so many guardias, murmured something to his daughter and disappeared. Tejada indicated Elena's bundle. "This is my son, Carlos Antonio."

The two guardias leaned respectfully over the baby, and offered their congratulations to the lieutenant. Hernández, himself a father, had the presence of mind to congratulate Elena as well. She thanked him, and then turned to her husband. "Papa's gone to get us a cab. Can you take care of the luggage?"

"Of course," Tejada agreed. "Why don't you take Toño and get away from the crush?"

"Jiménez, help the lieutenant with his bags," the sergeant ordered. "I'll take care of your ladies, sir." He offered one arm to Elena's mother, who looked at it rather dubiously before taking it.

Tejada felt as if an invisible weight had been lifted from his shoulders. He basked in the warmth of the May afternoon and the attentions of the men who had been his friends as well as his colleagues. Elena's broad and incessant smile told him that she was as relieved as he was to be back in Salamanca, and even the slightly awkward politeness between her parents and Hernández and Jiménez did nothing to dim his euphoria. The taxi ride to his in-laws' home was too quick for anything other than conventional questions about how the trip had been and explanations about timing. ("We arrived at seven on the dot even though I *told* Guillermo the Madrid express is never on time." "We made the connection fine, it was just that there was a twenty-minute delay in Zamora, and then we stopped for no good reason somewhere, not even a crossing, for ten minutes. Who knows what they have on their minds?") A few minutes before the end of the ride, Carlos Antonio, who had cooperatively slept for the last several hours, woke up and announced his displeasure at being hungry and jolted around. His grandparents admired his strong lungs, and his grandmother explained to Elena that she had set up Hipólito's old room as a nursery.

When they arrived, Elena retired immediately to nurse the baby, and Tejada busied himself unpacking their trunks. The family assembled for dinner a few hours later, when Toño was fed, changed, and contented. Tejada, always a little uncomfortable around his in-laws, felt the beginnings of constraint, but Elena was blissful, and her voice and face as she sat down and said, "Oh, it's *good* to be home" did much to make the meal a happy one.

Elena had written regularly to her parents since her arrival in Potes, so the Fernándezes knew most of what had happened since Tejada's promotion. Most of dinner was taken up with telling the extra details of the last few weeks: the damning evidence of Bárbara Nuñez at Márquez's trial, the way several neighbors had thawed toward Elena following Corporal Ortíz's promotion, and the temporary lull in the maquis' activities.

"So you think things will be easier now?" Guillermo Fernández asked his son-in-law when they had adjourned to the living room, and Elena and her mother had settled down to coo over Toño.

Tejada shifted, uncomfortable. Elena's parents had not asked about her kidnapping, but behind Guillermo's question Tejada heard the echo of the old man's plea the night before his daughter's wedding: "You'll take care of her, Lieutenant? She's all we have left." Tejada had been certain of his ability to care for Elena better than an old leftist could in the new postwar Spain. "I hope so," he said aloud. He looked over at Elena. She had handed Toño to her mother, and was leaning over him, smiling. "I'll know to be careful now, at any rate."

María de Fernández looked up and beckoned to her husband. "Guillermo, you haven't even seen Toño properly. Look, doesn't he look just like Hipólito at that age? The same smile, and the same long-fingered hands."

Guillermo Fernández got up and considered the baby. "Yes. But he looks like Elena, too. You had black hair just like that when you were a baby," he added to his daughter.

Tejada suppressed the urge to stand also. He could not quarrel with his in-laws' admiration, but he had hoped that someone would notice how much his son resembled him. He watched Elena and sought for the thousandth time the words to convey how much he would have missed her if she had been harmed by her kidnappers. He could not say to her in her parents' presence, *You're half my life, and Toño has become another quarter of it, and it scares me how little the things that I used to think were worth killing and dying for mean to me now.* He lacked the courage to say, *I should leave you here in Salamanca, because I couldn't bear it if anything happened to you in Potes, but I don't know if I could bear leaving you behind,* even when they were alone. "Let me hold him again," he said aloud abruptly.

Elena frowned. "You held him on the train."

"Only so you could get some sleep." The lieutenant defended himself. "Besides, he wanted to play peek-a-boo with me."

María de Fernández raised her eyebrows. "He wanted to?" She smiled wickedly, and Tejada thought that she looked like her daughter, and wished a little wistfully that she would be less rigidly formal when she spoke to him.

"Yes," he said. And then, stung by the skeptical silence, "Watch." He retrieved his son and passed a hand in front of the baby's face. "Peek-a-boo. Peek-a-boo."

"Aaah," said Carlos Antonio sociably.

"See," said Tejada triumphantly. "It works better with a tricorn. That covers his whole face, and you should hear him laugh when it's taken away."

Elena exchanged an amused glance with her mother, and took the baby back. "He's very clever for his age," she explained, returning him to María's arms. "And he's grown amazingly, too."

"He's, what, five weeks now?" Guillermo Fernández asked.

"He'll be six weeks on Tuesday," Elena said. "And he's already on a regular feeding schedule."

"Well, you look very well," her mother said. "Nighttime feedings aren't bothering you?"

Elena laughed and shook her head, blithely denying that she was disturbed at all. Tejada's definition of torture was beginning to include being startled awake at three-hour intervals, but he said nothing and tried to take comfort in his wife's happiness. He excused himself a little later and went to sleep, while Elena stayed up, talking to her parents.

Although he was a little resentful of the way they monopolized his son over the next several days, Tejada had to admit that Elena's parents were useful babysitters. The lieutenant had envisioned the ten-day leave as a chance to introduce the baby to the Fernándezes, and to see Sergeant Hernández again, but he discovered that it was also an opportunity to spend time with Elena, without the omnipresent infant. The Tejadas spent much of their vacation wandering through the old city together, or strolling through the park down by the river Tormes. Sometimes María de Fernández persuaded them to leave a sleeping Toño behind in her care. Sometimes they took along the ancient baby carriage that Guillermo Fernández had dug out of the attic.

The uninterrupted time together was a mixed blessing. It was easy to talk about Toño: about his intelligence, his charm, the clever things he had recently learned how to do, and his undoubtedly brilliant future. But Tejada felt there was a constraint between them when they talked of other things. Elena was so happy to be back in Salamanca that any reference to Potes seemed cruel, and he was nagged by the worry that he had never properly apologized to her for his threat to take Toño away. Besides, staying with her parents made him feel like an outsider, and reminded him again of what she had said about Vargas: talking to him had been "like being at home again."

Elena also felt the constraint, although she was not sure of
the reason for it. She knew that Carlos had started to take long
walks by himself when she stayed home to nurse Toño. She had
expected him to spend more time with former colleagues, especially Hernández, who had been kind to her just after her marriage, and Corporal Jiménez, who had worked with Tejada for
years, even in Madrid. But although he paid them a few duty
calls he was in a bad mood afterward, and he seemed to be
almost avoiding their company. She knew that Carlos loved the
baby, and was glad to be a father. But sometimes she wondered
with a little pang if he wished that Toño's mother was more
respectably conservative, or simply more beautiful and less hag-
gard with worry and childbirth and lack of sleep.

All of this was in her thoughts on the warm evening when she
and the lieutenant strolled down to the river to watch the sunset, pushing the baby carriage with them. They had only two
more days left in Salamanca, and a desultory conversation about
packing had carried them past the cathedral and university, as
far as the Roman bridge. Tejada lugged the carriage down the
steps to the path by the river, without asking if Elena wished to
go that way. She followed him, content to take a familiar path
one more time. They walked in silence for a little while, passing
under the arches of the ancient bridge, until they reached a
grassy space, surrounded by trees and leading to the sandy
shores of the Tormes. It was a favorite spot for both of them.
"Do you want to rest a little?" Tejada asked.

Elena nodded, and lifted Toño from the carriage. Then she
sat down, her back propped against a tree, cradling him in her
arms. Toño woke up as he was lifted, and gurgled. The lieutenant sat beside his wife, and leaned over the baby to gurgle
back. He straightened, and Elena smiled. "I think he's going to
be a linguist when he grows up," she said. "He likes to communicate so much."

The lieutenant nodded. "Like your father."

Elena heard the suppressed bitterness in his tone, and took his arm. "What do you think he should be?"

"I don't know. Anything but a guardia, I suppose."

Tejada sounded tired, and defeated. Elena squeezed his hand, longing to say something comforting without committing Toño to a career that she emphatically hoped he would not follow. "Listen to us! We're crazy to be worrying about careers already."

"Maybe." Tejada heard both her peace offering and her unspoken acquiescence that Toño should not be a guardia. He squeezed her hand back, and then looked up at the towers silhouetted against the twilight sky. After a few minutes he said with an effort, "It's really very beautiful here."

"Yes," Elena agreed softly, accepting the tribute to her home.

"And there are good schools," Tejada continued. "That's something to think about, for Toño's sake. He'll need a decent education."

"We have a few years before we have to think about that yet," Elena said, unconsciously echoing Bárbara Nuñez.

"Yes. But it's good to be settled in a place first." Tejada took a deep breath. "Would you like to live here? So we could be close to your parents?"

For a heart-stopping moment Elena thought that Carlos was exiling her again. Then she realized that he had said "we" and she was merely confused. "But you're settled in Potes. And even if you could transfer, I thought you didn't want to work with Captain Rodríguez."

Tejada kept his eyes on Toño. "I'm petitioning for discharge from the Guardia," he said quietly.

"*What?*" Elena stared at him. "Why?"

Tejada shrugged and snorted. "Isn't it obvious?" he asked, still avoiding her eyes. "It's only a matter of time before the maquis start up again. And when they do, what sort of man would I be if I put my family in danger a second time?"

Elena had always hated it that Carlos was a guardia, but now she discovered that she was unable to think of him as anything else. "But what would you *do?*" she demanded.

"I don't know. I could find a job as a clerk somewhere, I suppose. Or maybe be taken on as an associate at some firm. I don't remember much contract law, but it would come back to me." Tejada turned his head away from his wife's open-mouthed scrutiny, and stared at the darkening waters.

"But," Elena hesitated, "but you love being a guardia."

Tejada shook his head. "No, I don't," he said honestly. "I actually dislike a lot of parts of it. It would be nice to have a job that ends when you come home from the office."

"What about not wanting peace of mind?" Elena asked softly.

The lieutenant took a long breath that was almost a sob. The Tormes was broad and sluggish here, not like the bubbling streams of the Deva and Quiviesa, and the still waters did nothing to disguise the harsh sound. "I used to do my job because I thought it was important," he said slowly. "Because I thought it had some meaning. Some necessity. But I'm only a man. And now I don't care how important it is if it means that I might lose you."

"I don't think the maquis would—" Elena began.

Tejada gestured her to silence, one hand over his face. "I don't mean the kidnapping," he interrupted. "I meant . . . you agree with them, don't you? With the maquis. And if we stay in Potes you'll meet them again, and sooner or later you'll fall in love with one of them."

Elena gasped, uncertain whether to be amused or touched. "You're insane!"

Tejada finally met her eyes. He looked longingly at her. "Elena, being a guardia—especially in a place like Potes, where we're still at war—means violence, cruelty, all sorts of ugly things. You know that. If we go back, sooner or later I'll do something that will make you hate me. And you might easily decide one of them was a better man, like Vargas. And from there—"

"For the last time, I am *not* in love with Vargas!" Elena cried so vehemently that Toño whimpered in her arms.

Tejada felt a knot in his chest loosen. "You never said that before," he whispered.

"You never asked!"

The lieutenant touched her cheek. "Because I was afraid to," he said softly. "But if you really mean it . . ."

"You won't retire from the Guardia?" Elena asked, identifying the emotion that colored her tone as hope.

Tejada frowned. "Yes, I will. You still don't like it that I'm a guardia."

"If you do that you'll regret it within six months," Elena said flatly. "And probably hate me within a year."

"No," Tejada protested.

"Yes." Elena was firm, and suddenly very sure of herself. "You won't mean to, Carlos. But listen, I love you, and I don't mind being your wife, but there isn't a week since I've met you that I haven't thought of teaching, or missed being a teacher. That's part of who I am—who I was—and the Guardia is like that for you, only more so."

Tejada frowned, struck not so much by her argument as by her example. "That's not how most women feel. Not according to everything you hear and read."

"Most women lie," Elena said. "Probably because they're not as happy as I am. Honestly, I don't regret marrying you, and God knows I don't regret Toño, but you're so lucky, Carlos—" Her voice caught. "You're *so* lucky. You don't *have* to give anything up, not me or Toño or the Guardia. And you'll hate yourself if you do."

The misery of his long solitary walks through Salamanca, summoning courage to write a letter to Colonel Súarez, came back to Tejada, proving the truth of his wife's words. "It seems like a lack of imagination," he said slowly, but his voice was meditative now, and he spoke to Elena as he had spoken to her before Toño's birth, like a colleague whose judgment he trusted. "It's not even that I enjoy being a guardia. I just can't imagine myself as anything else anymore."

"You haven't actually asked for discharge yet, have you?" Elena demanded.

He shook his head and noted for the first time that the evening breeze smelled of sweet grass. Elena was a profile in the twilight, and Toño was a white mummy in her arms. "I was going to ask Torres to meet us at Santander instead of Unquera on Friday and drop the letter with Colonel Súarez when we got off the train."

"Ask him for a transfer instead," Elena urged. "Didn't he say that capturing Márquez was a good mark in your file? Surely he'd agree to move you?"

"I suppose. Although so much moving around in so short a period of time starts to look suspicious. But I could ask him to move me back to Salamanca, so Toño could be near his grandparents."

"I thought the corps didn't like to have officers serving in their home regions," Elena said heroically.

Tejada laughed, not because Elena had said something funny, but because the evening stars were beginning to twinkle over the dome of the cathedral, and the breeze smelled good, and he was happy. "I don't know if in-laws' homes count," he said wryly. "But I don't mind working in Salamanca. Or I could just request a transfer to a place where the maquis are less active, because of you and Toño. Somewhere with good schools for Toño and other children he could play with."

"And a pediatrician," Elena agreed. She sounded happy as well.

Tejada put his arms around her and the baby, and squeezed gently, unable to articulate his relief. "I'll tell the colonel that if he doesn't move us to civilization, I'll leave the corps."

Elena laughed, and kissed him. "Don't be silly," she said. "If we have to stay in Potes for a little while, we'll stay. Ortíz isn't experienced enough to command the post yet, remember? And Father Bernardo was going to help me get a school set up."

"That's true." Tejada took a deep breath and all of the things he had been trying to avoid thinking about over the last week poured happily out. "I've been wondering if maybe we should do something about the way we buy provisions. The system we have is fine if the entire force lives and works in the barracks, but with so many men spread out it's inefficient. I thought maybe I'd talk to Fermín about some way of having him handle the distribution and letting the ration coupons go through him. Or maybe I'll leave it to Ortíz, since they know each other, and Ortíz could use some practice dealing with administrative issues."

"What about letting guardias use coupons in the Monday markets?" Elena asked.

"Hard to regulate," the lieutenant said thoughtfully, shifting position. "But we could talk to the mayor and see what could be done." It was full dark by the time the Tejadas left the riverside, still discussing the mundane details of the lieutenant's command.

Their last days in Salamanca flew by, speeded by Tejada's sudden desire to talk to Hernández and Jiménez as much as possible, and by Elena's hour-devouring browses through the bookstores of her childhood, searching both for entertainment for herself and instruction for Simón Álvarez. She ended up taking one of her parents' old trunks for the books and stationery she had bought, and the extra space in the trunk inspired Tejada to buy a small radio he hoped would lessen her sense of isolation in Potes.

They left early on Friday morning, and the flurry of last-minute preparations and crises combined to make the whistle that signaled the train's departure a sign that brought intense relief. Elena leaned out the window as the train pulled out of the station, holding up Toño and making him wave good-bye to his grandparents with one hand. Impelled by the instinct of all rail travelers, Tejada forgot his reservations about his in-laws and leaned out the window to wave also. As Salamanca finally dropped from sight behind them Elena sank back into her seat and relaxed. Tejada sat back opposite her and smiled. "At least there's nothing more to remember for a few hours," he said.

"Thank goodness!" Elena agreed. "What time is Torres supposed to meet us in Unquera?"

"I told him five o'clock. So we should have time to have lunch and walk around a little."

"That will be nice."

Tejada grimaced. "Assuming the train is reasonably on time."

The train was not even close to on time, due to mysterious mechanical delays outside Zamora that made the lieutenant grind his teeth and mutter that things were better managed in various other parts of Europe. In fact, it was well after six when they finally reached Unquera. Tejada saw that their luggage was all off the train, and then began to wonder with a sinking heart whether he could leave Elena and Toño with the bags and find the Guardia post to call Potes and explain their delay. Elena agreed to this plan, and he stepped out of the dingy waiting room into the summer afternoon with a slight sense of guilt. The air smelled of lindens, and the distant sea. The loud honk of a horn made him look to the left. He was both startled and pleased to see a guardia vehicle sitting patiently at an intersection some twenty meters up the street. As he moved toward it, the truck purred to life and rolled up to him. It stopped as he drew level with it, and he saw that Guardia Torres was at the wheel. "Good to see you, sir," Torres said as he swung himself out of the truck. "Where's your lady? And the little one?"

In less time than Tejada would have believed possible, his family and luggage were safely settled in the truck and rolling away from the coast into the narrow gorge that led to Potes. It was a warm evening, and Torres drove with the windows rolled down. The roar of the rapids in the gorge was audible even above the hum of the motor, so the guardia had to raise his voice as he said, "I'm glad you're back. A lot has happened."

"Oh?" Tejada spoke sharply. "Have the maquis been active?"

"Oh, no, sir." Torres was apologetic. "I didn't mean anything like that. Just that Fermín had a shipment of soap, and Carvallo thinks that Araceli Caro is throwing herself at Ortíz now that he's a corporal, and Father Bernardo is talking about setting up a checkers tournament for the whole valley."

"The mayor's daughter, Araceli?" Elena said, startled. "Doesn't her father have something to say about that?"

"Real soap?" Tejada asked at the same moment. "Is there any left?"

"I told Fermín to save some for you. And it's not as if Ortíz has done anything. They've just talked during the evening *paseo* a couple of times. Father Bernardo asked if you'd be interested in the tournament, Lieutenant."

Tejada declined politely, but the conversation lasted until the steep walls of the gorge fell away into the green fields of the Liébana. Carvallo helped them unload their luggage when they reached Potes, and then drove the truck back to the post, promising to return to help move the trunks if he was needed. As it turned out, the guardia's aid was not necessary. Father Bernardo had been waiting at the *fonda* for them, and volunteered to help with the luggage. "I wanted to invite you to dinner," the priest explained, when Tejada thanked him for his assistance. "I thought Señora Fernández might be too tired from traveling to prepare anything, but it's always nice to have something to eat in the evening if you've had a busy day."

The Tejadas accepted the priest's offer with gratitude. It was twilight, and the first evening stars were just starting to twinkle as the lieutenant and his wife reached the parish house, along with their host. Dinner was all the priest had promised. The food was good and the conversation was friendly and general.

Toño woke up shortly after the plates were cleared, and Elena excused herself to nurse him.

"Your wife looks well," Father Bernardo said when the door had closed behind her. "Motherhood suits her."

Tejada nodded. "I think so," he said. "But it's probably our trip, as well. She was glad to see her parents."

"Very natural," Father Bernardo agreed. "But, if you'll allow me to say so, you look well also, Lieutenant."

"Fatherhood," Tejada said smugly, and the conversation turned to Toño until Elena returned with the baby, once more sleepy and silent.

The priest set out a plate of early strawberries for his guests, and was modestly pleased with their gratitude. "It's the least I could do," he explained earnestly. "I'm glad you're back. We were afraid we'd lost you after that business with the sergeant and everything."

Tejada and his wife exchanged glances. Then Tejada said lightly, "I wish all the people of the valley felt as you do, Father."

"Oh, I'm sure many do," Father Bernardo replied encouragingly. "Señor Rosas, for instance, must be pleased you've returned."

"It'd be nice if he showed it by building us a permanent barracks," Tejada said. "And maybe a school for Toño."

"I'm sure he's working on the barracks." Father Bernardo laughed. "As to the school, you know that I'd be happy to help with that."

"So would I." Elena spoke up from the armchair where she was cradling Toño.

The priest frowned, but Tejada looked at her with affection. "I know," he said. "Both of you just need the space to teach. And I think the Guardia owes Potes a school."

"Perhaps you'd better let Señor Rosas focus on the barracks first," Father Bernardo suggested gently.

Tejada nodded. "I'll make Señor Rosas speed up his blessed construction schedule!" he promised. "And if he starts clucking about Devastated Regions not having the manpower, I'll . . ." He paused, trying to think of something sufficiently awful to threaten to do to Rosas. "I'll build them both myself!" he finished finally.

Elena laughed. "You don't know the first thing about building anything!" she said fondly.

Tejada looked at the sleeping Carlos Antonio. "Maybe it's time I learned," he said.

Potes today is a thriving town of about twenty-five hundred people, a center for hiking, kayaking, and other adventure sports in the Picos de Europa, and a popular summer destination for Spanish tourists. The town is still the capital of the *comarca* of Liébana. The Torre del Infantado is currently being restored, but it retains its impressive silhouette. In the autumn of 1946, the Guardia Civil moved into the historic mansion, which had been completely renovated for its use, and where it is still housed. I would like to thank all of the citizens of Potes, who graciously swallowed their astonishment at the sight of a lone American visiting their town in the middle of February and shared their history and their memories with me.

I have adjusted their story somewhat to fit the needs of the novel. All my events and characters are completely fictitious, but I have tried to make the landscape of *The Watcher in the Pine* fairly accurate. Eusebio Bustamante's photographs of Potes before and after the Civil War, collected in the *Albúm de la Liébana*, capture both the beauty of the town and the devastation wrought by the fire of 1937. Mónica Álvarez Careaga describes the work of the General Directorate for Devastated Regions in Potes in her article "La reconstrucción de la villa de Potes (1939–1959)." Although Devastated Regions was a real entity, the harassed Señor Rosas is my own invention, and it must be said in fairness to his real-life counterpart, Juan José

Resines del Castillo, that the reconstructed plaza of Potes is an exceptionally beautiful spot.

The political climate of the story is also real. The end of the Spanish Civil War in 1939 signaled the beginning of a desperate guerrilla conflict between the Spanish Army, the Guardia Civil, and the Policía Armada (later the Policía Nacional) on one side, and the maquis, remnants of the defeated Republican army, and a few dedicated rebels on the other. The maquis operated throughout Spain, but they began their campaign in the north in Galicia and the Asturias. One of the most famous guerrillas of the region was "Juanín," Juan Fernández Ayala, a native of Potes. Born in 1917, Juanín was imprisoned at the end of the Civil War, and during the period in which *The Watcher in the Pine* takes place, he was in Santander's Tabacalera jail. He was released at the end of 1941, and took to the mountains shortly afterward. He was apparently a man of considerable courage and ingenuity and his exploits read like updated Robin Hood stories. He survived in the hills until a shoot-out with the Guardia in 1957. Today, the tourist brochures of the Liébana region hail him as a local hero. The Sten machine gun and Astra pistol taken from his body are on display in Madrid in the Guardia Civil section of the Museum of the Army, a bizarre tribute from his enemies. Although the action of *The Watcher in the Pine* takes place somewhat earlier than the years when Juanín was active, I have drawn heavily on Pedro Álvarez's biography, *Juanín: el último emboscado de la postguerra española*, for the setting and details of the guerrilla movement in Potes. Alfredo Cloux's Juanín Web page (http://es.geocities.com/los_del_monte) and its lively bulletin board were also invaluable to me, providing both sources of information and a chance to meet the children and grandchildren of the maquis (and their foes), as well as a few survivors of the period.

The maquis were most active in the early and midforties, especially the period between the Allied invasion of France and the end of World War II, when they hoped (and Franco's government feared) that the Allies would invade Spain as well, and topple the last remaining Fascist government in Europe. I am indebted to José-Antonio Vidal Sales's book *Maquis: la verdad histórica de la "otra guerra,"* a wonderful combination of oral history and analysis, for information about this period as well as the marvelous "Paisajes de la Guerrilla/Landscapes of the Guerrilla" (http://es.geocities.com/eustaquio5/index.html), a companion to Alfredo Cloux's Juanín page. Javier Corcuera's moving documentary *La guerrilla de la memoria* also sheds light on the maquis through interviews with the handful who still survive.

Franco's anti-Communism and loudly proclaimed neutrality at the end of World War II won him support in Britain and the United States, and by the time the first American military bases opened in Spain in 1953, the maquis had despaired of foreign intervention. Many fled over the Pyrenees to France. Others, like Juanín, were captured and killed by the Guardia. A few hid in the mountains as outlaws until the 1960s. Jesus Torbado and Manuel Leguineche's book *The Forgotten Men* tells the story of one, Pablo Pérez Hidalgo, who actually survived in the Sierra Bermeja until after Franco's death in 1975. Only after learning that a general amnesty had been declared by King Juan Carlos did he surrender to the Guardia Civil in December of 1976.

OTHER TITLES IN THE SOHO CRIME SERIES